QUIETUS

Book Four

The Pandemic Series

A novel by

Bobby Akart

Copyright Information

Thank you for purchasing
Quietus by Bobby Akart

For free advance reading copies, updates on new releases,
special offers, and bonus content,
Sign Up at BobbyAkart.com.

BobbyAkart.com

Other Works by Bestselling Author Bobby Akart

The Pandemic Series

Beginnings

The Innocents

Level 6

Quietus

The Blackout Series

36 Hours

Zero Hour

Turning Point

Shiloh Ranch

Hornet's Nest

Devil's Homecoming

The Boston Brahmin Series

The Loyal Nine

Cyber Attack

Martial Law

False Flag

The Mechanics

Choose Freedom!

Seeds of Liberty (Companion Guide)

The Prepping for Tomorrow Series

Cyber Warfare

EMP: Electromagnetic Pulse

Economic Collapse

DEDICATIONS

This book is dedicated to my darling wife, without whom life would be hopeless. Thank you for loving me. Bullie and Boom, seeing your wiggly butts at the end of a long day behind the keyboard makes it all worthwhile.

My friends and readers, please heed the warning of this series. A global pandemic can strike in an instant. I write this book to entertain you, but also to get you ready for the next global war.

Thank you for supporting me!

Finally, the Pandemic series is dedicated to the disease detectives, the shoe-leather epidemiologists of the CDC's Epidemic Intelligence Service, who work tirelessly to keep these deadly infectious diseases from killing us all. They are selfless, brave warriors, risking their lives and the loss of their families in order to fight an unseen enemy more powerful than any bomb.

ACKNOWLEDGEMENTS

Writing a book that is both informative and entertaining requires a tremendous team effort. Writing is the easy part. For their efforts in making the Pandemic series a reality, I would like to thank Hristo Argirov Kovatliev for his incredible cover art, Pauline Nolet for making this important work reader-friendly, Stef Mcdaid for making this manuscript decipherable in so many formats, John David Farrell and Kris Adams, who together with Marshall Davis, my producer, have brought my words to life, and the Team—whose advice, friendship and attention to detail is priceless.

The Pandemic series required countless hours of research. Without the background material and direction from those individuals who provided me a portal into their observations and data, I would've been drowning in long Latin words. Please allow me to acknowledge a few of those individuals whom, without their tireless efforts, the Pandemic series could not have been written.

Brant Goode, CDC CEFO Supervisor.

Colonel Mark G. Kortepeter, MD, a preventive medicine officer in the Operational Medicine Division at the U.S. Army Medical Research Institute of Infectious Diseases, USAMRIID, where he teaches the medical management of biological weapons casualties.

Rear Admiral Stephen C. Redd, MD, Director of the Office of Public Health Preparedness and Response (OPHPR) at the CDC.

Thank you and thank you for your service to humanity!

About the Author

Bobby Akart

Bestselling author Bobby Akart has been ranked by Amazon as the #3 Bestselling Religion & Spirituality Author, the #5 Bestselling Science Fiction Author, and the #7 Bestselling Historical Author. He is the author of sixteen international bestsellers, in thirty-nine different fiction and nonfiction genres, including the critically acclaimed Boston Brahmin series, the bestselling Blackout series, his highly cited nonfiction Prepping for Tomorrow series and his latest project—The Pandemic Series.

Bobby has provided his readers a diverse range of topics that are both informative and entertaining. His attention to detail and impeccable research has allowed him to capture the imaginations of his readers through his fictional works, and bring them valuable knowledge through his nonfiction books.

SIGN UP for email updates here:

eepurl.com/bYqq3L

and receive free advance reading copies, updates on new releases, special offers, and bonus content. You can contact Bobby directly by email (BobbyAkart@gmail.com) or through his website:

BobbyAkart.com

In the mid-twentieth century, a new weapon shocked the world with its ability to destroy the enemy.

For centuries, another weapon has existed…

One that attacks without conscience or remorse…

Its only job is to kill.

They are the most merciless enemy we've ever faced…

And they're one-billionth our size.

Be prepared to become very, very paranoid.

WELCOME TO THE NEXT GLOBAL WAR.

Biological weapons, delivered under the right conditions against an unaware, unprotected population, will, pound for pound and dollar for dollar, kill a million times more people than a nuclear weapon. A nuclear bomb doesn't come close to matching the potential footprint of a biological weapon.

Over the past half century, the number of new diseases per decade has increased fourfold. Since 1980, the outbreaks have more than tripled. With those statistics in mind, one has to consider the consequences of a major pandemic.

Death has come to millions of humans throughout the millennia from the spread of infectious diseases, but none was worse than the Black Death, a pandemic so devastating that uttering the words *the plague* will immediately pull it to the front of your mind. From 1347 to 1351, the Black Death reshaped Europe and much of the world.

In a time when the global population was an estimated four hundred fifty million, some estimates of the death toll reached as high as two hundred million, nearly half of the world's human beings.

This plague's name came from the black skin spots on the sailors who travelled the Silk Road, the ancient network of trade routes that traversed the Asian continent, connecting East and West. The Black Death was in fact a form of the bubonic plague, not nearly as contagious and deadly as its sister, the pneumonic plague.

Fast-forward five centuries to 1918, an especially dangerous form of influenza began to appear around the world. First discovered in Kansas in March 1918, by the time the H1N1 pandemic, commonly known as the Spanish flu, burned out in 1919, it took the lives of as many as fifty million people worldwide.

Why does the history of these deadly pandemics matter?

Because it has happened before and it will happen again—despite the world's advanced technology, or because of it. People no longer stay in one place; neither do diseases. Unlike the habits of humans during the Black Death and the Spanish flu, an infection in all but the most remote corner of the world can make its way to a major city in a few days.

Terrible new outbreaks of infectious disease make headlines, but not at the start. Every pandemic begins small. Early indicators can be subtle and ambiguous. When the next global pandemic begins, it will spread across oceans and continents like the sweep of nightfall, causing illness and fear, killing thousands or maybe millions of people. The next pandemic will be signaled first by quiet, puzzling reports from faraway places—reports to which disease scientists and public health officials, but few of the rest of us, pay close attention.

The purpose of this series is not to scare the wits out of you, but rather, to scare the wits into you. As one early reader said to me, after reading the Pandemic series, "I now realize that humans can become extinct. Not a comforting thought."

The Pandemic series is a new dystopian, post-apocalyptic fiction series from fifteen-time bestselling author Bobby Akart (the Blackout series, the Boston Brahmin series and the Prepping for Tomorrow series).

The events depicted in the Pandemic series are fictional. The events, however, are based upon historical fact.

Note: This book does not contain strong language. It is intended to entertain and inform audiences of all ages, including teen and young adults. Although some scenes depict the realistic threat our nation faces from a devastating global pandemic and the societal collapse that will result in the aftermath, it does not contain graphic scenes typical of other books in the post-apocalyptic genre.

I believe more of our young people need to lead a preparedness lifestyle. Studies show that our millennials do not have any of the basic survival skills. By writing this series free of vulgarities and gratuitous sexual innuendo, I've intended it to be suitable for everyone. Thanks.

PREVIOUSLY IN THE PANDEMIC SERIES

The Characters

Dr. Mackenzie Hagan ("Mac")

Dr. Mackenzie Hagan, is in her mid-thirties, tall, long blonde hair, slender, athletic build. She graduated from Virginia Tech with a Bachelor of Science degree before entering post-graduate study where she obtained a dual master's degree in Molecular Biology and Applied Genetics. She went on to receive her PhD in Microbiology from MIT and a Medical Degree from the University Of Chicago School Of Medicine.

After completing her residency, Dr. Hagan began her career in public service as an Epidemic Intelligence Service Officer at the National Center for Infectious Diseases. Her successes in fighting the West Africa Ebola outbreak lead her to the CDC where she served as the Associate Director for the Office of Infectious Diseases.

Dr. Hagan also holds the rank of Lieutenant Commander for the U.S. Public Health Service. As the daughter of a retired Commanding General of the United States Army Medical Research Institute of Infectious Diseases, Dr. Hagan often says infectious disease is in her blood.

Agent Nathan Hunter ("Hunter")

Nathan Hunter holds the formal title of Threat Reduction Specialist with the Defense Threat Reduction Agency, an arm of the Department of Defense based in Fort Belvoir, Virginia.

Hunter graduated with high honors from the Virginia Military Institute where he majored in International Studies with a minor in National Security.

Never a serious dater, Hunter is thirty-three years old, 6', 2", well-built and single. He lives in his deceased parents' estate on Lake Barcroft, Virginia. Upon their unexpected deaths, his father, a very successful defense contractor, established a financial trust for Hunter worth approximately one billion dollars.

Hunter served in the United States Army as an Operations Officer (Combat Support Squadron), Master Sergeant, First Special Forces Operational Detachment: 1st SFO Delta, also known as Delta Force in Fort Bragg, North Carolina.

At the DTRA, Hunter works with other members of the Project Artemis team to hunt terrorists, especially those engaging in bioterrorism, before they can act.

Janelle Turnbull ("Janie")

Janelle Turnbull is in her late twenties and single. Mac describes her as perky, but she is very serious about her career. Janie works for the CDC as a CEFO, Career Epidemiology Field Officer. Janie was educated as a veterinarian which attracted her to the CDC to study zoonotic infectious diseases. She currently lives in Atlanta. Her parents are still living, as is her younger sister, a student at Georgia Tech.

Major General Barbara Stinchcomb Hagan ("Barb")

Mac's mother and married to Thomas Hagan, her husband of forty years. The couple lives in Coos Bay, Oregon. Barb is in her early sixties and in good health.

She is a retired medical doctor who began her career at Denver Health where she met Tommy. After they were married, Mac was born and soon thereafter, Barb joined the United States Army. After several years of service, Barb rose through the ranks of USAMRIID, the United States Army Medical Research Institute of Infectious Diseases until she became Commanding General stationed at Fort Detrick, Maryland.

During the Ebola crisis, Barb became a political pawn and scapegoat for the current administration and the media. She was forced out of her post and retired.

Thomas Hagan ("Tommy")

Mac's father, Tommy, is a retired high school chemistry teacher. He spends his day gardening and tinkering around the house. He loves to hunt, fish, and train for the senior triathlete competition when he turns sixty years old. Tommy is a prankster and a jokester.

Supporting Characters of Importance:

President Tomas Garcia – In his final year of his first term, currently running for re-election. Indirectly responsible for the termination of General Barbara Hagan from her post at USAMRIID. Enjoys his brandy. Close friends with his Chief of Staff, Andrew Morse.

Chief of Staff Andrew Morse – Right-arm and close confidant of President Tomas Garcia. Has a unique ability to manipulate and keep the President on message.

Donald Baggett – Former accountant and political appointee of the President charged with cutting the budget of the Centers for Disease Control and Prevention. He is constantly at odds with Mac, who refers to him, privately, of course, as *D-Bag*, short for *douche bag*, due to his constant unwanted advances toward her.

Doctor Kwame Okoli – Native Nigerian who battled Ebola in Africa. He is currently on staff at Memorial Medical Center in Las Cruces, New Mexico.

USAF Master Sergeant Scott Jablonik – coordinator of Project Artemis within the Defense Threat Reduction Agency. Hunter's immediate superior.

Ali Hassan – Son of Abu Ali Hassan, a senior leader on the Islamic State Leadership Council. Ali Hassan is the mastermind behind the bioterror plot.

Doc Cooley – General practitioner in Breckenridge, Colorado who befriended the Hagans. He makes a living as a doctor but made his fortune as a poker player. Now he's a central figure in the fight to protect Breckenridge from the plague, and others.

Derek Cooley – Son of Doc Cooley. In his early twenties, and well-respected in Breckenridge.

Rulon Snow – Formerly of Utah, Snow was the number one for the leader of the FLDS Church. He was exiled after testifying against the prophet in Federal Court. He was granted property and cash to raise his ever-burgeoning family at Boreas Pass. He has two sons, Seth and Levi, who were the first-born into their new compound near Breckenridge.

Captain Kevin Hoover – Captain in the Colorado National Guard. He has a wife and two daughters. Capt. Hoover has seen the worst of what humanity has to offer following the spread of the plague.

Primary Scene Locations

Denver, Colorado – largest city in Colorado.

Fort Collins, Colorado – located an hour north of Denver. It is the location of the DTRA/CIA laboratory formerly operated by the CDC.

Breckenridge, Colorado – known as a ski resort destination. Population during the summer is just over four thousand residents. The population grows to nearly twenty thousand when the tourists and skiers begin to arrive with the first major snowfall.

Quandary Peak – A *14er*, terminology for a Rocky Mountain peak in excess of fourteen thousand feet. The Hagans have a second home just below the treeline near Blue Lakes at the base of Quandary Peak.

Cheyenne Mountain – location of NORAD and the hideaway for the President as part of Continuity of Government.

Star Ranch – The first of many safe zones around the country. A gated community, Star Ranch was used to house a select number of local citizens who would participate in the rebuilding effort.

Secondary Scene Locations

Guatemala – Location of the initial outbreak was in the jungle near the small town of El Naranjo. Mac and Janie begin their investigation when they meet the mysterious operative with the DTRA—Hunter. The CDC has a regional office in Guatemala City, about a mile from the United States Embassy.

Turkey – Several temporary camps for Syrian and Iraqi refugees were created in the western part of the country near Izmir, Turkey. In the surrounding countryside, migrant farms were established to pay the refugees and keep them busy during the day until they could emigrate to Europe.

Greece – In Athens, Hunter visits with his contemporaries at the Greek National Intelligence Service. By coincidence, Mac is investigating a case at the Hellenic Centre for Disease Control and Prevention. The two cross paths at a hotel and have dinner together. A spark of interest takes place after they overcome their first chance meeting in the jungles of Guatemala.

CDC – Atlanta – located near Emory University in Atlanta, Georgia.

White House – Washington, DC. Politics plays a pivotal role in all aspects of our lives and the center of the political universe is the White House.

Park Place on Peachtree – Mac's condominium in Buckhead.

Previously in The Pandemic Series
Book One: BEGINNINGS

The Pandemic Series begins with the kidnapping and interrogation of a young French research scientist in a remote biosafety laboratory in Franceville, Gabon. The terrorist cell run by Ali Hassan, the son of a top-level ISIS leader, also established a complex surveillance apparatus of the young scientist's family.

Forced to do their bidding in order to save the lives of his family, the French scientist modified the Madagascar strain of the pneumonic plague. His work was groundbreaking, although it was clearly a crime against humanity. In the end, he didn't save himself, or his family.

Initially, Hassan used the remote jungles of Guatemala as his testing ground. However, a series of events accelerated his plans as outbreaks of the disease occur in Trinidad and Greece.

Hassan, his trusted his allies, and thousands of sleeper cells around the world sprang into action. First, they secured their loved ones away from the harmful potential of the disease. Second, they issued a call to action—*the flag of Allah and jihad has been raised.*

Hunter and his comrades at the DTRA comprising Project Artemis began to chase leads and search for the bioterrorists. Mac and her fellow disease detectives at the CDC raced to identify the disease, and determine if a vaccine or cure was available.

As the disease spread and the death toll rose, Mac became increasingly frustrated with the President and his administration for not warning the public. She was admonished to do her job and not approach the media with alarmist statements. However, like her mother, Mac believed in transparency and the ability of the public to make decisions for themselves.

When the Congress set up special hearings on the Guatemala breakout and its potential impact on the United States, Mac made a decision. Wearing her dress white uniform indicating her status as a Lieutenant Commander in the U.S. Public Health Service, she decided to add to her attire. She added white gloves, an N95 particulate mask, and protective eyewear.

Her appearance immediately created a ruckus within the large gathering of media covering the hearings. It also raised the ire of the partisan congressman who support the President in his re-election efforts.

Perhaps it was Mac's attire, or maybe it was the typical partisan bickering which had consumed Washington, but the hearings immediately turned contentious. With the CSPAN cameras rolling, Mac was grilled with questions and placed under considerable pressure. She was asked to describe how the disease affects the human body and she gladly answered in excruciating detail.

Unscripted, but as if on cue, a man in the gallery began to cough up blood, causing a panic by all the attendees. During the stampede for the exits, the man vomited up blood, which immediately drew comparisons to plague-like symptoms. Throughout the ordeal, Mac sat silently, alone, staring at the CSPAN cameras which never turned off.

Meanwhile, in a thousand cities around the world, ISIS operatives continued to relentlessly pursue their Caliphate. As the mayhem took place in Room 2123 of the Rayburn House Office Building, Hassan and his trusted Islamic brothers approached the outskirts of Los Angeles.

From the final chapter of BEGINNINGS …

The rental car sped past the sign that read Welcome to Los Angeles, population 3,957,875.

"We are here, Hassan."

Hassan nodded. "We are everywhere, my brothers."

Book Two: THE INNOCENTS

The Pandemic Series continues with the world's population dwindling. After crisscrossing the planet in search of clues, Mac and Hunter realize this infectious disease is like no other, and with the jihadists implementing the plague as a tool of bioterror, there is not just one Patient Zero, but thousands.

Mac willingly followed in her mother's footsteps, electing to disregard her orders which came straight from the President of the United States. She rang the clarion bell, a warning to the world, that no one is immune or safe from the perfect killer.

Her heroic act got her fired but Hunter quickly came up with a viable alternative. Mac came on board with the DTRA and CIA at a covert laboratory located at a former CDC BSL-4 in Fort Collins, Colorado.

Mac and her family had significant roots there. Her Mom was a resident at Denver Health where Mac was born. The Hagan's owned a second home at Quandary Peak just south of Breckenridge in the Rocky Mountains.

While Mac worked on a vaccine and cure, Hunter was reassigned to the Denver field office of the FBI. He spent his working hours tracking the jihadists as they entered America, hoping to find the mastermind of the bioterrorist plot. During his off hours, Hunter was getting prepared for the inevitable — societal and economic collapse.

Darting around town from Costco to Walmart to REI Sporting Goods, Hunter systematically equipped the Hagan home at Quandary Peak for the impending apocalypse.

The day came when Hunter was face-to-face with his nemesis, Ali Hassan, the mastermind behind weaponizing the plague and advancing the final jihad. The two men locked eyes and Hunter took care of business. One dead terrorist, but one massive plague was waging the war.

Across the country, terrorist cells infiltrated airports, sporting events, and shopping malls, spreading the disease and infecting thousands, who in turn infected thousands more. They were winning and our governmental response was weak.

President Garcia slowly retreated into a bottle of brandy. His cabinet began to lose confidence in his leadership. The nation was a ship without a rudder, helpless to combat the most dangerous disease known to man.

Mac reached back to her days in college for solutions. She proposed an unproven remedy based upon her college thesis to Janie, who then provided it to her associates at the CDC. Despite Mac's warnings that the proposed solution was untested, out of desperation, the President and the CDC declared it to be a viable cure and began to inoculate American citizens.

The BALO vaccine was a bust and mac went back to the drawing board. In the meantime, the United Nations and the World Health Organization threw in the towel. A secretive Security Council meeting directive adopted during the Ebola crisis, and incorporated into law by the President, provided a drastic measure to save humanity.

From the final chapter of THE INNOCENTS ...

"It's from Homeland Security. Hunter, my God. They've declared a Level 6 Emergency."

"Don't you mean a phase six, based upon the WHO's pandemic

alert system?" asked Hunter.

"No, read it." Mac spun the monitor around for Hunter to read the short, two-sentence email. "Phase six is where the WHO considers the overall severity of a pandemic to be moderate to extreme. It's rarely used, but appropriate now."

Mac began to pace and then she got angry. She swept all the stacks of files off her desk and pounded the corner with her fist.

Hunter tried to console her, but she pulled away. "Mac, we know it's bad. I don't under—"

She threw her arms up and looked toward the ceiling. Then she turned to Hunter, arms crossed. "I thought this was the stuff of urban legend. You know a myth only made up on television."

"The situation is grave," interrupted Hunter. "Why are you so angry at them declaring a phase six pandemic?"

"No, Hunter. Don't you see? It didn't say *phase six*. They wrote *level 6* in the email."

"They?"

"Yes, see the bottom?" asked Mac as she spun the monitor on her desk for them both to see. She angrily tapped the part of the email indicating the signature field. "It's signed by the DHS and the UN. They've given up, Hunter. They know they can't contain it or stop it. The United Nations and our own government think this is an extinction-level event. It's over. My God!"

Mac walked back and forth through the room, hands firmly planted on her hips.

"Mac, what does level 6 mean?"

"Eradication, Hunter. *Level 6* is their code word for eradication of the diseased members of the species."

Book Three: LEVEL 6

In Level 6, book three of The Pandemic Series, the spread of the deadly strain of the plague has hit a brick wall, but not because it's burned itself out. Rather, the plague bacterium was running out of victims.

While the Hagans, Hunter and Janie attempt to get settled into a routine at their secluded mountain home at Quandary Peak, the government began to carry out the dictates of the Level 6 protocol. Their goal: Stop the spread of the plague. Their method: Eradicate those who are infected, or exposed to the disease.

Life for those lucky enough to survive became more difficult. The power grid went down, law enforcement was non-existent, and survival of the fittest became the norm. The death toll had risen to the point where less than ten percent of the world's population remained alive.

The government continued to operate from within the safe confines of Cheyenne Mountain and President Garcia makes a bold move to punish those responsible for the pandemic by ordering a nuclear strike against ISIS. While it obliterated the command-and-control structure of the terrorist organization, it would not necessarily stop the *final jihad*.

Meanwhile, Mac continued her work inside the laboratory built in the basement of their Quandary Peak home. As she focused on her testing, Hunter began to establish security for their home. Dead bodies and missing persons were brought to his attention. He got the sense there was evil lurking in the mountains and valleys surrounding Breckenridge.

His concerns came to the forefront when three major fires broke out on the ridges surrounding the town, one of which threatened Doc Cooley's ranch. Hunter and Tommy rushed to help their friends. Hunter became disoriented while fighting the fire and almost died. Tommy saved the life of a little boy but became infected with the plague in the process.

Despite all of their precautions, in a moment of compassion, Mac's father was now on the path of becoming a victim. Lying in the bed of what had become known as the Quarantine House, Tommy and his new friend, Flatus, fought the disease on their own. But gradually, the symptoms became worse.

From the final chapter of LEVEL 6 …

"Second day in a row, after I wake up," he said. "It's moving into my chest. I feel like I can't breathe. The chest pains have increased and I can't seem to shake the chills."

"I know, Daddy," said Mac as she fought back tears. Her father had lost several pounds in the last week and looked completely drained of energy. It hurt her to the core. "I've been working on this daily. It's the best I've got so far."

Mac displayed the six vials and picked up a syringe off the nightstand. She drew the vancomycin out of the first vial and was about to inject her father when he raised his arm.

"No, Flatus first," he said.

"What? Daddy, this is for you. I only have—" Mac protested.

"Honey, can you make more?" he asked as another coughing fit overcame him.

"Sure, of course."

Tommy waved his arm toward Janie. "Janie, you're the vet. Flatus first. He and I are a package deal."

Mac looked down at her father and she began crying out of pride. This man, who had raised her unselfishly throughout her life, was still thinking of others as he lay on his deathbed. The tears streamed into her goggles and mask. She was shaking from emotions as she turned and handed the needle to Janie, with a nod of approval.

Janie kneeled on one knee and injected Flatus in the shoulder. He panted, but never moved. He was feeling the effects of the disease now as well.

Mac regained her composure and calmed her nerves. She emptied another vial into a fresh syringe. She lifted her father's arm and wiped the sweat off with a cotton ball. Mac slowly inserted the needle into his vein and depressed the plunger.

Vancomycin-d-ala-d-lac entered his bloodstream and immediately, with every beat of her father's heart, moved throughout his body to fight the most vicious killer known to man.

The saga concludes in — Quietus
Enjoy!

EPIGRAPH

Throughout the millennia, extinction has been the norm and survival, the exception.

*****

Humanity, if it remains confined to this planet, will eventually succumb to an extinction event.

~ Elon Musk

*****

Death is the wish of some, the relief of many, and the end of all.

~ Lucius Annaeus Seneca

*****

Survival can be summed up in three words — never give up.

~ Bear Grylls

*****

God gives every bird its food, but He does not throw it into its nest.

~ J. G. Holland

*****

Here is the world. Beautiful and terrible things will happen. Do not be afraid.

~ Frederick Buechner

PROLOGUE

Quietus est ... he is quit.

Quandary Peak

Nothing was more emotional than preparing for the impending death of a loved one. Most were unprepared to understand the end-of-life process. Some remained in denial, refusing to express their loss openly. Others handled the pain by putting on a false front, by dealing with the business and legal aspects of a loved one's passing.

In a post-apocalyptic world, there were no distractions. No wills to write. No safe deposits and bank accounts to close. No friends and family to notify on Facebook. Sitting vigil at the bed of the one you love was very personal, intense, and spiritual. With the rate of death, it had also become a common, everyday experience for most.

Grieving a violent death was different from normal mourning behavior. Death caused by human intent left the bereaved loved ones with an obsessive need to assign blame, search for reasons, or dwell on the missing details of what happened and why.

Violence with your fellow man during the apocalypse will be a given. Humans were six times more likely to kill each other than the average mammal. Most animals used aggressive displays to ward off competitors for food or their mates without the intention of causing death. Predators kill for sustenance by preying upon species other than their own.

Man is different. Violence was part of our evolutionary process. Over time, however, humans became less prone to natural or even chaotic violence. Otherwise, we wouldn't have survived throughout the millennia.

But the ability to commit violent death, to take another human's

1

life, was buried deep within us, waiting for the right set of circumstances to come to the surface. What triggered our ability to kill our fellow man was in part biological, dating back to before humans existed as a species. Other triggers were ingrained from our social and cultural practices. After society collapsed, the ability to kill with little remorse most likely came out of our innate desire to survive.

Once infected by the plague, death was expected as part of the natural processes dictated by the disease. It wasn't death at the hands of violence per se. It was, however, a violent way to die.

Death was never easy to accept, and the torturous time associated with the dying process was unnerving. Around the world, humanity was experiencing death. Violent deaths occurred, to be sure. But the vast majority of the approximately seven billion people who died during the pandemic did so based upon the plague's timeline—in days nine through twelve after contracting the disease.

For the disease stricken, death came slow and it was agonizing. Some of the victims suffered alone, and others with available friends and families. There were no grief counselors. No toll-free hotlines to seek advice. Spiritual support from clergy was unavailable. Death was lonely and it hurt more with each passing day.

In some cases, their loved ones provided comfort. They sat watch at the deathbed, completely unprepared for what they were facing. Some found the experience of death firsthand to be, in many ways, similar to birth. It was the essence of life. For others, their unimaginable sorrow placed a sense of guilt upon the dying.

More than one dying soul wondered—would I be better off dying a violent death at the hands of my fellow man—quick and easy? Or perhaps I should die at my own hands to relieve the sorrow of my loved ones and unburden those who grieve for me?

After eleven weeks, the human race had dwindled to a fraction of itself, awaiting its release in the form of death. Day after day, mankind lurched toward the end—*the quietus*, seeking a final, merciful blow.

PART ONE

WEEK TWELVE

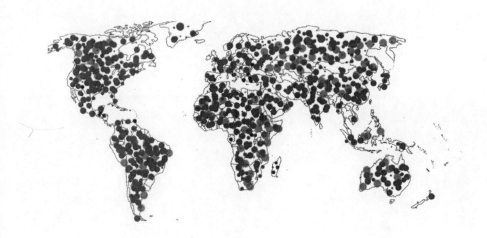

CHAPTER 1

Day Seventy-Eight
The Quarantine House
Quandary Peak

Overnight, Tommy's condition had worsened. Barb remained by his side throughout the night, taking catnaps in the chair when Tommy passed out from fatigue. Mac stopped in during the evening to sit with them while Janie and Hunter purposefully allowed the family as much time alone together as possible. It was agreed that the danger of contracting the disease was too great for constantly suiting-up in the protective equipment and then becoming exposed to the plague that was attacking Tommy's body.

He was in his second full day of being symptomatic. The plague bacteria had invaded Tommy's body like a thief in the night, wearing dark clothing and camouflaging itself to hide from the body's immune system.

The disease quickly adapted to its surroundings and began to seek nourishment. *Y. pestis* required iron, and Tommy's body had plenty of it within its hemoglobin and other proteins, including transferrin. The pneumonic plague, *the thief in the night*, committed a burglary. *Y. pestis* released a molecule that loves iron, so much so that it was able to physically rip it away from the transferrin protein and bring it back to the mother ship—*Y. pestis*.

With this nourishment, while Tommy was still attending to Marcus and feeling no pain, *Y. pestis* took up residency inside Tommy's lymph nodes. With each passing day, the lymph nodes began to scream to the body's sensory receptors—*Houston, we've got a problem*. The lymph nodes became swollen and the body began to react. For Tommy, the chest pains, fever, headache, and swelling were the first telltale signs.

His body was fighting the good fight. In this ninth day of the war, the plague bacteria were preparing to migrate through his bloodstream to the lungs. This was step one in a three-stage process, indicating the onset of sepsis and ultimately progressing to septic shock.

When Tommy awoke that morning, he complained that his heart was racing. Had he not been exposed to pneumonic plague, a physician might diagnose anxiety associated with an unknown malaise. However, the early signs of sepsis included a body temperature above one hundred one degrees, a heart rate greater than ninety beats per minute, and rapid, shallow breathing of more than twenty breaths per minute.

Tommy exhibited all of these symptoms and Barb determined he was in the first stages of sepsis. At Doc Cooley's instruction, Barb switched Tommy's IV fluids from normal saline to a thicker colloid mixture, which included albumin and dextran.

Barbara would now monitor for several signs of severe sepsis, which indicated Tommy's organs might be failing. As the *Y. pestis* bacteria began to increase in Tommy's bloodstream, the immune system would overreact, causing his blood vessels to begin leaking. Abnormal clotting would naturally result and the decreased volume then led to organ failure.

"Hey there, Tommy-gun," whispered Barb as her husband opened his eyes. She'd been giving him a cold-water sponge bath to help relieve the fever. "How're you feelin'?"

"Like a million bucks, baby," said Tommy with a chuckle followed by a gravelly cough. "You wanna get lucky with *the gun*?"

Tommy was licking his lips, attempting to produce saliva. When a person is in the final stages of dying, they are rarely conscious and usually breathe through their mouth. Tommy's mouth had dried out quickly, which made it uncomfortable to speak.

Barb kept a cold wet washcloth to wipe out his mouth, providing instant relief, which then allowed him to sip water through a straw. She also kept a tube of Blistex nearby to apply a couple of times an hour to prevent his lips from chapping.

She touched two fingers to her mask and then planted them on her husband's lips to pass along the kiss. He grinned and then closed his eyes again.

"Thank you for being with me," he whispered as he tried to open his eyes again. His body was weaker than the day before and he was no longer able to lift his arms. He was also physically unable to urinate into the bedpan provided by Doc, not that it mattered. His urine output had decreased to nothing, a sign that severe sepsis was imminent.

"Hey, are you up for some fresh air and a little sunshine?" she asked, trying to maintain an upbeat tone of voice. The temperatures had dropped into the upper thirties the night before, and Tommy's fever combined with the cold air to produce uncontrollable chills.

"Yeah," he strained to respond.

Barb limited the number of visitors to maintain a quiet, peaceful environment. The ever-present Flatus was fighting his own battles with the disease and lay on a bed Barb had created next to Tommy. She'd pulled a small loveseat out of a guest bedroom and scooted it next to Tommy's bed. Then she'd stacked sofa cushions to create a long series of platform steps to make it easier for Flatus to find a spot near his best friend.

It broke Barb's heart to see her men staring at each other, seeming to communicate, yet not speaking a word. *Are they encouraging each other to continue the fight? Or is it their way of comforting one another in preparation for the end?*

"Here we go," said Barb as she pushed open the windows in the room. A burst of cool, crisp air entered the enclosed space, unexpectedly invigorating both Tommy and Flatus. Flatus lifted his head and panted with a smile. Tommy reopened his eyes and took in his surroundings.

Some cultures call for a window to be open by the deathbed of a loved one to allow the souls of family members who have already died to come retrieve the person who is dying. It is their belief that closed windows trap the soul inside the room, preventing it from moving on.

"Very nice," said a reinvigorated Tommy. He turned his attention to Flatus. "Whadya think, buddy?"

Flatus winked at his bestie.

"Dear, do you wanna try something to eat? I can whip up some Cream of Wheat with sugar. Maybe some oatmeal?"

"No, thanks. Why don't you take a break? I know Mac and the others will be coming around soon."

Barb was puzzled by the request. She didn't understand why he would dismiss her. *Did I coddle or hover over him too much?*

"Tommy, I don't mind. I wanna be with you."

"I know. We've got a long day ahead of us. Take a walk, have breakfast, change clothes. Flatus and I'll be okay, right, buddy?" He reached his hand toward Flatus, who managed to wag his tail a few times. "See? Now scoot."

Barb studied her husband for a second. He wanted some alone time, but she didn't understand his reasoning. It was hard to grant his request, but she decided Tommy might need some time alone to prepare himself mentally. The process of dying required some preparation on his part as well. She decided to grant his wish.

"Okay," she acquiesced. "I'll go freshen up and come back in a new yellow suit I bought. You'll love it."

Tommy smiled and wiggled his fingers. "I love you, Barb."

"I love you more," she replied.

.

CHAPTER 2

Day Seventy-Eight
Quandary Peak

"What can I do to help?" Hunter asked Mac, a common question people ask when someone they care about is going through a traumatic, emotional time. Mac, on the surface, appeared to be holding it together. She recognized it was difficult for Hunter or Janie to know what to say to provide her strength and comfort. Mac had a plan to make it through the next few days. Immerse herself in the lab and continue to look for solutions.

"Knowing that you love me is all I need," she replied. "Try to stay with Mom. See if you can anticipate her needs without asking. Mom's tough exterior hides her true grief."

Hunter touched her face before she pulled on her protective headgear. He looked into her eyes. "Am I looking at the *Hagan tough exterior?*"

"Maybe." Mac blushed as she responded. She fought back the tears that had flowed when she woke up that morning. "I've got to put myself in another person's body for this, Hunter. Janie can't do it, nor can Mom. When I walk into that laboratory, such that it is, I'm Dr. Mackenzie Hagan, not Mac, the daughter of a wonderful father who is depending on me to save his life."

Hunter kissed her and touched her cheeks. "You're incredible. I promise to watch over both your parents today. Your work in that room is everyone's top priority."

"Thank you. I have to separate my emotions from the task at hand. Hand-wringing won't help my daddy. There are no arrangements to be made. And I can't just sit by his bedside, watching the clock, waiting for symptoms of pneumonia and septic shock to reveal themselves."

Hunter smiled and offered a fist to bump. "That's my girl, um, Dr. Mackenzie Hagan. Wow, you know something?"

"What?"

"I never call you Mackenzie. You've always been Mac to me."

"And I will be forever. Now listen, *Nate*, go take care of my mother. That's no easy task, soldier. Generals have a way about them."

"Okay. Okay. *Nate*, jeez. I get it," said Hunter as he gave her a final peck on the cheek. "Go find a miracle drug. I love you."

"I'll come down this afternoon when I'm finished," said Mac. "I love you back."

Hunter took the stairs two at a time in search of Barb. Mac rolled her neck to relieve the tension she held inside her and affixed her earbuds, which she attached to her iPod. Today, it would be her grand masters classical mix, starting with Mozart, followed by Bach, Beethoven and Tchaikovsky, who would be sure to keep her eyes open if she was exhausted after a long day.

Her mother assured her that Tommy's spirits were high when he was awake. His continued playful banter and interaction with Flatus was an encouraging sign. As part of his job, Hunter might have instigated the most deaths of anyone she'd ever met, but Mac had been around dying people more than the others.

It was common for depression and doubt to set in when someone was facing the end of life, particularly if they'd been the leader of the household. Her mother's military career might have taken priority over Tommy's teaching jobs, but within the Hagan family, it was understood he carried the weight of raising Mac and keeping their household running on all cylinders.

Although her father hadn't expressed any guilt for leaving the family under these circumstances, Mac and Barb agreed he was probably holding his feelings in. Barb promised to express her love and admiration for his accomplishments in raising their daughter. She would also remind Tommy that his dedication to their marriage enabled Barb to pursue her career to achieve the highest levels attainable.

All of this was important to maintain a cool head and clear heart as Mac studied her laboratory test subjects. She never assigned each mouse a name, as it was considered bad form to personalize a creature that would be dying soon. They were labeled by the date of the month and their numeric order by which they were infected. She then compartmentalized them accordingly.

Mac recreated the vancomycin d-ala d-lac formula that she had begun injecting into her father the day before. In the chaos of Tommy showing symptoms prematurely, Mac had failed to inject any of the mice who were symptomatic yesterday. They were now in the middle of a two-day freight train ride to their death.

It was her intention to spend the entire day in the lab, trying several variables to see what transpired. Mac had no illusions. Her father would likely be dead within forty-eight hours.

She carefully reached in and retrieved a weak, breathy subject. "Come on down, 09-03-01, you're the first contestant on the *Drug Is Right*."

She injected 09-03-01 and moved on to the next two lab mice from that day. All displayed the telltale signs of sepsis and pneumonia. She checked on her other mice who'd been injected with this same formula from the day before. They exhibited shallow breathing and their body temperatures were the same as the last check.

Last night, before they fell asleep, she and Hunter discussed life after her father passed away. It was a frank, emotion-filled conversation at first, but then Mac considered her future in the makeshift lab.

She promised to continue her work, hoping the drug could be useful someday on some level. Like the stock market crash of 1929, nobody could predict for certain when the precipitous drop in the world's population would bottom out.

Mac said it was likely this strain of the pneumonic plague would live on through a variety of hosts for eternity, or at least as long as she and Hunter lived. For that reason, she vowed to soldier on in her quest to find a cure, even if it was only for the benefit of their group.

So Mac made copious notes. She undertook a routine that was no different than the one she'd followed in college and continued during her career at the CDC. Somebody would find a way to use them.

CHAPTER 3

Day Seventy-Nine
The Quarantine House
Quandary Peak

Barb awoke to Tommy coughing violently in the early morning hours before dawn. He was complaining of chest pain and she checked his vitals. His blood pressure had dropped overnight. However, Tommy's heart rate was elevated. He felt clammy and his brow remained covered with droplets of sweat.

She was concerned Tommy was going into shock. Barb quickly elevated his feet about twelve inches above his head, using the seat cushion from her chair. She retrieved extra blankets and comforters from the closet and made sure he was warm and comfortable.

"I'm so thirsty, Barb. I need water," Tommy groaned.

"Honey, I'll get your mouth moist, but I have to be careful." Barb knew water might enter his lungs and hasten pneumonia.

She wet a washcloth and placed it around his mouth. "Can you bite down on it and allow the water to trickle down your throat?"

Tommy nodded and winced as he soaked his mouth with the fluid. He gave her a slight smile, indicating he had enough.

"Barb, this sucks."

He said it so matter-of-factly that she burst out laughing and added a few tears as her emotions slipped through the façade.

"Yes, sir, it sure does."

He tried to lift his arms to point, but the heavy blankets weighed him down. "Flatus. Thirsty, too."

Barb soaked the rag for him as well and wiped the drool off his mush. She allowed him to take in some water. Unlike Tommy, Flatus was able to lift his head and reposition in the chair. This encouraged Barb to provide him a small bowl to drink from.

"How's that, big boy?" asked Barb, showing genuine affection for the playful pup who was giving his life to be by Tommy's side.

His tired brown eyes blinked at her. She gently rubbed his head and down his back. Barb's gentle touch caused Flatus to relax and curl up nose to tail.

"Thank you, dear. Sit close to me, okay?"

Barb grabbed a chair from the dining room and carried it to his bedside. She sat and held his hand as Tommy continued.

"I'm leaving you in a mess. I'm sorry."

"Don't you apologize or feel bad for anything. You and I have shared a wonderful life together. Thank you for puttin' up with me all of these years."

He tried to laugh and then winced. Barb tried to get him to relax.

"Let's treat every last hour like it's a whole year. Whadya think?"

Tommy struggled to find the words, not because he was weak, but out of love for his family.

"I need to go, Barb. It's gonna get worse. So painful for you to watch."

Barb wiped his forehead again. She was concerned the fever and the pain he was suffering might be causing him to become delirious.

"I'm a big girl, Tommy. Don't worry about me. You make yourself comfortable."

Tommy closed his eyes and was noticeably trying to control his breathing. Barb continued to watch him as his breathing became shallower, like he was on the verge of falling asleep.

His eyes suddenly opened wide, startling her. His body jolted, making her think that he was having a seizure.

"Tommy, honey? Are you all right?" Barb was frantic. "Oh, God. Not now. It's too early. Not now."

Then Tommy asked something odd and out of context. "*Hamlet.* Do you remember *Hamlet?*"

Barb began to shed a few tears. Tommy was slipping away. She had discussed the loss of mental acuity with Janie and Mac.

"Honey, I don't understand. *Hamlet?* Of course I know *Hamlet.*"

Tommy nodded and forced out the word, "*Hamlet.*"

"Tommy, please rest. We don't need to waste your strength on Shakespeare, dear. That's way too heavy of a topic."

Barb doted over him by wiping his face and arms with a wet rag. She then grabbed another clean washcloth and doused it with cool water to provide him some hydration. He bit down and soaked in the moisture.

"Do you remember the story?" he asked.

Barb shook her head and grimaced. She wasn't sure if she should continue to insist upon his resting or humor him in his final hours. Studies had shown that talking to a person who is dying, even if they're in a coma, allows them to feel comfort while hearing your voice. She decided to recount the *Hamlet* soliloquy the best she could, if that was what her dying husband wanted. It was a play they'd enjoyed several times in their life together. She hoped her voice would calm him down and provide her some inner peace as well.

She began by saying the most famous line first, *to be, or not to be*, which opened the third act spoken by Prince Hamlet. Barb continued the story and Tommy was apparently drifting off to sleep when he interrupted her.

Like before, his eyes opened wide and his body shook slightly. It was as if Tommy's brain was overcompensating for his body's weakened state. He licked his lips and spoke.

"Remember the bare bodkin? Quietus?"

Barb's mind raced, searching for a response to his statement. She knew the phrase well, as it had been a frequent topic of conversation over a glass of wine at home.

Where is he going with this?

"Of course, dear," she finally responded. "We've debated what that line meant for years."

"Yes," said Tommy with a slight whisper.

She sat up in the chair and recited the line. "*When he himself might his quietus make with a bare bodkin.* We agreed the bare bodkin referred to a dagger. Quietus meant—" Barb abruptly stopped mid-sentence. *He wants to quit, or kill himself.*

Tommy nodded and looked directly at her eyes, mustering up the courage and strength to speak.

"Yes. Barb, I don't want to burden you. I want to go. Please help me go."

CHAPTER 4

Day Seventy-Nine
The Quarantine House
Quandary Peak

"Those were his exact words," started Mac. "Please help me go."

"Yes," said Barb, who'd just finished crying in Mac's arms.

After Barb got Tommy to sleep, she called from the checkpoint for Hunter to join her. Janie volunteered to suit up and join Tommy and Flatus to monitor their conditions. After a brief conversation with Hunter, he hustled up the ridge to retrieve Mac from the lab.

Just as the conversation was getting started, Doc Cooley arrived to check on his old friend. They brought him up to speed on Tommy's condition over the last twenty-four hours. He offered to examine Tommy, but they all agreed to allow their beloved patient the opportunity to rest.

"Mom, what does he want to do, commit suicide? Is he giving up on me?" asked Mac as she started to get emotional. For days, she'd kept her composure around everyone except when she released her true emotions around Hunter. But this was too much for her.

"Dear, don't assume that," replied Barb. "Your father was feeling remorseful because he believes he's leaving us in a world with his burdens. He'll be all right later."

Mac walked away and ran her hand through her hair. She had to put her emotions away and consider her father's feelings for a minute. She rejoined the group, who had been watching her.

"No, I'm sorry, Mom. The truth is we all know that Daddy will not be all right later. Not tomorrow, and for sure not the day after that. The day after tomorrow, he'll be gone. In the next day and a half, he'll suffer excruciating pain as his body fails him. It will be hard on him mentally and it will be hard on us as well. Daddy knows this."

"Mac, what are you saying?" asked Hunter.

"This is his way of asking us to help him go. He wants to die with dignity."

Barb began to cry. Hunter moved in to comfort her. After a moment, she wiped away the tears.

"It makes sense now. He doesn't want to come out and say the words *assisted suicide*. He wanted me to reach the conclusion on my own by using the line from Hamlet dealing with the bare bodkin, a simple dagger, and the Latin word *quietus*, meaning the final death."

Mac held her mother. The two hadn't shared many tender moments in their lives together, much less after Mac had become an adult. Now, as mother and daughter, they'd have to make one of the biggest decisions a family faces.

"Mom," said Mac as she pulled away, "what do we do? Everyone knows this is going to get worse. His body will begin to shut down with each passing hour. We can provide him a strong morphine cocktail to ease his pain, but all that will do is ignore his wishes."

Barb didn't say anything for a moment, which gave Doc an opportunity to counsel the family.

"Y'all know I think the world of all y'all. I don't believe anybody should have a right to die, but Colorado does have a law on the books that allows people to choose a fast and painless death in a manner that's good for them. It doesn't matter whether you call it right to die, or death with dignity, or a happy death. The end result is the same. The question is whether you grant his wishes or not. That's why folks create living wills in order to take the emotional aspect out of the decision-making process."

"Mom, do you guys have a living will?" asked Mac.

"I do. It was required by the Army. Your father never got around to signing one."

"Did he ever express his wishes to you?" asked Mac. "I mean, surely you guys talked about it if you created one through the military."

Barb took a few steps toward the house and attempted to peer through the window. She put her hands on her hips and kicked some stones at her feet.

"Yes, we did talk about it," she finally replied. "Once, after seeing *Hamlet*, we debated the meaning of the line I recited to him. The other occasion was when I signed my advanced directives."

"Well, what did he say? Also, what did you put in your living will?"

"Dear, we both agreed. We didn't want any extraordinary measures to keep us alive. Also, we agreed the best way to die with dignity is with the assistance of a doctor if we're terminally ill. I hope you understand. Neither of us ever wanted to be a burden on you in our final days. It had nothing to do with losing faith in your abilities or our love as a family. We just wanted to make things easy on our daughter."

Mac ran to her mother and they hugged each other for several minutes. Eventually, the crying subsided and they walked back arm in arm to a waiting Doc and Hunter.

"Doc, will you help us?" asked Barb. "We want to honor Tommy's wishes."

Doc hugged them both and explained their options. "Okay, things have changed since the days Dr. Kevorkian began shooting people up with potassium chloride. He'd first provide a painkiller and then the fatal dose of potassium chloride, which caused cardiac arrest. Today, there are two better, generally accepted and approved compounds used in states like Oregon, Washington, Montana, and California, which have all passed assisted-suicide statutes.

"This gets a little technical, but the option most often used is a lethal dose of phenobarbital, chloral hydrate, and morphine, which has to be compounded in the pharmacy. Likewise, a new mix using morphine, Valium, Inderal, and digoxin will work if the local pharmacy doesn't have the chemicals necessary to create the compound. The morphine will ease his pain and the Valium will calm his nerves and alleviate anxiety."

"The last two medications are for heart patients, right?" asked Barb.

"Yes, but in large doses, using the two together will dramatically slow his heart rate until it stops beating. Personally, I'd suggest the compounded mix of the three drugs in powdered form. It tends to have a bitter taste, but we might be able to add a little sugar or mix it with applesauce."

Barb laughed nervously. "If I know my husband, he'll wanna go out like John Wayne in some western movie. Mix it with a shot of your finest whiskey, Doc. He'll hold his nose and take it with a smile."

Everyone released some of the tension over Tommy's certain demise by laughing along with his wife of forty years. Barb gave Doc a hug and said, "Will you get everything we need?"

"Yeah, it'll take some doin'. The sheriff has that pharmacy under lock and key with twenty-four-seven armed security. The pharmacist may or may not do what I'm asking. He's funny that way. Don't you worry your little head none. I'll get 'er done and see y'all back down here in the morning, okay?"

"Thank you, Doc," replied Barb.

Mac hesitated and then hugged Doc as well. She still wasn't a hundred percent on board with the whole assisted-suicide concept— not when there was still a chance. After she visited with her father, she'd wrestle with the decision and get Hunter's opinion. If her mother insisted, then she'd have to decide whether the drama should be avoided in her daddy's final days.

CHAPTER 5

Day Seventy-Nine
Noah's Ark
Boreas Pass at Red Mountain

Boreas Pass used to be known as Breckenridge Pass when the Denver, South Park, and Pacific Railroad traveled through it, carrying miners from Denver throughout Summit and Park Counties. Few events in the history of Summit County and Breckenridge were more important than the 1882 arrival of the railroad. It connected the growing western town of Denver to the numerous gold mines that had sprung up throughout the Rockies.

The town of Boreas emerged near the rails running from the south into Breckenridge. Named for the Greek God of the North Wind, the perilous trail through the pass ran up to twelve thousand feet, battled fierce winds and steep, five percent grades.

Despite the brutal winters, the miners came and inhabited the valley. At one point, estimates approaching thirty thousand residents of Boreas Pass spent their days mining deep within Boreas Mountain, Red Mountain, and Mount Argentine.

During its heyday, at the time of the Civil War, Colorado mines produced two hundred thousand ounces of gold per year, leading to the creation of the Denver Mint.

Eventually the gold began to dwindle in supply and thousands of gold seekers became disappointed. They abandoned the mines and tried their hands at panning. The yield didn't justify the time spent for most of the prospectors, and the migration back to the Great Plains began.

Known as the go-backers, the ragged, foot-weary prospectors returned back east, crossing paths with the thousands who were headed west to seek their fortunes. Without gold, these new residents ultimately moved on to Nevada and California.

Make no mistake, there was still gold in the mountains, but it wasn't cost effective to mine it due to the high cost of machinery and labor. Prospectors of old could still make a decent living, but they were few and far between, except at Noah's Ark.

Rulon Snow had a business sense about him. When he was faced with life in prison, he made a business decision rather than an emotional one. He'd testify against the Prophet in that federal courtroom in Salt Lake City and he'd get paid for it.

In exchange for his testimony, the government provided Snow forty acres of seclusion on what they considered a pile of rocks. The Department of Justice didn't pay attention to the actual topography of the land, simply assuming it looked like the side of every rocky mountain.

What Snow received was a horseshoe-shaped meadow surrounded by steep cliffs. The meadow was fertile soil created by the constant erosion of the rocky peaks that surrounded it. Abandoned log cabins dotted the landscape, providing Snow decent enough lodging for his flock of three sister wives and their children.

In the rear of the property, at the base of Red Mountain, was a rock outcropping marking the entrance to the old Boreas Mine. After the mine was emptied of fifty thousand tons of copper ore in the roaring twenties, it was abandoned to the federal government during the Depression of the thirties.

As the story goes, the mine was shuttered in 1926 after a collapse in one of the shafts buried two dozen men alive. A rescue and recovery effort took place in the collapsed shaft, which descended just over a thousand feet at a steep incline into the mountain.

For days, the town assembled to dig out the collapsed rock and debris, eventually finding their way through to the other end of the shaft. What they found horrified everyone in Summit County.

Nothing. There were no miners. No dead bodies. No signs of activity. No new exits. The men had simply vanished.

As a result, the Phelps Dodge Corporation couldn't find miners to extract the copper ore. They would recruit men out of Denver who were unfamiliar with the tragedy. But as soon as they received their first paycheck and headed into Boreas for food and drink, they learned the story and never returned out of fear.

Phelps Dodge, the mine's owner, began to lose money, failed to pay their taxes, and soon under the Internal Revenue Act of 1934, gladly turned over the worthless mine to the IRS in exchange for a reprieve on their tax obligations.

Snow knew nothing of the story and the supposed ghosts of Boreas Mine. All he knew was that there was still gold in there. Over the years, he and his burgeoning family worked the mine. Unlike corporate mining operations, his labor was cheap, as in *free*.

The gold nuggets they found in Snow's early days in the mine were small, about the size of a dime. A one-gram nugget of this size was worth around sixty dollars. At first, the work was tedious because there was a learning curve. Within a few months, they were prospecting all day and discovering a hundred nuggets in a typical ten-hour work period.

Snow learned how to follow the veins running through the granite. The nuggets got bigger and the veins were richer. The pile of nuggets grew and then 2012 arrived. The price of gold hit $1,664 per ounce, which meant it was time for Snow to cash in.

He and his six sister wives, at that point, systematically traveled from Pueblo to Denver to Fort Collins to sell his nuggets. In a six-month time period, he amassed nearly a million dollars in cash, which he immediately used to fortify his compound.

He'd learned the lessons from the FLDS—Fundamentalist Church of Jesus Christ of Latter-Day Saints, in Utah and Texas. To maintain his way of life, he had to keep people out, but he also had to keep them in. As they recruited more sister wives and they bore children, security and privacy became his priorities.

Snow also had to feed the flock. He purchased food that could be stored for long periods of time within the bowels of the Boreas Mine. He stockpiled weapons and ammunition for defense of his family. If Snow didn't have it, he could afford to buy it, and he did.

When the plague cursed the planet, Snow pounced on the

opportunity. Now, eleven weeks into the apocalypse, he was thriving and his flock was growing as he took in more sister wives fearful of contracting the disease and seeking shelter.

Snow stood at the entrance of the mine and admired his accomplishments. Crops were being harvested. Fences were being patrolled. Horses were being trained. Seeds were being sown.

His brow furled as he thought of the first task before him. He unconsciously grabbed his belt, adorned with a heavy leather buckle, which had been passed onto him by his father, in more ways than one.

Spare the rod, spoil the child, Snow thought to himself as he contemplated the whipping he was about to administer to his beloved Seth and Levi for causing those fires. They had reeked of smoke the morning after the fires ravaged the mountains to their north. But it wasn't the fire that earned them their daily whoopin' since he'd discovered what they had done. It was the fact they had lied to him about it.

He made that clear to them each time he lectured them. Their punishment was confinement to the mine and a daily beating until Snow thought they'd learned their lesson.

Snow then hitched up his pants and turned into the mine with a smile on his face. After teaching his sons a lesson about lying, he was going to visit his prized possessions—the twins from Fairplay.

CHAPTER 6

Day Seventy-Nine
Conference Room
Cheyenne Mountain

It had been three days since President Garcia ordered the annihilation of the ISIS command and control structure hidden within the Qandil Mountains. The Minuteman III missile carried nearly five hundred kilotons of energy. Upon impact, it destroyed every structure within a twenty-two-mile radius. It collapsed the vast tunnel network built over the centuries by the Kurds and utilized by Hassan and al-Baghdadi.

The fallout was both deadly and troublesome. The health effects of nuclear explosions were due primarily to the blast, together with the thermal and nuclear radiation. The fallout consisted of weapon debris, fission products, and the tons of radiated soil, dust, and rocky material that spewed into the air for twenty-four hours following the attack.

The government of Iran screamed bloody murder. Through its allies on the United Nations Security Council, Russia and China, they called for the strongest condemnations of the attack and immediate sanctions on the United States.

To which President Garcia said *so what*. The nuclear attack upon ISIS was the equivalent of a giant stepping on an ant, but it was absolutely necessary to give the United States of America a win.

It had been very tense within the confines of Cheyenne Mountain over the past seventy-two hours. Some within the government openly questioned the decision and even voiced concerns over the President's mental stability. Others applauded the decision as a boost for the American psyche.

The military bases around the country enthusiastically cheered the move. Those new residents of the safe zones were all in support of the President. Even the poor and downtrodden who were forced to fight the ravaging plague and their fellow man were glad to hear of the attack.

With each passing day, as the fear of a retaliatory strike by Russia or China passed, President Garcia found a renewed vigor for his job and a love for the American people.

The first thing he did was abandon the bottle. Brandy had become his crutch to get him through the difficulties associated with being the leader of the free world.

Second, he returned to the daily briefings required to perform his duties. The alcohol no longer clouded his mind and his judgment. As a result, the paranoia of the plague lurking in the shadows or within every one of his cabinet members' breaths subsided. President Garcia was ready to get back to work.

"Good morning, everyone," announced the President as he entered the largest conference room in Cheyenne Mountain, an auditorium-style seating arrangement that allowed for PowerPoint presentations, podium speaking, and roundtable-style discussions in front of a large audience.

Nearly forty people were in attendance and responded to the President with a hearty good morning. While not all of the longtime government servants agreed with the President, most approved of his actions against ISIS. When word spread throughout the complex that President Garcia would cease to remain in isolation, spirits were lifted in anticipation of his speech.

The leaders of the U.S. government were ready to move on and look at this cataclysmic event in the rearview mirror. The group quietened down as the President tapped the microphone to make sure it was working.

"I think this mic is a little too much, considering the size of our group, don't you think?" asked the President with a laugh. He had dressed in a suit and tie for the occasion but immediately felt out of place. This was not a campaign address. It was a conversation with his top subordinates about the future of America.

He removed his coat and tie before he stepped off the stage. He walked around in front of the first row and hoisted himself up to sit on the stage with his legs dangling.

"Now, that's better," started President Garcia. "We've had a rough few months. By *we*, I mean all of us in this room. I've not been a very good leader, which is part of my job. My judgment has been clouded by fear of contracting the disease, among other things. That has changed and I'd like all of you to accept my apologies for being a less-than-stellar president."

"We're with you, Mr. President," responded his Secretary of Health and Human Services.

"Soldier on, sir," added one of the Joint Chiefs of Staff.

"I will, and thank you," the President responded. "My daily briefings will resume and all of you will be a part of them as we move forward. In fact, I've asked Mr. Morse to make these happen twice a day. The morning brief will continue to focus on international and defense issues. The afternoon briefing will focus on domestic issues and the challenges we face in rebuilding the nation. All of you will be required to attend rather than sending a subordinate. Our daily routines are much different than they were in Washington. Coordination and transparency within the Executive Branch will no longer be compromised.

"Let me begin by providing you an abbreviated State of the Union. First, on the foreign policy front. I made the decision to launch the nuclear attack against the Islamic State to send a message, but more importantly, to annihilate the enemy. I realize they have foot soldiers and sleeper cells around the world. But we believe their leadership council has been destroyed, and hopefully, their will has been destroyed too. Further, if our intelligence is correct, sadly, their wives and children would have perished as well. This will have a profound effect on the enemy. If they react in anger, they'll make mistakes and we will be ready for them.

"Second, while Russia and China have issued their—quote— *strongest condemnations of the attack*, it doesn't appear they intend to start a nuclear war. I've spoken with both Presidents and assured them our attack was both warranted and a onetime occurrence. Let me recognize the Secretary of State and his department for insuring that cooler heads prevailed throughout."

The group applauded as the Secretary of State nodded and waved his hand. The President knew the Secretary was one of the most vocal opponents of his decision to launch the Minuteman III. Recognizing him publicly was a way to give him credit for diffusing the situation while reminding the Secretary that the attack was a success.

"Domestically, I'm pleased to announce the safe-zone policy has worked with only a few exceptions. What happened at Fort Bliss was tragic and, in hindsight, avoidable. Tempers have calmed, potentially infected individuals have been quarantined, and order has been restored.

"Outside our military installations, the confiscation of private property, while unfortunate, has proven successful. Tens of thousands of community leaders have been placed under the protection of local law enforcement and the military. They will form the nucleus when it comes time to rebuild our nation. Which brings me to our final topic.

"Around the globe, the world's population has dwindled to a small percentage of what it was before the plague spread. The United Nations estimates seven billion people are now infected or dead. That leaves seven hundred million who can be saved absent a cure for the disease. Other sources, namely world governments, estimate the death toll to be even greater with survivors numbering under one hundred million.

"I don't want to come across as callous, but at this point in time, we have to focus on our own. I have no way of stating definitively what the population of the uninfected is in America. I can say we are going to use all of our efforts to find them. If the total is ten percent, as the U.N. suggests, then we have thirty million survivors to find and protect.

"The first challenge we face is where to protect them. The neighborhoods in the immediate vicinity of military installations like

Star Ranch here in Colorado Springs have been a success. I think we need to start thinking bigger. Let's consider finding towns that can be easily defended and cleared of the infected. Once these small towns can be identified as safe zones, then we'll tackle the issue of finding the uninfected and relocating them.

"I've tasked DHS with creating a plan of identification of potential safe zones, as well as a method to locate survivors who have avoided the disease. The Interior Department will assist in this endeavor as well.

"Lastly, there are numerous minor tasks to be assigned to each of you. I know all of you have questions, comments, and suggestions. Rather than voice them now, please see Mr. Morse after this meeting and schedule a time to sit down with me on an individual basis, even if it's for just fifteen minutes. I want us to be transparent, but we also have to be efficient. I will share my conversations with you during the morning and afternoon briefings, which will start tomorrow.

"Again, please accept my humble apology for the rocky start during these perilous times. Know that I have every confidence in your abilities to bring our nation back to her feet and follow our new policy of *America First*. Thank you."

CHAPTER 7

Day Eighty
The Quarantine House
Quandary Peak

Barb was like so many family members before her, sitting by the side of their dying loved ones, sometimes for days, processing the impending loss of their physical presence from their future. Then, the ill patient suddenly rallies, becomes more stable and even talkative.

It's human nature to grasp at what seems like a turnaround with a sigh of relief. Barb did not wake up on her own this morning. She woke up to Tommy's voice as he chatted with Flatus. Startled out of her sleep of just a few hours, her first thoughts were that her husband was going to hang on for a while. *But is he?*

"Tommy, are you feeling better?" she asked.

"Yeah, a little bit," he replied. "In fact, Flatus and I were just talking about it. I'm sorry we woke you. He said he feels about the same. I, on the other hand, have regained a little of my strength in my lungs, it seems."

Barb wanted to be jubilant. She wanted to sing from the mountaintops and call everybody into the quarantine house to witness the miracle. Then her medical training took hold and reality set in.

More often than not, a rally such as what Tommy was experiencing was actually a signal death was imminent. When working with the Ebola-stricken patients in Sierra Leone, she had experienced this before. Some patients wanted to talk, as Tommy was now. Others simply became more relaxed, yet tuned in to their surroundings and their fate.

On rare occasions, patients showed signs of physical stability where hours before they seemed on the edge of letting go. The rallies were momentary, or could last for days, depending on the timeline of the disease.

As she listened to Tommy speaking to Flatus, Barb recalled the effect these rallies had on the loved ones sitting vigil. She remembered one situation in West Africa where a man had withdrawn into himself, shunning the family members who gathered near him daily. They'd accepted that his time was coming soon. Then the man appeared to recover. He was even able to sit up and talk with them. There was a renewed spark in his eye.

He told his family to leave and get something to eat. He even asked for a bowl of groundnut stew, his favorite, which consisted of chicken and vegetables, flavored with groundnuts like cashews and peanuts. During the time it took the family to walk to the local restaurant and back, the man had died.

Barb's experiences with pre-death rallies in Sierra Leone had taught her to cherish those moments. She looked at it like a moment of clarity for someone who had dementia. A pre-death rally was one last time to connect with Tommy before the end, which loomed large on the horizon.

She stood and approached his bedside. He'd pushed off the heavy covers meant to slow the progression of sepsis and to help with his feverish chills. Tommy easily lifted his hand and reached for Barb's mask.

"I'd give anything to touch you one last time," he said as he rubbed her mask.

Barb welled up in tears. "Me too, dear. You seem to be feeling better. Yesterday, you could barely talk."

"Yeah, I got a good night's sleep. It must be the mighty morphine." Tommy laughed and coughed a little, which brought a frown to his face. The congestion in his chest was a reminder of the plague bacteria that invaded his body.

Barb was checking his vitals when she saw Doc Cooley position himself in the front yard where she could see him. He wisely didn't shout to her, but he held up a ziplock bag with several vials, reminding her of why he was there so early in the morning. *Doc Death* had arrived and she didn't want to dampen Tommy's good spirits.

"Dear, are you up for a visit from Mac?" asked Barb.

"Of course," replied Tommy. "Why don't you run get her and bring back some blueberry muffins. I think I could have one today."

Once again, Barb recalled her experience in Sierra Leone. There was no way she was leaving his side, especially to get food.

"No, I see somebody out front. I'll have them get her so you and I can visit some more. You stay put; I'll be right back."

"Ha-ha, very funny. I feel pretty good, but I'm sure not runnin' off anywhere."

Barb hustled out of the room and went onto the front porch. She waved Doc over to the west side of the house, where Tommy couldn't hear their conversation.

"How is he?" asked Doc.

"Actually, he woke me up," replied Barb. "He seems to have gained some of his clarity and strength to talk."

"Now, Barb, let me caution—" started Doc before she cut him off.

"I know, I know, Doc. It's just a pre-death rally, which is why I need your help. Would you please get Mac down here as quickly as possible? I'd like her to enjoy these few moments with her dad while he is talkative. It'll be a better way to remember him, you know?"

"I'll take care of it right now. Barb, I have the, um, the medicine we talked about yesterday. If Tommy is clearheaded, perhaps it would be a good opportunity to confirm his wishes."

Barb considered Tommy's suggestion. She knew in her heart what Tommy wanted, which was why she'd asked Doc about their options. She hated to ruin their final moment with Tommy while he was in this short spurt of energy to discuss whether they should hasten his death or not. This was a tough call that required Mac's input.

CHAPTER 8

Day Eighty
The Quarantine House
Quandary Peak

Mac and Hunter arrived within minutes after being raised on the radio by Doc and Janie. Doc met them in the yard and gave Mac the medicinal compound to be injected into Tommy's IV line. When Doc had prepared the compound at the pharmacy, he found some written instructions as well as notes on what to expect after the assisted-suicide drug was administered. He provided it all to Mac in a plain brown paper bag, together with some new syringes.

Hunter promised to wait on her to escort her back up to the house. He gave her a kiss, a few words of encouragement, and dutifully took a seat in a lawn chair outside the screened porch. Mac suited up and gave him a final wave before she went inside.

She found her mother in the dining chair at Tommy's side. He certainly looked better than yesterday. He immediately noticed her when she entered.

"Hi, dear," greeted Tommy as she came into his view. "Your mother and I were just talking about the time we were stationed in Heidelberg, Germany."

"You, you remember that?" Mac asked hesitantly. She looked to her mother, who shrugged.

"Of course. Barb had just taken over command of the 30th Medical. We went out to celebrate at a bräuhaus for some schnitzel and bratwurst. You insisted on buying a German dirndl to wear because you wanted to look like the Oktoberfest girl. Remember?"

"Wow, Daddy, that was a mouthful," Mac mused. She approached him and touched his face. Even through the antimicrobial gloves, he was still warm to the touch. "Of course I remember that. That was the first time you let me taste a beer."

"Yes, indeed," he added. "You said it was yucky."

"It was too strong," said Mac. "Speaking of strong, it appears you've found your voice."

"I got a good night's sleep, thanks to the drugs."

"He calls it mighty morphine," quipped Barb.

Mac checked his vitals again. She grabbed the spiral notebook she and her mother had been using to record his condition. The vitals were the same as yesterday, only he was more energetic.

Mac walked around the bed and examined Flatus. She opened his eyes and mouth. She then examined his lymph nodes for swelling. They were located at the back of the leg, near the leg joints at the hip, and at the side of his neck. They appeared to be the same as the day before.

Barb watched Mac's every move while Tommy appeared to remain in the euphoria of feeling somewhat better. The Hagan women caught each other's eyes and nodded. Mac turned her attention to her dad.

"Mom and I are going to put this fresh batch of vancomycin in the refrigerator. Would you like something to drink? I could have Mom crush some ice and feed you chips."

Tommy looked over at Flatus and smiled. "Yes, the gentleman and I will have some ice chips, please."

Barb and Mac exited the bedroom and pulled the door closed, leaving a slight crack. They overheard Tommy speaking to Flatus.

"This is where the Hagan doctors go and commiserate about us, buddy. They'll leave with a gloomy look on their faces, and when they return, they'll be all sunshine and rainbows. You'll see."

Barb and Mac looked at each other and smiled, shaking their heads in disbelief. Barb couldn't restrain herself.

"You do remember when I suggested the lockjaw option, right?"

"Hush, Mom," started Mac with a chuckle. "I remember. I'm gonna miss his jokes."

Barb took her daughter by the arm and led her into the kitchen. They put the vancomycin in the refrigerator and set the vials of compound created by Doc next to them. The two of them stared at the contents for a moment.

"Ironic, isn't it?" asked Barb rhetorically. "On the left side, we have the possible cure for the plague. On the right side, we have the cure for the pain and agony. Frankly, I don't know which is the right choice."

"He's improved, Mom. I think we should wait on the death option for now."

"Dear, you know not to get your hopes up. You've seen patients rally just before death during your time in the field."

Mac walked to the back door and stared off into the woods. Two deer were grazing on the uncut grass, but raised their heads and looked in her direction when they sensed her movement. She turned back to her mother.

"Doc suggested we talk to Daddy about the death-with-dignity option while he's having this moment of clarity. What do you think?" asked Mac.

"That makes sense, but he's having such a great morning, I hate to ruin it with talk of his demise. I know in my heart that's what he wants, Mac. I wouldn't have allowed Doc to go through the effort if I didn't."

Mac agreed with her mother, but she also recognized the clock was ticking. She opened the refrigerator again and stared at the vials of medication.

"Okay, let's not address it. I say we continue the vancomycin and the morphine drip. Mom, I have no illusions as to what happens next. If he continues to rest, maybe we'll get lucky and we'll have another opportunity to enjoy him like this one. We both know the clock's running out."

"I agree, dear. Let's give him his morning dose of antibiotics and painkiller. Maybe he'll have some more to say before he rests."

Mac grabbed a vial of vancomycin and a fresh syringe. She and Barb started back down the hallway when Barb grabbed her arm.

"Wait, I forgot about his ice chips. Help me, dear. It'll be faster to crush the ice together. I wish this fridge did it for us. We'll have to pound it in the sink to break it up."

Mac hesitated, looked toward the bedroom door, and turned to help her mother. A few minutes later, they returned to the bedroom.

Mac pushed open the door with her toe and immediately called out, "Daddy!"

Tommy was lying perfectly still, eyes closed, arms crossed across his chest as if he was hugging himself, his mouth gaped open, and drool was covering his pillow.

CHAPTER 9

Day Eighty-One
The Quarantine House
Quandary Peak

In the eleven days since Tommy had been infected with the disease, much had happened around the planet, but Tommy was the center of everyone's universe at Quandary Peak. When Tommy had rallied yesterday morning, Barb admitted to having a glimmer of hope. They knew they were correct in their diagnosis, but perhaps the strain was different, or even the bubonic form of the plague. Maybe, as Mac suggested, the medication was working.

Both of them felt guilty for panicking when they'd come upon Tommy in the bedroom—sleeping. When you're on deathwatch, your mind tricks you into false hope when there is a rally and confirmation of your expectations when your loved one appears to take a turn for the worse.

After Mac administered the vancomycin and morphine, the Hagan doctors returned to the living room and broke down emotionally. They cried for almost an hour, allowing their suffering to come to the surface. They took turns periodically to check on Tommy's condition. Both felt a sense of guilt in doing so. Barb and Mac were truly on deathwatch now.

Mac returned to the lab eventually and Barb returned to her husband's bedside. She refused to return to the house and rest. After yesterday's unusual wake-up call from a very talkative husband, she knew it was almost time.

"Barb, Barbara, are you awake?" asked Tommy, bringing Barb out of her slumber. Her eyes quickly adjusted to the morning light. Disoriented, she tried to remember what day it was.

Did I simply doze off during Tommy's rally? Or is this a sign of improvement? Is that even possible?

"What? Yes? Good morning, dear."

Barb had recovered the full use of her faculties and focused on her husband. He was lying awkwardly in the bed, tilted toward Flatus, who was also awake.

"Would you mind helping me straighten these pillows? I tried to prop up and got a little discombobulated. Would you please bobulate me?"

She tilted her head at him inquisitively. "Sure. But, Tommy, how are you feelin'?" She assisted him in leaning forward and she adjusted his pillows. He hadn't been able to sit up in four days.

"Not too bad. I think I slept a long time."

"You did," said a bewildered Barb. *This can't be happening. Not two days in a row.* "Let me check your vitals, okay?"

While Barb checked his blood pressure, which had risen closer to low normal ranges, and his heart rate, which was normal, Tommy had a conversation with Flatus. Flatus, who was normally quiet, responded with his own way of *talking*. Using his diaphragm to force air through his vocal cords, he created a variety of whining and groaning sounds, which he altered by moving his mouth.

Tommy mimicked the sounds and playfully patted the pup's head during the entire exchange. Barb shook her head in disbelief. She took Tommy's temperature. She looked at the first reading. Then she did it again. His fever had broken. It was still one hundred degrees, but that was better than the one-oh-two he'd been experiencing.

Nonchalantly, she turned away from him and beamed from ear to ear. Could it be that yesterday's rally was not a precursor toward death, but rather, a sign her husband was coming back to life.

She didn't want to get his hopes up, so she went about her routine. She got Tommy a cup of ice chips to share with Flatus and excused herself for a while. Since he was awake and feeling better, she told him she was gonna run up to the house and freshen up.

"Do you want me to send Janie in to watch over you guys?"

"Nah, we'll be fine. Right, buddy?" he replied while scruffing on his pal's neck.

"Okay," said Barb, holding her excitement, and guilt, inside. During yesterday's signs of improvement in Tommy's condition, she and Mac had focused on what the medical science dictated to them in their training. Tommy was simply having a pre-death surge in energy. What they failed to consider as being plausible was that Mac had found a cure for the disease.

Barb quickly and efficiently removed her gear and walked into the cool, fresh mountain air. Despite being slightly dehydrated herself, the cool air forced her to scamper into the bathroom located in a workshop building.

Tommy and Flatus were on the brink of death thirty-six hours ago, and now, after continuous treatment with the vancomycin cocktail, they were showing signs of recovery.

Barb shuddered, but not from the cold air. Rather, she contemplated the magnitude of what was happening. Her daughter might have discovered a cure, and most importantly, she'd saved Tommy. Had they not administered the correct dose in time, even half a day late, Tommy would have suffered from septic shock, pneumonia, and organ failure.

She scrambled toward the checkpoint to find Janie. Mac needed to hear the news.

CHAPTER 10

Day Eighty-One
Quandary Point Checkpoint

Hunter stood watch while Janie headed over to her picnic table perch at the bedroom window. Barb took a four-wheeler on loan from Doc and rushed to the house to speak with Mac. Hunter resisted the urge to go with Janie and see Tommy's condition for himself. He wasn't skeptical of Barb's revelation. She was levelheaded and not prone to exaggeration. Nor was she a person to allow her emotions to control her decision-making. Hunter believed there was improvement and he hoped for the best. The next twenty-four hours would reveal whether Mac had performed a miracle.

When Mac arrived, she drove down to the checkpoint and gave Hunter a kiss. They had a brief conversation about what all of this meant. While they spoke, they heard the sound of a vehicle approaching from town, so Hunter sent Mac scurrying toward the house to be with her father. He could handle the checkpoint alone.

The grille of Doc's pickup appeared around the bend and Hunter moved to block him from approaching the house. With Tommy's improvement, he wanted Barb and Mac to have time alone with their patient to assess his condition. Also, if the antibiotic concoction created by Mac was the real deal, they'd have to discuss what to do with this information. A cure for the plague created a lot of issues that Hunter preferred to address within his new family before announcing it to the world.

Doc's pickup slowed to a stop. Sheriff Andrews was on board with him.

"Hey, Hunter, do you want me to park here?"

"Yeah, Doc. Come on out and let me explain, okay?" replied Hunter, who then waved to the sheriff.

Hunter turned to look at the house and then casually led Doc and Sheriff Andrews down the road toward the checkpoint. He regretted the need to be secretive, but thought it was best for the group to discuss the ramifications of the morning's events first.

"How's he doin', Hunter?" asked Doc.

"He slept most of yesterday and all night," replied Hunter. "He had another moment of talkativeness, but then he was out again. Barb and Mac are by his side now, just in case. You know, one of those pre-death rallies you guys talked about yesterday."

Doc looked toward the house and then over at Sheriff Andrews, who frowned. "No, I absolutely understand where you're coming from. We'll give them time alone with Tommy. Based on the timeline, he could pass today or tonight."

"Thanks," said Hunter, relieved the doctor didn't insist upon an examination of Tommy or question Hunter further.

Sheriff Andrews joined the conversation and changed the subject. "I know you've got a lot on your minds down here and probably don't have time to search for news on the shortwave, but I wanted to let you know something major has happened."

"What is it?" asked Hunter.

"Garcia nuked ISIS," replied Sheriff Andrews.

"A real nuke? Where?"

"Yup. He blasted them in the mountains between Iran and Iraq. The word is spreading through the ham radio operators around the world. It happened four or five days ago. There weren't any press releases or statements. I guess the President had had enough and let 'er fly. I say good riddance."

"I agree," chimed in Doc. "It's about time we cut off the head of the snake."

Hunter rested his arm on the buttstock of his M4. "I can't imagine the entire leadership council of the Islamic State gathering in one place, or even in one set of mountains. But it makes sense. Prior to the pandemic spreading, ISIS fighters and their families everywhere were going into hiding. Their command and control apparatus went dark on the Internet. I guess they decided to hide in the mountains."

"Well, we got 'em," said Doc proudly.

Hunter shook his head. "I hate to put a damper on the enthusiasm, but the head of the snake you just mentioned is more like Medusa's head with many snakes. The tentacles of ISIS stretch into every corner of the planet. They have active cells all over North America. If the jihadists went into hiding in the Middle East, they went into hiding here as well."

"To do what?" asked the sheriff.

"Wait," replied Hunter brusquely. "They are very patient. Their predecessors, al-Qaeda, proved it by waiting for the dust to settle after the first World Trade Center bombing. 9/11 happened years later, after we'd let our guard down. The jihadists will wait, safely tucked away from the disease, and come out fighting using different techniques and weaponry."

"Like what?" asked the sheriff.

"They have a lot of options ranging from conventional warfare to biological and chemical options. The President shouldn't gain a false sense of security from this attack. For every al-Baghdadi, there are a dozen more right behind him."

CHAPTER 11

Day Eighty-One
Quandary Point Checkpoint

A gust of wind blew through the valley, carrying the smell of charred wood and smoke. This served to change the subject to the threats the men faced on a local level.

"Hunter, we haven't had a chance to talk since the fire was extinguished," said Sheriff Andrews. "Doc told me what you and Tommy did to help save his place and the lives of the folks up on Mount Argentine. On their behalf, and mine, please accept our thanks."

Hunter shyly shook his head and smiled. Throughout his years in the service and as an operative for the DTRA, he was used to receiving accolades from his superior officers. Because his work was always highly classified, most of the people he interacted with outside the military didn't know anything about his service to the nation. This was the first time a civilian had thanked him for his efforts.

"You're welcome, Sheriff. Tommy and I were glad to help. I take it everything is under control now?"

"It is," replied the sheriff. "We've had a few flare-ups, but the folks in town have been on the lookout by watching over the woods. Now their focus has turned to the how and why."

Hunter nodded in agreement. "Truthfully, while I'm working the checkpoint at night, my mind has wandered from Tommy's health to the events surrounding the fire. Clearly, this was the act of several arsonists, right?"

"No doubt about it," replied Sheriff Andrews. "The fire chief and I have walked through the charred remains of the woods where the fires appeared to have started. We found empty gasoline cans at the three locations consumed by the blazes. He was able to identify the exact locations where the gasoline was used as the igniter for the fires."

Doc Cooley repeated the fire chief's opinion. "There must have been at least three people or groups to create the fires in perfect coordination. We also discovered trails that traversed the mountain just above where the ignition points were located."

"Where do the trails lead?" asked Hunter.

"For the most part, they run parallel to the tree line," replied the Doc. "However, at Boreas Pass, they run through the woods toward Rulon Snow's place."

Hunter motioned for the men to take a seat on the hoods of the vehicles creating the blockade. The sun was out in force and the temperatures were quickly rising toward the upper sixties. Hunter removed a couple of layers of clothing.

"I've heard about this character in passing a few times," said Hunter. "What's his deal?"

Sheriff Andrews recounted the story of the trial and the plea deal. He was able to connect the dots through his initial conversations with Snow and his recollection of the national news reports during the trial in Salt Lake City.

"Basically, they're religious extremists no different than the jihadists who prey upon the weakness of others. Snow would send his sister wives into the Breck, seeking runaways or young girls who were disenchanted with their lives. We have no idea what he's doing up there. I know his numbers have grown substantially and, oddly, unlike what I know of other FLDS compounds around the country, his people appear happy. In the years since his arrival, I've never had anybody escape to tell horrible tales like what happened in Texas."

"He's tending to his sheep," quipped Doc.

"I'd be willing to bet his numbers have increased in the last couple of months," said Hunter. "People were looking for refuge and safety, especially the unprepared. Consider the number of potential refugees you might have turned away at the Boreas Pass roadblock. Most likely, they didn't trek all the way back to Denver or Colorado Springs. They might have turned to this guy, Rulon Snow."

"I agree, and that's why we need to take a renewed interest in his activities," said the sheriff. "We started to look for a pattern in the disappearances like you suggested. In light of what we just discussed, these disappearances could have a logical explanation. Folks who were outside our protective perimeter may have sought safety with Snow in his compound."

Hunter glanced at the four homes at the end of the Blue Lakes Road. Some of these people had been murdered while others had vanished. "Yes, or they met a fate similar to the residents who lived here."

"That's true," started the sheriff, adding, "Although this is a little out of their way."

Hunter thought back to his trip into town with Mac the day they had gone to the builder's supply. They'd followed a rusted-out pickup truck filled with chickens in the back. When he had been investigating the homes across the road from the quarantine house one day, he'd found empty chicken coops behind one of them. He relayed this information to Doc and Sheriff Andrews.

"It's possible that Mac and I were following the murderers that day. They were young men, dressed in pressed white shirts. I remember that now."

"Snow's sons?" asked Doc.

"Might be, but not his youngest. I had them locked up at the time, I believe," replied the sheriff. He thought for a moment and then added, "Let me think on that and look at my records. I may have returned them to the compound before that."

"Have you seen them again, Hunter?" asked Doc.

"Nope, just a couple of wayward hikers," Hunter replied. "Sheriff, is it possible Snow, or his people, set these fires?"

"I believe it's a strong probability. The two teens, the firstborn, as they're called, are wild hellions. They don't have to work in the Snow compound like the rest of the youngsters. He allows them to roam. I've picked them up on several occasions when they wander into town and get mischievous."

Hunter contemplated this for a moment and stared towards Red

Mountain. Now that they might've beaten the greatest killer known to man, the plague, was there an equally deadly threat, one born out of evil, a mountaintop away?

As his eyes slowly rose from the road up Hoosier Ridge, the faint, but familiar sound of a CH-47 Chinook tandem rotor helicopter approaching from the south grabbed his attention. The Chinook had frequently been used for troop deployments in Iraq during Hunter's brief tour of duty there.

The sound grew louder, catching the attention of Doc and Sheriff Andrews, as well as two young men perched high atop Hoosier Ridge—Seth and Levi Snow.

CHAPTER 12

Day Eighty-One
The Quarantine House
Quandary Peak

Unlike the last seven days in which Mac had tethered herself to the lab at the house, she'd spent a considerable amount of time doting on her father. On her only trip to the laboratory earlier, she'd made copious notes on the condition of the deer mice. All of them had either stabilized or were showing signs of improvement. In order to continue the experiment and provide further confirmation, she infected three more of the tiny creatures with hopes of curing them as well.

"Daddy, I don't know what to say," started Mac as she began to cry for the third time that day.

"Okay, allow me," said Tommy as he raised his hand toward Mac's gloved hand.

Although the prognosis for her father and Flatus was good, she and Barb would continue to wear protective gear while in the house. The plague bacteria was on all the surfaces in the master bedroom and guest bedroom where Marcus had passed away. The bacteria's normal lifespan outside a host was seventy-two hours, but there was nothing normal about this particular strain of *Y. pestis*.

"Please save your strength, Daddy. We have a long way to go before this is behind us."

"Dear, I know that. I'm not quite ready to go fishin', but I am strong enough to say thank you."

Mac interrupted him. "Daddy, that's not necessary. I did—"

Tommy interrupted her with a wave of a hand. "Now you listen to me, daughter with the strong will, which must've come from your mother's side of the family."

47

"Lockjaw," mumbled Barb, with a snicker. Mac stifled a giggle.

"Your mother and I have always been so proud of you and your accomplishments. You never gave up on me, or yourself. I firmly believe if any other human being were lying in this bed, you'd do the same for them."

"Thank you, Daddy," said Mac through her tears of joy.

He began to shed a few tears. "I only wish we could've saved young Marcus. He was such a sweet, innocent child. He deserved to have a full life. I've already had mine."

She squeezed his hand to comfort him. Stretching to bend over and hug her dad risked tearing loose a seam in her protective gear. She spoke in a lower voice as she hovered near his side.

"Daddy, everything happens for a reason. His death and your contracting the disease forced me to work harder. It's paid off. I couldn't save him, but he helped me save you."

Tommy nodded and squeezed her hand. "Mac, you begin saving the world one person at a time. You've given me the opportunity to live and now it's time to save other lives."

Mac wasn't prepared to address the issue of curing humanity just yet. There were a lot of factors to contemplate. "Daddy, you've inspired me all my life. It's because of you that I didn't give up. We're gonna focus on your recovery and making one hundred percent certain you've beat this disease. After that, we'll focus on everyone else. For now, you are our priority."

Tommy smiled and patted her hand as he leaned back against the pillows to rest. Before he closed his eyes, he added one more thing.

"I always knew you were destined to do great things. With greatness comes a tremendous responsibility to share your accomplishments with others. I know you'll find a way to do that."

CHAPTER 13

Day Eighty-Two
Quandary Peak

The next day, Mac woke up invigorated. She jogged down to the checkpoint, planted a morning kiss on Hunter, and then checked on her dad's progress. He'd slept well and was starting to get his appetite back, which was a great sign.

Flatus had shown remarkable improvement as well. He was now walking about the house and had even enjoyed half a bowl of Beneful grain-free purchased for him at Axel and Chloe's store. At this point, Mac had no doubt her final experimental mix of vancomycin with the peptides would cure a patient in Tommy's advanced stage after contracting the plague.

The next logical step in the process would be to perform clinical trials to test the vaccine in primates and then human volunteers. The clinical work Mac had been performing, somewhat out of despair, but mixed with luck, resulted in a pivotal moment in the life of a new medicine that would be followed by a period of gradually expanding tests on humans.

Trials on human test subjects were performed under strict oversight by the Food and Drug Administration. A principal investigator, in most cases a doctor, would administer the trials along with a team of nurses and scientists. It took months or years to do it right.

Mac made the mistake, in haste, to provide the CDC with the Bdellovibrio bacteria, or BALO, vaccine option. She'd warned them that her theory was based on her college doctoral thesis and required extensive testing to determine if it would be effective against the plague bacteria.

She had no idea that, out of desperation and political pressure, the

President would tout the BALO vaccine as a cure-all. When it failed to produce the desired results, confidence in the government and the CDC to find a solution plummeted.

A month later and after a couple more billion people dead, Mac had discovered the actual cure for pneumonic plague. The challenge facing her now was who could she tell about it and whether anyone would believe her.

That morning, Mac had another problem she began to consider. She'd only shared the details of her work with her mother, who was consumed with her dad's impending death. She doubted Barb retained anything Mac had told her. She discussed the lab experiments with Janie from time to time, but as a former veterinarian, molecular biology and genetic engineering were not exactly her bailiwick.

So Mac immediately set out to fill in her research notes and organize them to be used by others. She also created a duplicate journal to be locked in the gun safe. If something happened to her or the house, her experiments could be recreated.

As the day progressed, Hunter returned to the house and got some sleep. The two of them relaxed and talked about Tommy's miraculous recovery. They also discussed whether they should try to make contact with the government somehow. Hunter knew quite a bit about the continuity-of-government plan and the military's communications apparatus. He told Mac he'd give it some thought but agreed a few more days of studying Tommy's recovery was absolutely necessary before they took any additional steps.

After Hunter had napped, he took Tommy some oatmeal for dinner. Mac also wanted to start him on an electrolyte and vitamin regimen. Hunter delivered the box of food and vitamins to Barb. Once Tommy was settled in, Barb returned to the house.

Janie greeted her with a glass of wine when she entered the living room.

"You're an angel, Janie. Thank you."

"I think there's cause to celebrate, don't you?" said Janie.

Mac joined them with one of the cold Budweisers she'd been

saving for a special occasion. None of them had been in the mood for an adult beverage since Tommy became symptomatic.

"Guys," started Mac, "there are lots of issues to discuss, but I wanna focus on Daddy's rehab. Because the disease had advanced in his body, defeating the plague was just part of the battle. We need to start rehabilitation after the sepsis. We've got short-term considerations and there are also long-term effects."

Barb sat in the leather chair by the fire Hunter had built before he left. They were experiencing a bit of a cold snap in early September, resulting in some near freezing temperatures at night.

"I've dealt with the short-term plan of recovery," Barb said. "Rehab usually starts by slowly helping the patient to move around. He's been bedridden for days. His body will be stiff and weak. We'll want to build up his activities slowly. You know, starting with the basics like sitting up, standing, walking around, going to the bathroom. Basic daily functions around the house."

"Should we give him a heads-up on what physical symptoms he should expect in the next few days?" asked Janie.

Barb responded, "We can, especially because I don't want him to get discouraged by what he might think is a setback. He's gonna be fatigued, experience shortness of breath, and have general aches and pains. Depending how bad the sepsis was within his body, he might lose more weight and even lose some of his hair."

"Oh my, the silver fox won't like that," Mac said with a chuckle.

"Yeah, make no mistake," started Barb. "He is going to be a handful. Undoubtedly the most unruly and insubordinate patient any of us will ever encounter."

"Barb, what about continued medications? Same question to you, Mac. Does he continue the vancomycin?" asked Janie.

"Me first," replied Mac. "I think I will continue the antibiotics for the customary fourteen days unless I see adverse reactions. The potential side effects are unknown and actually should be part of a clinical analysis."

Barb finished her wine and Janie jumped off the sofa to quickly refill it. "Thank you, dear," said Barb with a smile. "Mac is spot on with respect to continuation of the antibiotic regimen. Typically, surgeries would be taking place during this recovery period in order to locate and control the source of infection. Obviously, we have to rely upon Tommy and his body to fight any lingering sepsis."

"We still have our work cut out for us," said Mac. "Long term, Daddy might have nightmares, panic attacks, and even insomnia. The post-sepsis effects are as much mental disorders as the fatigue and joint pains."

"That leads me to the last issue," said Barb. "When and how do we bring Tommy home?"

"I've thought about this," replied Mac. "Do you guys think he's still contagious?"

"His clothes and the house may still have active bacteria. Tommy wouldn't be contagious because the *Y. pestis* bacteria are being destroyed by the vancomycin d-ala d-lac," surmised Janie.

"I agree," said Barb. "He'll recover much faster here in comfortable surroundings. We can monitor him more closely as well. Whadya think?"

"Trust me, I want him home now, but we have to be careful," said Mac. "Let's give it two more days. We'll closely monitor his vitals and the post-sepsis complications. He'll regain his strength for the trip home by becoming more mobile at the quarantine house."

"What about the house and the bedding, etcetera?" asked Janie.

"It's gotta go," replied Mac. "I'll have Hunter take care of it."

"And Flatus?" asked Janie.

"Daddy made it clear the two guys are a package deal," replied Mac. "I don't see why they can't both come home together."

Barb nodded her agreement, as did Janie. The ladies clinked their wineglasses to close the consult about the most important patients in their lives.

CHAPTER 14

Day Eighty-Two
Bay of Fundy
Lubec, Maine

Military strategy and tactics are essential to the conduct of warfare. Strategy involves planning, coordination, and the direction of your resources to meet both military and political objectives. Tactics is an art form. The great tacticians on the battlefield are able to make quick, short-term decisions regarding troop movement and the deployment of weapons in order to gain an advantage.

The great military theorist Carl von Clausewitz once said *tactics is the art of using troops in battle, but strategy is the art of using battles to win the war.* Throughout history, especially as the technological age advanced military capabilities, tactics became better known as operational strategy. It became difficult to differentiate between strategy and tactics as they became one and the same due to advanced technology and a third, overarching objective—geopolitical relations.

With advanced technology at their disposal, nation-states like Russia used cyber warfare as a precursor to a ground war. Their intelligence services used cyber tools to disrupt the critical infrastructure of a nation, as they did in Estonia, Georgia, and Ukraine. Their next step was to initiate a hot war, where they could easily overtake a country while its government was in disarray.

Abu Hassan was a student of war. He'd studied Genghis Khan, Julius Caesar, and Sun Tzu from ancient times. He admired Napoleon, Patton, Rommel, and Confederate General Nathan Bedford Forrest, who had one primary strategy—*get there first with the most men.*

When Hassan and his son had devised the strategy for the war on the West, the final jihad, they envisioned a two-pronged approach. In the past, they'd relied upon psychological warfare via social media.

Terror absolutely worked, despite what Western politicians proclaimed with words touting a nation's resolve and lack of fear. Public beheadings and executions grabbed the attention of Western media looking to make headlines.

The final jihad took a different strategy. The Islamic State's social media prowess was not used. Instead, they successfully killed off the bulk of the infidels through his son's ingenious plan to use bioterrorism. The scheme worked far greater than Hassan envisioned. It was a battle tactic that surpassed America's nuclear arsenal in its ability to inflict collateral damage on the enemy and their citizens.

While the likely death of al-Baghdadi in the nuclear attack was unfortunate, it only served to strengthen the resolve of tens of thousands of ISIS fighters around the world. With Western civilization and the infidels that inhabit it on the brink of extinction, it was time for Hassan and his jihadists to sneak in without detection to deal the final blow.

The next phase of his strategy came at a tremendous risk to his fighters. Prior to the initiation of the bioterror attack that spread the pneumonic plague like wildfire throughout the planet, communications with his fighters went dark. Four days ago, that changed with these words—*nahn qadimun*, we are coming.

Hassan's ship sailed the thirty-four hundred miles across the North Atlantic to the Bay of Fundy, a body of water on the northeast coast of Maine and tucked between two provinces of Canada. There he would reunite with the largest number of ISIS sleeper cells in the world.

Canada was proud of its achievements in creating an open society, welcoming to all, especially Syrian refugees in their time of need. While America focused on protecting its southern border, Canada quickly became the interim destination of choice for radical jihadists.

ISIS efforts in Canada were hugely successful in advancing the caliphate. Their leadership effectively spread the concept of jihadism among the faithful. Sharia law was adopted throughout most of the Muslim community in Canada.

Their biggest success of all was in their recruitment of misfits, especially disillusioned youth. It was easy, actually. Hassan instructed his key operatives to use a tactic that preyed upon young Canadian men.

He'd have his operatives say, "You're sixteen years old. You don't have a girlfriend. You're not doing well in school. Your family is either on your case or ignoring you altogether. We'll send you to Syria. We'll give you a concubine and you can have sex all the time. Do you want adventure? We'll give you a gun to shoot at people. When you're ready, we'll send you back to Canada, or even better, how about we get you a place in the United States? Just remember who *your real friends* are."

The recruiting technique was simple, but it worked. Thousands of ISIS terrorists in Canada had avoided the pandemic as instructed. They'd assembled their teams and weaponry as Hassan's strategy dictated.

Hassan and al-Baghdadi made alliances with al-Qaeda and Hamas. Their loyalists worldwide were brought into the fold. However, the biggest number of recruits came from within the Muslim religion. There were hundreds of thousands of Muslim faithful who believed in the concept of Sharia and the establishment of a caliphate, but who disagreed with the radical jihadist tactics.

As the pandemic widened across the planet, those Muslims on the fence joined the jihadists as they sought safety and protection from the disease. They were told it would come with a price—follow us or you will be cast out among the diseased infidels. Most chose jihad.

When the American NSA was at full strength, they claimed to have eyes on the bulk of Muslim extremist travelers who'd returned to Canada and the United States as part of the Islamic State's migration into North America.

But the NSA was not at full strength, nor were any of the other moving parts within the nation's intelligence apparatus. His operatives could move at will without the threat of detection by law enforcement for so long as they could avoid being infected. One of the potentially fatal flaws in Hassan's strategy was the probability his fighters could contract the disease.

He overcame this by preparing all of them mentally and financially to avoid outside human contact through social distancing. He cautioned them in advance to be prepared for radio silence for many weeks. Over the years, ISIS had acquired thousands of portable satellite communication devices, using devices made by Hughes, Iridium, and Garmin. These handheld units were standard issue to his fighters.

In advance of the release of the plague by his son, his fighters were instructed on the protective gear to purchase and the proper techniques for avoiding the disease. Hassan had no illusions as to the troop strength he'd have to work with. He was sure to have attrition before and after the implementation of the second phase.

It didn't matter. His jihadists were willing to die for the caliphate. They had the element of surprise. Their primary target—American military installations—most likely made his task easier. He was beginning to receive intelligence from around the country. The conclusion was predictable.

The U.S. government protected their own first. They gathered up their military assets and bundled them together in a nice, neat package within the confines of their bases. They made a perfect target for the dirty bombs and rocket-propelled grenades his operatives had assembled.

Just as the plague marched across America's southern border and the Mediterranean, he would lead the final jihad into America from sea to shining sea.

We are coming!

CHAPTER 15

Day Eighty-Three
Cheyenne Mountain

President Garcia was pleased with the change in attitude throughout his cabinet and senior advisors following his apology and words of encouragement a few days earlier. There appeared to be a renewed commitment on the part of everyone regarding a rebuilding effort. The death toll was still grim, but the losses worldwide appeared to be stabilizing.

"Andrew, you've kept a pulse on this," started the President as he met with his Chief of Staff and two of his domestic cabinet members. "What's your theory on why the estimated death toll appears to be slowing? Has another country found the cure and not told us about it? That's a possibility, you know."

Morse leaned back in his chair and dropped his pen on the notepad in front of him. He had aged in the two months since their arrival in Cheyenne Mountain. His eyes told the story, dark and sullen from lack of sleep and excessive worry. He was allowed to bring his wife and children into the compound, but the oldest kids and their families were scattered around the country in military installations.

"Mr. President, the plague is running out of hosts," he answered dryly. He allowed his words to settle in on the President, who sat across from Morse next to the secretaries of Homeland Security and the Interior. Interior Secretary Rhonda Ryan had not been a regular attendee of the meetings until recently as she coordinated with DHS in identifying future safe zones.

"That's a pretty grim assessment," said the President. "Sadly, it's a logical determination. Those who've successfully survived this pandemic without our assistance are spread across the country in

57

isolated areas where they can distance themselves from others. The vast majority of deaths in the United States have occurred in the cities and surrounding suburbs. Would you agree, Rhonda?"

"Yes, Mr. President," replied Interior Secretary Ryan. Secretary Ryan was born and raised in Missoula, Montana, but had lived in several western states, including Denver. Prior to being named Interior Secretary, she was Idaho's junior senator.

She continued. "Per your directives, I coordinated with DHS and military installations around the country. We began what amounted to a grid search-and-rescue mission. Using available National Guard units, we've deployed helicopters in areas surrounding our military bases. Under normal circumstances, we'd supplement the choppers with land assets, but we all agreed our ground units would spend more time fending off desperate, infected people than we would looking for communities of survivors."

"How did you establish your search pattern?" asked Morse.

"Naturally, we focused on areas around the choppers' base of operations," replied Secretary Ryan. "Without stretching their fuel and range capabilities, we identified small towns with populations from five hundred to five thousand."

"Why did you limit your options?" asked President Garcia.

"In my conversations with DHS, I learned that most municipalities greater than five thousand were too large to cordon off and they experienced a much higher rate of death than those with a lesser population. We targeted towns larger than five hundred because they'd be most likely to have multifamily housing and medical facilities. Smaller towns would be able to sustain an influx of American refugees."

"Good," added the President. "Tell me you have found some options."

"Of course, we're still in the middle of our analysis, but if I may use the Rocky Mountain states, which I know so well, as an example, I can—"

"Use Colorado, please," interrupted the President.

"Yes, Mr. President. That's an excellent choice. If we take into consideration the ski resort towns like Aspen, Vail, Breckenridge, and Gunnison, we could house as many as seventy thousand refugees in those four towns alone."

"Do they fit the criteria?" asked Morse.

"In fact, they're better than ideal, depending upon their current circumstances regarding the disease and death tolls."

The President was intrigued. If his Interior Secretary was right, Colorado would become the model for the rest of the nation. The government could continue to operate within the safe confines of Cheyenne and he could show the American public there was a hope for a future.

President Garcia looked at Morse and smiled. "Lay it out for us, Rhonda." The President leaned back in his chair and clasped his fingers behind his head as Secretary Ryan continued with her proposal.

"Here is why the resort towns of Colorado, and any resort destination, are ideal candidates for what we have in mind. Whether the destination is a winter locale like Aspen, or a summer destination along the lines of Galveston, Texas, the population swings vary with the season. Aspen has to be geared up to handle ten times more visitors in the wintertime than their normal population of roughly five thousand. In the summer, when skiing is not an option, the thousands of hotel rooms and condos remain unoccupied. However, the infrastructure of the town must accommodate the high temporary population levels during the so-called tourist season. Each of these communities have law enforcement, medical facilities, and utilities to accommodate a small city of over twenty thousand, despite their full-time population of five thousand or less.

"Beach and coastal communities are similar. Whether it's Galveston Beach or Myrtle Beach in South Carolina, the hotels stand relatively empty in the winter and are full in the summer. Using these criteria, we could start the rebuilding effort by creating larger safe zones in these resort communities where temporary housing, such as hotels and condos, are abundant."

The DHS Secretary added, "And, if properly selected, our military personnel could provide adequate protection against those who are carrying the disease and the roving gangs that have developed around the country."

"Gangs?" asked the President.

"Yes, sir," the DHS Secretary replied. "The criminal element will always find a way to exploit a weakness in our law enforcement structure. As society collapsed, criminals and the desperate formed alliances—roving gangs—to move across the countryside. Some simply scavenge for food and supplies together with a safe place to ride out the pandemic storm. Others take it to another level of human depravity, which is sickening."

"Can't something be done about this?" asked the President.

"Of course, given time," replied the DHS Secretary. "We've adopted an approach that protects our personnel until the rebuilding effort is ready. As much as I'd like to unleash the power of our military onto American soil to combat these thugs, I verily believe we can do more good for survivors by following through with the safe-zone plan first. Then we'll hunt down the criminals."

Morse leaned forward. He'd been fairly quiet during the conversation, taking in the recommendations of these cabinet members. President Garcia knew his friend well. *Andrew was processing the information and formulating a policy.*

"We need to be methodical about this, Mr. President," Morse cautioned. "May I suggest we choose one of our best options, the closest to home? Cheyenne Mountain, that is. Madame Secretary, which resort town would you suggest?"

"Breckenridge is the closest," she replied. "It fits all the criteria and our flyover indicated perimeter security is in place."

"However, they've endured a major wildfire," interrupted the DHS Secretary.

"What?" asked the President.

"Sir, our reconnaissance revealed that a major wildfire scorched a couple of thousand acres stretching along the east side of the town across three mountain ridges. It must have been a tremendous blaze. I had the NSA pull satellite footage of the area and we watched it. It took a monumental effort, but the town pulled together to extinguish the flames."

"Air support?" asked the President.

"No, sir. Their local fire department is too small to have their own air tanker like the Lockheed P2V. They did it the old-fashioned way, it appears, using firebreaks, clearing the deadfall that fuels the fire, and constant monitoring of flare-ups."

"Wow," exclaimed the President. He stood up to stretch his legs. He wandered around the conference table and observed the activity on the operations center floor. "Resilient. The community pulled together to protect themselves and never asked anyone for help."

"Yes, sir," added the DHS Secretary.

"What's the first step, assuming Breckenridge is our best option at the moment?" asked the President, looking toward the Interior Secretary.

"Sir, if I may?" asked the Secretary of DHS.

The President nodded.

"We've already surveyed the area with a Chinook. As we've said, the locals appear to have instituted roadblocks at all inbound roadways, which is a good sign. But we can't know for certain whether the town is *clean*, so to speak, until we send in a contingent to inspect conditions on the ground."

"How many personnel would you use?" asked Morse.

"For the protection of our troops, I'd suggest two platoons to enter on both sides of the town simultaneously. We don't want to frighten the residents, but we must have a show of force."

"Why's that?" asked the President.

"I'll tell you why," started Morse, whose tone disturbed President Garcia. "Because the locals might say *thanks, but no thanks.*"

CHAPTER 16

Day Eighty-Three
Noah's Ark
Boreas Pass at Red Mountain

Rulon Snow wasn't in a hurry to receive Sheriff Andrews and his ragtag group of temporary deputies who awaited him at the front gate of the compound. He knew why they were there and no amount of threats or flashing of Summit County sheriff's badges were going to result in his turning over of his two beloved, albeit mischievous, sons.

If the sheriff planned on using force to take his boys into custody, he'd be in for a rude awakening. Since the truce had been reached between the sheriff and Snow, his compound had grown considerably. The young men in their late teens he'd lured to become part of his flock had grown up and were fiercely loyal to Snow.

They'd been well trained in the use of firearms, alternative weapons, and hand-to-hand combat. The young men had fully adopted the Fundamental Church of Latter Day Saints ideology, and while he wasn't sure they'd take a bullet for him, he was certain they'd defend their home when the time came. As he ambled up to the gate and saw that Sheriff Andrews and his men had not drawn their weapons, he knew the time was not today.

"Hello, Sheriff, how may I help you today?" asked Snow.

"Rulon," started Sheriff Andrews, who incorrectly voiced Snow's name as ru-lon. This had infuriated Snow in the past, but he didn't correct the sheriff, instead opting to allow the mispronunciation to fuel his resentment against all forms of law enforcement. He would never forgive those federal prosecutors in Salt Lake City for bullying him into that plea deal, despite the fact that it resulted in a far better life for him than he would've endured on the FDLS compounds that remained under constant scrutiny back home.

Sheriff Andrews said, "I'd like your permission to speak with a couple of your boys."

"Which ones, and why?" asked Snow.

"Seth and Levi," replied Sheriff Andrews. "We've had a serious situation arise and I'd like to ask them about their possible involvement."

"Now, Sheriff, if you're referring to those fires, I can assure you the boys don't play with matches. The fires were probably started by a careless camper, or even one of your own trying to cook out when they shouldn't be."

"Rulon, I don't need to explain my reasons. This is a law enforcement investigation. Because of their past history of run-ins with the law, we can take them in. I wanted to give you the opportunity to produce them and spare the embarrassment for the boys."

Snow bit his tongue. You pick and choose your battles, so he lied. "The boys aren't here, Sheriff. They went with their older brothers to the Mission in Colorado Springs to purchase supplies. We take care of our own, you know."

"When will they be back, Rulon?" asked the sheriff, who appeared disgusted with Snow's response.

"As you know, Sheriff, the apocalypse is upon us and these brave young men have left the safety of our compound to help me tend the flock. When they return, I'll speak with them, but as far as I know, they've been good boys and haven't left the compound since you brought them back that day."

"Rulon, I'm serious about this. One or more arsonists burned most of Bald Mountain and quite a bit of Mount Argentine. You can smell the fire from here. If they had something to do with it, they need to be punished."

Snow looked down and began to chuckle as he kicked a few rocks at his feet. "Sheriff, you and I have a pretty good agreement that has served us well for years. So far, we've managed to live up to our end, as I appreciate you living up to yours. I know the boys can be badly behaved at times. Heck, they're young teens. Now, I punished them for looking upon that shameless hussy lying nude in public, as I'm sure her husband punished her for tempting my boys' tender curiosity."

"Rulon, I'm serious—" started Sheriff Andrews before being interrupted by Snow.

"However, Sheriff, you've got no cause to accuse them of arson. Nor do you have any proof. I'm sorry, but if you want to speak to my sons when they return from the city, you'll have to have a court order or warrant. Unfortunately, I've learned how the legal system works and I must insist upon the proper documentation."

"Come on, Rulon. You know the courts aren't operating. Heck, we don't even have a judge anymore."

"Well, perhaps you should come on back when you get one. We'll have to speak on this at another time."

Snow spun away from the gate. Without ordering them to, the guards immediately slid the gates shut and lowered the four-by-eight rough-sawn post, which slid into cast-iron rungs. The gate protected the Snow compound from intruders, and justice.

*****

High above Noah's Ark, perched on a bluff jutting out of Red Mountain like a couple of gargoyles, Seth and Levi took turns spying on the confrontation through their binoculars.

"Whadya reckon they want, Seth?" asked Levi.

"You and me, probably."

"Are we gonna be in trouble," asked Levi nervously.

Seth, the alpha dog in this pack of two, had studied the body language of the sheriff and his men after the guards locked the gate. Seth's instincts told him the sheriff was frustrated and defeated.

"They won't be back. Looks like whatever the prophet said caused them to leave. We might oughta slip back into the mine before he finds out we snuck out. I can bribe our way out until the prophet forgives us for what we done, but he might get doubly mad if he knew you and I were sneaking off without his permission."

"How much longer you reckon he's gonna punish us?" Levi asked.

Seth shrugged and hoisted himself out of his crouch. He was about to slip the binoculars into his backpack when he decided to look toward the setting sun over Quandary Peak. He gazed upon the desolate beauty over the snowcapped peak, and then he slowly lowered the glasses down toward the checkpoint where Janie and Derek were standing watch.

"Hopefully, not much longer, brother. I'm gettin' bored."

CHAPTER 17

Day Eighty-Four
The Quarantine House
Quandary Peak

For two days, Tommy had been an exemplary patient, heeding Mac's warnings about trying to recover too quickly. At this stage, a relapse into a bout with the plague was not of any concern. But Tommy's body had been brutally attacked from within. Sepsis and pneumonia were both dangerous illnesses that required constant monitoring. Now that he and Flatus were no longer infected with the plague bacterium, they were ready to return home for further rehab.

Janie suited up and prepared Flatus for release from the quarantine house. Although Flatus was weak, he was recovering faster than Tommy. Janie attributed the speedy recovery to the fact he'd been infected later than Tommy was and the difference the high altitude made on the dog's heart rate. Mac confirmed this over the last two days as she tested the deer mice subjects. The quick recovery in the rodents was remarkable.

Janie took him into the master bathroom, which had effectively doubled as a decontamination chamber. He stood patiently as she scrubbed him down with a medicated pet shampoo purchased by Hunter and Mac on their trip into town several weeks ago. With a good rinse, Flatus shook off the excess water and eagerly moved into the screened porch. Janie followed her normal routine and finally let Flatus into the fresh air.

He was beside himself. He'd run as fast as he could in one direction, stop to look around, and then run in another. Flatus spied a patch of tall fescue and raced to it, sliding to a stop on the moist blades. He rolled around, kicking his legs in the air. Flatus was one happy pup.

"Flatus, seriously. You need to relax," shouted Janie. She turned her attention back to the house, where Tommy was standing in the window, watching the spectacle.

"You ain't seen nuthin' yet, young lady!" shouted Tommy. "I'm gonna do the same thing, in my birthday suit!"

"No, you will not, husband," said Barb as she playfully grabbed his hair and gently tugged him away from the window. "The only time you're going to be naked is while I wash you in the tub. There are a lot of germs and bacteria to scrub off you, mister."

Barb led Tommy by the arm toward the bathroom. She guided him to the toilet seat and propped him against the tank while she ran the bath. As she got it ready, she double-checked that his clean clothes were set in the screened room. Tommy had lost a lot of weight. His favorite Army sweats would fall off him now. Hunter had offered some of his clothes as a replacement.

"Barb," started Tommy with a serious tone, "when will I be out of the woods? I mean with the sepsis."

"We need to give you another week or so to declare total victory over the plague and its minions, sepsis and pneumonia. Honestly, without full medical treatment and the ability to look inside you, we're working in the dark here. Your recovery will require very careful monitoring, but each day that passes gets us a step closer."

"Should I go to a hospital?"

"I've talked with Doc about that. The hospital has all of the necessary equipment, but it's not fully functional due to lack of personnel. The vast majority of full-time health care workers lived in Dillon, which is outside the town's protective perimeter. Sheriff Andrews tried to get a cooperation agreement with Dillon, but it was a no-go. They're very protective of their own town's borders and the specialists from every profession that reside there."

The water was ready and she helped Tommy get undressed. Barb was shocked at his condition. He'd lost at least thirty pounds in the last two weeks. She made a mental note to keep him on a bland, high-calorie diet with a focus on carbohydrates and fats. While protein was essential to build and repair muscle tissue, it could be difficult on the kidneys to process.

Tommy slid into the tub of warm water and a few tears appeared on his cheeks as he studied his emaciated body. "I almost died, Barb. You guys saved me, but what's left to save? Skin and bones?"

She gently sponged him off and washed any plague remnants off her husband's body. Periodically, she'd allow some warm water to stream into the tub, which she'd use to rinse him.

"Dear, you see skin and bones and I see the man of my dreams from forty years ago when we first met. I see a loving husband that I took for granted far too often and wept over night after night the last two weeks while you were on the brink of death. I see a loving father who adores our daughter. I see my best friend, and he's alive, skin, bones, and a heart of gold."

CHAPTER 18

Day Eighty-Four
Quandary Peak

Hunter came to the quarantine house to assist in transporting Tommy home. Tommy was too weak to walk long distances, so Hunter picked him up, carried him to the Defender and drove him up Blue Lakes Road.

Hunter had a full morning of chainsaw work to make a path for the vehicle to pass. He'd created a trail around the barricade he'd created for security purposes. The four-wheeler loaned to them by Doc Cooley could navigate through the woods, but the path was too precarious to risk transporting Tommy. Hunter cut up the trees and said he'd find a way to recreate the road blockage later. For now, it was time to celebrate Flatus and Tommy's return.

"I'd prefer a glass of that vino, but this chocolate shake is pretty good," said Tommy as everyone finished toasting his return. He sat in a leather chair near the fire with a hand-crocheted blanket they'd kept at the house for years.

"I bought the shake powder on one of my runs to Costco," started Hunter. "It's made by a company called Optimum Nutrition. While I never anticipated this use, I thought it would be an excellent way to provide us replacement meals full of vitamins, carbs, and protein."

"Well, I'll have no problem packing on the pounds with this stuff," said Tommy as he enjoyed another sip.

Barb clinked glasses with her husband and beamed with happiness. The group had agreed to dispense with the medical talk, as they'd already decided upon a rehabilitation program for Tommy as well as medical monitoring of his condition. The rest of the evening was intended to talk about how fortunate they were and to look toward the future.

For an hour during dinner and drinks, they forgot about the apocalypse that had descended upon the world. While Tommy was feeling good, they tried to keep the conversation lighthearted until discussion of the elephant in the room came up at Tommy's request.

Tommy reached for his daughter, summoning Mac to join his side. She set down her wine and sat on the leather roll-top arm of his chair. She gently rubbed his shoulder.

"Dear, we have to make a decision about what happens next," Tommy began with a serious tone. "What you've accomplished is right on par with the discoveries of vaccines for polio and smallpox, if not greater. The world is becoming extinct from the plague and you've discovered a cure. We have to tell someone."

Mac looked to Hunter. This had been a nightly topic between the two of them before they went to bed. Her mother had been staying with her dad at the quarantine house and hadn't really been a part of the debate. Hunter took the lead in the conversation.

"Mac and I have discussed this several times since your recovery. I'm trying to wrap my head around the logistics of this. It is fortuitous that the center of our government is basically down the road from us at Cheyenne Mountain. I know very little about the complex. Barb, have you ever been there?"

"No, I haven't, but I do know from conversations with those who have that you won't get anywhere near the entrance on a good day, much less under these circumstances. You're going to have to approach someone on the outside with sufficient clearance to help you. Perhaps you could start at Peterson Air Force Base."

"It's all we've got," said Hunter.

Mac gave her opinion somewhat sarcastically. "Okay, we'll just stroll up to the gate and say hey, I'm Mac and I've got the cure for the plague. Would you mind letting us in?"

"It's gonna be a challenge, dear," admonished her mother. "We have to get this information to the government."

"What if they won't listen to me, Mom? They probably think I'm a crackpot. Heck, they may have a shoot-to-kill order on me, or something." Mac was standing defiantly next to the fireplace with her arms crossed. Hunter knew where she was coming from because they'd gone down this road before.

Hunter approached her and took her by the hand to lead her back to the sofa. She drank some wine and allowed him to speak.

"Yes, there are several challenges in addition to the contact issue. First, we need to get there alive. We will face trouble on the road. There will be checkpoints like the one we established. There could be gangs like the Vagos, who are encamped just down the road from us."

"Exactly," Mac chimed in. "How can I take Hunter away from here with a threat like that less than two miles down the road? Something could happen to us out there, but it's also possible that you guys could be threatened while we're gone. We would've saved Daddy's life and left you guys unprotected trying to save a bunch of strangers." Mac began to cry now and Hunter comforted her.

"There are too many unknowns," added Janie. "We don't know where to go and who to see. I think we can protect the house with Doc and Derek's help, but then we'd have to disclose why Mac and Hunter are leaving for the city. That can create additional problems when the sheriff and Doc insist upon stockpiling the cure for the plague for the people in town before Mac leaves."

"Janie's right, I don't have enough compound to protect everyone," said Mac, wiping away her tears. "This needs to get into a laboratory and it needs to be refined. I've got the formula in my journal, but I only have enough of the actual vaccine to save one person, maybe two."

Tommy raised his hand, as a way of asking everyone to be quiet. "All of you swore an allegiance or an oath to protect Americans and also humanity. I know there are risks and I don't want harm to come to either one of you, but there comes a time when we all have to step up and make sacrifices. Hunter, I've asked you this before. Can you protect my daughter?"

"Yes, sir, with my life if necessary."

"Mac, can you be as convincing as you were the day in Washington when you stared down that camera and told the world the truth?"

"Yes, Daddy, of course."

"Then you both have to try. Our safety is not a concern. We'll be fine. You have the ability to save millions of lives, Mac. There should be no question about what has to be done."

PART TWO

WEEK THIRTEEN

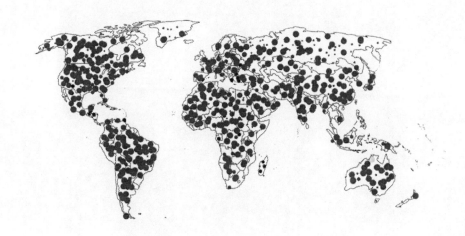

CHAPTER 19

Day Eighty-Five
Quandary Peak

Hunter and Mac were at a crossroads. The group consensus was clear—the vancomycin compound created by Mac could save humanity. But everyone respected Mac and Hunter's decision on how to move forward. It was their lives at risk as they ventured outside the relative safety of Quandary Peak, all things considered.

Most often, when someone speaks of being at a crossroads in their life, they mention two paths—right and wrong. Mac and Hunter were venturing out into the unknown. Their crossroads would involve choices resulting in life and death, their own. In a post-apocalyptic world, a simple mistake or miscalculation could get you killed.

The trip from Quandary Peak to Colorado Springs was a hundred miles, give or take. The first half involved winding their way through the ridges and mountain peaks until they reached the small town of Hartsel. From there, it was a straight, flat divided highway into Colorado Springs, where the real fun would begin, as Hunter explained while they reviewed their route on a map they'd purchased at Walmart weeks before.

Mac exchanged tearful good-byes with her parents and Janie. Barb provided Hunter a strong, lengthy hug, never saying a word. When they broke their embrace, her eyes locked with his, telling him everything that was in her mind. He nodded and gave her a reassuring smile.

I know, Barb. I love your daughter and promise to bring her home safely.

As Mac entered the Defender, Tommy waved to Hunter for a few final words. Hunter joined him at the top step of the front porch and sat down next to him. Tommy's voice was still a little weak, so

Hunter leaned in to listen.

"Son," he started, calling Hunter the endearing term for the first time, "I know that calculated risks are part of what you do. Risks are a lot different from being crazy. Just because you two come up with a plan that's so completely crazy it might work just because it's completely crazy is, frankly, completely crazy. Am I making sense?"

Hunter started laughing and put his arm around the older man's shoulders. "Tommy, have you been in the mighty morphine again? You've gotta trust my judgment, okay?"

Tommy nodded as a tear found its way out of the corner of his eye. "I know I made this big rah-rah speech last night at dinner, but I'm gonna be selfish here. All I care about is my daughter's and your safety. The world has turned their backs on Barb and Mac before. This is their last chance to accept my family's help. All I'm saying is don't do anything crazy."

Hunter lowered his head for a moment and thought. After a moment, he decided to tell Tommy something he'd intended for another time, but felt a father deserved to hear now.

"Sir, I love Mac more than life. I will never place her in danger and I promise to bring her back just as you see her now." Mac was sitting in the front seat of the truck, having a final laugh and conversation with Janie and Barb. The sun was shining through the sunroof, illuminating her blond hair. To Tommy and Hunter, she looked angelic.

"Tommy, I will bring her home safely, but in return I hope you'll give me your blessing and approval to marry your daughter as soon as I can convince her to say yes."

Tommy began to laugh. "Now I know you're crazy. As beautiful, smart, and successful as she is, I never thought Mac would marry. She's like Barb, married to a microscope and those dang germs. Let me tell you something, I'd love to have you as a son and Barb would as well. If you can convince the half-tamed bronco to marry you, then you'd have both of our unequivocal approvals."

"It's a deal," said Hunter, extending his fist to bump with Tommy's. "My final word to you is this, Tommy. I hate the prospect of leaving you guys behind. Do not let your guard down. I believe there's something bad, evil running around these mountains. They killed right down the road and set fire to the ridges near town. Promise me you'll stay frosty, okay?"

"You bet," replied Tommy. "You guys save the world and I'll protect the fort. Go!" Tommy shooed Hunter off the porch and he trotted over to the truck. He gave a final good-bye before he and Mac headed out.

Hunter made a quick stop to roll some of the cut tree logs to fortify their blockade of the upper half of Blue Lakes Road. It would be a second deterrent to anyone approaching the house by car, in addition to the checkpoint down the street.

At the checkpoint, they explained to Derek's men that they needed to see the mayor of Fairplay about his missing daughters. The men didn't question Hunter and dutifully moved the cars out of the way, allowing them to pass.

As they left Quandary Peak full of anticipation and fear of the unknown, the greatest emotion of them all, they discussed what was reasonable to expect when they arrived in Colorado Springs. Mac was hopeful that the large military presence around Cheyenne Mountain and at Peterson Air Force Base would have resulted in order being restored.

Hunter hoped for the same. His concern was not so much the city and surrounding suburbs. The map revealed several potentially perilous locations along the way that could impede their progress.

He maneuvered the Defender through the twists and turns of Route 9 as they dropped in elevation in their descent into the valley. They passed the neighborhood sign for Timber Ridge and Hunter eased around a blind curve until he jammed on the brakes, throwing Mac forward in her seat.

"What?" she asked, looking frantically around the truck.

"Look, down there," said Hunter, pointing to several burly men sitting on their motorcycles blocking the road about a hundred yards in front of him. "It appears the Vagos have set up their own roadblock."

77

"What do we do?" asked Mac.

Hunter studied the situation further. He calmly turned around and reached into the backseat, where he retrieved his AR-10.

"Mac, after I leave, get in the driver's seat and be ready. If this goes bad, turn around and go home. If it goes well, then follow my signal."

"Are you gonna shoot your way through?" she asked.

"That will be their choice," Hunter replied as he exited the vehicle and began walking down the incline toward the bikers. Then he muttered to himself, "We've been gone all of five minutes and here we go."

CHAPTER 20

Day Eighty-Five
Timber Ridge
Route 9
Alma, Colorado

Hunter was almost upon them before the men, smoking cigars and focusing their attention in the opposite direction, heard his voice. The only thing that prevented Hunter from shooting them in the back was the lack of a suppressor and the twelve to fifteen other men a quarter mile away in the front yard of the Timber Ridge clubhouse. Hunter feared they could close the gap before Mac could get the truck down the road to pick him up. It was too great a risk when he had better, quieter options.

"Good morning, gentlemen," said Hunter, causing the men to fall over themselves as they turned around. One moved to grab his shotgun leaning against his Harley, but Hunter encouraged him to stop. "Don't do anything rude like that, my friend. All three of you will be dead before your hand reaches the gun."

The men looked toward the other members of the gang for help. They were preoccupied as well. The bikers were digging through clothes and storage boxes in the front yard of the building like a gang of shoppers at a rummage sale on a Saturday morning.

The men began to raise their arms. "Nope, don't do that either," said Hunter. "You guys are gonna keep doing what you're doing, okay? Enjoy your cigar, stay relaxed, and let's have a little talk. Fair enough?"

"Yeah, man, whatever," replied the smallest of the three. He took a deep draw on his cigar and blew smoke in Hunter's direction. Hunter smiled at the man, mentally thanking him for revealing his attitude and identifying himself as the first to die in the event of trouble.

"Good," said Hunter. "This is very simple. We need to pass without trouble from you or your buddies down there. Don't you agree that sounds easy?"

The men didn't speak and Hunter continued to study their movements, but especially their eyes. The eyes, as they say, were windows into the soul. Hunter was familiar with the thousand-yard stare when a person seemed to be looking through you rather than at you. An adversary who was considering his options to attack might be unresponsive to simple questioning, which was why Hunter took the tack that he did.

The man's snarky responses initially followed by silence and the targeted stare told Hunter he had a problem. In only a few seconds, Hunter knew the man was in an alternative reality, one which typically ended in a violent encounter because that was what the Vagos Motorcycle Club knew—violence.

Hunter had no options, but he'd known that when he approached the men from behind. He was perfectly capable of winning a gun battle. He had the high ground on the dozen or so bikers down the street. His weapon and superior weapons skills could take them all out in seconds. But he knew there were more within Timber Ridge.

They would likely chase them through the winding road into Fairplay. The motorcycles were faster and could outmaneuver the Defender. It was not a good option. Hunter had to calmly diffuse the situation and he would focus on the only one of the three who had spoken.

"Guys, I don't want to kill all of you and your buddies down there," said Hunter, which drew a sarcastic laugh from the men. Hunter patted his automatic weapon and raised it slightly. "But, trust me, that's what I was trained to do. Let me ask you something. Do any of you want to die today?"

Two of the bikers stepped backwards slightly. Only the mouthy one stood his ground. He continued to provide Hunter a death stare. He stepped back with his right leg and began to flex his fingers. He gritted his teeth as he spoke.

"Ain't nobody dyin' today but you, boy."

Hunter ignored him and decided to pick off the two weaker members of the group. He looked them each in the eye and determined they weren't interested in a fight. Hunter spoke to them.

"Boys, I don't think you share the same attitude as your friend here. I want you to slowly and calmly join your friends down there as they pilfer through those boxes. Don't raise any alarms or I'll shoot you in the back. Are we clear?"

The burliest of the three bikers spoke up and addressed the mouthy one. "Yeah, man. Look, Jaws, let the man be. He don't want no trouble."

Jaws, that's appropriate, Hunter thought to himself as he continued to focus on the leader who did all the talking.

"Shut up, Jesse," said Jaws. "Go on. This is between me and him."

The two bikers began walking down the embankment towards the group at the clubhouse. Hunter waved his arm to Mac, instructing her to pull forward. He placed his palm facedown as if he were patting the top of a desk, cautioning her to come in slowly.

"Good choice," said Hunter bluntly.

"Are you military?" asked Jaws.

"Yeah, Delta," replied Hunter. He glanced to his right to watch the men descend the slope. They looked back in his direction but were following his instructions. "You?"

"1st Cavalry Regiment," he replied.

"Dragoons?" asked Hunter.

"Yeah, honorable discharge twelve years ago. Did three tours in the desert," Jaws said as he pushed up his sleeve to reveal a tattoo depicting an iron horse. "You ride?"

"Yeah, I've gotta '90 Fat Boy," replied Hunter.

"Classic ride, man. First year they were made."

"Yeah, it's back East," added Hunter.

Hunter tilted his head, trying to process why this guy was caught up with a violent bunch of thieves and drug users like the Vagos. A lot of vets came home with nothing waiting. Their girls moved on.

Jobs were not available. And the VA turned their backs on soldiers with mental disorders as a result of battle.

The low rumble of the Defender's exhaust indicated Mac was getting closer, and within half a minute, she'd be in view of the bikers down the hill. Hunter took a chance and lowered his weapon.

"Sorry for interrupting you boys. Say, what are you doin' with these guys?"

"Survivin'," replied Jaws. His reply was curt.

Hunter reached for his left pocket, which caused the man to tense up.

"No worries, brother," said Hunter as he pulled out a roll of hundred-dollar bills and handed them to the man. "I just wanna pay the toll. Plus, your friends are gonna need to know why you let us through. You can show them I paid my way and tell them you've created a friend who's tight with the Summit County sheriff."

"So?"

"Better times are ahead, Jaws." Hunter used the man's name to gain his favor. "If you fellas are looking for a place to ride out the next phase of this storm, you're better off on the right side of the law. Right now, scavenging, looting, whatever you wanna call it, is expected to an extent. When this is over, those who kept violence out of the equation will fare better with the sheriff than those who caused harm to others. Make sense?"

"Yeah."

Hunter began to back away as Mac quietly pulled alongside of them. Jaws glanced toward Mac and then his head turned toward the other bikers, who were now walking toward the roadblock. Mac leaned over and opened the passenger door for him. He slowly backed away from the confrontation with his rifle ready if need be.

"My name's Hunter. I'll be coming back through here soon enough. I want you to tell your friends I'm reasonable and can be an ally. Trust me. You don't want me as an enemy."

"That ain't up to me," the man replied, nodding back over his shoulder at the men starting to trot up the hill.

"You can sell it," said Hunter, staring back at the man as he closed the truck's door. Mac started to pull away as Hunter finished. "I see it in your eyes."

CHAPTER 21

Day Eighty-Five
Fairplay, Colorado

Every small town across the country had its claim to fame. If you'd envisioned an old west mining town with wooden porches overhanging the fronts of stores and businesses, or a grizzled old guy leading a burro down the street, then it might've been called Fairplay. As Hunter approached the outskirts of town and a welcoming committee, which included two Park County sheriff's deputies with their weapons raised, he wondered if he'd been thrown back into the late nineteenth century. Beyond the roadblock, a dust-covered street was devoid of vehicular traffic but was bustling with pedestrians and burros.

"Hunter, what year is it?" Mac asked facetiously.

"Yeah, no kiddin'," Hunter replied as he eased to a stop. The windows of the Defender were rolled down and he quickly put his hands in clear view of the deputies.

"State your business, friend!" shouted an older deputy, who pointed his rifle directly at Hunter. The younger, thinner version of the old guy left himself open more than the older deputy. Their facial features were very similar. Probably father and son, Hunter surmised. He stuck his head out the window so the men could hear him twenty-five yards away. If they got trigger-happy, this distance was beyond the accuracy range for most shooters.

"We're just passin' through, but I'd like to say hello to Mayor Weigel and Sheriff Williams if they're around."

"Gimme a name!" the deputy shouted back.

"Tell him my name's Hunter, a friend of Terry, um, I mean Sheriff Andrews." Hunter purposefully stammered over Sheriff Andrews's

84

name to imply that he was on a personal, first-name basis with the man. Although he'd never informally addressed the sheriff as Terry, he could have if he wanted to. Hunter always preferred to show respect to those in law enforcement by using their formal title unless they insisted otherwise. "I met the mayor and your boss up at Quandary Peak."

The two men looked at each other and the younger man slowly backed away and jogged toward town. After a few minutes, Mayor Weigel appeared wearing jeans and a flannel shirt. He looked exhausted.

"Mayor, my name is Hunter. Do you remember? We met when you and the sheriff came up to Quandary Peak."

"Yes, absolutely!" exclaimed the mayor. "Fellas, let 'em pass. This fellow might know somethin' about my daughters."

Hunter and Mac were welcomed into the center of town, where several of the locals gathered around to look at the Defender. The truck was beefed-up with grille guards and tires designed to climb mountains. The roof rack gave it a safari wagon appearance. It was a far cry from the burros and horses that appeared to be the new mode of transportation in Park County, Colorado.

Hunter introduced Mac to Mayor Weigel and they got caught up to speed on the search for his missing twin daughters—Karen and Terri. The mayor was distraught, as could be expected. They'd disappeared over three weeks ago and the daily searches had been called off.

He admitted the roadblocks were primarily for asking folks questions about the girls' whereabouts and secondarily to protect the town from thieves or looters. As he put it, there wasn't much left to steal.

As the three of them finished their conversation, Sheriff Williams pulled up and rolled down his window. Mac was introduced and then the sheriff pressed them about why they were headed for Colorado Springs. Mac lied and told the sheriff they were going to the Air Force base to retrieve her cousin although they weren't quite sure the sheriff bought it.

Hunter also told him about the two encounters with the Vagos MC bikers. One of those unholy truces that both the sheriffs of Park and Summit counties seemed to enjoy making was created with the Vagos gang as well. Hunter said he wasn't sure it would last, but for now the bikers seem content to remain in Timber Ridge.

Sheriff Williams offered Hunter assistance in getting to the outskirts of Colorado Springs. "You're gonna encounter roadblocks all the way to Woodland Park. They're manned by local law enforcement as well as the ranchers along Highway 24. I've gotta tell ya, it may just be sixty-some miles, but it'll take you more than a day to talk your way through them all, seein' as how you're not locals."

"Do you have any suggestions, Sheriff?" asked Hunter.

"I have better than that, but it will require a favor in return," replied Sheriff Williams, who glanced over at the mayor. "I'll send a deputy with you as an escort clear down to West Colorado Springs. We'll be a little out of our jurisdiction at that point but not within the chaos of the city."

"Chaos? I assumed with the military presence, Colorado Springs would be relatively benign compared to Denver," said Hunter.

"Logic would tell ya that, but as they secured Olympic City, folks fled Denver, seeking refuge. A lot of the bad element came along with them." Olympic City was the nickname adopted by Colorado Springs because the U.S. Olympic Committee and a major Olympic training center were located there.

"How bad is it?" asked Mac.

"Transients everywhere. Infected and used-to-be infected, as in dead bodies, too. If you survive the desperate people looking for food or drugs, you might rub shoulders with a carrier of the plague."

"Wow, okay," said Hunter, who was genuinely surprised at this revelation.

The sheriff continued. "Listen, I don't mean to scare you folks off from retrieving your cousin, ma'am. I just wanted to warn you that the areas outside of the military-secured areas are very unsafe."

Hunter shook his head and looked over to Mac. She raised her chin and showed her resolve. Despite the risks, they had no choice.

Hunter only wished he could trust somebody with lots of firepower to escort them to the front of Cheyenne Mountain. Unfortunately, they probably possessed the most valuable commodity on the planet and he couldn't trust his fellow man to do the right thing.

"You offered to help in return for a favor. What is it?" asked Hunter.

"Okay, and I haven't even told Johnny this information yet," said the sheriff as he glanced over to the mayor, who immediately came closer to listen. "I've been up Boreas Pass, nosin' around this morning. Now, Johnny, I have nothing but one old farmer's story, but I believe the twins might be up there."

"Well, we gotta go get 'em," said the mayor.

"Johnny, I've got three deputies and a bunch of broken-down old codgers that can barely walk to the bathroom. Rulon Snow has a small army up on that mountain. We're gonna need Terry's help and this fella here."

"Let's do it right now!" said the mayor.

Now Hunter was in a pickle. They had to stick to their plan. He somehow had to hold the mayor off.

"Okay, Mayor, I understand that you're anxious," started Hunter. "I don't blame you. But we could get your girls killed if we go in there outgunned. Her cousin is in the military and we can bring some soldiers back with us."

"I see," said the dejected mayor.

"Sheriff," Hunter said, directing his attention to the older law enforcement officer, "if you can get us to the outskirts of Colorado Springs, I can take it from there. Try to get a message to Sheriff Andrews and compare notes. He knows this Snow person pretty well. When I get back, we'll pay the man a visit. Fair enough?"

"Deal," said the sheriff with a nod. "Stay here and I'll round you up an escort and a letter on my stationery vouching for your character, which should help you get safely through any military checkpoints."

"Thank you, sir!" said Hunter. He rolled up the windows and spoke to Mac.

"How many lies have we told today?" she asked with a noticeable chuckle.

"Enough to get us closer to Cheyenne Mountain. Somehow, I think we'll need the practice to get to the powers that be."

CHAPTER 22

Day Eighty-Five
Highway 24
West of Colorado Springs

It had been five weeks since they'd left the outskirts of Denver for the presumably safer confines of the Breckenridge area and Quandary Peak. With the collapse of society, the massive death toll, and then the power grid shutting down, Mac and Hunter could only speculate as to what the world looked like outside their bubble.

They caught their first glimpse of death, raw and open, when they passed through the small town of Woodland Park, fifteen minutes west of Colorado Springs. Nestled in the midst of thick stands of aspen, pine, and spruce trees, the community used to thrive as one of the gateways to the unspoiled wilderness of the Pike National Forest at the base of Pike's Peak.

They had been driving nearly eighty miles an hour during the last stretch of highway before they entered the town. The deputy turned on his emergency lights and slowed abruptly as they arrived in town.

Hunter remained on alert, studying the old-west-style storefronts built to resemble the downtown of Tombstone, Arizona. There was no movement. No curious onlookers. No stray dogs or cats. Nothing.

Only death. Bodies were strewn about in various stages of decay. Some were partially covered with sheets, while others were half in and half out of doorways or windows. Buzzards picked at the remains of a rotting corpse in the middle of the highway. The deputy rolled down his window and slapped the side of his patrol car, startling the voracious birds for a moment. As soon as Hunter slowly inched past the body, the buzzards were back for their meal.

"Hunter, this is bizarre," started Mac. "The town is just, um, dead. I think everyone is dead."

Hunter let the reality set in. A community of maybe five to seven thousand residents, family, and friends, all succumbed to the plague.

"Maybe the survivors are hiding, Mac," he added. "If they were smart, they wouldn't approach the corpses. They're filled with the disease for a period of time after death. Frankly, if you don't have the security capabilities to defend your town, I can't think of a better way to deter looters than to leave diseased-ridden bodies out in the open. I wouldn't want to step foot out of the car in this place, would you?"

"Nope. It's surreal. You'd think there would be somebody around."

"What's happened across the planet is unimaginable to me," said Hunter. "I don't know what to expect when we hit a city the size of Colorado Springs."

"If it's like this, I might freak out," said Mac.

The deputy in front of them rolled up his window and began to pick up speed as they cleared the last of the abandoned businesses at the end of town, including a gas station that looked like it had been hit with a bomb. It had been completely leveled, and the rusted, charred remains of a dozen vehicles stood nose to tail where the fuel pumps once stood.

"Just do the math," Hunter began as he did the calculations aloud. "Colorado Springs is a fairly large metropolitan area of probably half a million to three-quarters of a million people. You and Janie ran the numbers. What did you call it?"

"An epi curve. We plotted the incidents over a certain time frame and it helped us form a hypothesis as to the death toll based on the transmission of the plague."

Mac paused for a moment as the deputy slowed to a stop ahead of them. An accident was blocking the highway, leaving a serpentine path through the abandoned cars. Hunter steered with his left hand and slowly dropped his hand behind the armrest to reach for his rifle.

The deputy cleared the crash site and picked up speed again as they wound their way through ridges on both sides of the highway.

"Okay," said Hunter as he pulled his arm back and breathed a sigh of relief. "What was the number at this point, eighty-some days into the pandemic?"

"One percent or less," replied Mac.

"A big city like Colorado Springs has probably gone from seven hundred fifty thousand to seventy-five hundred."

"Many of whom could be sick and dying," mumbled Mac as she leaned against the window and watched the sun peek over the tall canyon walls. "It's hard to fathom small towns like this one being that hard hit."

"Denver, Atlanta, New York, and Chicago would be much worse," added Hunter. "The smaller communities, like Breckenridge, which sealed itself off from the world, are the new population centers."

"When you think about it, a small group of a few dozen people could move into a town like Woodland Park when this is all over and own the whole—"

BOOM !

The sound of a high-powered rifle reverberated off the canyon walls, followed by several more gunshots. The sheriff's car ahead of them swerved left, then right as the deputy began to lose control.

"Hold on, Mac!"

Hunter jammed on the brakes as the patrol car turned sideways in front of them until the wheels grabbed the pavement and sent it rolling over and over until it landed on its side and slid down the steady downward slope of the highway.

The gunfire sounded like thunder rolling through the valley as bullets struck the hood of the Defender and ricocheted off the roof rack. Hunter jerked the wheel to the left to avoid hitting the patrol car and bounced off the concrete divider separating the narrow east- and westbound lanes of the highway. He was almost clear of the wrecked patrol car when he ran out of room.

A stalled car stopped his progress and they were trapped between the guardrail, the patrol car, and the stalled sedan. Hunter threw the Defender into reverse and mashed the gas pedal in an attempt to extricate themselves from the trap.

The shooters were too fast. They shot out the rear window of the Defender and the right rear tire.

Mac shrieked as broken glass pelted her from behind. Hunter reacted quickly, putting the truck back in forward, and pulled back to the overturned patrol car. He created a wedge by positioning the passenger side of the truck to where the shots were coming from.

He pushed open his door and rolled out of the truck.

"Mac, quickly! Crawl out this way!"

Mac inched across the center console on her belly, dragging her rifle with her. They both fell to the asphalt and rolled under the edge of the Defender for cover.

Several more rounds came their way, blowing out the glass on the passenger side of the truck and tearing up the back of the small sedan across from them.

Hunter assessed the situation. Based upon the initial shots fired, the trajectory was coming from above them on both sides of the road. The impact of the most recent rounds indicated the shooters were behind them. He'd positioned the Defender to create a barrier between the shooters and their position.

He quickly looked up at the canyon walls to the south and the lower-lying slopes to the north. Then he took in the scene on the ground. There were several stalled cars along this stretch of highway. They weren't parked because they were out of gas. They had been disabled by gunfire. Tires were flattened. Fluids had leaked from engine blocks. A body lay facedown in the middle of the highway just below their location. The woman had been shot in the back.

"Mac, this is just the beginning. They'll be coming for us next."

CHAPTER 23

Day Eighty-Five
Highway 24
Cavern Gulch
West of Colorado Springs

Hunter maneuvered himself so he could open the passenger door to the backseat. He was able to grab their backpacks and his rifle before several rounds peppered the roof of the Defender, two of which imbedded in the back of the driver's seat.

"They're using green tips," Hunter surmised, referring to the steel-piercing rounds used in AR-15s and AR-10s. The lack of rapid fire told him they were using hunting rifles rather than a semiautomatic rifle like the AR-15. If they were part of a group, Hunter decided, the battle-ready firepower would be coming their way soon.

"This is an ambush, Mac. Disabling the vehicles from above is just the first step."

Mac rose into a crouch and hid behind the front wheel and the engine block. She'd pulled the charging handle on her AR-15 and was looking from side to side for movement.

"They didn't hesitate to shoot a cop car either," added Mac.

Hunter slid her backpack along the ground to her and she quickly put it on. He rummaged through his pack and pulled out a six-inch fixed blade in a sheath and strapped it to his right leg. He also retrieved a shoulder holster and removed the paddle holster from his khakis and reinserted his sidearm under his left armpit. Finally, he retrieved an olive-drab, military-style ammo belt, which he stretched around his waist. He didn't have a full chest rig, but the molle belt allowed him to insert several magazines for his AR-10, Mac's AR-15, and his handgun.

Mac didn't have the same gear as Hunter, so they'd have to work in close proximity to each other in case he needed to provide her a resupply of ammo. He didn't plan on leaving her side anyway, but he chastised himself for not acquiring additional gear for her use.

"Hunter, what about the deputy?"

Hunter looked in both directions and ran in a low crouch toward the roof of the patrol car, which was crushed inward. His movement went unnoticed, which confirmed his suspicions that the snipers were above and behind the car pileup.

A portion of the shattered windshield had peeled away from the patrol car's frame. Hunter avoided the broken glass and stuck his head inside to check on the deputy. The young man had been killed by a single bullet to the head. Hunter dropped his chin to his chest and pulled away from the car.

He now had a better view of the road in front of them. There was a long stretch of open highway with more abandoned cars. He and Mac were both in excellent shape and he considered their options.

Hunter quickly found his way back to Mac and gave her an assessment.

"He's dead, Mac."

"Geez. He was such a nice kid. This pisses me off, Hunter," she growled. "Can we get these guys?"

"I'm mad too, but that's not what we're here for. We've got two options."

Mac chuckled. "Two? You're pretty optimistic or crazy. Which is it?"

"Your dad said crazy." He laughed as he pulled his backpack around and began to rummage through it.

"What?"

"I'll explain later," he replied. He reaffixed his pack and showed Mac a simple clip-on visor mirror he'd purchased at Walmart. He also handed her a white tee shirt. "I'm gonna get in position, and when I give you the signal, I want you to throw this shirt as high in the air as you can. I'm hoping you can draw their fire."

"Got it."

Hunter eased to the rear bumper of the Defender, which was

wedged against the concrete barrier. He positioned the mirror just past the fender where he could see the tops of both ridges. The snipers were well hidden, but all he needed was a general idea of where they were. He'd never get a clear shot at them.

"Okay," he said to Mac. "Now!"

She tossed the shirt into the air, and as expected, the shooters reacted. He saw their muzzles flash nearly simultaneously as bullets rained down upon them, but flew harmlessly over the top of the truck. Now he had them spotted.

Hunter turned to Mac and waved her to his side. "Hold the mirror with your fingertips so that you can see from the ledge on the left side of the road all the way to the top of the ridge on the right side. I'm gonna do the same thing. Mac, this is important. Watch for a flash of light. From here, it'll look like somebody lit a cigarette. You have to focus, okay?"

"I'm ready. Go for it," she replied.

Hunter tied the tee shirt on the end of his rifle and quickly moved across the front fender of the truck with the tee shirt just above the hood. Two shots rang out, followed by a third. He stood up once he was behind the back end of the patrol car.

"Did you see them?" asked Hunter.

"Yeah, and something else too," she replied.

"Whadya mean?"

She was still looking through the mirror, but the angle was tilted lower. "There are five or six guys walking down both sides of the highway. They're spread out, maybe ten feet apart."

Hunter rolled his eyes and banged the back of his head against the trunk lid of the patrol car. He dropped to the pavement until he could look under the frame of the Defender. He saw three sets of feet spread apart, as Mac had observed. That meant the other men were across the barrier.

"Come join me," he said to Mac. She walked back to him, being careful to keep her head below the truck's windows. She slid next to him and they stood with their backs to the trunk of the patrol car.

Mac was breathing heavy. "What's the plan?"

"We could jump the concrete barriers and dash thirty yards for the scrub brush and aspen trees over on the shoulder of the westbound lane, but we'd be exposed for a considerable amount of time."

"I'd cover you and then you'd cover me, right?" suggested Mac.

Hunter smiled. He was impressed at how Mac was holding it together. Taking on live rounds in a gun battle was a lot different from her days playing combat games at Paintball Atlanta. However, the principles applied were the same.

"I don't like it," said Hunter. "There are too many shooters. Our cover fire may take the guys approaching us out momentarily, but the snipers will be a real problem. At least one of them is a great shot. He hit the deputy in the forehead from a distance while the car was moving at a pretty good clip. The snipers worry me more than the guys approaching—"

Hunter was interrupted by shouting.

"Hey, down there!" yelled one of the gunmen.

"Y'all need to give it up! Come on out with your hands high and empty."

"Maybe you'll live!" said another.

The men were getting closer and laughing. They were taunting Mac and Hunter.

"Plan B?" asked Mac.

"Look at this," said Hunter. He grabbed her by the hand and they eased to the hood of the patrol car, where they could see down the highway. The cars were scattered every twenty yards on both sides of the eastbound lane from the barrier to the canyon wall. "If we can neutralize the snipers with cover fire, you and I can run from car to car."

"Bounding overwatch," said Mac. "You cover me and I'll cover you."

"You've got the concept. You learned that playing paintball, right?" asked Hunter.

"Yep, sure did. I'm ready. Who's first?"

Hunter loved this woman.

He thought through a pattern first. If they stayed at a low crouch, they could make it to the front of the small sedan next to them first. After that, he'd send Mac to the vehicle while he covered her.

"Shoulder your rifle and we'll crawl like spiders to the front of this car. Stay low. Me first."

Hunter slung his rifle's strap over his neck and got on all fours on the ground. He walked on his hands and toes until he got to the front of the small Nissan. They didn't take on any fire, so he waved Mac forward to join him.

"So far, so good," she said.

One of the men shouted at them again. They were close.

"Last chance, people! Sheriff, don't try to shoot it out with us. It won't end well for you!"

"Time to go, Mac," insisted Hunter. "I'll lay down cover fire and slow the roll of these jerks. Get in front of the minivan and I'll join you."

Mac had her white CDC cap on. She turned it sideways and put on her Ray-Bans. "Love you!" she whispered, tapped him on the shoulder and began to run down the road.

Hunter immediately opened fire. The explosive NATO 7.62 rounds blasted out of his AR-10 in short three-round bursts toward each of the sniper positions. The approaching men began to yell and the sounds of footsteps could be heard as they sought cover. Neither of the snipers got off a shot.

"Go!" shouted Mac from her cover position.

Fully trusting her abilities, Hunter took off to join her. Her AR-15 sounded like cannon fire as Mac quickly squeezed off a couple of rounds toward the cliffs. Her aim was effective because the snipers were stymied again.

While they caught their breath, a few rounds were fired wildly in their general direction. The snipers had lost track of their targets.

"Mac, from here out, we don't stop for long, okay?"

"Okay."

"We get in position and keep the fire headed in their direction. They're gonna lose interest in us. Most likely, they only want the contents of our vehicles."

Mac craned her neck to identify their route down the highway until the road curved to the right. "I've got our route. If we can make it to the curve at the bottom of the hill, I don't think they'll follow us."

"I agree," said Hunter. "Although you never know where the bend in the road might take you."

He turned to steady his aim at the sniper's position on the ledge overhang. This time, he was gonna try to score a hit.

"Go!"

Mac took off and Hunter hesitated just a millisecond until he saw the slightest of movements through his scope. He squeezed the trigger and allowed the rounds to pepper the shooter. Without waiting for the results of his shots, he whipped his weapon to the right and sent a hail of gunfire in the vicinity of the other sniper. As he did, the wail of a man falling fifty feet to his death filled the canyon.

This battle was over.

CHAPTER 24

Day Eighty-Five
Cave of the Winds Park
West of Colorado Springs

They jogged down the mountain several minutes until they were certain to be clear of the threat behind them. For the next hour, they barely said a word as each of them processed what had happened at Canyon Gulch. Hunter knew war and what man was capable of doing to one another. Mac had learned through the plague pandemic how ruthless people were just to advance an ideology. What they'd just experienced was how little human life was valued by some. The snipers on those ridges and the men advancing toward them were killing indiscriminately, not in self-defense or through some warped justification in the name of survival. They simply wanted to take what any passersby had in their possession. They were killing without qualms or misgivings.

Hunter glanced at his watch and walked backward for a moment to catch a glimpse of the setting sun. "It's gonna be dark soon and we don't want to enter the city after dark."

"Wouldn't it be safer if we weren't seen?" asked Mac.

"That's logical thinking, but I suspect any survivors are on edge," replied Hunter. "They know their surroundings and we don't, which provides them an advantage. I also suspect the lights aren't on, making it difficult to choose our route toward the nearest military installation."

"Based upon the map we studied, we're probably six to eight miles away from the outskirts of town," added Mac.

Hunter led them a little farther down the road until the road opened up with a view of West Colorado Springs. He looked up toward the top of the ridges, which were not near as high in elevation as the area they'd just passed through.

They made their way around a sweeping curve and the city opened up before their eyes. Mac picked up the pace to pass him slightly.

"I can't decide if I'm excited to see where we're headed or scared to death," said Mac. "What do you think?"

"I wish we had a car," said Hunter bluntly. "Being mobile gives us lots of options. We could rest for a while and then slip into some of these neighborhoods. A car would allow us to get around town faster and locate military personnel, who hopefully will help us."

"Would you feel better if we rested for the night?" asked Mac.

"Yeah, probably. But I'm torn. As it gets darker, we'll start looking for a spot."

They walked another half hour, barely over a mile at their leisurely pace. Each time they approached an abandoned vehicle, they had to confirm there wasn't a threat waiting for them inside, or a plague-stricken corpse. On a couple of occasions, vehicles were found that appeared to be clean, but they had been locked by the owner after having run out of gas.

Hunter was getting discouraged as nightfall crept in and he searched for a place to sleep for the night. He'd brought a couple of mylar blankets in his backpack, but they'd be insufficient against the evening's upper thirties temperatures. They needed a house or building to get out of the elements and he didn't want to wait until dark to secure a place.

After another fifteen minutes of walking, they came to a traffic signal with a single road turning off the highway next to a sign indicating the entrance to the Cave of the Winds Mountain Park.

The cave, discovered in the 1880s, had a unique limestone entrance that created winds from the inside of the mountain. As explorers went deeper into the face of the mountain, they discovered enormous caverns inside. After additional excavation and the advent of electricity, the Cave of the Winds was opened to the public. Soon a lodge was built to hang out over the canyon below and zip-line rides were created to send screaming tourists on a trip of terror to the bottom.

Hunter looked at the destination from another point of view. It was a nonresidential area, which might provide them some shelter for the night. Plus, there might be maintenance vehicles on the property if they could locate the keys.

"Do you have enough energy to hike up to the top?" asked Hunter as he looked up the winding road, which traversed the side of the ridge about a thousand feet. "I think it will give us a clear view of the city and it might provide better shelter than sleeping in a house full of plague bacteria."

"Lead the way," said Mac. "I think we're both in better shape than we were five weeks ago. I'm finally used to the altitude, how about you?"

"Absolutely," said Hunter as they started the trek up the mountain. Periodically, he'd glance over his shoulder, looking for signs of movement below them. It was eerily still. "The first week was brutal, and then all of a sudden, I didn't experience the shortness of breath anymore."

As the two of them reached the top of the ridge, Mac exclaimed, "Whoa, look at this place!"

Hunter picked up the pace and started a half jog towards the facility. The zip-line ride contained a bottomless chair attached to the cable. Called the Bat-A-Pult, the attraction dropped those fearless souls who enjoyed the thrill from the top of the mountain twelve hundred feet to the valley below.

"No way!" shouted Mac, who picked up the pace and jogged past him. "Do you think we could get it working?"

"I doubt they have power, but what a ride! It reminds me of dropping out of that helicopter in the Gulf of Mexico."

"What helicopter?" asked Mac as she looked over the safety rail to the base of the mountain. Hunter had never told her the details of their mission, so she was unaware of the risks he had taken.

Hunter walked closer to the building and didn't find any cars in the parking lot. Just the same, they needed to be careful. "Mac, let's clear the building and then we'll see if we can find anything useful. Let's go."

Together, they walked the perimeter and looked for evidence of looting or any occupants in the building. It was remarkably untouched. They approached the front door, a wood and glass patio-style door that was locked. Hunter shrugged, picked up a large piece of limestone from the landscaped area at the front, and broke out a pane near the handle.

With his left hand, he reached in and quickly turned the lock. He flung open the door and led the way, his rifle barrel swinging back and forth, ready to fire upon anything that moved. Mac walked in behind him, looking under the counter of the cash wrap where the registers were located at the front of a gift shop.

Hunter went left toward the children's play area and Mac cleared the gift shop. It was a one-story building with vaulted ceilings. Each of them opened closet doors to find them stuffed with merchandise, but no people.

Hunter declared this part of the interior to be clear. He whispered to Mac, who joined his side, "I don't see any evidence that this building has been touched in weeks. That means it's clean, right?"

"Yes, Hunter, but look," said Mac, directing his attention to a winding stairwell at the rear of the gift shop. "There's an upper level. Looks like a restaurant." She pointed to a sign on the wall, which read *Caver's Café*.

Hunter moved quickly past Mac. They moved upstairs together with Hunter taking two of the wood steps at a time. Mac continued to watch their backs, allowing Hunter to deal with threats head-on.

A quick glance at the large dining area revealed neatly arranged tables and chairs and an incredible view of Colorado Springs. Mac remained in the dining area while Hunter entered the kitchen and food storage pantry. After a minute, he emerged from another entrance.

"We're clear, Mac. This place has a lot of food like those big #10 cans of vegetables and lots of condiments. The walk-in freezers and coolers are locked up, but I imagine the food is spoiled anyway."

He walked through the dining room and stood by her in front of the windows facing the city. After a brief moment, she left his side and walked out onto the balcony.

"Hunter, check it out. They have those tower viewers. You know, put in a quarter and you can see all the way to the city."

Tower viewers were large metal binoculars that were mounted on a steel base and stalk. They were coin-operated, usually requiring a quarter to view locations in the distance. When payment was required, there was a time limit of a couple of minutes. The ones located at Cave of the Winds were free.

Mac and Hunter positioned themselves behind their own viewer. These particular devices enabled them to change magnification and had a wide range of motion although Colorado Springs was seen through a narrow gap in the mountain ridges.

Hunter liked the directories provided with the units. They showed specific attractions in the field of vision, which included Cheyenne Mountain. He adjusted the focus and the height to allow him to study the situation on the ground between the base of the mountain and NORAD. There was a road that ran along the mountain to their immediate south along the outskirts of a large residential area. That road would give them a straight shot to where they needed to be.

"Mac, originally, I thought we should go to the Air Force base, but it's on the other side of the city. I have a better idea. Let's go right to the front door of Cheyenne Mountain. There's a road that winds its way along the neighborhoods and comes out fairly close."

"So we're gonna stay for the night?" asked Mac.

"Yeah. Let's establish a secured perimeter. I wanna look in those storage garages out back for a ride, and then we'll check out the kitchen."

"Nacho chips and cheese, with jalapenos," said Mac. "Movie theater food."

"Sounds delicious," said Hunter with a laugh.

"No, seriously. I saw bags of tortilla chips and a large can of that Rico's fake nacho cheese. It won't be hot, but it never is by the time you get to your seat in the theater anyway."

Hunter laughed and put his arm around her neck. "Let's get our chores out of the way and you can whip me up a gourmet post-apocalyptic dinner."

CHAPTER 25

Day Eighty-Six
West of Colorado Springs

It was early in the morning, about an hour before sunrise, when Hunter woke up next to Mac. His back was sore from the accommodations, which consisted of the two of them crawling into a wooden play fort created for the children who visited Cave of the Winds. It had two-inch foam pads as a base inside and they used Terror-Dactyl pillows from the gift shop to rest their heads on.

Before they went to sleep, Hunter made an interesting discovery by looking through the viewers. Parts of Colorado Springs had electricity and they were residential neighborhoods, not military installations. Because of the distance and the mountains, which obscured his field of vision, Hunter wasn't able to specifically identify the locations, but one was along the road he'd identified the day before as their likely path to Cheyenne Mountain.

Mac began to stir, so he welcomed her awake. After they worked the kinks and soreness out of their muscles, they rummaged through the café's kitchen in search of anything that resembled breakfast.

A search of the pantry produced honey buns, and the employee break room rewarded them with a four-pack of Starbucks Double Shot cans of espresso. This was a score worth all the gold in the mountain.

The sun was just peeking over the horizon when they loaded up in the white Ford F-250 utility truck parked inside the shed. It was full of fuel and the rear had additional gas cans, albeit empty. The truck also had a toolbox attached to its bed. This would provide them some additional cover in the event they got ambushed like the day before.

"Saddle up, cowgirl," said Hunter as he encouraged Mac toward their new ride with a gentle nudge.

Mac, who was still not a morning person despite the end of the world as they knew it, moped to the passenger side. Hunter suspected she'd be hard to get started, so he snuck his second Double Shot into his pocket to reward her when she was ready to go.

They were both in the truck, buckled up, and ready to head out when he presented her with the extra can of espresso.

"You do love me," she purred.

"I know you, too," he said with a laugh. "I'm hoping this will get your blue eyes wide open to help me navigate and watch for trouble. But, yes, I do love you."

Hunter took off down the hill and ignored the solar-powered flashing red light that greeted him at the highway. Things would be moving quickly now and he was glad to get started just as the sun brightened the sky.

By his calculations, they'd turn off the highway in about two miles and then follow the base of the adjacent mountain. He had no idea how to get to Cheyenne Mountain and knew that the military probably had a significant presence around it. He'd brought his credentials from the FBI and the DTRA. Mac had stuck her CDC and temporary CIA identifications in her backpack as well. These forms of ID might not have helped them with the thugs in the shoot-out yesterday, but they would carry some weight when they approached law enforcement or the military.

The highway flattened out and Hunter knew he was getting closer to the road he sought when he began to see residential rooftops in all directions. The highway divided and more stalled cars appeared, as well as corpses. Dozens of buzzards picked at the rotting flesh, causing Mac to look away.

"If it's like this here, imagine in the center of the city or around those high-rise condos," said Mac after regaining her composure. She reached into the storage compartment behind her seat and retrieved her backpack. She pulled out two masks for them to put on, as well as their nitrile gloves. "Just in case."

Hunter nodded and steered with his knee for a moment while he affixed his gear. They traveled another mile, rounded the final bend, and then Hunter abruptly stopped.

In front of them was a group of a dozen or more men, women, and children walking up the highway. They were pushing shopping carts and pulling toy wagons full of clothes. One pregnant woman pushed a stroller with a toddler strapped in.

"My God, Hunter."

"Breaks my heart, Mac. But we have to be careful. Never underestimate any contact."

Hunter eased down the shoulder of the road to allow the group plenty of room on the other side. As they got closer, an emaciated man waved to them. Mac stared at the procession and then gently touched Hunter on the arm.

"Hunter, can we talk to them?"

Hunter exhaled and half shook his head. "Okay, but have your gun ready. Do not assume these people are safe because they look like they've got one foot in the grave. They may not look infected, but that doesn't mean they're not armed."

Hunter rolled down his window. "Where you folks headed?"

"We heard it was safer up toward Cascade and Woodland Park," replied a man wearing mismatched clothing and sneakers. The clothes hung on him as if he'd lost forty pounds.

"It's not," replied Hunter. "We got shot at up in Cavern Gulch, this side of Woodland Park. The town looks like everyone is dead from the plague. I have a better place for you."

"Where's that?"

"Up ahead, there's a place called Cave of the Wind, do you—"

"I know it," the man said. He looked down at the ground. His teary eyes looked directly at Hunter. "I took my family there when they were alive. This here's my family now." He turned and waved his arm at the rest of the refugees in the group.

"It's not much farther," continued Hunter. "At the traffic signal, you'll have to turn up the hill. It's a pretty tough walk, but it'll be worth it. There's quite a bit of food and some clothes in the gift shop. It's also fairly secure."

107

"Thank you, sir!" exclaimed one of the women.

"God bless you," said another.

The group began to walk up the road when Hunter hollered at the man, "Do you know where the military checkpoints or camps are located?"

"The closest National Guard location is at Star Ranch on the way to NORAD. They made it nice for the muckity-mucks and left the rest of us to fend for ourselves."

"What's Star Ranch?" asked Mac.

"It's a gated subdivision, but now it's one of the safe zones. None of us belonged, so now we're leaving."

The man began to walk again and Hunter asked him one more question. "How do I get to Star Ranch?"

"Down a bit and to your right," he replied. "Follow the base of the mountain. They'll find you before you find them. No matter what you do, don't go straight into town. You'll probably die."

Hunter placed the truck into drive and coasted down the hill toward *civilization.*

CHAPTER 26

Day Eighty-Six
West Colorado Springs

"Hunter, what's happening here? Who's being quarantined, the ill or the well?" Mac rolled down her window and took in the sights and sounds, or lack thereof. There were no vehicles in operation. No steady hum of machinery or air conditioners distracted her senses. All her mind could soak in was a major city, bleak and desolate and a shell of its former self.

"Last night, I took another look through those viewer things," started Hunter. "There was a neighborhood in this direction that was lit up. At first, I thought it might be related to Cheyenne Mountain, but it's not far enough south. It's gotta be the Star Ranch place that guy was talking about."

"Hunter, the road's blocked!" said Mac, pointing ahead as Hunter took a slight curve through the outskirts of a neighborhood.

Hunter stopped short of the eight or ten parked vehicles, which took up the entire street. Landscape boulders in the front yard of the home to his left blocked their truck's path through the grass, and the steeply rising ridge on their right prevented any route around the obstruction.

"I don't see anyone, but that doesn't mean they're not there," said Hunter.

"There was a street that turned left back there," added Mac. "Let's try it. We can work our way south, even if we have to drive through yards."

For the next thirty minutes, Hunter and Mac looked for ways through the maze of neighborhood roads. Someone had meticulously planned and positioned vehicles throughout the side streets to prevent, or at least slow, access toward the south. Stymied, Hunter stopped and shut off the truck.

"Fine, people, you win!" Hunter voiced his frustration. "It's not that we're in some hellfire emergency to get there although the longer we're out here, the more dangerous it is."

"They're forcing us closer to town," interrupted Mac.

"Exactly, and farther away from the base of the mountain where I think Star Ranch is located. Mac, how do you feel about walking?"

"More risky and slower," she replied. "But we'll never get there at this pace. Plus, remember what that guy said about them seeing us before we see them. We're not sneaking up on anybody in this jalopy."

Hunter reached into his pocket and pulled out his cell phone. He and Mac carried them constantly for their iPhones to use as a camera and for their GPS capability.

"In case things go bad, we can find our way back here. Actually, I like walking up to the front door better. Even a slow-approaching vehicle puts soldiers on edge."

Hunter and Mac donned their backpacks and began to walk through the neighborhood back to the road, which meandered along the base of the mountain. At first, they were diligent in using parked vehicles as cover to avoid detection by anyone living in the homes along the way. Eventually, they walked down the middle of the street. They didn't see a single living human being during their first hour of walking until they came upon Cheyenne Mountain High School.

A white, nondescript utility van was parked on the rise above them as they walked down the sidewalk through several trees. After they'd passed the parked van, it suddenly started up, which sent Mac and Hunter scrambling for cover, with each hiding behind their own oak tree.

The van backed up out of their field of vision, then sped off toward the south end of the parking lot and out a back exit.

"What was all that about?" asked Mac.

"I dunno," said Hunter as he jogged ahead to join her. "I'm pissed that I let my guard down, though. Here's the thing. They didn't have to reveal themselves. We'd already passed them."

"Yeah, they could've just waited for us to walk off," added Mac. "No, they were up to something and seeing us caused them to panic. But hey, at least they didn't shoot at us. That's progress."

"Or maybe they're some kind of advance scout for those guys," said Hunter, nodding down the road toward two Humvees speeding in their direction.

"What do we do?" asked Mac.

Hunter gauged their speed as they approached. The soldiers appeared to be on a mission to get somewhere, but not necessarily to confront them. "We're here to make contact with the military; there's no time like the present. Hold this for me." He handed Mac his rifle.

He stepped out into the road and waved his arms to get the attention of the driver. He'd already pulled out his DTRA identification and his temporary FBI credentials to provide them evidence of credibility.

The Humvees never slowed down, roaring past Hunter and throwing a stinging mist of gravel and dust onto his face.

"Well, all righty then." He chuckled, looking at Mac in disbelief. "I suppose they've got bigger fish to fry. We'll keep goin'."

Hunter retrieved his rifle and they started in the same southerly direction, periodically walking through yards and hugging the base of the mountain. They began a long stretch adjacent to a golf course, using the cart paths instead of the sidewalk to continue their trip. They climbed up an embankment and found the road again, when they heard the distinctive roar of the Humvee's tires behind them.

Hunter and Mac ran up the incline and ducked into the driveway of a McMansion overlooking an open field.

"Do we try it again?" asked Mac, but Hunter never had a chance to answer.

"Drop your weapons!" a voice boomed over a loudspeaker behind them.

At the top of the rise, a dozen soldiers were advancing toward them with their rifles illuminating their bodies with red dots from their laser sights.

"Slow and easy, Mac," said Hunter. "Follow my lead by keeping your arms and hands away from your body and gently lower your rifle to the ground like this."

Hunter firmly gripped his AR-10 and slowly crouched to the ground before setting it on the concrete driveway. Mac followed his lead.

"Don't shoot!" hollered Hunter in response. "We're going to remove our sidearms. Two fingers, okay? We're both active-duty military, so we know the drill." Mac was, after all, a lieutenant commander in the U.S. Public Health Service.

"Slowly," the man behind the loudspeaker bellowed.

Simultaneously, Mac and Hunter unclipped their holsters and removed their weapons, once again gently laying them on the ground. Hunter held his hands high and wide over his head. Mac did the same. He knew the best way to keep from getting killed by law enforcement or the military police in a tense situation was to comply with their commands. It was just that simple.

The Humvees caught up with them and screeched to a halt at the end of the driveway. Within seconds, Mac and Hunter were surrounded.

CHAPTER 27

Day Eighty-Six
Star Ranch
Colorado Springs

It took fifteen minutes of convincing for the sergeant in charge of these men to accept that Mac and Hunter weren't infected with the plague. One of the soldiers put on a mask, gloves, and goggles and approached them with an electronic forehead thermometer. When both of their temperatures read normal, the sergeant declared them to be safe, a potentially deadly mistake but not in this case.

Mac was placed in the back of one Humvee and Hunter was placed in the back of the other. Their weapons were taken away and a sergeant who didn't identify himself placed their backpacks and rifles on the hood of each truck. Mac couldn't discern what he was saying to the listener on the other side of the military radio, but he constantly referred to their identification and periodically held them up to compare their faces to the images on the laminated cards.

The sergeant hung up the phone and began to rifle through Hunter's backpack, brusquely unloading the contents on the hood of the truck. When he grabbed for Mac's backpack, she began yelling at him.

"Hey, be careful! There are medications in there!"

The sergeant glanced up at her, but disregarded her shouting. As he dumped the contents onto the hood, the aluminum case rolled out of her backpack and slid off the side of the truck. It landed hard on the concrete and tumbled over until it rested against the curb.

Mac disregarded the soldier's order and pushed the rear door open and scrambled out of the Humvee, shouting at the sergeant, "You idiot! You stupid fool! Do you realize what you might have done?"

Mac was yelling as she ran to retrieve the case. Two of the soldiers standing guard over them rushed to intercept her, but she got there first. She cradled the case in her arms like it was a child, not saying a word, but her eyes fired cannons at the soldiers.

"Take it easy, everybody. Take it easy!" shouted Hunter, who also exited the back of his Humvee. "Sergeant, tell your men to stand down."

"I don't take orders from you!" he yelled at Hunter. Then he motioned his men toward Hunter. "Get him back in the truck, now!"

Hunter struggled against the soldiers as they gripped his arms and pushed him back toward the Humvee. "Sergeant, do not make a mistake that the world will regret! We need to speak to your superior officer immediately."

Mac was now being restrained and one of the soldiers wrestled the case away from her. He handed the case to the sergeant.

"What's in here?" asked the sergeant, who turned it over and over to examine the casing. "Where's the key?"

"We can't open that," replied Mac. "You see my ID. I'm with the CDC and I also work for the CIA. You're way over your head here, Sergeant. If you open this case, people will die, including yourself. It contains samples of the plague as well as something else that I must get into the hands of my superiors at the CDC or at least notify the Secretary of Health and Human Services of its existence."

"You're lying." The sergeant began to walk away. "This is just some BS ploy to get into Star Ranch. Let me guess, you wanna nice house with a pool like the rest of them."

Mac struggled to pull away and was successful for a moment. She moved closer to the Humvee until she was restrained again.

"Sergeant, look at me! Don't you recognize me?"

The sergeant studied her face and shrugged. "Just another pretty girl. You look like that chick on the show my daughter used to watch on TV."

"Blake Lively," Mac interrupted. "Yeah, I get that a lot. Please set the case down and listen."

The sergeant's attitude softened and he complied.

Relieved, Mac continued. "I testified in front of Congress two months ago. Do you remember the uproar?"

One of the soldiers restraining Mac spoke up. "Sarge, I remember that. It caused the Capitol to go on lockdown. Don't you remember? She was wearing her lab outfit and the guy seated in the hearing room started spewing blood. Turned out to be a false alarm."

"Yeah, I remember now," said the sergeant. "I thought you got fired."

"No, Sergeant. I was reassigned to the CIA. You know how these things work. They never tell the public the truth."

"True dat," mumbled the other soldier, who held her right arm.

The sergeant wandered around the front of the truck and looked to the sky for guidance. "Here's what I'm gonna do," he began. "I'll take you to the officer in charge of Star Ranch. My orders are to escort you outside the perimeter you walked through. You can make your case to him. That's all you get from me."

"That's all we ask," replied Mac.

Mac's gear was loaded into the front seat of the Humvee. The driver gently placed the aluminum case in the passenger seat by itself and the sergeant rode shotgun in Hunter's vehicle. After a short drive, they passed through a series of HESCO barriers, which blocked the divided, boulevard-style entrance into Star Ranch.

Within the barrier's perimeter, but outside of a newly erected chain-link fence with concertina wire, there were several dozen tents on both sides of the entrance to Star Ranch. People were milling about and having casual conversations with one another. When the Humvees stopped short of the gate and the soldiers disembarked with their weapons pointed in their direction, the conversations ended and everyone scurried back into their tents.

Mac and Hunter were ordered out of the trucks and told to stand to the side. Their backpacks were set on the ground next to them, but their weapons were taken into a temporary guard station, along with the case carrying the vancomycin.

A man emerged from behind the steel gates and walked through the guard station. He had a spirited conversation with the sergeant and at one point took the case from him.

"He's got bars," said Hunter. "I'm guessing he's the lieutenant that gave the orders to have us escorted out of here. Now he's pissed."

"No question about it," said Mac. "Here he comes."

The lieutenant glared at them as he studied their government-issued IDs. He shook his head as he stuffed them in his pocket. "If you two are full of crap, I'll shoot you myself. Got it?"

Mac and Hunter returned his stare without responding.

"Got it?" he shouted, startling Mac, who jumped back slightly.

Hunter, on the other hand, took a step forward. "Lieutenant, you run this up the chain of command and get me the officer in charge of this facility. Or you give us back our things and let us go. We'll find someone who will appreciate what we've done for this country and we'll let them know how we were treated—"

"Lieutenant, what's going on here?" came a voice from behind the guard station. A uniformed officer approached the group. "Who are these people?"

CHAPTER 28

Day Eighty-Six
Fort Drum, New York

Jamal Al-Nashiri and his men moved swiftly and decisively, with the quiet knowledge of knowing one's fate and being prepared to face it with honor. Al-Nashiri led the assault on Fort Drum during the night raid, but he was not in front of the two dozen men who were strategically placed around the massive military reservation in upstate New York and barely thirty miles from the Canadian border.

Al-Nashiri was one of seven high-value detainees released by President Garcia after he took office. Fulfilling a campaign promise of shuttering the United States military prison at Guantanamo Bay, Cuba, once and for all, the President personally visited the facility, which created an uproar in the media.

The contentious and rocky start to his presidency resulted in the release of sixteen detainees under cover of darkness via a flight to Bermuda. In a secret deal made with the Bermudian government, four prisoners were released into their custody and the rest were dispatched to Saudi Arabia, Iraq, and Oman.

Jamal Al-Nashiri and three fellow detainees remained in the custody of Bermuda authorities until a rare, late-October hurricane bore down on the island. Hurricane Nicole, a category five storm, approached with maximum sustained winds of over one hundred twenty miles per hour. The storm surge threatened the entire island, prompting pre-storm evacuations to the U.S. and Canada.

Because of the international notoriety of Al-Nashiri and his associates, they were transported to Canada for safekeeping until the storm threat passed. They were never returned.

Using Canadian attorneys assigned to them, Al-Nashiri and the three other detainees filed a civil action against the country for

117

violating their rights under Canadian law, wrongful detention and damages resulting from their incarceration at Guantanamo Bay.

The case became a battle cry against the U.S. government's handling of terrorists, interrogation techniques, including waterboarding, and the ongoing military presence in the Middle East. The attorneys moved the cases through the Federal Court of Canada, ultimately reaching their Supreme Court.

In a stern rebuke of U.S. government policies, the Supreme Court of Canada ruled in favor of the terrorists, stating *the officials at Guantanamo offended the most basic Canadian standards about the treatment of prisoners of war.*

The court, disregarding Al-Nashiri's crime, which was using a grenade to blow off the face of an American soldier on the streets of Fallujah, ordered the four terrorists to be released and a compensation of two million dollars, Canadian, in damages.

Today, Al-Nashiri advanced toward the perimeter of Fort Drum as his operatives surreptitiously moved into position with the weapons purchased and assembled using the damage settlement paid by the Canadians. His Jeep Wrangler's thirty-two-inch off-road tires bit into the uneven terrain, kicking up gravel, but advancing him closer to the rise across the Black River from the base.

Al-Nashiri tightened his grip on the steering wheel as it jostled back and forth every time it hit a rock or fallen tree limb. Periodically, he'd glance back at his cargo, three Russian-made RPG-29 Vampirs captured by ISIS fighters during the Syrian Civil War.

The Vampir was a shoulder-launched, unguided, tube-style rocket launching system with a range of fifteen hundred feet. Its projectiles were thermobaric antipersonnel rounds, which created an explosion in the form of a sustained blast wave. When the rocket detonated, it used oxygen surrounding the target to create intense pressure at the point of contact. It was deployed primarily against tanks, but the thermobaric round was ideal for closely grouped targets.

The southern perimeter gate of Fort Drum came into view as the lights in this military oasis shined bright compared to the surrounding towns. Fort Drum had been fortified with twelve-foot-high chain-link fencing and razor wire. It looked more like a medium-security prison than it did a military base in America.

He silently cursed the lights giving those guarding the compound an unfair advantage of seeing farther than his fellow jihadists.

But it would not matter.

Al-Nashiri's answer to their technology was not to fight it but, rather, to overwhelm it and deceive it and those who depended on it. His fighters carried similar weapons to his as well as AK-74 assault rifles built in Venezuela. The AKs were built with an added bonus—a GP-25 grenade launcher attached to their short barrels. The lightweight launcher was capable of firing a forty-millimeter grenade and then could be quickly reloaded.

Their targets included diversionary and primary locations. His operatives had studied Fort Drum for days to learn its footprint and vulnerabilities. He checked his watch. It was 4:00 a.m.—almost time.

Using binoculars, he surveyed the fence line that stretched along the southern perimeter. The well-worn grassy road created by the patrolling Humvees was quiet. Tonight, there were no patrols.

The plan was simple. Al-Nashiri would use his three Vampirs to fire at the southern entry gate. He would then move easterly along a path they'd discovered during their reconnaissance toward where the Wheeler-Sack Army Airfield was located. His targets would then become their Apache helicopters, the sworn enemy of the Taliban, with whom his father had served proudly.

Al-Nashiri and his operatives would also target Fort Drum's critical infrastructure by destroying its large generators and solar array. The fuel depot near the airfield would also be hit with the rocket-propelled grenades.

His instructions to his men were straightforward—hit your targets hard and fast in multiple sections along Fort Drum's southern perimeter. When you're able to break through the security fencing, then enter with reckless abandon under the strength of Allah and kill everyone you see.

If the defenses held, their efforts would still be a success, as many of the infidels would die and Fort Drum would be crippled. At this point, nothing on earth could stop their attack, and his fighters were waiting for the fuse to be lit.

Al-Nashiri's fellow jihadists had planned, rehearsed, prayed, and rehearsed again. They'd accepted the inevitable outcome of their actions. Some yelled, some cried, some sweated, some were calm, and some chanted in Arabic. But, at the given time, they would charge at the infidels in their quest to achieve the final jihad.

The time had come. Al-Nashiri fired his first RPG-29 Vampir. The rocket zoomed overhead and was followed by several others to his left and right.

Armed with white phosphorous incendiary heads, the projectiles arced toward their targets, undetected until it was too late to react. U.S. military installations never anticipated an attack such as this, especially in a post-apocalyptic world. Had this been a major base in the Middle East, like Bagram, base defenses like the Phalanx Close-In Weapons Systems would have reacted instantaneously. Their deadly accurate 20mm Gatling guns would have decimated the RPGs before they crossed the Black River.

But only a single shout could be heard from Fort Drum, a lonely voice at the southern gate that yelled *incoming* before he was killed by Al-Nashiri's first shot.

Gunfire erupted in many places along the perimeter as his fighters engaged patrols who scrambled into position. More rockets were fired at the gated entries at First Street and Great Bend Road. His men could be heard shouting instructions to one another in Arabic, and *Allahu Akbar* was included as they joyously attacked the infidels.

The return fire from the Americans was sporadic, indicating their momentary confusion. This was expected, but Al-Nashiri knew the advantage would be short-lived. Within minutes, the barracks on the northwest side of Fort Drum would empty and thousands of soldiers would be joining the fight.

His goal was not to annihilate the enemy but, rather, to humiliate and demoralize them. He picked up the pace, now running through the path created in the woods, the two remaining Vampirs bouncing on his shoulder.

He took up a position at the Great Bend roadblock, steadied his aim, and fired. The rocket sailed through the air and struck its target, as evidenced by the screams of the men who once stood guard there.

Headlights illuminated below him, and his fighters drove through the gate in a black Ford F-250 pickup truck. They opened fire on anyone who came into their field of view and then the men turned into the heart of the installation, launching their grenades into the cluster of helicopters at the airfield.

Al-Nashiri had one more important task, so he ran back towards his original position near the Jeep. He frowned as bullets zoomed over his head, but wildly off the mark. The Americans were finding their footing, he thought to himself as he broke out into a run.

With his fighters now fully engaged within the perimeter, it was time to give his men an advantage. He set his sights on the electricity substation that served Fort Drum exclusively. Two large transformers sat in the middle of the fenced-off area, together with several sets of power lines, which ran toward large solar arrays to the north side of the electric generating plant.

His two final shots would be the death blow to Fort Drum. By destroying their electricity, he'd destroy their will. He checked his Vampir and the PG-29V tandem-charge warhead, which was one of the few warheads that could penetrate the Americans' battle tanks. He'd used it before and knew its capabilities.

Al-Nashiri took his aim, whispered, "*Allahu Akbar*," and launched the first PG-29V. Within seconds, it found its mark. The explosion caught him by surprise.

The combination of the rocket's impact with the breaching of the transformers lit up the sky with maddening force. Bursts of fire, cement, fencing, and power lines sailed into the air. The blast swallowed the light of Fort Drum like a distant star getting sucked into a black hole.

Al-Nashiri stood in stunned disbelief as a strange silence overtook the base. A temporary ceasefire, of sorts, was put into effect for a few seconds as the masses of humanity who resided at Fort Drum contemplated what had just happened.

The lessons of Fort Drum would be taught to those alive in the future to learn them. When fighting someone who did not care if they lived or died, the fanatics eventually succeeded.

Al-Nashiri picked up the final PG-29V with its special payload and loaded it into the launcher. He studied Fort Drum as his ISIS fighters waged jihad. He prepared for one final blast to seal the fate of as many infidels as possible.

He pulled the trigger and the rocket-propelled grenade that had been modified to carry radioactive materials as part of its payload sailed high into the air toward the barracks. The explosives detonated on impact in the middle of the four buildings and temporary housing tents.

As it detonated, the radioactive material vaporized, propelling it into the air in all directions.

Al-Nashiri heard the screams and realized they were not that different from the ones he recalled as a child following a drone attack that bombed his village.

"Only the beginning," he mumbled as he watched the carnage below.

CHAPTER 29

Day Eighty-Six
Star Ranch
Colorado Springs

Neither Mac nor Hunter was able to sleep. After Captain Hoover had instructed them to wait in this holding tent, nobody had returned. On two occasions, Hunter and Mac asked to use the latrine, which they were granted access to, but they were escorted and advised not to speak to anyone. It was now approaching ten o'clock and Hunter was growing restless. He began to pace back and forth, drawing a rebuke from Mac.

"Hunter, technically speaking, as a lieutenant commander in the Public Service, I outrank you," started Mac. Earlier in the day he'd referred to her as being *active-duty military*, so she decided to pull rank and use it to her advantage.

"Huh? Maybe, I guess. So?" he stammered a reply as he kept walking from one side of the twelve-by-twelve structure to the other.

"When I started at the CDC, I followed some of my mom's advice while other suggestions were ignored, which ultimately got me into hot water." Mac was trying to get Hunter's attention, to no avail.

"Are you talking about the congressional hearing?"

"No, I'm talking about being an employee of the government," she replied. "Patience is an absolute quality every government employee must have. It's kinda like the beard you've been growing."

Hunter stopped pacing and sat down on one of the folding chairs provided them by the soldiers. "Why are we talking about my beard?"

"If you have the patience to grow a beard, then you should have the patience to deal with the government," she replied. "You've been lucky in the past because the DTRA was all about shortcuts and rapid response. You don't know bureaucratic red tape like I do."

"I'm patient," he mumbled.

"No, sir, you are not. Waiting is one thing, but having the ability to maintain a good attitude and a clear head requires patience."

"Mac, we have the cure for the plague and these guys are jacking around trying to make a decision," Hunter insisted.

She reached out and touched his face and scruffed his beard with her fingertips. "Your beard is fully grown, and the government will get to us in due time. Wearing out the floor won't make it happen sooner."

He managed a grin and nodded his head. "You're right," Hunter said as he reached for her hand.

Mac gave it a squeeze. "See, being patient has given you this important moment of clarity."

"I don't get it," he said.

"Yes, you do. After calming down, you acknowledged that I'm right. I am, and I always will be. First rule of any relationship is the woman is always right. Sometimes we may be confused, misinformed, stubborn, and maybe a little emotional on occasion, but no matter what, we're never wrong."

Hunter started laughing. "I guess Barb told you that too."

"Nope, Daddy did. He said it was the key to a long-lasting marriage."

"Oh, kinda like the happy wife, happy life thing, right?" said Hunter with a chuckle.

"Wow, patience is paying off for you. Look how much we've accomplished in just a few minutes," said Mac before Hunter pulled her close to him and planted a smooch on her lips.

She began to giggle as he tickled her ribs, when the ill-tempered lieutenant interrupted them. He cleared his throat to announce his presence.

"Ahem. I want you both to listen carefully," he grumbled. "The captain wants to speak with you inside the perimeter. Leave your things and I will have an aide bring them to you. Don't say a word, understand?"

Hunter and Mac exchanged a quick look and both nodded their

response. The lieutenant opened the flap of the tent for them and they were greeted by two unarmed men wearing khakis and polo shirts.

"Follow us, please," they said in unison.

Mac and Hunter were led to the rear of the guardhouse and through an iron gate that was part of the original neighborhood entrance. In front of them was a large two-story brick home with a circle drive in front. A variety of military vehicles were parked on the pavement and around the side of the home.

The first thing that struck Mac was the fact the neighborhood had electricity. She casually turned to look over her shoulder into the valley where the downtown area of Colorado Springs was located and it was dark except for a couple of fires burning around the area. On the far eastern side of the city, a faint glow could be seen reflecting off the cloud cover. She speculated that was Peterson Air Force Base.

They were led up several stone and concrete steps and past two armed guards who flanked the double door entry. They were quickly taken inside, where they were greeted by the officer who had calmed the situation down earlier.

"Dr. Hagan, Sergeant Hunter, my name is Captain Kevin Hoover. I'd like to start over and welcome you to Star Ranch."

Hunter nodded and Mac smiled as a sense of relief came over her. She didn't want to admit it to Hunter, but the whole spiel about being patient was a load of crap. She was nervous—not because of the time it was taking, but because of how they might be treated. Her work was contained in that case and she'd lost control of it along with her notes.

"Thank you, Captain," said Hunter. "I don't blame your men for doing their job. The world wasn't a very safe place before the pandemic; it sure isn't now."

Captain Hoover gestured for them to enter a formal living room, which was once impeccably decorated but now contained half a dozen maps tacked to the wall. Four of the maps were from the property assessor's office, identifying the improved lots in the subdivisions commandeered by the government and within Captain Hoover's control.

"Would you like a drink?" he asked.

"Water for me," said Hunter.

"Sergeant, I have just about anything you could want, including beer, wine, sodas, etcetera. Seriously, don't be shy."

"I appreciate that, Captain. Water is fine."

"Yeah, me too," said Mac. Mac sensed Hunter was still on edge. When he avoided alcohol, it was because he wanted to stay sharp. This was an important step and she wanted to keep her wits too.

Captain Hoover asked his aide to retrieve the bottled waters and he walked over to a desk, which contained Mac's case. He returned it to her.

"I apologize for the rough treatment by our sergeant. He's experienced a lot outside Star Ranch. We all have."

The aide returned with the water and efficiently retreated out of the room, closing the door behind him. Captain Hoover tugged at his collar as if it was strangling him. He exhaled before continuing.

"Let me start by telling you where we stand," said Captain Hoover. "Obviously, I have confirmed your identities through Cheyenne Mountain. Both the DOD and the CDC, a Dr. Spielman, I think, has vouched for you both."

"He's alive?" Mac asked excitedly. "I mean, um, so much has happened. I wasn't sure if they were compromised in Atlanta."

Captain Hoover sat in a Queen Anne chair across from them and leaned against the cushioned back. "I don't know the details. Information is hard to come by, even for us. Apparently, hundreds of people began to gather outside the CDC facility in Atlanta. That became thousands before the governor was able to assemble sufficient National Guard units to assist.

"The crowd was demanding answers and a vaccine. They grew impatient and stormed the building. It got pretty ugly and the director and some of his staff were removed by helicopter off the rooftop. That's all I know."

"Where is he now?" asked Mac.

"I don't know, but it must be somewhere within radio contact. We should know more by tomorrow."

Hunter set his water on the table in front of them. "What happens tomorrow?"

"At some point, and trust me when I say I don't know when, they'll set up a closed-circuit conference call with the both of you. I'm authorized to provide you a place to stay, but you'll have to be on a loose form of house arrest."

Hunter looked to Mac and nodded. "Completely understandable."

"Actually, let me explain because it's for reasons other than you might think. I have no concerns about you as a threat of any kind. Just the opposite, actually. I've been provided your service record, Sergeant. It's nothing short of incredible."

"Doin' my duty, Captain," Hunter added.

"Here's the problem," Captain Hoover continued. "The government seized this community weeks ago to create safe zones for the people they deemed necessary to start a rebuilding effort when the time comes. As a result, homeowners were removed, some by force, and others know their days at Star Ranch are numbered. In those tents outside are the new residents. We keep them segregated for fourteen days as part of our quarantine process. When they're cleared, then we will remove another family and move those people into their homes."

"I can see how that might get contentious," said Mac.

"Oh, yes," said Captain Hoover. "These residents don't realize it, but they're being sent out to survive on their own. The military provides them a vehicle with a full tank of gas and enough MREs to last two weeks. They can go anywhere they want, but they can't stay here."

Hunter shook his head. "This is not our nation's finest hour."

"I can't disagree with that, Sergeant."

"Please, call me Hunter."

"Okay, brother. My friends call me Cappy. Listen, I hate this, too. I did things, following orders of course, that kept me awake at night for weeks. Here's what I know. My wife and babies are sound asleep upstairs. They're surrounded by good soldiers, my men. Nothing is more important to me than that."

Mac smiled at Captain Hoover and then did something completely unexpected. "Captain, I have the cure for the plague."

Hunter snapped his head to look at her. She calmly smiled at him and then turned her attention back to Captain Hoover.

"I'm not a psychologist by any stretch, but my career requires me to be around a lot of troubled, hurting people. I can see that in your eyes and hear it in your voice. I want you to know we may have the ability to bring the suffering and death to an end. That's why we're here."

"Doctor, I hope so. The only things preventing me from opting out of this ugly mess are lying with their gorgeous little heads next to their mommy. If you have the cure, then I'll help you get it in the right hands."

Mac reached for Hunter's hand and squeezed it, an unexpected show of affection in front of the captain. "We'll do everything you ask. We can all talk more tomorrow. It's late and you should spend some time with your family, even if they're sleeping."

"Roger that."

The three of them stood and Captain Hoover was about to open the doors to the living room when he added one more statement. "Also, they're going to talk with you about Breckenridge."

"What about it?" asked Hunter.

"We'll talk tomorrow," replied Captain Hoover as he swung the doors open, ending the conversation.

CHAPTER 30

Day Eighty-Seven
Cheyenne Mountain

It was 3:00 a.m. and President Garcia had just received a phone call informing him of the attack on Fort Drum. Prior to the pandemic, the concept of a president being awakened in the middle of the night to be informed of a crisis or a matter that presented a clear and present danger to the safety of the United States was largely a myth and only used in fiction. The wake-up calls were often unnecessary, but there had been occasions where an overzealous national security advisor felt obligated to provide a president bad or unexpected news despite the fact there was little that could be done by the commander-in-chief.

Most often, the wake-up call was done as a matter of political optics, like the time President Ronald Reagan's staff caused an inside-the-beltway uproar by failing to wake the president after two F-14 Tomcat fighter jets shot down two Libyan MIGs in the middle of the night.

President William Clinton was a notorious night owl. He was more likely to wake up his staff than to have them wake him up. When he received the phone call at 3:00 a.m. in '98 to finalize the Northern Ireland peace agreement, he was said to be sitting up in bed, wide awake.

President Garcia had been sleeping much better since he'd abandoned brandy as a crutch to make it through the day, and night. The physicians at Cheyenne Mountain provided the President a gradually decreasing dose of Valium to assist him with the withdrawal symptoms and the sleepless nights.

The afternoon of his inauguration, the President instructed Morse in no uncertain terms that he was to be awakened in a time of crisis, perceived or otherwise. He could always go back to sleep, but he never wanted to leave the impression on the American people that he was asleep at the wheel.

After he was informed of the Fort Drum attack, and despite the fact it had been brought to a conclusion, he insisted upon gathering Defense Secretary General Denise Keef and the Secretary of Homeland Security into the conference room.

When he arrived, coffee was ready as well as a variety of pastries. Every seat in the operations center was taken and images of the devastation at Fort Drum filled the screens. Security cameras had provided footage of the attack, which had concluded just an hour ago. The President stood at the glass and listened as General Keef conducted the briefing.

"Mr. President," started General Keef, "the base is secure and the threats have been eliminated. As daylight comes in the east, the base command will dispatch patrols into the surrounding areas to learn more about how the attack developed. We have to learn from this, sir, in order to protect our other installations."

"Casualties?" the President gruffed.

"Precise numbers are unknown at this time, Mr. President," responded General Keefe. "We're estimating several hundred, perhaps more than a thousand."

"What else?" the President asked his Secretary of Defense.

"One of the big issues we're facing is Fort Drum's electrical supply. It has been destroyed, sir. The transformers were taken out with an RPG designed for a tank. Under the overall circumstances, I don't think they can be repaired or replaced."

The President looked to the Secretary of Homeland Security. "What are our options?"

"Mr. President, Fort Drum is one of the nation's largest in the Northeast. If we cannot restore power, it cannot be properly secured and maintained. Our best bet is to relocate the Army to the US Army Garrison at Fort Devens in upstate Massachusetts. There are several other military options within the state. It'll be crowded, but workable."

The President turned back to the monitors to study the footage. "Is this an isolated event or part of an orchestrated attack?"

General Keef spoke up. "Sir, the attack appeared to be well planned, coordinated, and they used advanced weaponry, including a dirty bomb. As you know, our intelligence apparatus is not performing its function up to our normal high standards. We are more reactive than proactive right now."

"General," interrupted the President, "with the information you have, give me your best calculation of what we're dealing with here."

"I believe it's the beginning of a ground war against our military, Mr. President—on American soil. The beginnings of this final jihad, as ISIS calls it, started with the creation of the plague pandemic. The logical continuation would be to bring the battle to us rather than defend their territories in the desert. This is their chance, Mr. President, to turn the tide of the war we've waged for decades."

"Are you fortifying our bases—their potential targets?" asked the President.

"Sir, we believe every military installation is a hard target for their advanced weaponry, but we should also be prepared to defend our soft targets," replied General Keef.

"Soft targets?"

"Yes, sir. The safe zones."

CHAPTER 31

Day Eighty-Seven
Star Ranch
Colorado Springs

The night before marked the first time Hunter and Mac had slept together without fear or preoccupation with the events that had enveloped their lives. The sun was on full display as Hunter pulled back the silk curtains of the impeccably decorated master bedroom of the home they'd been escorted to last night.

While he stretched and wondered if coffee was an option in the kitchen, he noticed the activity near the front gate. The vehicles parked in front of Captain Hoover's headquarters were being moved out and driven to different points throughout Star Ranch. Armed soldiers now flanked the gated entrance along the HESCO barriers. A Humvee with a fifty-caliber machine gun mounted on its turret backed into the entrance to block access.

"Mac, wake up. Something's wrong. Mac!"

She slid up in bed and reached for her clothes on the floor. "What is it?"

"Hoover's men are scramblin' around. It's all hands on deck. I'll be right back."

HESCO barriers ran down the hallway and entered every upstairs bedroom. He looked out of the windows, trying to catch a glimpse of where the other Humvees were going.

"Hunter, where are you?"

"At the end of the hall. They're fanning out throughout the neighborhood. They must've had a breach in their perimeter security."

Mac looked in the mirror of what appeared to be a young girl's bedroom. She adjusted her clothes and joined Hunter at the window.

"Should we—" she began before being interrupted by a pounding on the front door.

The door opened and a voice bellowed from below, "Sir, ma'am, Captain Hoover needs to see you immediately. Please join me on the front porch."

They scrambled down the winding staircase and Hunter searched for his shoes. He'd left them upstairs. While he ran back up, Mac asked the aide, whom they'd met the night before, what was going on.

"I'm sorry, ma'am, Captain Hoover will explain. Your belongings are in the HQ."

Hunter ran down the stairs to join them. The aide led them to Captain Hoover's office in a fast-paced trot. The trio paused momentarily as a forklift ambled by them, headed up the street in the direction of the mountains.

Two Army AH-64 Apache helicopters roared from north to south above them with a deafening roar. A Jeep was driving through the neighborhoods with one of the soldiers shouting through the bullhorn, advising the residents to remain in their homes until further notice.

When they arrived at the house, men and women in uniform were moving briskly from room to room and then out the front door. The aide led them back to the living room, where they'd sat with Captain Hoover the night before.

"Mac, look," said Hunter, who stopped her and pointed to the top of the stairs. A young child, probably Captain Hoover's oldest, was standing on the landing alone. She was holding onto the balusters, watching the activity.

"Where's her mother?" asked Hunter.

"I'll take care of it," replied Mac. She left Hunter's side and raced up the steps. Hunter watched for a moment and then joined the aide, who'd reached Captain Hoover's side. The aide noticed Mac was missing.

"Where's your friend?" he asked, looking past Hunter.

"She'll be along," replied Hunter and then he ignored the aide.

"Cappy, what's happening? Did you have a breach?"

Captain Hoover took Hunter by the arm and pulled him to a corner behind the desk, where there was no other activity. "We took a hit last night. Fort Drum was attacked in the middle of the night. Those cowards hit our barracks with an RDD."

"A dirty bomb?" asked Hunter. RDD was an acronym for radiological dispersal device. "Radiological? Are they sure?"

"Certain enough to order us on full alert here," replied Captain Hoover.

"Why here?" asked Hunter.

"Because we're sittin' ducks like every other military base and safe zone created by the President. I get the concept of the safe zones, but putting everyone in one place makes us vulnerable to attack."

Hunter studied Captain Hoover. The man was frenzied and probably over his head to an extent. His role with the National Guard as the plague spread throughout Denver had had a profound effect on him. Hunter questioned whether he was up to the task alone.

"Cappy, I don't know what they disclosed to you from the DOD, but counterterrorism is my deal. Let me help you."

Captain Hoover took a deep breath and responded, "I know what the DTRA does. Here's what I learned about the attack. They launched missiles at Fort Drum, using RPGs or something similar. We don't have the details because they hit and ran."

"They confirmed the radiation?"

"There was little physical damage in the vicinity of the RDD impact other than that caused by the explosive charge. But the contamination was widespread. They knew exactly where to target to have maximum impact."

Hunter shook his head and looked grim. "They'll have to abandon the base. The intent is to flush us out of our nests."

"I'm afraid so," said Captain Hoover. "If it happens here, every one of these people will leave one form of poison and walk right into another. My job was to protect them from the plague, not radiation."

"Cappy, we've got to assume they're going after military

installations first. If the attacks are going to have the biggest effect on the nation's psyche, ISIS will try to destroy people's confidence in their protectors—the military."

"Do you think we're good?" asked Captain Hoover.

"No, I didn't say that. Their MO is to strike fear in the hearts and minds of Americans. Whoever they didn't kill with the plague could die by running out of their safe places into the disease's arms. All it would take is one successful attack on a location like this and any hope of rebuilding America could be lost."

The lieutenant from the night before and two of his men stood on the other side of the desk. They were awaiting orders from Captain Hoover. For a moment, an awkward silence overtook the group until Hunter took control.

"I need maps of the surrounding area. We have to expand our perimeter. Captain, may I have permission to direct your men?"

"Absolutely."

"Okay, Lieutenant, listen up. Here's what needs to happen," started Hunter.

CHAPTER 32

Day Eighty-Seven
Star Ranch
Colorado Springs

Mac wasn't a mother, but she was a kid once and knew what it was like to grow up in a loving home. She couldn't recall her parents arguing, nor did she detect any form of hostilities between them. Not all children were so lucky.

Children were like sponges, absorbing the world around them, especially when there was turmoil swirling through their eyes. They were sensitive to the tensions between parents and any adults in their lives. This applied constantly because oftentimes parents became so immersed in their own emotional states that they acted as if the kids were invisible.

Regardless of age, kids could sense something was wrong. Whether a heated argument occurred between family members or perhaps it was the stress caused by a bad financial situation, children often took on the burdens and pressures of their parents.

Mac learned this firsthand in Western Africa during the Ebola outbreak. Children in Africa during that time stood quietly as their parents suffered and died. They knew real pain caused by the loss of a mother or father. They considered ways to make it better, but because of their age and physical limitations, they couldn't.

At the top of the stairs, a little girl, maybe three or four years old, stood alone, watching her father run back and forth through the foyer in a frenzy. Mac had no idea how long the child had been standing there, or where her mother was, but she recognized the look of depression and stress on her face.

Mac ascended the wide stairwell and approached the child slowly before sitting on the floor next to her. The girl looked at Mac for a

136

moment and then turned her attention back to the activity below.

"Would you like to sit down with me? It might be more fun to watch that way," started Mac.

The smallish child gave Mac a puzzled look. She looked back downstairs and then shrugged, collapsing onto her butt with her legs crossed in front of her.

"My daddy's busy," she managed to speak a few words.

"He sure is because he is a very important man. My name is Mac. I'm a doctor."

The little girl was interested in this topic. "What kind of doctor? People or dog doctor?"

"Before I answer, will you tell me your name? We can't be friends unless you tell me your name."

"I'm Melissa. My daddy is a soldier."

"Yes, I know. My mother is a soldier too."

The girl giggled. "Mommys can't be soldiers."

"Oh, yes, they can. She used to be a general, but now she's retired."

The girl simply nodded her head. Mac wanted the little girl to feel safe but her biggest concern at the moment was why she wasn't being watched by her mother.

"Melissa, where is your mommy?"

"She went to bed. She said she just wanted to sleep."

"Melissa, don't move. I'll be right back. Promise?"

"Okay."

Mac jumped off the floor and ran toward the end of the hall, where a set of double doors led into the master bedroom. She didn't bother to knock and flung the doors open.

"Mrs. Hoover!" she exclaimed as the doors opened wide. Captain Hoover's wife was sitting on the floor with her back against the bed, holding her baby. An opened prescription bottle lay on the bed and a dozen bright red capsules were scattered about.

Mac ran into the room and grabbed the bottle. "Did you take any of these?"

The woman kept sobbing. Mac fell to the floor onto her knees directly in front of the crying woman.

"Mrs. Hoover!" she shouted. Mac grabbed her face with her left hand and shoved the bottle at her. "Look at me! Did you take any of these?"

The woman shook her head and whispered, "No."

"What about the baby? Did you give them to the baby? Answer me!"

Mac was incredulous, but she had to snap this woman out of it before she said anything else. She immediately recognized the red capsules as Seconal. Secobarbital was a powerful narcotic used to help insomniacs, which Captain Hoover apparently was experiencing. Its street names were *reds* or *red devils*.

"No. No. I couldn't, um, I would never do that." The woman began to wail.

Mac looked around where the three of them sat on the floor to make sure there weren't any pills around her. She got up and began to scoop all the drugs up into her palm. She glanced to make sure little Melissa was still sitting where she'd left her a moment ago. Then Mac rushed into the bathroom and attempted to flush the pills down the toilet, but it wouldn't flush.

She rattled the handle repeatedly and then realized the water wasn't working. The family had several one-gallon jugs of water sitting in the bathtub. Mac quickly poured two gallons into the toilet bowl, causing the weight of the water to activate the flushing mechanism. The toilet flushed on its own and took the red devils away.

Mac had to decide what to do next. Obviously, this woman was so distraught that she was contemplating suicide and leaving these two beautiful children behind. Her husband, who seemed on the brink of losing it himself, had told Mac he couldn't sleep because of the terrors he'd witnessed in Denver. The sleeping pills were probably used by him to escape the horrific memories of what he'd witnessed.

She wasn't sure what was going on and why the soldiers were scrambling, but the last thing Captain Hoover needed right now was his wife attempting suicide. Mac decided to bring Melissa back into the bedroom and calm the situation down.

"Hey, Melissa, your mommy decided not to take a nap after all. Come in here for a moment because I have a fun idea."

Melissa shrugged and said, "Okay."

Once she was inside the bedroom, Mac closed the door behind her. She took the baby out of Mrs. Hoover's arms and helped the new mother off the floor. She'd recovered her composure but was still crying.

"I don't know what came over me," she said through her sniffles. "Kevin told me what happened and it was, like, the last straw. I couldn't take it anymore."

"What's your baby's name?"

"Amy."

"Melissa, would you like to help your mommy for a minute?"

"Okay."

Mac looked around the room and there was no crib or place to put the baby. There was a car seat lying on the floor in the corner of the room. Mac took the baby and strapped her in so she couldn't get into anything.

"Here we go, Amy," said Mac as she gently put the infant in the car seat. "Melissa, you guys pretend you're going on a ride to the zoo, okay. I'm gonna talk to your mommy because I have an idea."

"Sure. Come on, Amy. Let's go see the monkeys first."

Bad choice, Mac thought to herself.

She quickly checked under the bed to make sure none of the pills were on the floor within the children's grasp. Then, Mac rose up out of her crouch and turned to Captain Hoover's wife.

"Come with me," Mac said brusquely as she led the woman into the bathroom and closed the door behind them.

"I wouldn't have gone through with it. It's just that—"

"Now you listen to me," started Mac. "People are dying gruesome deaths out there. You don't have the right to quit. Do you hear me? I almost lost my father the other day. I cried and cried at the thought of life without him. Is that what you want for your babies? How selfish are you?"

Perhaps Mac had been a little rough because the woman broke down in tears again. "No. I love my girls."

"Enough to leave them behind?" Mac asked as she kept her face directly in front of the distraught mother.

"No, I'm sorry. I was just so upset."

Mac decided to soften her approach. She didn't want to drive the woman into looking for more pills. "I get it. It sucks right now. But look at me," said Mac as she forced the woman to look into her eyes. Mac tried to read her to see if this was a onetime lapse in moral judgment. "Do you love your husband?"

"Yes, of course. I love Kevin more than anything."

"Then focus on what you have with him and not what's out of your control. You, your husband, and those two precious little girls are your universe. Forget the rest."

She stopped crying and reached for a towel on the vanity. "I'm so weak."

Again, Mac gave her a pep talk. "No, you're not. You wanna know why?" Mac, who was at least six inches taller than the mom, bent down to look into her eyes.

"Why?"

"Because you couldn't go through with it. If you were weak, you'd be dead. Instead, you chose the lives of your husband and children instead."

Mrs. Hoover nodded her head and gave Mac an unanticipated hug. The two women held each other until the new mother whispered, "Thank you."

"Are you okay now? I've got to go downstairs for a minute, but I'll be back, okay?"

She nodded and then got a fearful look on her face. "Are you gonna tell Kev? He has so much pressure on him."

"No, I'm not. That's up to you. When the time's right, you'll find the strength and you'll deal with it together. Right?"

"Yes."

"Okay. Go play with your children. Hold them close. I'm gonna talk to the guys for a minute and then we're gonna go to the house we slept in last night and have a tea party for Melissa. She needs to get away from this. All of this. It's too much for a little girl. It's too much for a new mom also."

CHAPTER 33

Day Eighty-Seven
Star Ranch
Colorado Springs

Hunter had just emerged from the living room, where he and Captain Hoover provided final instructions to the National Guard contingent, when Mac came bounding down the stairs to greet him. She had a frazzled look on her face.

"Is everything okay up there?" he asked.

She leaned in to his ear and whispered, "No, not even close. Hoover's wife was on the verge of suicide. She'd closed herself up in the master bedroom with her baby and a bottle of Seconal—sleeping pills."

Hunter calmly said, "Did she take them?"

"No, I think she was going to and couldn't go through with it. Hunter, I've got this under control for now, but she's pretty unstable still. I don't think we should tell her husband. It should be up to them to work it out."

"I agree. The man's under an inordinate amount of stress. Mac, I've seen PTSD in various stages. Cappy's on the edge of losing it. I'm not kidding."

"His family is too," said Mac as she looked past Hunter's shoulder. "Here comes Hoover."

"Good morning," he said, addressing Mac. "Hunter, I think we're ready."

Hunter nodded and looked to Mac.

Mac said, "Cappy, listen. I was just upstairs, talking with your wife and Melissa. You know, this is kinda busy and disruptive for your girls. Would you mind if I invite them over to the house you provided us? There are two girls' bedrooms there with toys and dresses. Us girls could get away for a day. Whadya think?"

Captain Hoover thought for a moment. "I think they'll be safer here with the guards posted downstairs."

"Cappy," started Mac as she moved closer to establish physical contact. She lowered her voice, forcing him to focus on what she was saying. "The girls are scared. Look around you. They know something is wrong and they're frightened. Trust me. I'll take good care of them."

Captain Hoover looked upstairs to the empty hallway and back to Mac. "Okay, I trust you. Let me get your weapons. But I wanna send one guard for my peace of mind."

"I can't argue with that," said Mac. She kissed Hunter on the cheek and touched his face. "See ya later."

Hunter followed Captain Hoover into the dining room, where his aides were seated, making notes. Hunter chuckled at the fact the government's penchant for filling out forms and keeping inventory hadn't gone away even during the apocalypse.

Something had been troubling him throughout their preparations that morning. He'd always had a knack for putting himself in the mind of a terrorist. That'd kept him alive through the years as he participated in a variety of missions.

ISIS always sought out targets that provided maximum media exposure. The media firestorm created by a truck plowing into pedestrians or a suicide bomber in an open-air market was an effective way to get the message to the malcontents of society looking to join a group driven by hate.

The attack on Fort Drum the night before was warlike, not propaganda driven. It had all the markings of an insurgency operation where a smaller force, David, takes on the mighty United States military, its Goliath.

ISIS was conducting classic guerilla warfare using ideological soldiers who conducted hit-and-run campaigns aimed at tearing down America's confidence. Like 9/11, what was happening now was years in the making.

He thought about Mac's lecture to him yesterday about patience.

The sleeper cells had been waiting for the appropriate trigger event to attack America. The plague gave them an ideal scenario. Out of fear of dying, they huddled together for protection.

Give us your huddled masses.

This provided the terrorists easy targets to inflict maximum psychological damage. To defeat an insurgency, conventional military tactics like search and destroy had to be abandoned. A clear and hold approach made the most sense and Captain Hoover was successful in doing so.

Or was he?

Hunter abruptly turned and went inside to locate Captain Hoover. Mac was escorting the girls down the stairs with her sidearm firmly attached to her belt and her AR-15 slung over her shoulder. Hunter gave her another kiss and patted young Melissa on the head with a smile.

Captain Hoover kissed his wife before Hunter quickly pulled him aside. "Show me the map of your perimeter."

They went into the dining room and moved the aides out of the way. Captain Hoover unfurled a large taped-together map of Star Ranch and the surrounding neighborhoods. There was a dotted line made with a permanent marker that ran haphazardly around the neighborhoods.

"Cappy, within this perimeter, are there any other civilians besides those in the tents out front?"

"Sadly, no," he replied. "Initially, my orders were to secure Star Ranch. Later, I was told to displace all civilians within the dashed line. Once in a while, our patrols observe someone moving about and we send out a couple of Humvees to run them off."

"Like yesterday," Hunter interjected.

"Yes, on the north side we had reports of a large group of teens breaking into homes. Our units were dispatched and we ran them off. They reported you waving in the road as they went by."

"What about vehicles? I wasn't able to find a way through your makeshift barricades, which was why we were walking."

Captain Hoover rose up from being hunched over the map. "I

inspected them myself. It would take a tow truck to make a path. Other than that, we disabled every vehicle in the surrounding neighborhood so they couldn't be used to breach our inner fencing around Star Ranch. Why?"

"We saw a white panel van, the old style, parked at the high school," replied Hunter. "We'd just walked past it when it pulled out of the parking space and headed toward the back of the school in a hurry. Could your men have missed it?"

Captain Hoover turned his attention back to the map. He pointed to Cheyenne Mountain High School. "Are you talking about here?"

"Yes, and then they took off toward the west behind the school. Where do these roads lead?" Hunter traced his fingers along a twisted, winding road that headed due west into the mountains and then reversed itself toward Star Ranch again.

"Those are old mountain roads that aren't used except by hikers who like to take photographs from Seven Falls Inspiration Point."

"Do you have a topo map?" asked Hunter.

Captain Hoover was growing impatient. "No, but I can approximate elevations if that's what you wanna know. Hunter, what are you drivin' at?"

"The van we saw yesterday breached your perimeter somehow. It's big enough to carry weaponry and ISIS operatives. Let me say one more thing. When Mac and I walked past it, we were below grade and probably out of their field of vision. They took off in a hurry, not because we'd just walked by. It was because they knew you were coming."

"How so?" asked Captain Hoover.

"Lookouts," replied Hunter, who began to wander through the dining room toward the foyer. "You said your Humvee patrols ran off the teens?"

"Well, actually, they were gone when we got there. They vandalized a couple of homes and must've heard us coming."

Hunter grimaced. "Or they were warned as part of an orchestrated test of your defenses. They have eyes outside your fence but also within your perimeter, Cappy. Yesterday was a dry run to gauge your

145

response time. Mark my words, today there will be another diversion, or two, at the outside perimeter. Ignore them. The real attack will come closer to home."

CHAPTER 34

Day Eighty-Seven
Star Ranch
Colorado Springs

"Here's what I suggest we do," started Hunter as he spoke to Captain Hoover and his top officers. "They'll raise a big ruckus at the outer perimeter with the intentions of drawing you away from the fences surrounding Star Ranch. We're gonna pretend to take the bait with two decoy vehicles. We need offensive capability outside the fence anyway."

Hunter walked along the wall of maps in the living room. The aerial photographs of the surrounding neighborhoods provided to the Guard by the local property assessor were invaluable. He reached for a yellow Post-it notepad and started tearing them off. He covered some of the houses nearest the entrances to Star Ranch in yellow and then he picked up a pink pad off Captain Hoover's desk and covered other homes that were farther away.

Hunter continued. "I would be willing to bet the houses I've identified in yellow are already occupied by jihadists with rifles and maybe even RPGs. If they had access to rocket-propelled grenades at Fort Drum, I'd assume they have them deployed elsewhere.

"There are half a dozen houses at the north gate that are possibilities. We'll send out three Humvees with four troops in each. Break them up into teams of two and assign a house. When the diversion begins, have the Humvees charge out of here but immediately circle back and clear these locations."

Hunter turned to Captain Hoover. "Do you have anyone proficient in long-range shooting, even sniping?"

The sergeant who had brought Hunter in answered. "Four or five. They're not military issue, but we confiscated a variety of hunting rifles, including a couple of Remington 700s, from the residents in Star Ranch."

"You disarmed them?" asked Hunter.

"Yes," replied Captain Hoover. "The situation was too volatile. I personally dealt with a man who was prepared to shoot anything that moved to keep from being dislodged from his home."

"Doesn't matter," grumbled Hunter. "You need to send your best shooters to the upper levels of these homes on the northern perimeter of the neighborhood. Quietly and systematically move all the residents out of these homes along the outskirts into other, more secure houses. Have your shooters focus on these houses marked in pink. Watch for open windows, movement behind curtains, or a rifle barrel sneaking a peak. Sergeant, they must not hesitate. Once the battle begins, light 'em up!"

"Got it. I'll get my men started," replied the sergeant.

The room cleared, leaving only Captain Hoover and his lieutenant with Hunter. Hunter thought for a moment. In Afghanistan, the Taliban were very effective in using the high ground to extend the range of their RPG attacks on American military positions. The location of Star Ranch was set at the base of a ridge.

"Are there any balconies upstairs looking out of the back of the house?"

"Yes, in the master bedroom," replied Captain Hoover.

Hunter pushed past the other two men, grabbed his AR-10, which leaned against the wall next to the desk, and ran up the stairs two at a time. He found the double doors leading into the master bedroom and made his way to the outer balcony. Captain Hoover and his lieutenant caught up with Hunter a moment later.

Raising his rifle toward the ridge to the west, Hunter eyed the terrain through his scope. He slowly moved the barrel from left to right and back again. He lowered the rifle and then focused on a particular location toward the right side of the ridge.

Pointing to a peak high above the last row of houses in the neighborhood, he asked, "Does that road lead to the inspiration point you were referring to?"

"Yeah, it's called Cheyenne Mountain Highway, but it's not much of a highway," replied the lieutenant. "It can be accessed through our western perimeter gate or the long way from the roads we identified on the map earlier. From our gate, it takes about ten minutes. Going the long way would take someone an hour."

Hunter gave the mountain one last look through his scope. "If my hunch is correct, they're already there. Waiting."

"That's on the maximum end of an RPG's range," offered Captain Hoover. "But they've gained at least a thousand feet, if not more, in elevation."

"It provides the perfect vantage point to see how things unfold below so they can target us to their advantage. Let me think for a minute," said Hunter.

As he began to turn away from the balcony, he spotted a little boy playing alone in the yard behind the house next door. The child was oblivious to the threats around him. It was also a reminder that everyone needed to take cover. There would be bullets raining on their heads at any moment.

As the three men descended the stairs, Hunter asked, "Do the Apaches patrol this side of Colorado Springs daily? I mean, is there a discernible pattern or established schedule?"

"Yes, usually first thing in the morning," replied the lieutenant.

Hunter raced down the stairs and into the living room, where he once again studied the aerial maps. On the backside of the ridge, there was a long valley that ran north to south. It was ideal for what he had in mind. Only time would tell if his hunch was correct. Part of him hoped his theory was wrong and this entire morning was an overreaction to the attack on Fort Drum.

"Cappy, we need to order an air strike," began Hunter. He traced his fingers along the valley and then tapped his fingers on the map where Seven Falls Inspiration Point was located. "Provide them the coordinates for Inspiration Point. Instruct them to fly low through this valley before they identify their target—a white van, older model, but it doesn't matter. Cappy, they'll need to have the element of surprise or the jihadists will get off a shot. I don't need to impress on anyone how devastating that will be."

"I agree. Johnson!" shouted Captain Hoover to one of his aides. "Get me the colonel on the phone. It's urgent."

Hunter continued. "I think we need to mount up and be on the northern gate to lend a hand. We may or may not have a firefight coming our way."

The lieutenant drove Hunter and Captain Hoover through the neighborhood. It appeared deserted as the residents were told to find a basement or secure location inside their house that was away from doors and windows.

Initially, the colonel questioned Captain Hoover's orders, who strategically left Hunter out of the conversation. Convinced, the colonel ordered the strike and suggested it would happen within the hour.

Once they arrived at the gate, Hunter took up a position behind the HESCO barriers and studied the homes across the street. The afternoon was a beautiful, peaceful sunny day until the explosion.

To their north, black smoke began to trail into the air. The lieutenant received reports of a car exploding at their perimeter fences.

BOOM!

Another, louder blast could be heard, apparently closer than the first one. The lieutenant gave the order and the three Humvees carrying a dozen guardsmen headed out of the north gate. Hunter joined three soldiers along the gate. He encouraged them and told them to focus on movement in the windows.

Where is the air strike?

Seconds passed, and then they turned into a minute. Hunter watched and listened. His years in the desert and firsthand combat experience didn't fail him.

Hunter wished the National Guard had a stealthy RAH-66 Comanche at their disposal, but Captain Hoover assured him they did not. The Apache was built for performance. Its blades were designed to maximize their uplift force—speed and weight capacity. The AH-64s had two engines with four blades, a main rotor and a tail rotor. While they couldn't sneak up on anyone, their speed and agility enabled the pilot to use the terrain as cover.

Against the quiet background, the Apache could be heard, but its speed didn't provide the terrorists much time to react. Once the chopper rose up the canyon walls, it would be game over for their attackers.

Hunter listened for the thirty-millimeter articulated cannons to open fire on the van. Each Apache was equipped with twelve hundred of these high-explosive rounds, which could be fired in less than two minutes. The sound, which reverberated through the valley, was unmistakable to combat vets who'd served in the Middle East.

The pilot left nothing to chance as he unleashed two Hellfire missiles on his target. Bypassing the seventy-millimeter rockets, which were more than sufficient to do the job, the pilot opted to send a message, and get even, for the attack on Fort Drum.

The twin blasts destroyed Inspiration Point and the white van full of rocket-propelled grenades and small-arms munitions, which were detonated by the impact. Debris and smoke flew into the air, giving the appearance a mini-volcano had erupted on the ridge. The soldiers on the front row of HESCO barriers became distracted by the sudden burst of the rockets and looked to see the results.

Hunter, however, did not. He watched the windows of the homes across the way. In the upper windows of the second house down, he detected movement. The ISIS operatives were also looking toward the blast.

Hunter didn't hesitate. Shocking everyone around him, he sent three rounds through the glass, shattering the window and the chest of the gunman, who came tumbling into the front yard.

He continued to search for targets, immediately spotting another one in the same house. The powerful NATO 7.62mm rounds overwhelmed the shooter and killed him before he could raise his weapon.

The firefight had begun in earnest. The National Guard snipers apparently detected movement in the little pink houses, as Hunter called them, which constituted homes in the distance with a clear line of sight to Star Ranch. Gunfire flew over their heads from the sniper positions behind them.

The terrorists were now engaged, returning fire but directing it at the front gate rather than the homes occupied with civilians. Hunter's plan was working. The sound of flash-bang grenades could be heard as the teams in the three Humvees began to move into the terrorist-occupied homes outside the secured perimeter of Star Ranch.

The soldiers at the front gate took on sporadic gunfire, but the bulk of the firefight was now taking place inside the houses across the street. After fifteen minutes, the gunfire ceased and the National Guardsmen began to walk into the front yard.

Hunter took a deep breath and relaxed when he heard Captain Hoover report, "All clear." He was always aware terrorist cells or lone-wolf jihadists were capable of terrorist attacks against Americans on their own soil. But this was different. This had all the markings of a hot war.

CHAPTER 35

Day Eighty-Eight
Cheyenne Mountain

"Mr. President," announced Morse as he entered the conference room, "the linkup is ready, sir. We'll use the microphone here in the center of the table, and as soon as I turn on the monitor, the live feed will appear."

"Will the doctor be accompanied by Sergeant Hunter from the DTRA?" asked President Garcia. "I'd like to personally thank him for the role he played at Star Ranch yesterday."

"Yes, sir," replied Morse. Morse turned on the monitor, and the dining room at Captain Hoover's headquarters appeared on the screen. Hunter and Mac sat at the table, watching one of the aides scramble around to make sure the communications link was operable.

"Testing, testing," he said into the triangular device in the middle of the dining table.

Morse leaned over the conference table and mimicked the aide's words. "Testing. Testing."

He received a thumbs-up from the aide and gestured to the president.

"Mr. President, we're good to go. When you're ready to speak, press this button. Otherwise, you'll be able to hear them at all times, but you will be muted on their end."

The President leaned forward, pressed the button, and spoke into the device. "First, I'd like to thank you, Sergeant Hunter, for your efforts in assisting our guardsmen in the defense of Star Ranch. We promised those folks safety and an opportunity to rebuild this great country one region at a time. I'm told your insight was instrumental in repelling the attack."

Hunter spoke into the microphone. "Thank you, Mr. President, just doing my duty, sir."

"Well, thank you, on behalf of the American people and myself."

The President released the button and spoke to Morse. "I assume he can be present for the rest of this conversation, or do I need to clear the room?"

"Sir, I instructed Captain Hoover to vacate his staff from the home altogether during this teleconference. Sergeant Hunter, who I understand might be romantically involved with Dr. Hagan, is privy to her work. He has a very high security clearance, sir."

"Okay, we'll let him stay," said the President, who once again pressed the button. "Dr. Hagan, my time is limited, so I want to get right to the point. I suspect a lot of wheels will be set into motion after this conversation, but one of the things I want to promise you is this. You and I will have a face-to-face private conversation regarding General Hagan, your testimony in front of Congress, and my relationship with the two of you. I believe it is long overdue, and unfortunately, circumstances dictate it may have to wait a little longer."

Mac pulled the microphone in front of her. She'd used the devices on many occasions while at the CDC. She was aware anything said by her would be picked up on the hot mic.

"Mr. President, what I hope for today is to establish a fresh start and a good working relationship, for the good of the country."

"I couldn't have said it better myself, Doctor. Please, in layman's terms, if you don't mind, explain to me the results of your work."

For the next five minutes, Mac walked the President through the science and the results of the testing. She became emotional when she discussed the manner in which her father became infected and the remarkable recovery he'd made. At one point, she left her seat and placed her iPhone in front of the camera in the dining room. She scrolled through the images of Tommy during his last two days of the illness until the morning they pulled out of Quandary Peak.

"That's remarkable, Dr. Hagan," said the President. "Please don't take this as a sign of any disrespect, but are you absolutely certain of your findings? I mean, can there be any other explanation?"

"I understand, Mr. President. These are questions I asked myself repeatedly as my father's condition improved. I wish I had the forethought to bring the laboratory mice so I could provide you live test subjects, but we had our hands full getting here anyway."

The President released the microphone button and turned to Morse. "What do you think, Andrew? She's burned us a couple of times before."

"Mr. President, in the spirit of providing a fresh start to both sides, I want to give her a chance. She can join Dr. Spielman at Stapleton, and if it doesn't pan out, we'll show her the door—again."

The President chuckled. "Wow, Andrew, that's harsh. Three strikes and you're out, right?"

"Yes, sir. If it works, you'll be a hero. If it doesn't, nobody will know except the skeleton crew working in the lab."

"What about this fella Hunter?" asked President Garcia.

"I have plans for him that will help advance another agenda. According to our man at Star Ranch, Hunter is well-respected in Breckenridge by the local authorities. Let's use him as a liaison, a way to bridge the gap for shipping refugees to the town. General Keef is concerned the town may reject our request to fill their hotels and condos with Denver's displaced residents. Frankly, I wouldn't blame them, but we'd force the issue militarily if we have to. We'll secure his assistance as part of your approval for Dr. Hagan to be accepted into the fold."

"I like it," said the President. "The chess games never end, do they, Andrew?"

"No, sir, they don't, and I have an even bigger gambit in mind, which we'll discuss after this call."

The President leaned back in his chair and smiled. "I'm intrigued. Let's wind this up."

Mac and Hunter appeared to be getting fidgety and the President was anxious to finish his conversation with Morse, so he got right to it.

"Dr. Hagan, I want to thank you for your efforts and I want you to know I believe you've been successful."

"Thank you, Mr. President," said Mac. "I'm anxious to get to the CDC and continue my work."

"Yes, of course," started President Garcia. "About that, and Chief of Staff Morse will make the arrangements, but we will be reuniting you with Dr. Spielman as quickly as possible. Sergeant Hunter, because this is a matter of national security above your current clearance, you won't be able to accompany Dr. Hagan. However, I'm prepared to provide you an escort back to, um, where did you say you lived?" The President attempted to feign lack of knowledge of their prior whereabouts.

Hunter hesitated. Suddenly, he didn't trust the President, but he played along.

"South of Breckenridge, sir. I can manage on my own, but I'll need a new vehicle and an ammo reload."

"Absolutely not, Sergeant Hunter. You're a hero in my book and a valuable asset to this nation. I'll have the arrangements made. If you wish, you may retrieve your belongings and any family members as well. We'll provide you a home at Star Ranch while Dr. Hagan performs her work."

Hunter glanced at Mac before responding. He couldn't wait to get her alone to discuss his suspicions. He replied to the President, "We'll discuss it, sir. Thank you for the offer."

The four participants in the teleconference exchanged thank-yous and good-byes, leaving President Garcia and Morse alone for a moment.

"Well done, Andrew!" the President exclaimed after Morse had shut off all communications to Star Ranch. "Now, let's discuss what really happens next."

CHAPTER 36

Day Eighty-Eight
Cheyenne Mountain

The President and Morse ordered lunch and then continued their conversation.

"Okay, we send the doctor to Stapleton and we take her friend back to Breckenridge, right?" asked the President.

"Yes, sir. It appears he hesitated, but I'll send the colonel in charge of that Guard unit to convince him. Guys like Hunter will respond to a *full bird* before he will to us."

President Garcia looked onto the operations floor, which had been frenzied with activity since the attack on Fort Drum. Their immediate focus had been on securing military installations. Now they had to protect the safe zones as well. Until the revelation by Mac, the President was worried about his available military forces being stretched too thin handling predominantly local law enforcement duties and traditional National Guard functions.

"If Dr. Hagan has in fact developed a vaccine—" started the President before being interrupted by Morse.

"Sir, it may seem like semantics, but there is an important distinction between the words vaccine and cure. Dr. Hagan has found a cure, which means it can only be used to treat the diseased. We have no idea what side effects there might be and the optimum time to begin treatment."

"Fine, cure, vaccine, whatever. As long as it works. I want Spielman and HHS to be in the middle of every move she makes. Andrew, you dropped a hint during our conversation and I want you to spill it now." The President took a big bite of his favorite sandwich, tuna and cranberry on whole wheat.

Morse pushed his plate away and wiped his chin with a white cloth napkin. He washed down his Reuben sandwich with a Coke and began.

"Tomas, I'm about to speak with you as a longtime friend and former client," started Morse. "This conversation is purely hypothetical and never happened between the President and his Chief of Staff."

"Well, Andrew, you've certainly got my attention. Do I need to worry about recording devices?" The President jokingly looked under his plate and felt under the table with both hands.

"No, this is strictly between a couple of old buddies. Fair enough?"

The President laughed and gestured to Morse with his hands to proceed. He pushed his chair away from the conference table and casually crossed his legs like he was sitting with his old friend in a cigar bar somewhere.

"I'm listening, old buddy," the President said with a chuckle.

"What if, arguendo, this was the only cure known to man on the planet?"

"Said like a true lawyer," interrupted the President. "But, okay, for the sake of argument, we're the only ones who possess the cure. Go ahead."

"And this cure needs to be refined, tested, tested again, etcetera, etcetera," continued Morse, rolling his hands over and over again. "What if we didn't want to risk harm to the citizens of other nations during the human trial testing, opting instead to risk American lives, you know, just to make sure the cure in fact worked without risking the lives of others."

"Andrew." The President laughed. He was picking up on Morse's train of thought. "Off the top of your head, what is the normal lead time for bringing a new pharmaceutical drug from conception to market?"

"Mr., um, Tomas, it's my understanding, from what I read in the papers, that it takes twelve years for a drug to travel from the research lab to the patient. Keep in mind that only twenty percent of drugs are approved for human usage."

"Well, Andrew, what if a hypothetical, benevolent President and leader of the free world ordered the process to be expedited to, say, one year while human trials were conducted on Americans only, you know, for the sake of avoiding unnecessary risks to other countries' citizens."

"That's right. Safety first," added Morse.

"Isn't it logical that the precipitous drop in the American population would halt, but sadly, the drop around the world would continue?"

Morse also leaned back in his chair and responded, "Hypothetically, I believe you're right. It might have the unintended consequences of creating a world in which the United States could overwhelmingly dominate—socially, economically, and militarily."

"But this domination would come with substantial risk to the American citizens who were a part of the clinical trials for the next year, or two."

Morse grinned. "True, but consider this. In a year, or two, as you suggest, the hypothetical President could share the cure with the rest of the world's population, you know, that remains."

CHAPTER 37

Day Eighty-Nine
Star Ranch
Colorado Springs

To say their first few days in Colorado Springs were eventful would be an understatement. As a dot on the *i* and a cross to the *t* of their experiences, Mac and Hunter assisted Captain Hoover's family through a very difficult time.

Mac had spent much of her free time with Chrissy Hoover, discussing her potential postpartum depression and the overwhelming feelings she had due to the pandemic. They also discussed what it was like to be the family member of a soldier who was suffering inside.

Hunter had several one-on-one conversations with Captain Hoover in which he discussed the telltale signs of post-traumatic stress disorder. Although Hunter was admittedly inexperienced at relationships, he and Captain Hoover had some genuine conversations about the loving and caring a man should give his wife.

Together, Mac and Hunter impressed upon the couple that their feelings were expected and not a sign of weakness. They also assured them they were capable of working through it. As the day came to a close, they were finally left alone with a couple of Budweisers.

"Mac, I don't want to rehash this because I don't think we have a choice. But I don't trust the President. This is a man who has proven time after time to have an undisclosed agenda. I don't want to be a tool in whatever game he's playing."

Mac took a small sip and let out a slight belch, followed by a giggle. "I think you're being paranoid. Besides, what other options do we have? He's the man at the top. It's not like we can auction off the cure to the highest bidder. I suppose we could've negotiated a sweeter compensation package."

Hunter laughed. "Mac, we didn't get any compensation package. You're being taken away from me to god knows where, and all I know is that there will be a house for us and your parents when I return from Breckenridge."

"I realize that's a lot of unknowns," said Mac. "I still don't see that we have a choice. We have to do what we have to do. I'm sure when you return from the mountains, they'll bring me to you."

Hunter finished his beer and crushed the can with his fist. "They don't want to screw with me if they don't."

Mac handed him her beer. "Here, you drink it. I don't want any more."

Hunter took the beer and gave her kiss. "Wow, this is true love. It's almost full. Do you have a fever?" He held his hand to her forehead.

"Nah, I just wanna be ready for tomorrow. The colonel said we'd be leaving right at sunrise."

Hunter shook his head. "See, this is what I mean. He gave us absolute zero idea as to where you're going. Back to Atlanta? Fort Collins?"

"All he said was there would be a military escort to the airport," replied Mac. "I'll know when I get there."

"I still don't like it," said Hunter. "I'm gonna miss you. I'm already having separation anxiety."

Mac hugged him around the waist and Hunter pulled her close for a kiss.

"Okay, you big baby," said Mac. "You'll be fine without me. At least I'll know you're safe with Hoover riding along. I trust him, and you guys work well together."

"Yeah, he's a good guy and I'm glad they're working things out," said Hunter as he gave her another hug. "I think we need to get to bed. It's a big day tomorrow."

"Hunter, it's only seven o'clock."

"Yup. Come on."

CHAPTER 38

Day Ninety
Denver International Airport
Denver

Mac's driver informed her it was ninety miles from Star Ranch to Denver International Airport. A convoy of four vehicles transported her to Peterson Air Force Base, where she was loaded into a helicopter and flown directly to the tarmac adjacent to the main terminal.

The first thing that struck Mac as odd that morning after she arrived was the lack of operating flights. The facility appeared on the surface to be deserted except for a handful of Humvees driving around the perimeter of the airport with fifty-caliber machine guns mounted on top and operated by National Guardsmen.

To the untrained, uninformed eye, DIA was abandoned. Of course, Mac soon learned otherwise.

DIA was nestled on a fifty-four-square-mile parcel of land in northeast Denver. Surrounded by farmland, it was the second largest airport in the world behind King Fahd International in Saudi Arabia.

Prior to the collapse, Denver's airport served over fifty million passengers a year and had recently completed a massive project called an *aerotropolis* just to the west of the runways. Based upon a derivative of the Greek words *aero*, or flight, and *metropolis*, generally meaning large town, the highly anticipated airport-driven economic development was hailed as a success by some, and a boondoggle by others.

The concept was innovative, blending a central commercial district, in this case, an airport, with commercial businesses, services, and residential areas to serve the airport. The community had been thriving and then it died, along with ninety-nine percent of the rest of

Denver's inner city.

Now, apparently deserted, the military patrols appeared to protect the buildings comprising the airport so that someday normal flight operations could resume.

"Did I miss my flight?" quipped Mac to the soldier sitting to her left as the helicopter flew in hard and fast toward a clearly marked helipad on the tarmac. He ignored her while the pilot set the chopper down flawlessly, causing Mac to look out her window to determine if they were in fact on the ground.

After the helicopter's blades began to slow, her escort opened the door and helped Mac step onto the concrete tarmac. She carried nothing except her backpack containing her journal and the aluminum case, which continued to protect the cure for the plague.

A blast of wind blew debris in her direction, causing her to cover her face with her arm. The gravelly mix peppered her cheeks, stinging them slightly. The airport's lack of use was apparently offering itself up to the barren landscape from which it came.

Mac attempted twice to make conversation with the soldier, and each time he ignored her. She wasn't sure whether the man was rude or under orders. Either way, she followed him through the doors leading into the building and then down some stairs, which opened up in the baggage claim area.

Artwork adorned the walls of the airport and one in particular caught her attention. Under the circumstances, it was a grim reminder of the post-apocalyptic world in which she lived.

A mural depicting a large green soldier with an eagle symbol on his hat, a bayonet-tipped gun, and a large curved sword stood menacingly over a scene that appeared to be the artist's rendition of poverty and distress. A woman clutching her baby and children sleeping in ruins were *guarded* by the soldier.

Mac's first impression of the mural was that it was indicative of a police state where military oppression ruled the day. She looked at the placard revealing the name of the mural—*The Children of the World Dream of Peace.*

She stopped and stared at the artwork. To label it as dark was an understatement. "I disagree. Those kids aren't dreaming about peace. They're afraid of oppression."

The soldier gently nudged Mac from behind with his arms and rifle. This startled Mac, who apparently gave him a fearful look.

"We need to keep moving."

She nodded and caught up to her escort. He continued past the baggage claim area and approached a beige door located between the men's and women's restrooms. The steel door had a keyed lock and a pass card swipe machine next to it. The door was stenciled with a combination of letters and numbers—BE64B.

The soldier stopped and stood to the side as her other escort joined her. They both looked around the vacant baggage claim area to confirm they were alone.

"Ma'am," said the talkative escort, "please turn around."

Mac obliged but listened to the sounds of a keycard swiping the terminal and the lock cylinders turning inside the door. The door popped open.

"Okay, ma'am, this way."

Mac took one more look around and stepped into what she thought was a utility closet servicing the two restrooms. Once again, she was surprised.

A dank, dusty hallway appeared before her. Footprints, all leading in, could be seen on the dusty concrete floor. Cinderblock walls rose on both sides of her to a concrete slab ceiling. A series of pipes ran the length of the hallway, as well as galvanized steel light fixtures that appeared every thirty feet or so—for as far as the eye could see.

The tunnel, Mac would later learn, stretched three miles away from the main terminal some one hundred and twenty feet below the ground to an area northwest of the airport. It took them nearly an hour to walk the entire distance, without a word spoken between the three of them.

At the end of the hallway, the entry routine was repeated. Mac turned around, the lock's mechanized sound filled the air, and the door opened. This time, Mac's eyes grew wide and her mouth fell open in amazement. She blinked twice and then leaned against the doorjamb to take it all in.

"Ma'am, are you okay?"

"I-I'm not sure," she replied.

CHAPTER 39

Day Ninety
Stapleton Underground Bunker
Denver

Mac thought she'd just stepped up to the reception desk of a massive, sixteen-story hotel, only it was upside down in the sense that the lobby was on the top floor and the hotel stretched toward the center of the earth below them. She slowly walked toward a polished brass rail sitting atop a Plexiglas barrier and peered over the edge without getting too close. The building, or cellar, or bunker, whatever it was called, dropped hundreds of feet straight down except for walkways, which traversed the interior.

Then she looked upward to a series of tubes and large vent fans, which spread across the ceiling. The tubular skylights provided a pathway for the sun to provide diffused natural light while the fans provided an exhaust for stale air.

Mac was suddenly dizzy and wobbled on her feet a little. She closed her eyes to get her bearings and regain her balance when a familiar voice brought her back to normal.

"Dr. Hagan, are you a sight for sore eyes!" exclaimed Dr. Tom Spielman, the director of the CDC and her former boss.

Mac rushed to greet him and provided him an impromptu hug, a personal gesture considered wholly inappropriate and taboo at the CDC, but somehow not untoward under these circumstances.

"Dr. Spielman, I'm so glad you're—" started Mac before she caught herself. "It is so good to see you, naturally. Although all of this is a little, um, weird, maybe?"

Dr. Spielman began to laugh. "Indeed. It's very sci-fi and futuristic. Trust me, some of this is borderline weird science. Let's get you properly checked in and then I'll show you around."

He led her back to the desk, where Mac showed identification. She was fingerprinted and provided them a retina scan. While she waited for a laminated ID badge, Dr. Spielman explained the need for security.

"This is probably the most secretive government installation in the world. To begin with, and you probably didn't notice because the descent was very slight, but during the three-mile walk through the tunnel, you dropped more than a thousand feet below ground."

"I thought I was in *The Twilight Zone*," interrupted Mac. "It's a good thing I'm not claustrophobic."

"I remember, I was brought in the same way," said Dr. Spielman. "Whenever you leave the *Den*, which is the nickname for the facility underneath Denver's Stapleton Airport, you'll take different tunnels and exits. Security tries to mix things up so people on the surface don't establish a pattern."

Mac continued to look around in amazement. "When do I get to leave the Den?"

"Excuse me, Dr. Hagan," the receptionist politely interrupted before Dr. Spielman answered. "Here is your ID and a welcome packet. Everything you need to know about the facility is enclosed as well as your room assignment and keycard. Dr. Spielman, will you instruct Dr. Hagan on security protocols, including the use of the biometric and retina scan locks?"

"I will, thank you," he replied. Dr. Spielman gestured for Mac to follow him and the two began to walk around the perimeter of the upper floor. He continued. "First, let me say this. I'm as anxious as you are to discuss your findings and check out what's in that case you're cradling like a baby. But here's what we learned right away after our arrival—the government is just as infuriatingly slow and deliberate here as it was in the so-called good old days. Although resources are surprisingly vast considering the world as we know it has ended, we do have our limitations when it comes to the activities of the CDC."

"Dr. Spielman, I'm amazed this even exists," added Mac. "How did they keep it a secret?"

Dr. Spielman chuckled as he led her toward an elevator. "Well, they didn't do such a great job, but in typical government fashion, together with a willing media, they covered it up. Trust me, conspiracy theories abound, even within the present occupants. Here's what I know."

The elevator arrived and they stepped in. Mac noticed the numbers descended from 1 at the top to 16 at the bottom. "See, this is bizarre. I take it we're on the first floor, but if we want to go to the bottom floor, we go up to floor sixteen, um, I mean down to floor sixteen, right?"

"Exactly." Dr. Spielman laughed. "Let me show you to your room and we'll get your things put away. Then I'll take you around and you can see the amenities."

As the elevator dropped, Mac processed what she'd heard so far. She then began to realize nobody knew where she was, a very uncomfortable feeling.

Ding! Ding! Level 6. A computerized voice announced their arrival.

"Here we are," said Dr. Spielman. "All of our co-workers are housed on this floor."

"Couldn't they have chosen a better floor than *level 6*?"

Dr. Spielman led the way out of the elevator and they turned to the left. He ignored her question for a moment and then said, "Why's that?" He didn't look at Mac, choosing to nonchalantly peer over the railing as they ambled down the walkway.

She wasn't sure how to interpret his reaction. *Does he not know about the Level 6 order? Is he pretending not to know?*

There was an awkward silence between them until they reached her room, which spoke volumes to Mac. Her first inclination was to look around the ceilings and walls for cameras and microphones. This whole thing, the Den, as they called it, smacked of something out of George Orwell's *1984*, and suddenly, she didn't like it.

"Okay," started Dr. Spielman. "Here's our first opportunity to use the advanced security system to gain access to parts of the complex. Your ID badge operates like money within the facility, which is odd because everything is free. In any event, when you make purchases in the commissary or eat in the various restaurants, you'll scan your ID. Movies, the video game corral, and the health club also require your ID badge to be scanned.

"To enter secured areas for which you've been provided clearance, such as your room and the CDC facilities on the floor above us, you'll use a combination of this retina scan and the fingerprint scanner below it. You must do both simultaneously to activate the lock mechanism. Go ahead, give it a try."

Mac leaned into the retina viewer and adjusted her head to fit her eyes within the rubber cups. Then she felt around the wall and found a similar device to insert her index finger. She pressed the glass with the tip of her finger and the sound of locks popping indicated she was successful in gaining entry.

"Very good, Mac. It takes a few times to get coordinated so that you don't look like a newbie. We've all gone through it."

He pushed the door open for her, extended his arm into the room and flipped on a light switch. The interior was designed like any Comfort Suites hotel room with a king-size bed, a television, a couple of dressers and a separate seating area complete with a desk.

Mac hesitated before entering. A small bathroom was to her left next to a tiny closet. The room was small, sparsely decorated and impersonal. She missed Quandary Peak.

"Here's the best part," said Dr. Spielman. He walked to the end of the room where floor-to-ceiling curtains were drawn closed. He pulled them open and more light filled the room. A ten-foot-wide, curved panel AQUOS television was mounted on a concrete wall behind a glass pane window. A continuous video loop of outdoor, nature scenes played. "It's not the real thing, but it is a reminder that our world exists above here and that the good work we do on the floor above us is for a good cause—the American way of life."

Mac was creeped out. She wanted to leave now. She was prepared to dump her journal and vancomycin vials on the bed, race back through the three-mile-long hallway of doom, and burst onto the desolate runways above the Den.

The American way of life? What does that mean?

"Mac, I can see you're a little overwhelmed," said Dr. Spielman. "Why don't you let me take the case to the lab while you take a hot bath and maybe a nap? We can continue this later. Like I said, we've got plenty of time."

No. No, we don't.

"I'm okay, Dr. Spielman. I'd rather continue, if you don't mind. Listen, a moment ago, you made reference to *we* earlier."

"I'm sorry?" asked a confused Dr. Spielman.

"Upstairs, or on the first, well, whatever. You said when *we* first arrived. Are there more of us from the CDC?"

"Of course, let's go upstairs," he replied, pointing his finger upward, "to level 5 and I'll show you the lab and the new CDC."

CHAPTER 40

Day Ninety
The Den
Denver

"By executive order, the President incorporated the Combat Casualty Care Research Program into the continuity-of-government plan," started Dr. Spielman as he and Mac made their way to the elevator. "This opened up the CDC's scope of responsibility beyond disease control to also include deployment of life-saving strategies, new surgical techniques, biological, and mechanical products."

They stepped into the elevator together and Mac asked, "Practically speaking, what does that mean?"

"Well, a lot more work for me, for one. The CCCRP used to fall under the purview of the Army through the Institute of Surgical Research. The government has contracted considerably, for obvious reasons, and the various agencies within the military and under Washington's control have now been consolidated where possible. For example, USAMRIID, your mother's old stomping grounds, now falls under the newly constituted CDC."

Mac chuckled, trying to take her mind off conspiracy theories and back toward her purpose for being there. "That's a lot of new responsibility, sir. I assume you got a hefty increase well beyond my GS-15."

Dr. Spielman let out a hearty laugh. "I made the mistake of asking that question when the Secretary of Health and Human Services came around to provide us an orientation. He said my raise was measured by my ability to stay alive. Nice, huh?"

"Yeah." Mac laughed. "Money's worthless now anyway."

"For now, but at some point I'm sure they'll make it up to us."

They exited the elevator and entered an empty hallway with

double doors to their right and left. They were flanked with fake areca palms, plastic versions of the ones Mac recalled slapping her in the face that fateful day she walked through the rain-soaked forest in Guatemala. In a way, she felt she was venturing into the unknown again.

"To the right are the administrative offices and conference rooms. To the left is the lab. Since you asked about the others, let's go meet up with some of your old co-workers."

Dr. Spielman encouraged Mac to practice her entry through the secured locks and she did so flawlessly, earning her *like an old pro* accolades.

He led the way and was briefly interrupted by a receptionist, who handed him two phone messages. He explained there was an intranet phone system tied directly to NORAD. It was used on an as-needed basis only and only by senior level department heads. Mac took that to mean phone privileges weren't included in her *compensation package.*

The hallway for the administrative wing of the CDC moved along the interior of the curved structure. Each floor's walkway was open to the interior and the amenities, which were seen every fourth floor spanning the middle of the building. He finally reached another set of double doors, which led them into the new operations center. There, she was greeted with a familiar voice and a big smile.

"Oh my gawd," said Sandra Wilkinson, the eighteen-year veteran of the Office of Public Health Preparedness and Response and duty officer in the CDC's former Division of Emergency Operations. She jumped up from her desk and ran to give Mac a hug. "Dearie, thank God you're alive. This is such great news."

Mac laughed and returned the woman's bear hug. "Yeah, last time I saw you I was being escorted out of the building. It's so good to see you, Sandra."

"Honey, everybody knew that whole thing was a farce. Privately, we all cheered you on. Publicly, we were expected to ignore you, per instructions from you-know-who."

Mac glanced around the room at the faces who were observing the joyous reunion. She was looking for one face in particular.

"Where is Baggett? Did he make the trip?" asked Mac.

Dr. Spielman cleared his throat and casually walked away from the two of them toward a water cooler.

"No, honey, he bit the dust," replied Wilkinson. "During the riot, he tried to sneak out the back door and headed for his car. The mob found him and beat him to death. They stole his wallet, watch, and car in the process. It was an ugly way to go for an ugly man, I'm afraid."

"Whoa," was Mac's only response. She despised D-Bag, but she'd never wish that fate on anyone. She looked past Wilkinson and saw a young man waving in her direction. Her mind was fuzzy from the newness of it all and she was having difficulty placing the young man. He approached her from his station.

"Dr. Hagan." Henri le Pen introduced himself using the King's proper English rather than his native French. "Do you remember me?"

"Of course, Henri. I'm so glad to see you here safe and sound."

"Yes, it is interesting how we greet one another. Before, we might say how was your weekend? Now we greet a friendly face by saying glad to see you are alive. Incredible times, no?"

"Yes, Henri. Most incredible." Mac walked farther into the room and looked around. It was almost an exact replica of the Emergency Operations Center at CDC-Atlanta.

Dr. Spielman returned to her side. "Remarkable, isn't it?"

"It's almost like a clone of the former EOC," replied Mac. "How did you do it?"

He led her back toward the door and said, "Wait'll you see the BSL-4. I'll give you the background along the way."

Mac stopped and gave her old co-workers another hug. She whispered into Sandra's ear, "I want to meet with you later. I have a lot of questions."

"As well you should, honey. My room is six-two-six, but don't come tonight. It's too soon. We'll find each other tomorrow once your routine is established."

Mac, stunned by Wilkinson's words, pulled away and acted

nonchalant. "Bye, guys," said Mac shyly. "I guess I'll see you guys around."

As they walked out the door, Mac glanced back and saw Sandra whispering to Henri. Several other members of the staff approached the two of them immediately to inquire about her, Mac assumed. She looked forward to her visit with Wilkinson the next day.

Dr. Spielman led Mac around the entire floor occupied by the CDC until they reached the lab. Again, he urged her to open the doors on her own, which she did. *Her world* opened up before her eyes.

Unlike the administrative offices, all of the walls were made of thick glass. The space was divided between a research laboratory, the BSL-4, and several workspaces and meeting rooms. At the moment, the laboratories were unoccupied, but she did see mice in cages lined up along the far wall.

"Primates?" asked Mac as she stared into the rooms.

"I wish," replied Dr. Spielman. "All we have to work with are typical laboratory mice. I'm working on making primates available to us before we consider human trials. It's a process, you know."

"Hey, there's Michelle!" noted Mac. Through the glass, in the research laboratory, she spotted Jamaican-born CEFO Michelle Watson, who headed up the team tracing back the origins of the young teen who died in Greece after traveling there from Libya. They exchanged waves and big smiles.

"There are others scattered throughout the floor, Dr. Hagan. Over time, I don't doubt you'll run across them all. Let me show you to the office I've been saving for someone like yourself."

"What do you mean?"

Dr. Spielman gestured to an open office, which was beautifully decorated. It contained mahogany furniture, was adorned with upscale décor, and had a seating area including a sofa.

"This is pretty fancy," said Mac. "Are you saying this is for me?"

"Maybe, it depends. We'll spend some time together over the next several days and then you'll have to tell me whether all of this is right for you." Spielman waved his arm around the room and back toward the hallway.

"Well, of course, I don't know. I mean, it's all very impressive, even though I'd have to get over living like a mole in the ground. But, Dr. Spielman, I have my mom and dad. Then there's Janie. And Hunter, he's my, well, boyfriend and I love him."

Dr. Spielman sat in the chair across from her desk. He pointed toward the executive chair, which awaited an occupant. "Take it for a test drive."

Mac set the case containing the vancomycin on the desk, releasing her hold on it for the first time since she'd left Star Ranch hours ago. She slowly sat in the chair and swiveled around a little bit just to get the feel of it.

Dr. Spielman continued. "Of course, Janie is welcome to join us and I hope you'll convince her to do so. Your parents, it is my understanding, will be offered a home within Star Ranch. As for Sergeant Hunter, I'm sure there will be a place for him within the military arm of the government, but I'm not so sure he's needed here. My guess is a man of his capability would become extremely bored handling security duties at the Den."

He knows about Hunter and his capabilities?

"Sir, he is very important to me," said Mac. "I'm not sure I could function without him."

"Listen," started Dr. Spielman as he rose out of the chair. "We have a lot of important details to discuss, not the least of which is contained in this case." He took it into his hands.

Mac felt a jolt run through her body, a twinge of seller's remorse. *Why is my gut screaming WARNING at me?*

175

PART THREE

WEEK FOURTEEN

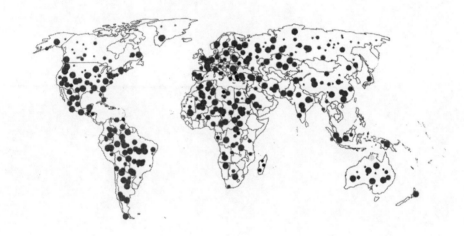

CHAPTER 41

Day Ninety-One
West of Colorado Springs

At Hunter's suggestion, Captain Hoover spread the four Humvees across both sides of the divided highway and had them separate, leaving plenty of distance so the snipers who were perched on the cliffs of Cavern Gulch a week ago couldn't get clear shots at all four vehicles at once. Hunter, who distinctly recalled the sniper's positions, exited his Humvee and walked behind the lead vehicle, which included a manned fifty-caliber on top.

Hunter was provided a ten-round magazine with tracer rounds for his AR-10. He intended to fire upon the positions on both sides of the road to identify the locations, and if fire was returned, the soldier operating the Ma Deuce would light them up.

The Humvee moved to the far right shoulder of the highway to avoid two dead bodies rotting in the road. Hunter grimaced as he recognized them from the group leaving Colorado Springs. These two didn't follow his advice to seek the relative safety of the Cave of the Winds Park. They were murdered and they had nothing to give their killers.

The convoy was now into the kill zone created by the snipers. His Defender had been ransacked. All the doors were open, the glove box contents had been thrown onto the seats, and the windows had been shattered out of petulant anger.

He looked through his scope to observe any signs of movement on either side of the canyon walls. It was completely still. He tapped on the back of the Humvee, a signal advising them to stop. Hunter gave instructions to the soldier, who kept his weapon trained on the cliffs.

"I'm gonna fire two rounds into each of the positions. First left

179

and then right, in order to get a reaction. If they're up there, they'll return fire, so be ready."

"Yes, sir."

The loud report of Hunter's rifle destroyed the silence. His first two rounds shattered rock and dirt where the sniper had been killed on Hunter's last pass through Cavern Gulch. Nothing.

He quickly moved to the other side of the Humvee and shot in the general direction of where the other sniper was perched the week before. Again, no response.

Hunter provided direction to the soldiers. "It appears they've moved on. Let's continue slowly through the canyon's divide for about a mile. They may have taken up new positions, but I don't see any new, disabled vehicles. Once we reach the opening on the west end, it's pretty much clear sailing to Fairplay and Route 9."

The four-truck convoy continued, taking nearly twenty minutes to clear Cavern Gulch and the graveyard of bodies and vehicles left behind. Hunter tried to stay sharp, but his mind wandered to what had become of humanity. He continued to scan both sides of the roads with the intent to identify shooters, but instead his eyes focused on the death and depravity resulting from their murderous activity.

What is it about human nature that prevents us from helping one another rather than committing atrocities like this? Are we naturally violent and prone to fight one another?

Given the long, awful history of violence between varied groups of people, it was easy to think humans were predisposed to war. For three months, Hunter had seen what man could do to one another—unspeakable things, beyond the ravishing of the population as a result of the plague.

Is it a natural result of our advanced technology, which produced weapons of mass destruction beyond the comprehension of man a century ago?

Hunter chuckled to himself as he considered the tools of war used in World War I. Rifles and machine guns were most common, with artillery and mortar considered the newest technology. The aircraft were lucky to fly, much less have a considerable impact. Just a century later, a single tick of the clock in the history of mankind, many nations of the world possessed rockets that could leave earth's atmosphere and return with a vengeance, annihilating the entire population of some countries with a single nuclear bomb.

Did we use this technology to deter one another, or to outgun our enemies?

Hunter immediately recalled conversations with Mac about the plague and other infectious diseases. A tiny bacterium or virus, a silent, deadly enemy only one-billionth our size, possessed the killing ability of all the nuclear weapons on the planet. With a nudge from man, the plague bacteria was propelling itself across the planet toward a sixth extinction-level event, yet individuals focused their cruel intentions on murdering innocents as they tried to find a way to survive.

"Sir, it appears we've made it through to where the highway is clear," said the soldier, who brought Hunter out of deep thought.

"Yeah, okay. Hang on," Hunter responded and jogged back to the Humvee carrying Captain Hoover and his superior officer, Colonel Frank Clements.

Captain Hoover flung the door open behind the driver of their Humvee, inviting Hunter to join them.

"Thank you, Sergeant," offered Colonel Clements. "That was a disgusting display of what's wrong with this world."

"Yes, it was," added Hunter. He leaned forward to address the driver. "We shouldn't have any problems from here to Fairplay. There are a few towns, but they've been abandoned, or the people have all died. The lead vehicles should be aware of an ambush, but it was clear a week ago."

The Humvees roared ahead and the group rode in silence for twenty minutes. A sign indicating they'd entered the city limits of Fairplay caused the drivers to slow and raise their awareness levels. At the roadblock, which was maintained by Sheriff Williams and another man who was not in uniform, Hunter exited the Humvee and conducted a quick conversation with the sheriff.

He explained what had happened to the deputy on the way to Colorado Springs. When the deputy hadn't returned, they'd sent out two truckloads of men to find him. They had encountered the group who had just killed the man and woman walking up the highway. The sheriff's men chased them into the scrub brush and down a ravine, where they executed them all. As Sheriff Williams put it, *my jail may be empty, but it's too good for vermin like that.*

Sheriff Williams asked Hunter why he was being escorted by four Humvees. Hunter tried to respond, but found himself at a loss for words, as he didn't have a good answer. While it was true there were potential obstacles along the way, such as Cavern Gulch or an encounter with the Vagos bikers, Hunter hadn't voiced those concerns to Sheriff Williams when they'd passed through Fairplay the first time. In reality, Hunter didn't know why he was being accompanied by the colonel and all of the guardsmen.

He returned to the Humvee with a puzzled look on his face, as well as a very big question on his mind. He decided to bring it up as soon as they were on their way.

"So, Colonel, I appreciate the ride up here to speak with my group, but I have to ask something," started Hunter. The colonel didn't reply and stared at the vehicle leading them up Route 9 toward Breckenridge. Hunter glanced in the direction of Captain Hoover, who he'd just realized had remained silent the entire trip. Hunter pressed the issue. "In addition to you and Captain Hoover, there are fifteen soldiers in this mission and three Humvees with a potent accessory mounted on their tops. Isn't this a little bit of overkill?"

"Sergeant, I know you want to spend some time to gather up Dr. Hagan's family and her associate from the CDC. We wanted to insure your safety both to and from your place up here."

"Colonel, I certainly appreciate that. It just seems like a lot of firepower, that's all."

Hunter glanced at Captain Hoover to gauge a reaction. His new friend frowned, shook his head and looked down at his boots. Hunter tried to pick up on the cause of Cappy's concern, but Colonel Clements began to speak.

"While we're here, Sergeant, there will be one other thing you can assist us with."

"What's that?" asked Hunter.

"The President has ordered us to take control of Breckenridge."

CHAPTER 42

Day Ninety-One
Route 9 to Breckenridge
Alma, Colorado

"What?" demanded Hunter. "What does that mean?" Hunter's tone of voice startled the driver, who unconsciously slowed down, leaving a widening gap with the lead Humvee.

Colonel Clements shifted in his seat to look at Hunter directly. "Sergeant, the President has now shifted his focus to rebuilding our nation. Your Dr. Hagan has provided us the first crucial element of the effort. Our next step is to reestablish law and order, as well as a safe place for survivors to live without fear of dying in a massacre like we saw back at Canyon Gulch. Towns like Breckenridge are an integral part of the President's plan."

"Breckenridge has done just fine without the government's help," said Hunter. "They've secured their borders, unlike our government, which has contributed to the death toll, I might add. They've managed to feed their own, which is far more than I can say for our government. People who've managed to avoid the plague are dying of starvation, dysentery, and common diseases that ordinary medical treatment and nutrition could have addressed."

The colonel shot back, "Sergeant, I would remind you I am still your superior officer for so long as you are part of this man's Army. I would caution you to hold your tongue or run the risk of losing our support!"

Hunter was incredulous. "Are you threatening me? You know what? Screw you! How's that for insubordination? Driver, stop the truck. I want out!"

Captain Hoover stepped in to diffuse the situation. "Hunter, you have to understand. Rebuilding the nation will be for the greater good even though it might ruffle some—"

"Wait! Are you in on this? Come on, Cappy, really? Did you know this was the real purpose of driving up here?"

"Now, hold on, Hunter, it's not like that."

Hunter was shouting now. He'd sensed something was off about the trip and he was pissed Cappy was in on it. "What's it like, then? If this is such a great idea and for some *benevolent purpose*, then what's with all the secrecy, huh?"

The driver interrupted the argument. "Colonel, we've got trouble ahead." The driver accelerated and spoke into his comms to advise the two tailing vehicles to close the gap and be ready.

Ahead, a dozen members of the Vagos motorcycle gang were holding the soldiers of the lead Humvee at gunpoint. All of the military personnel, including the soldier manning the fifty-caliber machine gun, had been caught by surprise. They were lined up in front of the Humvee with their hands on their helmets.

As the remaining vehicles in the convoy pulled closer to the standoff, Hunter's driver waved the other two Humvees around before slowly pulling to a stop.

Hunter couldn't resist taking the opportunity to be snarky. "I guess these guys didn't get the memo about the takeover, Colonel."

Colonel Clements ignored Hunter and spoke into his portable radio. "Can you get a clear shot on the gunmen?"

Hunter shook his head. This wasn't going to end well, nor would the *Invasion of Breckenridge*. He decided to diffuse the situation because he wanted to get to Quandary Peak and be done with this charade.

"Tell your men to stand down. I've got this," said Hunter as he quickly exited the truck. He left his weapon behind and strutted up the incline toward the roadblock.

Hunter marched between the twin Humvees blocking the two-lane highway and approached the bikers. He was pleased to see that Jaws, the former soldier, was among the men holding weapons on the guardsmen.

"Hunter, right?" asked Jaws and then commented to his fellow bikers, "He's cool, boys. Let him pass."

"Yeah, Jaws. I'm with these guys," Hunter replied as he pushed past the soldiers and walked up to Jaws, who had positioned himself behind three parked vehicles in a formation similar to the one Hunter had established at the Blue Lakes Road checkpoint. "I see you've beefed up your security."

"Yeah, got the idea from up the road," said Jaws. "These boys gotta pay a toll, too."

Hunter looked around and spoke in a loud whisper. "Man, are you nuts? I've got a full-bird colonel back there with me. They won't hesitate to open up those Ma Deuces and tear you to ribbons. I can keep that from happening, but you gotta call off the dogs."

Jaws looked past the detained soldiers at the menacing fifty-caliber weapons pointed in his direction. He leaned in to Hunter and whispered, "I gotta collect a toll or the boys will think I'm weak. I didn't tell you before, but this is my pack. I'm runnin' things here."

Hunter wasn't surprised. His steely look from their prior encounter spoke volumes of his ability to lead men, both soldiers and bikers. *Time to negotiate.*

"Whadya want? I've got more cash," Hunter began.

Jaws looked around at his fellow bikers, a ragtag group sportin' a variety of shotguns, primarily sawed-off, and a thirty-eight-caliber revolver. "I need weapons."

"Come on, Jaws. The military's not gonna turn over their weapons," said Hunter. He thought for a moment. "All right, here's what I'm gonna do. You and I are straight, right?"

"Yeah, man. We're cool."

"I'm gonna give you my AR-10, on loan for now. Got it? It won't do you any good anyway 'cause you'll never find ammo for it."

Jaws looked confused. "What's the point? I'd love to have it, but you're right, none of these houses are gonna have the rounds for it unless I can get lucky and find some .308. I need something more common, like these fellas' M16s." He pointed to the rifles lying on the ground at the guardsmen's feet.

"Not gonna happen," said Hunter. "I'm gonna give you the AR-10 and I'll bring you a couple of guns later on to trade it back, with a full ammo can. If we're friends, then we can help each other. Fair enough?"

Jaws appeared to be thinking it over. Hunter hoped the ex-grunt would see that he and his fellow Vagos were in over their heads.

"Yeah, let's make it happen," said Jaws.

"You owe me," quipped Hunter.

"Wait, why? How do you figure I owe you?" asked Jaws.

"I just saved your collective tails!" Hunter laughed as he left before Jaws could respond.

Hunter jogged down to the Humvee, retrieved his rifle and said to the colonel, "I've negotiated a settlement for us to pass. I need your word that your men will stand down."

"They held guns on the United States military," the colonel bristled. "I will not tell them to stand down."

"Colonel, yes, you will," said Hunter. "You can't blast your way through this. Likewise, you can't just waltz into Breckenridge and take over either. You think this situation sucks, the people of Breckenridge will bow up even worse."

The colonel didn't immediately respond and then Captain Hoover spoke up. "Hunter, will you at least help us make our argument to the town?"

"Fine, but no promises, Cappy. I have very little pull over these guys," Hunter said, nodding toward the bikers. "I have even less with the people who live in the Breck."

"If you're on board with us, Sergeant, then I'll stand down," said the colonel.

"Yeah, fine."

"Why are you taking your weapon?" asked Captain Hoover.

"Trade bait," replied Hunter as he jogged back up the hill with his rifle.

One crisis at a time.

CHAPTER 43

Day Ninety-One
Quandary Peak

After a minute of grumbling from the colonel about giving in to the criminal element, the convoy was on its way for the remaining five-minute ride to Quandary Peak. Hunter assured the driver there wouldn't be any further complications, so they took the lead. Hunter wanted to be the first person out of the truck when they hit Blue Lakes Road so he could explain to his people about the military presence.

The driver slowed the Humvee to take the final S-curve approaching the checkpoint. He pulled up to the vehicles, which were positioned exactly the way Hunter had left them when he and Mac had pulled out a week or so ago. Only now, nobody was standing watch.

"Something's wrong," muttered Hunter. Before the driver pulled to a complete stop, Hunter instinctively grabbed for his rifle and remembered it was gone. He flung the door open, hit the pavement, and pulled his sidearm as he raced between the parked vehicles.

"Janie! Derek! Where are you guys?" Hunter looked up toward the abandoned houses. He knew that Derek and Janie practiced dry-fire drills in the houses during their shifts at the checkpoint. He'd admonished them to stay close to the roadblock. They might hear a car coming but not necessarily someone or a group on foot. They might have ignored his instructions while he was gone.

Frantic, Hunter jogged up the road toward Breckenridge and began looking around the terrain in search of a clue. He called out again, "Anybody? Janie! Are you guys here?"

"Hunter, what's the deal?" shouted Cappy, who was making his way through the cars. "How do we move these cars out of the way?"

Hunter holstered his weapon and returned to the checkpoint. "Cappy, this roadblock has been manned continuously since we set it up. Something's wrong."

"Maybe your friends back there had something to do with it," said Cappy.

"No," Hunter shot back. Then he wondered. *Don't assume.* "I mean I hope not. Get your men. Hurry."

"Can't we move the cars?" asked Cappy.

"No. The guards on duty keep the keys in their pockets rather than in the ignition. If they're attacked, hiding the keys serves as one final delay-and-deter mechanism of our security."

Hunter started up the incline toward the quarantine house in which Tommy and Flatus had lived long enough for Mac to find a cure. Hunter cupped his hands over his mouth to create a megaphone effect.

"Hey! Janie! Derek! Anybody!"

He was making his way to the second house when he heard a groan coming from behind a toolshed there. He started running toward the sound. He caught a glimpse of a leg hanging out of the shed, wedged against the swinging door.

"Don't move!" shouted Hunter as he drew his weapon. He approached cautiously, moving his eyes in all directions to detect any sign of an ambush. He had seen the Taliban use this technique to entrap U.S. soldiers in Afghanistan. They'd pull on the heartstrings of the troops by pretending to be injured while the trap was sprung.

He pointed the weapon at the center mass of the prone body while he opened the toolshed door with his left hand. The body was barely moving, but the man was still alive.

"Derek!" exclaimed Hunter, who took one last look around the inside of the shed before putting away his weapon. He knelt down beside Doc's son and slowly turned him onto his side.

"Arrrgh," Derek moaned, his throat appeared to be filled with fluids as he gurgled out the painful sound.

Derek's face was a torn, bloody mess. Hunter looked around the shed and grabbed an old beach towel off a tool bench. He sniffed it to make sure it wasn't soaked with chemicals or gasoline and then he used it to gently wipe off Derek's face.

"Hunter, what've ya got?" asked Cappy, who suddenly appeared at the entrance. "Does he have the plague?"

"No, he's one of our people," replied Hunter. "Tell your men to fan out and look for Janie, or anyone else for that matter. The houses are clean, disease-free."

Cappy left and directed his men per Hunter's instructions just as Colonel Clements arrived at the shed.

"What can I do, Sergeant?" he asked.

"Colonel, please help me pull his body out. He has a head injury, so we need to do this slowly. I'll brace his head and shoulders."

The colonel positioned himself between Derek's knees and grasped him around the legs. Hunter counted down, "Three, two, one, lift." Although Derek was slipping in and out of consciousness, his body felt like dead weight. The two men struggled to carry him through the narrow entrance of the shed but successfully moved him to a patch of grass nearby.

Hunter felt in Derek's pants for the keys to the vehicles. He pulled them out and handed them to the colonel. "Please move the cars out of the way. Then we need to get his father, who's a doctor. Send a Humvee up the highway about three miles to a driveway on the right with four large wagon wheels marking the entrance. They're painted white. Tell them to ask for Doc Cooley and let them know Derek has been badly injured. Colonel, they need to hurry."

Hunter rolled up the beach towel to make a small pillow for Derek's head. He ran for the house and kicked open the back door, which had been locked. He found more towels and soaked them in water. He started down the hall toward the bathroom in search of first aid supplies but reversed his position. He had to stabilize Derek before he could consider any kind of treatment. The young man's face was badly battered. Hunter's first goal was to keep him breathing.

As he raced back to Derek's side, he spotted a shovel in the tall grass near a path into the woods. He darted in that direction and then caught himself. *You can only do one thing at a time.*

"Cappy! Over here!"

Hunter reached Derek and wiped the rest of the blood off his face. "Derek, Derek, can you hear me? It's Hunter. Hang on, buddy, we're gonna get you fixed up. Your dad will be here in a minute. Just hang on. Can you hear me?"

Derek's body lurched and then his chest heaved as he began to cough up some blood. This was not good. Captain Hoover and one of his men ran up next to Derek.

Hunter pointed to his left and toward the trail. "Over there. See if that shovel is—just check out that shovel."

"Derek! Stay with me, buddy. I need you to hang in there!"

Hunter continued to wipe Derek's face and kept his throat clear. With Captain Hoover's help, he turned Derek on his side to prevent him from choking on his own fluids. Hunter applied continuous pressure to Derek's wounds to stem the blood loss, but there were so many gashes it was almost impossible.

One of the soldiers returned with a wooden-handled shovel. The blade was covered in blood and bits of flesh.

"Cappy, have them check the woods. Janie might be in there! They always worked the checkpoint together."

Captain Hoover took the soldier and summoned more men to assist. They charged down the trail and fanned out. Hunter returned his attention to Derek.

"Derek, can you hear me? Can you tell me what happened?"

Derek didn't respond, or maybe he couldn't, thought Hunter. He gently wiped the blood off Derek's throat and saw the discolored skin from the massive bruise that had formed. He might have a crushed windpipe or larynx.

Captain Hoover's men continued to scour the woods, looking for Janie, when Hunter heard the roar of the Humvee's tires returning with Doc Cooley. The vehicle kicked up dirt as it raced into the backyard and skidded to a stop. Doc spilled out of the truck with his wife.

"Oh my!" she screamed as she scrambled to Derek's side. In her frantic haste, she stumbled and fell onto her chest. With tears streaming down her face, the hysterical mother crawled on her hands and knees to join her son, ignoring the blood dripping from her chin.

"Honey, let me in to check on our boy," said Doc, putting on his best pretense of being calm and cool. "Hunter, what happened?"

Hunter explained how he'd found Derek and what he'd done to make him comfortable. Doc examined his son's face, head, and throat. He checked Derek's pulse.

"We don't have much time," he whispered in a barely audible voice. Doc let out a sigh and reached for his wife's hand. "I'll do what I can, darling."

"How can we help?" asked Colonel Clements.

"We need to get him to the hospital," replied Doc. "It's his only chance."

"Corporal!" shouted the colonel. "Let's get this young man loaded up. Drive these folks to the hospital *posthaste!*"

"Yes, sir!"

Doc cradled his son's head in his hands as Hunter and the corporal lifted his body. They carried him to the colonel's Humvee and laid him across the backseat. Hunter ran into the house and retrieved a comforter from one of the beds to keep Derek warm. Doc was concerned he might go into shock due to the blood loss.

"Doc, I'm sorry," said Hunter as he gave the distraught father a hug.

Doc looked around the yard at the new faces in uniform. "Hunter, where's Janie?"

Hunter ran his fingers through his hair, forgetting they were covered in Derek's blood. "Doc, I don't know."

CHAPTER 44

Day Ninety-One
Quandary Peak

"Captain Hoover, we followed the trail all the way down the ridge to where it crossed the road and picked up on the other side. We found three sets of footprints at one point and there were signs of a struggle. We also found this." The soldier handed Captain Hoover a camouflage hat with a strip of Velcro on the front to hold a patch. The patch was missing, but Hunter recognized the hat.

"That's mine," said Hunter as he took the cap from the soldier. He turned it over to examine the inside, hoping there were no signs of blood. "Janie always borrowed it because she wanted to fit in with the guys when she worked the checkpoint. There was an American flag on the—"

Hunter stopped in mid-sentence as the faint sound of a dog barking echoed through the valley between the two massive mountain ridges.

"Hunter, didn't you say that you guys had a dog?"

"Yeah, that's Flatus. Let's go!" shouted Hunter as he took off toward the front of the house. He yelled back over his shoulder, "Bring the trucks! You'll have to move some logs out of the way to get through. Hurry!"

The entire contingent scrambled to follow Hunter up the road. Captain Hoover ran after Hunter and the rest took to their vehicles. The entire group arrived at the deadfall of trees across Blue Lakes Road. Hunter pointed out the cut logs he'd used to fill in the gaps a week ago.

"These can be rolled out of the way," he instructed as he hurdled the logs, taking a glance to the left to confirm the Jeep was still parked below the blockade. He shouted back to a trailing Captain

Hoover, "Hurry. Driveway is up half a mile on the left."

"Corporal, come with us," ordered the captain as he jumped over the logs in pursuit of Hunter. The two soldiers chased after Hunter, who was now fully acclimated to the higher elevations. Captain Hoover and his corporal were accustomed to Denver with an elevation half that of Quandary Peak, so they lagged behind.

Hunter took a trail he'd cut through the woods to provide a shortcut to the house. The barking sounds coming from Flatus grew louder for a moment and then they subsided until he couldn't hear them.

This concerned Hunter, so he drew his sidearm and cautiously entered the clearing at the yard. The first thing he noticed was the front door standing wide open. He ran to the entryway and cautiously entered the room. The house had been ransacked. Food was strewn about the kitchen, as the cupboards had been hastily emptied onto the floor and countertops.

The knife drawers were open and Tommy's carving knives were dumped into the sink. Hunter moved with trepidation toward the Hagans' master bedroom. He had entered too many closed bedroom doors during this nightmare and immediately braced himself for the worst.

He turned the knob and pushed the door open. It was empty. With his gun leading the way, he checked the corners and under the bed. He made his way to the master bathroom and found it empty as well.

When he returned to the great room, he found Captain Hoover and his corporal panting, trying desperately to catch their breath. Hunter knew the feeling, so he didn't judge. He motioned with two fingers for the corporal to take the stairs and check the loft bedrooms. He nodded to Captain Hoover to finish searching the main floor while he descended the stairs.

What he found downstairs caused him to shake his head in disgust. All of their stored food and supplies had been knocked over and thrown about. Whoever raided their home had taken a hammer to Mac's lab and broken the Plexiglas panels that had prevented the plague from escaping during her experiments. He secretly hoped enough of the bacteria had survived on the laboratory's surfaces to infect them in the process.

Flatus was barking again. Hunter made his way through the debris and ran through the rear doors into the backyard. He could hear Flatus over the side of the ridge toward Monte Cristo Creek.

"Clear!"

"All clear!" shouted Captain Hoover from the main level, loud enough for Hunter to hear.

"Backyard, Cappy!" Hunter yelled as he burst through the doors into the warming sun. "Flatus! Come here, boy. Flatus! Here!"

The barking intensified as Flatus got closer. Hunter ran to the back fence railing and looked into the ravine. Flatus was tearing up the path, barking the entire way.

"There! I see somebody!" yelled Captain Hoover from the deck above Hunter. "Corporal, follow that trail."

Hunter didn't hesitate as he ran toward the path, almost crashing into Flatus as he reached the backyard. The dog was panting heavily after having made several trips up and down the ridge. Hunter admired the tenaciousness of the pup, which was also recuperating from the plague disease. Beyond that, Flatus exhibited an unconditional loyalty to their group that could never be found in their fellow man.

Hunter leaned down and took a moment to rub his neck and accept a few slobbery kisses. He spoke to Flatus in a calm voice. "Come on, boy. Show me the way."

Flatus responded with a gentle gruff, and off he went tearing down the trail, much faster than Hunter would even consider.

"Hundred yards down, Hunter!" shouted Captain Hoover, who remained atop the deck to keep an eye on the movement in the woods.

The corporal caught up to Hunter just as they reached a small clearing in the trees. What he found brought him both a sense of relief and heartbreak. It was Barb and Tommy, badly bruised and bloodied, but alive. They were huddled together against a rock, shivering from the cold morning.

Flatus ran back to Hunter and gruffed one last time before he collapsed on the ground. "Corporal, go back up the hill. We need a few more of your men and two large blankets out of the house. We've got to keep them warm to avoid hypothermia and we'll need to carry them up the hill. Tell Captain Hoover to quickly build a fire."

"Yes, sir," said the corporal, who ran up the hill like he'd caught his second wind. Flatus stood as if he felt the need to give chase, but Hunter patted his leg, signaling him to join his side. "You did good, Flatus. Stay here with us now."

Hunter knelt in front of the two frightened seniors. It was easy to forget that Barb and Tommy were both in their sixties now. Despite their excellent conditioning, their bodies were not very accepting of a beating, nor were their psyches.

"Guys, save your strength, okay," started Hunter, and they both nodded as Barb's usually tough exterior broke down into tears. "Is anything broken, or do you have any open wounds?"

Tommy reached toward his ankle. Hunter studied his face and then gently felt for any bones extruding from his bare feet. His toes were turning blue and his ankle was very swollen, but it didn't appear to be broken.

"Good, it's not broken but is badly sprained," started Hunter. "We'll get some ice on it and it'll be good as new."

Tommy cleared his throat and then whispered, "No ice, please. It's already frozen."

Hunter chuckled and lovingly touched the side of his friend's face. A knot protruded from his forehead. "We'll get some ice on this too, or is your brain already frozen?"

"Very funny," Tommy replied with a grimace. He looked to Barb, who continued to shed tears.

Hunter pulled the end of his long-sleeve tee shirt over his unbloodied hand and wiped Barb's tears. He wiped off the remnants of Derek's blood onto his khakis and took Barb's hand in his.

"Where does it hurt, Barb?"

She let out a deep breath and closed her eyes. "My ribs and chest.

The savages kicked me in the—" She stopped talking and began to cry again. With each deep gasp of air, she moaned as she continued to whimper. Tommy reached for his wife and squeezed her shoulder in support.

Hunter reached forward to feel her ribs, but she pulled away ever so slightly. She began to bawl despite the pain. Hunter became overwhelmed as sorrow overtook him. He listened to her words before his blood began to boil inside him.

"They kicked my breasts—over and over again. They said I was too old and worthless."

Tears streamed down Hunter's cheeks. He leaned into the middle of the loving couple, whom he now considered his parents. He wrapped his arms around them and pulled them together as the three became one.

"I love you guys and we're alive," said Hunter as he stifled his thoughts of revenge. Mac's parents needed his compassion, not the scary side of him that could come out when he was angry. "We're gonna make you both better, and I'm gonna make this right, I swear to you."

"We love you too, son," whispered Barb.

CHAPTER 45

Day Ninety-One
Quandary Peak

Hunter paced the living room as Tommy and Barb were attended to by a medic that was part of Captain Hoover's unit. They were covered with cuts and multiple bruises, but the twisted ankle was the worst of the physical injuries. Hunter's main concern was their emotional state. It had been a traumatic experience, but it was necessary for him to gather the details.

The medic had completed his examination, and the Hagans sat wrapped in fleece blankets, sitting on the fireplace hearth. Hunter brought them coffee before he began to ask them questions. He asked the soldiers to give them some privacy, so Colonel Clements and Captain Hoover exited the house and distributed coffee to the soldiers.

"I want you to know how sorry I am for not being here for you both. Mac and I debated whether we should leave. I'm truly sorry that we did."

Tommy was more emotionally and physically capable of speaking. Barb was upset and agitated, plus her bruised ribs prevented her from taking a deep breath.

"Do not second-guess your decision," said Tommy. "We all agreed it was necessary, but tell us, is Mac okay? You're alone."

"Yes, she's fine and there's a lot to tell you. Let's just say we've made a deal with the President, and with fingers crossed, it will work out for all of humanity. She passes on her love, and, Barb, she wanted me to let you know she'd be working with Dr. Spielman again. Apparently he made it out of Atlanta."

Barb smiled and then flinched in pain as she reached her left hand up to Hunter. He squeezed it and encouraged her to put it back down. "Thank you, Hunter. Good news."

"I have to tell you something else and this is going to be painful," started Hunter. "When we came upon the roadblock, it was abandoned. We found Derek badly beaten with a shovel. I sent for Doc, who examined him. Guys, Derek's in real trouble. He's fighting for his life."

"Oh no," muttered Barb. "Janie?"

Hunter scowled because he truly feared for Janie's life. "I'm sorry. She's missing."

"My god!" said Tommy. "What's wrong with these people?" He put his arm around Barb, who began to cry again. She couldn't suffer any more sorrow.

Hunter pulled up an ottoman and sat directly in front of them. As Mac had admonished before, pacing the room didn't help matters.

"Please, I know all of this is horrible, but we have to find Janie. She's in real danger."

Tommy nodded his head. "Let me tell you what happened. It was still dark outside, maybe an hour before the sun came up. I heard a noise and Flatus did as well." The tired pup raised his head and looked up at Tommy. Hunter instantly wished Flatus could tell him what he'd seen.

Tommy continued. "The sounds came from behind the house, maybe around the greenhouse. Flatus and I went out these doors onto the deck. I thought it was a critter that I could just shoo away, so without shoes on and dressed in pajamas, like an idiot, I wandered down the stairs and into the backyard with a stupid broom.

"That's when I was hit in the back of the head by a kid, um, a teenager, actually. I blindly chased the boy, who was laughing at me, and then he pushed me down the hill until I rolled against a tree. Another teen joined in and kicked me. Flatus started barking at them and they ran back toward the house."

Flatus got up and sat next to Tommy in solidarity. Tommy rubbed his neck. "Several minutes passed and then I heard Barbara scream," continued Tommy. He looked to his pained wife and smiled. She nodded for him to continue.

"I'll relay to you what she was able to tell me earlier. She came out looking for us and they jumped her on the back deck. They forced her down the stairs and knocked her down into the yard. That's when they were, um—"

Barb interrupted and whispered, "That's when they were shouting at me. They dragged me to the trail and pushed me down the hill. I rolled for a hundred feet before my back crashed into a boulder."

Tommy continued. "I had twisted my ankle at that point, but I tried to use the trees to come back up the hill. About the time I reached Barb, the boys, who couldn't have been older than sixteen, showed up and began throwing sticks and rocks at us. They were laughing, calling us sinners and heathens. Flatus ran toward them, barking and growling, but they attacked him with rocks too."

"Hunter," said Barb through her sniffles, "they were driving us down the ridge and deeper into the ravine toward the creek. It was sadistic. Their cackling laughs were evil. These boys were enjoying torturing us, so we tried to get away until all of a sudden it stopped."

Tommy comforted his wife, who buried her head in his shoulder. He wrapped his arm around her. "We waited a long time, hoping they wouldn't come back. We weren't sure we were physically able to climb up the mountain anyway, but when Derek and Janie didn't come looking for us, and the cold set in, we became scared. That's when we tried to claw our way up the ridge."

Hunter had been exposed to so much in his years of military service and then as a covert operative with the DTRA. He'd seen bravery on the battlefield and among men who knew they might be taking their last breaths. He stared into the tired, courageous eyes of Mac's parents.

In that moment, he learned that bravery was not the absence of fear, but how you triumph over it. Barb and Tommy had been afraid, but they'd conquered their fear to survive. That made them heroes as much as anyone he'd served with.

He stayed with them for another minute or two and refilled their drinks. They assured him they were fine and he encouraged bedrest.

He also promised an armed soldier would remain with them until he returned.

"Where are you going?" asked Tommy.

"I need to find Janie and I'm certain I know where to look. You guys get your rest and I'll be back when it's over."

CHAPTER 46

Day Ninety-One
Breckenridge

The Humvee convoy left for Breckenridge. At Hunter's insistence, two soldiers were left behind to patrol Blue Lakes Road from the Route 9 checkpoint up to their house, with instructions to periodically check on the Hagans. He also informed Colonel Clements of a change in their arrangement.

As they drove into town, Hunter told them the history of Rulon Snow as it had been relayed to him by Sheriff Andrews and Doc Cooley. He also began to tie the loose ends together of the strange happenings around Breckenridge. With Janie's abduction and the taunts hurled at Barb, Hunter was beginning to put together a working theory.

Hunter explained his thinking to the colonel and Captain Hoover. "This guy, Snow, is trying to ramp up his seed bearer program using local women he abducts. I hope I'm wrong, but Janie was selected by these two punk boys of his. Most likely, so were the daughters of the mayor in Fairplay and other local women around Breckenridge who've gone missing."

"Why hasn't the sheriff done something?" asked Captain Hoover.

"It's a long story, but until the pandemic hit, the two kept their distance from one another," replied Hunter. "I think the fire was the last straw. The two firstborn sons of Snow in his new compound have been running around these mountains, causing problems. Now, with the sheriff preoccupied, they've increased their activity to arson, kidnapping, murder, and probably rape."

The colonel stared out of the window as he processed the information. "Listen, Sergeant. You know I'm here on a much larger mission than the one you're suggesting. While I certainly understand the plight this town faces, my orders come pretty much directly from the President. He wants this town for refugees."

"Colonel, I get that, and reluctantly, I'm gonna try to help sell it. But you have to understand. Doc Cooley is very influential here, much more than me. Once he learns the Snow boys were involved, he's gonna charge after them himself and expect everyone with a weapon to be by his side. This is an opportunity for you to prove you offer something more than twenty thousand strangers pouring into their community. You offer them hope and security as well."

The colonel nodded his head just as they entered the south side of Breckenridge. A handful of people were walking toward the center of town in the middle of Main Street and moved aside, stopping to gaze at the unusual sight of moving vehicles, much less the Humvees with fifty-caliber machine guns mounted on them.

"What's our first stop?" asked Captain Hoover.

"I think we need to start with Sheriff Terry Andrews and let me fill him in," replied Hunter. "After that, depending on what the sheriff says, I think we need to check on Doc Cooley and his son. I hope Derek is alive and can recover from this. He and Janie have become close. They deserve better than what happened to them."

The Humvee slowed as they entered the center of town, where a large crowd had gathered. Most of the men were holding rifles as they listened to Sheriff Andrews speak while standing on top of a park bench at the entrance to Blue Lakes Plaza, a pedestrian park leading from Main Street to the Breckenridge Riverwalk.

The Humvees inched forward and Sheriff Andrews stopped speaking. Hunter, Captain Hoover, and Colonel Clements exited the lead truck. They walked toward Sheriff Andrews and Doc Cooley, who stood on the sidewalk next to him.

A hush came over the crowd as the entourage greeted one another. Hunter quickly made the introductions and then he turned to Doc Cooley.

"How's Derek?"

"He's stable, but he's exhibiting symptoms of intracranial pressure—brain swelling. We don't have the personnel to properly conduct an MRI, but based on the nausea, headache and his irregular breathing, it's pretty apparent that he's in trouble. The good news is the pharmacy had both mannitol and hypertonic saline that can be used to reduce the pressure by removing excess fluids from his body. We're keeping him calm with a little Valium and his mother's love."

Hunter gripped the man by the shoulder and looked into his eyes. "Doc, I've come to know Derek pretty well. I've served with some real warriors in my career. I think your son is as resilient as any of them."

Doc patted Hunter's hand. "Thanks for saying that. I hope you're right. He was able to tell me something."

Hunter looked around at what was clearly a lynch mob. "I gathered that."

"It was one, or likely both, of the Snow boys. They tricked him into the shed, and when he opened the door, they clobbered him with the shovel. Hunter, I've had enough."

"We all have!" said a man standing behind Hunter.

"Yeah, they tried to burn us out. It's time to put a stop to this crap!" shouted a woman behind the sheriff.

The sheriff moved to calm the mob. "Now, listen up, folks. I agree and we are gonna do something about this. Let me talk to our visitors and see what they have to say. Y'all go home for now and come back around five o'clock. I promise you I'll have a full explanation and an appropriate plan."

The Breckenridge locals began to grumble because they were hyped up and ready to go. One of the men responded, "Sheriff, we trust you, but we've all had it. I, for one, am tired of living under the threats that man Snow and his family poses for the Breck and my family."

"Yeah!"

"Me too. I'm fed up!"

The crowd was rarin' to go. The sheriff held his hands up, hoping for calm. "All right then, come back at five. Let me talk to these fellas and I promise you nothing's gonna happen in the meantime. Go on. I'll see you all back here later. Go on, now!"

The crowd slowly dissipated and the sheriff led Doc, Hunter, and the two military officers toward the Riverwalk, where the water was flowing at a pretty good clip. At the railing overlooking the river, the group took in the beauty of the river before the sheriff spoke first.

"Okay, gentlemen, give me one reason for not unleashing the angry mob on that SOB Snow and his people."

"Experience," started Colonel Clements. "We're going to do it for you, but I have to tell you, there is a price."

CHAPTER 47

Day Ninety-One
Noah's Ark
Boreas Pass at Red Mountain

Janie was trembling as she pressed herself hard against the bolted wooden door that sealed off her exit from the room—only, it wasn't a room, really. She'd caught a glimpse of it as she was shoved inside by her handlers, the two women who pretended to be her friends but acted more like her captors. The dark space where she'd been locked into was a cave or a dug-out hole inside the middle of an abandoned mine.

Somewhere within the underground labyrinth of connected mine shafts, she heard the sheer terror of a woman as her screams echoed off the walls. Janie closed her eyes and opened them quickly, hoping this was a nightmare. When she suddenly realized she was biting down on her hand, it confirmed she was fully awake. She'd unconsciously bit down hard enough to draw blood from the cuts she'd sustained while being attacked and dragged up the mountain.

Within seconds, the screaming stopped. The resulting silence was deafening. Janie pressed harder against the door, trying to hear. In the dark, she fumbled for a handle, but there wasn't one.

The door has to have a handle; otherwise you couldn't get out, right?

Janie gathered the courage to move away from the door and follow the cold, wet wall around the perimeter of the room, using her hands. Her legs bumped into a simple wooden table against the wall. She felt around the top in search of a lamp, but all she found was a single candlestick sitting in a holder. A box of matches sat within the bobeche designed to catch the wax drippings.

Janie lit the match and the room illuminated. Awestruck at its frightening appearance, she stood stunned for a few seconds until the burning match began to burn her fingertips, bringing her back to the present.

She lit the candle and threw the burning match angrily onto the floor. She took in her surroundings. It was a dug-out hole in the wall of the mountain. The ceiling was low and the space small, barely large enough for the antique iron bed, the simple pine side table and a dresser, which included a pitcher of water and a bucket, which she assumed was her toilet.

Janie immediately walked to the dresser and opened the drawers. Several white and pastel cotton dresses were neatly folded inside with some fur-lined moccasins.

She made her way to the bed and flopped onto it out of exhaustion. She began to recall the events that led to her abduction. Derek had heard a crashing sound emanating from the toolshed and the two of them ran up from the checkpoint to investigate. Janie was supposed to watch the woods in case anyone came out after them.

Derek had barely moved the door when the shovel blade came out of the opening and sliced into his face. Stunned, Janie tried to run toward the shed, but out of nowhere, she was tackled from behind.

Her gun flew out of her hands as she got pinned to the earth, knocking the wind out of her. Now she was helpless. The man on top of her yoked Janie's hands behind her back and tied them together with an extension cord. She managed to let out a scream, which distracted Derek, whose face was already bloodied.

She saw the boy pounce out of the shed with a grin on his face and slap Derek across the throat with the shovel's handle. Derek fell to his knees and grabbed at his neck. The teen didn't hesitate as he let out a guttural scream and swung the shovel as hard as he could to the back of Derek's head, knocking him half in and half out of the shed.

The boy danced around Derek's feet, waving the bloody shovel over his head, screaming, "Home run, home run," before spinning around and heaving the shovel toward the woods like an Olympian might toss a hammer down the field.

He then turned to Janie with a devilish grin. "Stand her up, Levi," the boy demanded as he approached Janie, who was in a state of shock, staring at Derek's lifeless, bloodied body. He walked around her and played with her hair. He touched her face, her neck, and then everywhere else he decided to touch.

Janie began to cry as she relived the moment. It wasn't her safety and what might inevitably happen to her in the midst of these crazy people, but it was her lasting memory of Derek, a guy she'd fallen for, who was left behind, facedown in a pool of blood.

For several minutes, she whimpered as quietly as possible, hoping her captors would forget about her. The boys had turned her over to the older women, who immediately stripped off her clothes, using a long hunting knife. Then they bathed her while she stood there defiant, fighting back the tears.

Finally, Janie was wrapped in a thin, white cotton gown and shoved deep into the mine to this room. In her confusion, Janie didn't pay attention to her surroundings. The women cut the cord off her wrists, drawing blood on her back with the tip of the large knife, and then pushed her into the room. Within seconds, the door was slammed closed and the sound of a steel latch sealed her inside.

Now, she sat there, frightened, recalling the details of what was said and where she had been taken prior to this mine shaft. Somehow, Janie held out hope the memory could help her escape or aid in her rescue. She was deep in thought when she heard a girl's voice.

"Hey, new girl, can you hear me?"

Janie thought she was mistaken. The tension in the air screamed at her. *How can I be hearing a voice? They told me not to talk, or there would be punishments.*

"It gets better, you know. At first, they'll break you. But if you're *compliant*, as they like to say, you'll get a better room and good food too."

Janie wrapped the robe around her and tied the front. She pushed her ear against a crack in the door and listened. Then she spoke to the voice on the outside.

"They told me not to talk."

"I know, but we've learned they leave us alone after the prophet has visited for the evening."

"Who?" asked Janie. "The prophet?"

"Yeah, we don't know his real name. We don't know any of their names."

Janie thought about the girl's words. "What do you mean by we? Are there more of us?"

"Lots, my name is Terri. I'm in here with my sister, Karen. We're from—"

"Fairplay, right?" interrupted Janie. "Your father came around our place, looking for you. Whoa, that's been a month ago."

"Could be, we've lost track of the days. I miss Daddy," said Terri Weigel as she began to cry.

Janie felt terrible for the girl and her twin sister. They were so young. "Hey, my name's Janie."

There was silence for another few seconds, then a chorus of replies came from the mine shaft. Janie couldn't determine if they were real or ghosts, because they were so weak and faraway.

"Rachel's my name."

"I'm Becky."

"Olivia."

"Emma."

"My name is Sophia."

"I'm Charlotte."

"My name is Emma too."

The women's whispered voices continued to provide their names until they were too far away for Janie to hear them. She was suddenly filled with despair.

Why are they doing this? Who are these people?

Then Janie got the courage to ask the Weigel girls. "Hey, what does this prophet want from us? Please help me understand."

The answer was unnerving in its terrifying simplicity.

"They want our babies," replied Terri.

"But I don't have a baby."

"You will," said Terri before pausing. "Eventually."

CHAPTER 48

Day Ninety-One
The Den
Denver

Mac's first full day working at the Den, the government's secret facility several thousand feet below the runways at Stapleton Airport, might've resembled any employee's first day at work for a new job. Most of the morning was spent being introduced to her co-workers, some of whom were with the CDC, but most of whom had been brought on board from USAMRIID at Fort Detrick.

Through casual conversations with her counterparts, she learned more about the government's plan to recall all military personnel and their dependents to the vast network of military bases around the country. Star Ranch was the pilot community for civilians who would assist in the rebuilding effort once the plague could be contained, or now, thanks to Mac's efforts, cured.

Mac was careful to choose her conversations and wary of another person's intentions when asking her innocent questions. Sandra Wilkinson didn't strike her as a conspiracy-minded person in the past when they had worked together in Atlanta, but she certainly was now.

Mac slept until seven o'clock this morning when a wake-up announcement was made over the speakers in the facility. *No one warned me of that.* Anxious to observe the routine of the hundreds of people within the Den, she got dressed and found a mess hall on the eighth floor.

In addition to the ground floor, which had a weight room, a running track and a movie theater, the facility had several other common areas used by all of the residents of the Den. At the fourth, eighth, and twelfth floor, in the center of the structure, massive steel cross supports spanned the interior like spokes on a bicycle wheel.

Built on top of these spokes was a commissary and several restaurants. Each of the three common areas had a twenty-four-hour facility that served traditional foods. The fourth floor also had an Asian restaurant. The eighth floor served Italian fare. The twelfth floor contained a Mexican cantina, without the tequila, much to Mac's chagrin. In fact, there was no alcohol or weapons allowed within the facility.

While she was eating a bowl of cereal with a plate of canned fruit, Sandra Wilkinson slid into the chair across from her. The two casually sipped coffee and talked about the events that had transpired in Atlanta. Wilkinson, like the other survivors from Atlanta who were airlifted to Denver, had given a round-the-clock effort to finding a vaccine or a cure for this strain of the plague.

Mac's BALO proposal was modified, tweaked and tried again on residents of Atlanta. The failure of the drug to produce a cure resulted in the riot that occurred at the CDC campus.

When the crowds started to gather and the Georgia National Guard announced they could no longer guarantee the safety of the CDC employees, Dr. Spielman gave the order to dismantle equipment and transfer data onto portable hard drives. The staff worked for twenty-four hours to prepare for an evacuation of both equipment and personnel.

A dozen scientists and another dozen support staff were whisked away from the rooftop of their building via helicopter, taken to Dobbins Air Base in Marietta, and then immediately flown to Denver's Stapleton Airport via military transport.

"We were held in the terminal for seventeen days as part of their quarantine protocol, but the medical eval involved more than that," said Wilkinson. "We were visited on multiple occasions for one-on-one conversations with government psychologists."

"So if you didn't have the plague, you were good to go unless you were crazy?" asked Mac.

"Pretty much, honey. As I look back on it, the questions regarding our ability to live in an enclosed, underground building like this were mixed into the other inquiries about family, friends and suicidal tendencies. It made sense, you know. If you boil it down, we're trapped underground. It ain't right."

Mac laughed. "Well, underground, yes. But not really trapped."

"Yes, trapped," added Wilkinson bluntly. "Mac, nobody leaves here. I've heard of people claiming to lose it after months of being underground and they end up being medicated in the infirmary for a while before they appear around the facility in other jobs."

"Dr. Spielman never told me that," said Mac.

Wilkinson continued. "He will, as soon as you ask to leave. Have you read your orientation packet? You know, about the furloughs?"

"No."

"Mac, when you volunteered to come here, did they not tell you these things?"

"No, Sandra, they didn't. In fact, I had a hard time falling asleep last night and I thought about all of the unanswered questions I had asked Dr. Spielman. In hindsight, he was very evasive and I should have pushed him for answers."

"Honey, I'm sorry to be the bearer of bad news, but those questions should've been asked and answered before you agreed to come here. It's too late now. I doubt Spielman has the sole authority to send you out of here anyway."

Mac slumped in her chair, dejected. She understood the need for secrecy. She doubted whether most members of Congress knew about the Den, much less the public. Mac had a high security clearance and could be trusted.

Why wouldn't they tell me about these restrictions?

"Mac, who recruited you to come here?"

"The President."

"What, honey? Our President? Garcia? He recruited you to come here. I didn't think you two would ever be on speaking terms after, you know."

Mac laughed. "Well, he loves me now. Sandra, you have to keep this quiet until after lunch, agreed?"

"Sure, honey. What is it?"

"I've developed a cure. I've been working on it since I was fired.

My father contracted the plague and so did his dog. I cured them both. That's why I'm here."

Wilkinson leaned back in her chair and momentarily smiled before a look of gloom came over her face. "I knew you'd do it. But that presents a bigger problem for you, honey."

"How so?"

Wilkinson leaned into Mac. "You've given the president the keys to the kingdom, and now he can charge the rest of the world a king's ransom for the cure."

"He wouldn't do that. I mean, he can't, right?"

Wilkinson patted Mac on her knee in a Southern, motherly way. "Oh, honey. You didn't learn anything from what happened in Washington, did you? If you trust this President, then you've obviously failed history class."

CHAPTER 49

Day Ninety-One
The Den
Denver

Earlier, Mac had spent a few more minutes with Wilkinson, who warned her about the cameras tucked in every room and the potential for strangers approaching her in casual conversation. The facility was full of snitches reporting information back to the department heads to gain favor. While living in a hole in the ground didn't have that much to offer, Wilkinson had said, better meals, more free time, and the promise of escorted trips into the heavily guarded Jeppesen Terminal were worth tricking someone into saying too much.

Jeppesen, the aboveground terminal of Stapleton, was where the department heads had face-to-face meetings with members of the military in a private conference room. The government employees who'd *earned* their *perk* to visit above ground were allowed to sit in a cordoned-off section of the terminal, which had a uniquely designed peaked roof providing a snow-capped mountain effect. For an hour, the *chosen ones*, as Wilkinson called them, were allowed to look out the plate-glass windows, hoping to catch a glimpse of wildlife or humanity. However, being exposed to natural light was the greatest perk of all, Wilkinson surmised.

One of the things Mac had learned from her years in public service was jealousy ran rampant throughout the ranks of government employees. The government pay scale and advancement system fostered an atmosphere that rewarded those who endeared themselves to their superiors, often at the expense of others.

Mac didn't need the aggravation of being tricked because she was new. She now had one goal in mind—get out of the Den.

The information received from Wilkinson and her own

214

observations dictated her actions at the noon meeting with Dr. Spielman and the other scientists. Mac had an idea that would make her indispensable.

Before the meeting, she approached Dr. Spielman in his office, regarding the offer to be assigned the prime office space. He'd never specifically said what he had in mind, but whatever the position was, she intended to take it if it gave her the opportunity to get out of there.

"Dr. Spielman, yesterday you tempted me with a pretty sweet carrot in the form of that office. I assume it comes with some level of responsibility beyond my normal capabilities."

"It does, Mac. Just a moment. I want to shut this door so we can talk privately."

While Mac waited, she leaned forward and studied some of the paperwork on his desk, looking for a hint or a clue of any nefarious activity. Dr. Spielman returned and she quickly averted her eyes from his desk, but not before she saw a document labeled *CABLEGRAM* on the stationary of the World Health Organization.

"Clearly, these circumstances and this facility are highly unusual. Yet they resemble a scaled-down version of what we did at the CDC. The only difference is we've incorporated the USAMRIID functions and some of their personnel under one roof, or floor, in this case." Dr. Spielman chuckled at his sly remark.

"Yes, sir," said Mac, who was all business. "At the moment, are you supervising all of these activities?"

"I am, and now, thanks to your miraculous discovery, which I'm anxious to hear about in more detail, my workload has doubled."

"Dr. Spielman, how can I help? Shall I coordinate with the WHO and other foreign health protection agencies in distributing the vancomycin formula?"

Dr. Spielman pushed back in his chair and gripped the arms slightly. "We've not been able to make contact with the WHO, and other governments are in disarray. Most don't have the same continuity-of-government protocols our nation has established."

Mac frowned and then swallowed. She decided to continue to

---

ferret out his plans for her. "Are there any other tasks you can assign to me to take the burden off your shoulders?"

"Obviously, I need you to oversee the development, testing and production of the drug. Today, the development and testing phase will begin in earnest. I'm pleased to tell you that we have government zoologists capturing primates that survived the plague outbreak at the Denver Zoo and they're bringing them here for our test purposes."

"That's great news, sir. I'm anxious to get started and will help you in any way," said an exuberant Mac.

"Mac, I want to speak to you on a personal level for a moment, if I may?"

Here we go, thought Mac. "Of course, sir. Please do."

"Your perseverance on behalf of this nation should be commended and rewarded."

"Sir, that's not necessary," interrupted Mac. "I never lost my will to fight for a cure that could save humanity. Sounds like a lofty goal, but it was real."

Dr. Spielman studied Mac for a brief moment before he spoke. "At the CDC, our mission was to protect our nation and its citizens against health, safety, and security threats. Now, thanks to you, we're on the cusp of saving millions of Americans."

Mac listened intently, but he sounded like he was making a speech to a new group of epidemiology recruits. She wanted him to get to the point.

He continued. "By accepting this position, you are taking on a great responsibility to the American people, but especially your government. The Chief of Staff expressed concern to me about your loyalty to this project and the President. Mac, you need to understand, you're one of us now."

"What do you mean?" she asked.

"Prior to the pandemic, our government operated on a hierarchal system that was out of control. By sheer attrition, the layers of management have shrunken considerably. As my number two, you would become a phone call away from the president. That makes you one of us."

Mac was genuinely bewildered by this conversation. Dr. Spielman seemed to be talking in riddles. "One of us, sir?"

"Yes, Mac. We will enjoy responsibilities and perks that are not available to the others in the newly constituted CDC."

Perks, there's that word again.

He continued. "What that means is private conversations with that busybody Sandra Wilkinson have to cease. They will be used against you to undermine your position."

How did he know about that? It was just a few hours ago. "Sir, I knew Sandra from the EOC in Atlanta. We were just catching up on a few—"

"Dr. Hagan," said Dr. Spielman sternly, which made Mac jump in her chair slightly. *I guess the personal talk is over.* "Are you able to separate yourself from the others and remember who the two of us answer to?"

Here came the first of many lies Mac would tell over the next few days. "Absolutely, sir. I am one hundred percent loyal to you. Rest assured, I will follow your lead on everything."

"Good. Now, let's you and I go to this lunch meeting, where you will brief the team on your findings. This afternoon, I will make the announcement that you're the new principal deputy director of the CDC."

Mac gulped. She didn't know who to believe. Sandra Wilkinson seemed so convincing, yet she was very conspiratorial.

Was Sandra setting me up so she could get a peek at the natural light above the ground?

But, then, could she trust Dr. Spielman? He had been evasive in his prior responses. As part of her acceptance of any position she offered, she was going to insist upon time with Hunter, but the topic never came up.

Two things struck her about their twenty-minute conversation. One had to do with Dr. Spielman's focus on their nation and American citizens. Mac thought their goal was to save all the people in the world, not just theirs. The other had to do with his interaction with the WHO. The cablegram on his desk proved he wouldn't hesitate to lie directly to her face.

How am I supposed to separate the truth from the lies? She needed Hunter's advice and would find a way to manipulate her way out of the Den.

CHAPTER 50

Day Ninety-Two
Noah's Ark
Boreas Pass at Red Mountain

Hunter left the negotiating—or arguing, which was a better characterization—regarding the military's occupation of Breckenridge up to the sheriff and Doc. He and Captain Hoover drew on their experience as a covert operative and platoon leader respectively to create a plan to attack the Snow compound and save the people held there.

They did not have the benefit of a map or any details regarding the layout of the compound, which basic reconnaissance would provide. As Sheriff Andrews pointed out again, nobody had escaped the Snow compound thus far because he assumed they were remaining with Snow of their own free will. He now second-guessed this theory because it was apparent Snow, or at least his sons, were kidnapping women and holding them captive.

It was a completely dark evening, as the new moon provided no ambient lighting. A beautiful blue and green aurora lit up the northern sky, which drew the attention of Hunter as they hiked along the tree line of Red Mountain. He wished Mac was there to enjoy the incredible sight.

Armed with full chest rigs and automatic weapons, Hunter and Captain Hoover set out at midnight along the many trails created by the Snow teens. Using a compass and the benefit of night-vision goggles, the men worked their way up Boreas Pass until they reached a clearing above the compound.

The sheriff provided the men some of the gear used for riot control and SWAT team activities. He laughed as he issued the flash-bang grenades, pepper spray, and bulletproof vests. The closest confrontation Breckenridge had ever experienced that could be labeled a riot was when Deep Roots Gardening Supply ran out of marijuana seeds during their first day of operations. Demand was much larger than their supply, resulting in a skirmish between the local potheads.

Captain Hoover tested his communications with Colonel Clements but was having difficulty. "Hunter, let me try your radio," said Captain Hoover.

Hunter backed off the edge of the cliff overlooking the compound and moved closer to his partner. Captain Hoover keyed Hunter's mic and received the same static in response.

He reattached the mic to Hunter's rig and grumbled, "Maybe they need to be in range. These mountains are wreaking havoc on our comms."

"Yeah, or it's that," started Hunter, pointing over his shoulder at the aurora. "I always laugh when people get all excited about the beautiful aurora. The news cameras show the beauty to all of their viewers and everyone shares their pics with The Weather Channel. One of these days, that beautiful aurora is gonna turn deadly, fry all of our electronics, and cause a massive blackout."

Hunter got up from his crouch and started down the trail toward the back side of the compound, where several small cabins were scattered against the woodsy backdrop. Based on their conversations with Sheriff Andrews and a few of the locals, Snow assigned housing based upon importance within his community. During their briefing earlier, the owner of the builder's supply said he hadn't seen the Snows make any lumber purchases in a couple of years, so he doubted there had been any new construction.

That led the group to one conclusion—Snow was using the mine as a prison.

Hunter and Captain Hoover had the advantage of a dark, early morning hour and night-vision goggles, a device Hunter called the great equalizer. Whenever the DTRA undertook a mission at an unfamiliar location, night vision, which was usually not available to their targets, allowed the operatives to move through a building or street without detection. While the enemy might have the benefit of local knowledge, in the middle of the night, Hunter could see what they could not, thus leveling the field of battle.

Hunter stopped as they reached the clearing, barely forty feet from the first log house. He checked his watch. It was just after four a.m. They had two hours to clear the mine of any guards, free the women, if in fact that was where they were, and hustle them to the safety of the woods.

At dawn, the Humvees would roar up the driveway in formation and shred the compound's fortified gate with fifty-caliber bullets and grenade launchers. Sheriff Andrews, on behalf of Summit County, had taken advantage of the Department of Defense transfer of four-point-three billion dollars' worth of surplus and used military equipment to local law enforcement agencies around the country.

By declaring Summit County a hotbed of illicit marijuana growers, he'd received a dozen M16s, six .45-caliber pistols, twelve Mossberg 590 shotguns, and two grenade launchers. He offered up all of the above in the effort to take down Snow.

Hunter and Captain Hoover needed to begin their part of the mission now. Their goal was to extract the women from the mine and get them into the safety of the woods before the front gate was breached.

"Cappy, our plan can be executed without comms," said Hunter in a whisper. "Let's work with our silenced weapons and clear the mine first. Once we've located the prisoners and have them freed, we'll sneak them back here."

"What if the compound rises before dawn?" asked Cappy. "We know nothing about their routine. Hunter, we really should have conducted some surveillance first."

Hunter didn't respond right away since he knew Captain Hoover was right. He was taking a risk because he was being protective of Janie. He had seen the worst of what mankind had to offer and he wasn't going to subject Janie to it for one minute longer than necessary.

"Yeah, I get it. Are you ready?"

Captain Hoover patted him on the back and the two men emerged from the woods together. Using the night scope attached to the M4 he took from the sheriff, Hunter walked sideways through the cleared area against the woodsy backdrop. He and Captain Hoover had both dressed in woodland camo clothing to blend in with the aspens and pines behind them.

After two hundred yards of maneuvering through the tall, wet grass, they reached the entrance of the mine. Hunter crossed over the opening of the mine as a burst of cold air rushed down the face of Red Mountain. The air pulled the decades-old musty smell out of the mine shaft past his nostrils.

Hunter crouched next to the massive posts holding the entrance open. He turned his rifle inside the mine and searched to identify any guards. Sixty feet into the mine was an open area furnished with an old sofa, a couple of plastic stackable chairs, and a simple wooden table. A kerosene lantern produced a faint glow revealing a card game being conducted.

To the left, and slightly out of his field of vision, two men were standing alone. After a moment, they returned with a plate full of sandwiches for their candlelit meal. Hunter looked around the interior of the mine shaft for evidence of electrical wiring. Their ability to make sandwiches confounded him, but it didn't matter. It was go time.

CHAPTER 51

Day Ninety-Two
Noah's Ark
Boreas Pass at Red Mountain

Hunter raised two spread fingers to Captain Hoover and then put them together and pointed them toward the right, indicating the locations of the hostiles. He entered the cave slowly, walking heel to toe down the slight decline. Periodically, a concrete curb had been created with weep holes on both walls next to it. These were designed to catch excessive water runoff, which would prevent the mine from flooding.

The men continued to play cards, blissfully unaware of Hunter's advance. He was close enough to take the shot, but then he paused. Just past the men's location, a series of single lightbulbs hanging from a cord in the ceiling ran down the center of the mine's shaft.

Hunter traced the wire back to the opening and then to the left, where the men had emerged with their sandwiches. He quickly glanced upward to make sure he hadn't missed the wire.

Captain Hoover stopped across the shaft and dropped to a knee. "What's up?" He whispered the question.

"The power comes from the left side. There might be another entrance to the mine. I'm gonna drop these two, but prepare for their buddies to appear from the left side like mice out of a hole in the wall."

"Hit 'em, and I'll pick off the mice," said Captain Hoover.

Hunter inched forward and chose the closest target first since he was partially obscured by the mine's wall. Two rounds spit out of his suppressed M16, exploding into the man's back and ricocheting throughout his chest and vital organs. The dead man fell face-first into the table, causing the kerosene lamp to crash onto the floor.

The second target sat upright in stunned silence, receiving a round to the chest and one to the face before tilting backward against the floor with a crash.

What happened next caught Hunter by surprise and instantly meant they were in grave danger. A man with a hunting rifle stepped into the clearing and got off a single round, which flew between Hunter and Captain Hoover, who were both crouched on one knee.

Captain Hoover quickly dispatched the shooter, but the damage was done. The loud crack of the gunshot echoed through the mine shaft and was most likely heard by those in the compound. The guys were trapped with only one way out—firepower.

Hunter thought quickly. He had to hope there were only the two entrances into the cave. If they could gain control of the point where the three dead men now lay, releasing their blood down the mine shaft, they could hold off Snow's men until the Humvees mounted their frontal assault—in just under two hours.

"Hurry," ordered Hunter as he moved deeper into the mine. Another person burst into the opening and Hunter immediately shot him in the head. "Stay low."

The two men walked against the walls, keeping their bodies as low as possible to avoid providing an easy target.

Captain Hoover was the first to spot the arm pointing a handgun around the carved-out opening of the mine's wall. He raised his weapon to shoot after three quick shots were sent in their direction, missing low, but still putting them at risk from a ricocheting bullet.

The shooter pulled his arm back quickly, but Hunter trained his rifle on the exact position in case he got a second chance. The instant the hand reappeared, Hunter squeezed the trigger, dislodging the weapon from the shooter's hand, together with three of his fingers.

The man began to wail in pain, and this was when Hunter first realized all of the shouting taking place both within the mine and outside it. As they approached the apex of the two mine shafts, Captain Hoover killed the other man, who was lying on the floor, gripping his bleeding appendage. The shaft to their left rose up a slight incline and into the night sky, but was now empty.

Women were screaming and pounding on their doors. They were shouting for help and begging to be released. As badly as Hunter wanted to locate Janie and the others, he needed to deal with the threat posed by Snow's men first.

"Cappy, can you see their cells?" asked Hunter as he waved his rifle back and forth, searching for targets to come down the mine shaft. "From the sounds of their voices, they must be down at least two or three hundred feet."

Captain Hoover rifled through the pants of the dead men until he found a large ring of keys attached to one of the men's leather belts. "Hunter, I've got the keys."

Hunter quickly weighed his options. They could hold off an attack for a while as long as they managed their ammo. He looked around at the weapons left by these men, which included three handguns and a hunting rifle.

If Snow and his men rushed the mine from both directions, he couldn't hold them off alone. However, they wouldn't have time to release all the women in the middle of a shoot-out. From the sounds of their screams and excited calls for help, there could be two or three dozen cells to find and unlock.

He couldn't delay his decision any longer because Snow was surely mounting an assault. "Cappy, go find Janie and let her out. Janie only, okay. If you let them all out at once, they'll come storming up here in a panic and get us all killed."

"You got this?" asked Captain Hoover.

"Yeah, but hurry."

Hunter continued to watch both entrances to the mine for signs of movement. It had been fifteen minutes since they'd entered the cave and five minutes since Captain Hoover had gone deeper into the mountain to locate Janie. *Where are Cappy and Janie?*

Hunter glanced over his shoulder and thought he saw the shadow of a man approaching and took a little extra time to make sure it was Captain Hoover.

"Welcome back," said Hunter.

"Yeah, sorry," said Captain Hoover. "I started calling out for Janie and pretty soon everyone's name was Janie."

"Did you find my Janie?"

"He sure did," said Janie, who was wearing a pale pink cotton dress. Her look startled him somewhat.

"Come here," Hunter said and he reached his left arm out to hug her. Captain Hoover took the point while the two spoke. "Janie, are you okay? Did they hurt you?"

"No, thank goodness. Hunter, you have no idea what these bastards are doing here."

"Well, we're putting an end to it, but we've had an unexpected hiccup."

Janie looked at the four dead bodies spilling blood at her bare feet. "Hunter, can we help the others too? They're being raped."

"I figured as much," he replied. "Yes, we're gonna take everybody, but I need your help. Cappy, hand me the—"

Hunter stopped talking when the power to the mine's electricity system was cut off. The women shrieked and Captain Hoover cursed as he stumbled over the dead body just below Hunter.

Hunter quickly raised his weapon to view the twin openings through his night scope. There was no activity, yet.

"Here, sling this rifle over your shoulder," said Hunter, handing her the dead man's gun. "Also, get your shoes on."

"We don't have any. They took everything and left us with these Amish-looking dresses."

He turned to Janie even though they couldn't see one another in the darkness. "Janie, you have to keep them calm. Impress on them that if they come charging out of here, they'll die as soon as they smell the fresh air of the compound. Can you do that?"

"I think so, Hunter. The mayor's twins are here—from Fairplay. I'll get their help."

Hunter pointed his scope down the shaft to a point where the drop became more pronounced. He flipped on his red laser sight and pointed to the point.

"Put on these goggles, Janie, and get used to them," he instructed as he handed her the night-vision gear. She fumbled with the straps but eventually adjusted them to fit her head.

"Okay, it's all green, but I can see," she muttered.

"Now, look down the shaft and locate my red laser light. Do you see it next to those railroad tie supports?"

Janie raised her chin up and down in an attempt to get her bearings. "Yes, yes. I see it."

"Good. Janie, bring them to that point but no farther. If we have to shoot our way out, I don't want them to get caught by stray bullets. Okay?"

"Okay! Thank you, Hunter," she said as she cautiously walked down the mine toward the despondent women, who feared they'd been left behind.

"Don't thank me yet," Hunter mumbled as she got out of earshot.

"What's their next move?" asked Cappy as Hunter squatted next to him.

Hunter tried to think like Snow. The man was vile and wicked, but the enslaved women represented a valuable commodity, an asset to a deranged man who would conceive of such a heinous crime. Snow wouldn't risk the lives of his seed bearers.

"I think he'll wait us out," replied Hunter. "He doesn't know how many of us are down here, but must assume we're acting alone since the compound hasn't been attacked. I believe these are the only two points of entry to this shaft."

"We hope, anyway," added Captain Hoover.

"Yeah, but assuming that's the case, he knows we'll slaughter his men if they charge down either entrance. In his mind, eventually, we'll have to give up."

Captain Hoover looked at his watch. "I'm guessing the colonel didn't storm the gate because he couldn't hear the gunfire down here. If we can just manage to hold them off for thirty minutes, then we can move the women out of here."

Suddenly, a bright flash and the sound of a rumble came from the top of the mine shaft where Hunter and Captain Hoover had entered almost an hour ago.

A wooden barrel had been lit on fire and was crashing down the shaft towards them. It slowed as it began to crash over the concrete curbs used to control water into the mine. Every ten feet, it broke apart, spilling the oil and gasoline mix inside it. The fire spread down the shaft, creating a massive blaze and temporarily blinding the men.

Gunfire echoed down the shaft as Snow's people opened fire. Bullets zinged past their position as they used the second entrance to the mine as cover.

"Good," said Hunter over the noise.

"Really?" Captain Hoover chuckled.

"Yeah, that gunfire is just as loud on that end as it is down here. I'd be willing to bet the colonel is less than ninety seconds away from blasting that front gate in."

CHAPTER 52

Day Ninety-Two
Noah's Ark
Boreas Pass at Red Mountain

Hunter waited until he heard the explosions of the grenades being launched at the gates. When he heard the first Ma Deuce open up and the accompanying screams from the people in Snow's compound, he knew it was time to move. Plus, he was afraid they'd follow up with another barrel of fire down their only exit option.

"Cappy, make sure Janie has gathered up all the women and then send them up this shaft. I'm gonna make sure the exit stays clear of fire and debris. These girls may not have any shoes, which will make it impossible to escape."

"Got it," said Cappy. He slowly backed into the mine, where Janie was keeping the women calm. Hunter heard his voice before he jogged up to the exit. "I'm Captain Hoover with the National Guard. We're all getting out of here, but you have to follow my directions, okay?"

The women began to thank him, but Hunter couldn't take the time to listen. He was on his own and on a mission to keep their path clear. He kept his weapon pointed at the open sky in front of him, preparing to shoot at the first sign of movement.

As he reached the opening, he heard the familiar sounds of war. Gunfire filled the air, barely drowning out the screams of agony as people were wounded within the compound.

At the entrance, he immediately fell to the ground. Hunter slid on his stomach to look for any shooters around the mine. He knew most untrained assailants usually shot higher than their target. Very few would target an adversary skimming the ground on his belly.

Hunter slithered out to the wet grass at the entrance and was both surprised and pleased to find it abandoned. Snow's men must've determined the greater threat to be the three Humvees, which had now entered the compound.

The gunners manning each Ma Deuce were relentless as they ripped up the turf in pursuit of Snow's gunmen. The log cabins were no match for the powerful fifty-caliber rounds as they sailed through doors and windows and embedded into bodies inside.

Sheriff Andrews and the colonel agreed, everyone within Snow's compound was culpable in the abduction, imprisonment, and likely rape of these innocent women. As a result, for this mission, there was no such thing as rules of engagement and collateral damage. This was the apocalypse, which left no room for margin of error.

After the gunners on the Humvees held their fire, screams like wild Indians filled the air as the posse formed by Breckenridge's residents entered the compound. Personally, Hunter found this aspect of the operation unnecessary, but it wasn't his call to make. Despite the apocalyptic world they lived in, there was a point in every battle where the enemy was clearly defeated and some semblance of mercy should be shown. Hunter doubted the townsfolk were showing restraint.

"Cappy, it's over!" shouted Hunter. "Come on out."

Hunter heard the silent footsteps of the innocent victims of Snow's depravity coming up the mine shaft. A Humvee drove up through the grass and illuminated Hunter. He shielded his eyes from the headlights and waved to the truck.

A door swung open and Colonel Clements strutted up the hill toward Hunter. Sheriff Andrews and Doc Cooley followed his lead.

"Well done, Sergeant!" said the colonel, providing Hunter a snappy salute. Hunter returned the salute just as the women, led by Janie and the Weigel twins, emerged from their prison.

"Terri, Karen, it's me, Doc Cooley. Are you young ladies okay?"

The Weigel girls ran to his side.

Doc addressed Hunter. "I've been their doctor since they were still in diapers." He hugged them both.

Janie held Hunter around the waist, and they stood out of the way to let everyone exit. A school bus ambled up a path to the top of the hill and several women from Breckenridge emptied out carrying blankets for the girls to stay warm.

Hunter looked to Janie and smiled. "Mac would be proud of her Janie doll."

"I miss my friend," added Janie.

"Yeah, me too," said Hunter. "Come on, let's get you home. Barb and Tommy got roughed up by these thugs too."

The two of them walked through the grass despite Hunter's offer to carry Janie to keep her feet warm and dry. She told him she didn't care because it made her feel alive.

Just as they were about to reach the Humvee, Janie looked ahead and saw two bodies in the grass, lit up by the rising sun. She broke away from Hunter and walked up to the dead boys.

"Hunter, they're the ones. They beat Derek and kidnapped me. Seth and Levi were their names. Rot in hell," shouted Janie as she spit on them.

Janie began to cry and Hunter defied her earlier request. He scooped her up to put her in the back of the Humvee. He whispered in her ear, "I wish I could've taken the shot that put them down."

"So do I," said Janie. "Did they kill the prophet?"

"Who? Oh, you mean Rulon—?" Hunter started to ask when a throaty scream surprised them from the woods in front of them.

Snow raced out of the woods toward Hunter and Janie with a machete in his hand. He lunged at Hunter, who easily avoided the man's attempt to slice him with the machete while deftly setting Janie down at the same time.

As Snow stumbled past, Hunter punched his throat with his right hand, causing him to clothesline from the blow. Snow lay on the ground, gasping for air, eyes wide as they stared toward the sky.

Janie calmly grabbed the machete and dropped to both knees beside him. She held the machete to his neck until it drew blood.

"This is for Derek and all the women you raped," she growled as she used surgeon-like precision to sever his carotid artery.

231

Janie stood over his body gushing blood through his fingers and down his neck. She threw the machete on Snow's chest. "We can go now, Hunter."

CHAPTER 53

Day Ninety-Two
Quandary Peak

Hunter stood on the front steps of their home at Quandary Peak with Captain Hoover as they discussed the day's events. Hunter assured him that an armed sentry was no longer necessary. He had coordinated a new guard rotation for their checkpoint at the bottom of the ridge, and after their efforts against Snow at Noah's Ark, the residents of Breckenridge seemed anxious to pitch in to the security effort.

"Hunter, I don't think the President is gonna waver on his orders to use Breckenridge as a safe zone and, in a way, a sanctuary city for survivors," said Captain Hoover. "I hope the sheriff and the other town leaders will understand. This is going to happen, so at least try to agree on terms most favorable to the town."

"Like what?" asked Hunter.

Captain Hoover took Hunter by the arm and walked towards the side of the house where he couldn't be overheard by his driver.

"The colonel let me in on their points of weakness, which could help delay or slow the process," started Captain Hoover. "Your people can insist upon a quarantine period of sixteen days. Colonel Clements will have to give on that. Naturally, the quarantine area would have to be restricted, nearby, and monitored twenty-four seven. The government is prepared to give on all these points."

"Eventually, they'll be allowed in," interrupted Hunter.

"True, but it'll take the military at least a week or more to identify an area to hold refugees, set up temporary housing for them, and assign a contingent. I know because it took Star Ranch a while to get up and running in a neighborhood full of homes with perimeter fencing already in place."

Hunter pulled down his sleeves as a gust of cool wind pushed down the southern face of Quandary Peak. The cold weather came quickly in the Rockies, he thought to himself as he glanced at the snowcapped peak.

Captain Hoover continued. "At best, they'd be able to introduce five hundred, maybe a thousand at a time—every few weeks."

"A lot could happen in three or four weeks," said Hunter, wondering when the President would be announcing the cure and a plan to inoculate the sick. This refugee proposal might go away before it was implemented.

"I'm leaving two men and a Humvee behind for a couple of days while they make sure Snow's people are all captured and jailed. They'll be heading back to Star Ranch. Shall I instruct them to pick you up?"

"Yeah, I'll be ready to go. Janie is supposed to come with me to help Mac, but I'm not sure how she'll feel about that now with Derek being injured. I'm about to discuss it with everyone."

Captain Hoover and Hunter clasped right hands and bumped their chests in a bro-hug. The two had become brothers after fighting side by side twice.

Hunter stood outside the house for a moment and thought of Mac. He walked through the front yard and circle drive, hands in his pockets and kicking loose gravel. The safest course of action weighed heavily on his mind. In the past, he'd charge in to any crisis and become the catalyst to sway a decision one way or the other. Now, he was looked up to by Mac's parents and Janie. They would defer to his experience for guidance. He turned his face to the sky and said, "Mac, I really need you right now."

He finally wandered inside and found the Hagans laughing with Janie as she retold the story of cutting Snow's throat. This disturbed Hunter and caused him concern for Janie's sanity. To his knowledge, this was her first kill. Joking about the manner of the kill, which was extremely personal, did not feel right, especially for someone of Janie's gentle, jovial character.

"Everybody doing okay in here?" he said, announcing his

presence, which had been ignored when he walked in. "Janie, how about you?"

"Hey, I'm fine. We were just rehashing your daring rescue and the final coup de grace! He was an animal and I put him down!" She and Tommy exchanged high-fives.

Hunter had flashbacks to his days in the small barracks constructed as part of the many forward operating bases he'd worked out of while deployed in the Middle Eastern theater. After a good day on the battlefield, especially when a team had taken out a high-value target, the comradery and celebrating was over the top. It helped ease the tension from a warrior's body after risking his life for the mission. Janie was not unlike any other warrior who had succeeded in battle. If this were *Game of Thrones*, there would be ale and a turkey leg for all.

"Hunter, is the military pulling out?" asked Tommy.

"Sort of. They left a couple of men behind to make sure there are no stragglers from the Snow flock roaming the woods, seeking revenge. They'll head back to Colorado Springs but will stop by here to pick us up. The original plan was for us to receive a new home at Star Ranch."

Barb hobbled to the kitchen to retrieve the bottle of chardonnay on the kitchen island. "Hunter, would you like a glass?"

"No, thanks. I'm gonna hit the sack after we talk about our options."

Tommy took the lead on the conversation. "Hunter, you've told us a lot about Star Ranch. It sounds nice, but it isn't permanent in our minds. We live there at the whim of the government, which might displace us at any time and without notice. We know how this president operates. He may have offered this to induce Mac to come on board, only to snatch it away when he's done using her."

"What Tommy's beating around the bush to say is we're gonna stay here," interrupted Barb. "This is our home, and despite recent events, we feel safe here."

"Barb's right," added Tommy. "We got too comfortable and let our guard down. What those two teens did to us was unconscionable, but we've learned from it and we'll adjust our lives accordingly."

"Janie, you've been through a lot, so nobody would expect you to make a decision right now," said Hunter. "Besides, we don't have to leave for a couple of days."

Janie pulled her knees up to her chest and curled into a ball on the sofa. Her demeanor had changed once she wasn't leading the conversation about the death of Rulon Snow. It was if she was uncomfortable talking about the realities of life.

"I know Mac probably needs me, and I definitely want to talk with her about it. But I'm worried about Derek and I'd like to go into town to see him if you think it's okay."

"I'll drive you myself," said Hunter, who planned on closely observing Janie for PTSD. "There is no need to rush into a decision."

"How about this, for purposes of reaching a decision," said Janie. "If I ride into the city with you, would they be able to bring me back after I talk with Mac?"

"I'll insist upon it," replied Hunter. "For now, let's call it a day and tomorrow we'll start fresh. Deal?"

"Stamp it," said Tommy, slamming his fist on the fireplace hearth.

CHAPTER 54

Day Ninety-Three
Cheyenne Mountain

The President and his Chief of Staff had just received another report of a terrorist attack against a military installation. This time the target was the Letterkenny Army Depot in South Central Pennsylvania near Harrisburg, the state capital. The facilities at Letterkenny were used to store and decommission tactical missiles and ammunition. Unlike Fort Drum and Star Ranch, the terrorists did not target a highly populated base. Letterkenny was being protected by a company of ninety soldiers, whose primary focus was the prevention of civilians breaking into the facility and looting.

In a surprise attack, ISIS operatives successfully engaged the nighttime sentries and overwhelmed them at the gate. Jihadists detonated two suicide bomb vests in the barracks, killing forty-six soldiers and severely injuring the rest.

According to the survivors, as many as thirty terrorists entered the base and commandeered six 900 Series five-ton trucks, three medium tactical vehicles and a variety of shoulder-fired missiles, including a dozen RPG-7s seized by the U.S. military in the Syrian Civil War. Despite a heated gun battle with the uninjured twenty soldiers who engaged them, the terrorists managed to escape into the night relatively unscathed.

The President was furious with General Keef, who attempted to defend the military's inability to take the fight to the enemy due to the risk of contracting the plague while outside their respective bases.

"Mr. President, we want to hunt the vermin down and make them pay for what they've done to our country," said a standing General Keef before she left the conference room. "In the process, we could lose more of our people to the disease, both while they are in the field and when they return to their families on the base."

"General, if we can't hunt them down, can we at least secure our facilities across the country?" asked Morse.

"Sir, I've raised this issue previously," replied Keef somewhat condescendingly. "While the jihadists are willing to expose themselves to the disease because they do not fear dying, our personnel are hiding behind fences and walls, sitting ducks to their attacks. Mr. President, just like our country's decision to hunt radical Islamic terrorists on their turf following the attacks of 9/11, they have chosen to bring the fight to us, using the pandemic as cover. The only way to defeat this enemy is to unleash the wrath of our military, but we can't do that unless we can insure their safety from the disease."

"Thank you, General," said President Garcia. "That's all for now."

General Keef exited the conference room and the President watched her march down the walkway overlooking the operations center.

"She's right, you know," said Morse, breaking the silence. "She wants to let the dogs out, but the risk of contracting the disease is too great. Once we deploy troops from the protection of our bases, we may not be able to let them back in."

The President swung around and slammed the top of the conference table with his hand. "We've got the cure. Why can't we use it to heal our people if they contract the disease?"

"Mr. President, they've only been working on it for a couple of–"

President Garcia dropped himself into a chair at the head of the table, causing it to partially tilt backwards. He had gained weight since he'd stopped drinking, opting instead for comfort foods in the form of sweets.

"Tell them to pick up the pace," he demanded. "Besides, I thought our great Dr. Hagan had already determined the formula. What's the holdup?"

"Sir, my understanding from Spielman is that the formula needs to be tested on various subjects, including monkeys, and then hu—"

The President was frustrated. "Andrew, didn't she represent to us this vanco—um, whatever it is. This drug, does it work or not?"

"Yes, sir. According to Spielman, the drug should work, but they know nothing of side effects and the usual concerns about interaction with other medications. He says he needs—"

"Andrew, are you kidding me?" The President was shouting now, his temper returning from his old days of drinking. "Sit down and listen to me carefully. We have the ability to save every diseased American on our soil. I'll be damned if I'm gonna allow these terrorists to kill the remaining survivors using, let me emphasize, our own weapons!"

"Sir, I can contact Spielman about expediting production, but it goes against our prior directives to develop the vancomycin slowly."

"Andrew, we don't have to slow walk the production for our own people. We need to hide it from the rest of the world until we can set our plans in place. But first, we have to defend Americans and keep them safe or they'll lose confidence in yours truly. I've still got one eye firmly affixed to the big prize—making America the world's only economic and military superpower."

"Mr. President, I'll set up a conference call with Spielman and Hagan for tomorrow morning. Would you like to participate?"

The President started laughing. "No, Andrew, of course not. Have you forgotten the first maxim of politics—plausible deniability?"

CHAPTER 55

Day Ninety-Four
The Den
Denver

Mac had always been driven. Throughout her career at the CDC, she was never one to seek attention or accolades. Her self-worth was based upon preventing the spread of, and the fighting of, infectious diseases. Her work ethic had been noticed by those around her and she was quickly labeled as a loner in the lab. During those final weeks in Atlanta when Donald Baggett hovered over her, watching her activities, she'd kept to herself, confiding only in Janie.

Only a handful of people at the Den knew of her approach to tackling a problem. In those first few days, Mac was labeled as standoffish and even rude. At first, old acquaintances like Sandra Wilkinson and Michelle Watson defended her demeanor. With each passing day, Mac's paranoia overtook her and she kept her distance from them as well.

She spent every waking hour in the lab, testing the mice and the newly introduced primates captured at the Denver Zoo. Her formula for the vancomycin d-ala d-lac had remained the same because it was too early to consider adjustments. The CDC rushed her BALO vaccine upon the public at the President's insistence and it was a failure. This time, armed with her clinical notes from a successful test patient, her father, Mac intended to get it right.

Mac was in the lab early this morning, long before the Den's big-brother PA system issued its wake-up call over the loudspeakers. The human body adapted itself to sunrises and sunsets. When underground, the body lost touch with the natural sleep cycle. In just a few days, she'd become a morning person and didn't know it.

She was making some notes on the charts of the newly infected primates when Dr. Spielman tapped on the window to the BSL-4 to get Mac's attention. He mouthed the words *my office now* and pointed toward the other side of the circular facility.

Mac immediately felt apprehensive. She couldn't recall a single time in her life when she'd felt more insecure and paranoid. Her career revolved around handling deadly, incurable diseases, but she approached every risk with caution and comfort in knowing she could protect herself by following the proper protocols.

She was in a different world now and she was alone. She constantly reminded herself that no one knew where she was and she had no ability to reach out to them. Her mother was unavailable for counsel and her father's jokes couldn't lift her spirits on a bad day.

And then there was Hunter. She'd never known love before and she'd finally opened herself up to the prospect when the perfect man came along. She missed his touch and his friendship. As she went throughout the decontamination process, she resolved to raise the issue with Dr. Spielman. She was prepared to demand access to her family.

Mac approached the entrance to Dr. Spielman's office, fully resolved to fight for time outside the Den. However, the conversation never got that far.

"Mac, come in and shut the door, please," ordered Dr. Spielman. He checked his watch. "Take a seat."

"What is it, Dr. Spielman?"

He held his hand up to stop her from talking. Then his phone began to ring. He pressed the speaker button and answered.

"Good morning, this is Tom Spielman."

"Please hold for Mr. Morse," announced a female voice on the other end of the line.

Mac's eyes widened as she heard those words. Dr. Spielman returned her surprised look and shrugged.

"Tom," said Morse, "do you have Dr. Hagan with you as well?"

"I do, sir. We're ready."

"I'll get right to the point," said Morse. "We need to accelerate the manufacture and distribution of the cure created by Dr. Hagan. The

National Guard is making arrangements now to take control of a local drug manufacturing facility and make it available for your use. Questions?"

"Andrew, there are considerations we haven't discussed when it comes to mass production of the drug. Currently, we have our chemists reviewing Dr. Hagan's compound and her clinical notes. We're not prepared to declare the drug reproducible or stable based upon our limited confirmation of her research."

"Hagan, does your drug work or not?" asked Morse.

"Well, yes, sir, it did work on my father, our dog, and the laboratory mice at my disposal," she replied.

"Then I don't understand what the problem is," he added.

Mac hesitated and took a deep breath. "May I speak frankly?"

"Young lady, it appears you know no other way. Go ahead."

Mac gulped. *I guess I deserved that.* "Mr. Morse, I am almost one hundred percent certain that the vancomycin formula will be successful. There are still many trials to run on the primates and then human test subjects."

"Run them, but chop-chop about it."

"Well, sir, I don't want a repeat of the failed BALO experiment. That option should have been tested before being used on human patients."

Morse cleared his throat. "Hagan, we'll take the blame on that one. We sought a politically expedient solution and it was a risky move. This is different. I need to have your assurances the new drug is capable of performing. People's lives will be put at risk based on your answer."

"Well, sir, not to be difficult, but the people to be inoculated with the vancomycin drug will have to be in the infectious and near symptomatic stage of the disease. In other words, their lives will be at risk before they receive the vancomycin injection."

The microphone went silent, prompting Mac to whisper to Dr. Spielman, "Did he hang up on us?" Half a minute passed before Morse returned to the line.

"Tom, our initial policy regarding distribution of this new drug has not changed. I respect Hagan's concerns about prematurely introducing this proposed cure to the public. For that reason, we will only distribute the final, approved drug to our military and their dependents after they sign a waiver. In essence, we'll test it on our own until we're satisfied that it should be available for wider distribution."

Mac wasn't expecting this. Her only reason for raising the issue about the viability of the vancomycin compound was to remind everyone the drug was new and untested. She'd come to the Den with the intention of creating a cure for all of infected humanity, not the government's chosen few who already enjoyed the protection of the military behind the fences and protective perimeters of their safe zones.

Lest we forget, there are sick human beings around the planet. Are we gonna let them die?

"But, Mr. Morse, the vancomycin is intended to help the plague-stricken people on the streets. I don't see how it is needed for the disease-free populations within—"

"Dr. Hagan," the chief of staff barked into the speakerphone, "there are a number of factors in play here that are beyond the scope of your duties. Your job is to produce this drug. This administration's job is to distribute the drug in the best interest of our great country. Can you do your job? We can certainly do ours."

Mac bristled at his harsh attitude towards her. She slowly closed her eyes and suppressed her anger. Morse's outburst reminded her of why she didn't like him.

Dr. Spielman sensed Mac's frustration, so he took over the remainder of the call. "Andrew, we're here to serve the American people and will follow your instructions. We have some logistics to work out, and I can assure you, Dr. Hagan and myself will be on the same page."

"Good. Do you agree, Dr. Hagan?"

"Yes, sir," replied Mac through gritted teeth.

"Tom," started Morse, "I'll send over the details on the Upsher-Smith Laboratories facility for your perusal. We are in the process of having the National Guard secure the facility and a one-block perimeter for safety reasons. We don't want a repeat of Atlanta."

"Thank you," said Dr. Spielman. "Will you have an equipment list available as well?"

"It will be on its way to you shortly," replied Morse. "Please review this with Dr. Hagan and let me know what other materials or equipment you'll need to create one hundred thousand doses of the vaccine."

"Mr. Morse, let me be clear about something so there is no confusion here," interrupted Mac. "This is not a vaccine in the sense it acts as a preventative medication to stop a person from becoming infected. The vancomycin compound is a cure, designed to treat someone already exposed to the plague bacterium. The patient must test positive for the disease in order for the vancomycin to be effective against it."

The silence returned to the speakerphone. Mac waited patiently for the Chief of Staff to return. *Is the President in the room too? Why isn't he participating in the phone call?*

"At what point must the diseased patient be in the timeline before the vancomycin can be effective?" asked Morse.

"I don't know. I've only used it on my father and he was in the third day of being symptomatic. Had I waited one more day, he would have suffered organ failure and died."

"Are you saying a patient has to be on the brink of death before you can administer the drug?" he asked.

"Sir, all I'm saying is we don't know until we test it further," replied Mac.

The silence returned. Mac attempted to whisper to Dr. Spielman, but he shook his head and raised a finger to his pursed lips. Morse came back for one final statement.

"I want you to move forward, Tom. I also want you to provide us a detailed memorandum of the disease's timeline, including a day-by-day symptoms tracker. Hagan, I want you to formulate your best guess as to the earliest and latest points in time during the disease's progression that your new drug will be effective."

244

"My best guess, Mr. Morse?" she asked.
"That's what I said. Now, get to work."
The call was over.

CHAPTER 56

Day Ninety-Five
The Den
Denver

Mac was on her way to a 9:00 a.m. meeting with Dr. Spielman to discuss the mass production of the vancomycin da-ala d-lac. She had produced vials of the compound in her lab at Quandary Peak, but she'd never been involved in the manufacturing and distribution of a medication on this level. After their teleconference with the Chief of Staff the day before, Dr. Spielman had dismissed her from his office and she went about her day. She preferred to stay busy to keep her mind off Hunter and her family, but as she worked, certain statements made by Morse and Dr. Spielman stuck in her mind.

Not that he was required to do so, but Morse never provided an explanation for skipping the testing process and jumping straight into production. By doing so, they ran the risk of a public health debacle like the rollout of the BALO vaccine.

Dr. Spielman seemed genuinely surprised at the advanced timetable for the manufacturing of the drug. During his back and forth with Morse, Mac got the distinct impression that the President's previous policy was to move slowly with the vancomycin's development. Now, they were full-speed ahead but only for distribution to those already protected by security and, therefore, uninfected. It just didn't add up.

"Good morning, Dr. Spielman," announced Mac after tapping on his door. "I brought an extra coffee if you'd like it."

"Yes, please. Thank you, Mac." He gestured for her to sit down.

"You look tired, sir," said Mac. "Are you worried about the President's directive?"

"Sort of. He wasn't on the line with us, but Morse speaks for him.

246

I'm concerned for the viability of the drug for all of the reasons you stated. But I'm uneasy about the manufacturing process. None of us have any experience with this and the National Guard is having difficulty locating the Upsher-Smith employees. I need someone to oversee the operation that has at least a minimal amount of experience in creating the proper formula and dosage. I studied our roster last night, and unfortunately, the only person available is you."

Mac's heart raced. *Is this my ticket out of here?*

"Sir, part of my duties at the CDC, at least when I was wearing my lab scientist hat, was to create test vaccines for use at our sister laboratories around the world. When we came across that particularly virulent strain of hemorrhagic fever in Central Africa several years ago, we had to tweak the ribavirin formula in order to stop the effects of Lassa. It took a lot of long hours in the lab, but I was able to disseminate the drug all over the world in the event symptomatic patients slipped out of the hot zone."

Dr. Spielman nodded his head. "I know this, Mac, and this is why I'm in a predicament. Selfishly, I need you here. But to follow through with the President's orders, I need you overseeing the manufacturing process."

"I'd be glad to do it, sir."

He sighed before continuing. "It's not easy to transport people in and out of the Stapleton facility. You haven't been around long enough to meet people or get to know them on a personal level, but most of our staff doesn't have anyone outside of the Den. If I assign this task to you, we'll have to find alternative housing for you until someone else can be trained."

Mac tried to contain her elation. Inside, she screamed *SCORE!* Outwardly, she put on her best Diane Sawyer, faux-concern look.

"I understand, Dr. Spielman. Perhaps they have sleeping quarters at Upsher-Smith. Or better yet, I could stay at Star Ranch with my family."

"That's a long, risky commute, Mac. I don't know if that's a viable option."

Mac thought fast. "Dr. Spielman, I happen to have a boyfriend that is very good at what he does. I can't imagine being in safer hands than having Hunter escort me back and forth to work every day. Plus, I can assure you that his security capabilities will surpass ten of the National Guardsmen assigned to the facility."

Dr. Spielman contemplated Mac's suggestion. He scribbled some notes and then wrote the number 14 on a page, which he then circled.

"Based upon my calculations after reviewing the information on the Upsher-Smith production capabilities, it will take fourteen days to produce the first one hundred thousand doses requested by the President. I think you could take somebody under your wings during that time frame, which means I could have you back here afterwards."

Two weeks with Hunter was better than nothing, but then Mac thought of a way to extend her duty out of the Den.

"Sir, have you considered using military jets to transport samples of the vancomycin together with our clinical notes to other major laboratories around the world, starting with the WHO?"

"That is an option, but it's not going to happen for a while," replied Dr. Spielman. "Even before this new development, the President intended to release the information to the rest of the world many—"

Dr. Spielman caught himself mid-sentence and stopped, feigning a cough to clear his throat. He looked down at his notes and then took a quick glance at Mac's face. Finally, he continued. "Let's take one step at a time, okay? I'll put in a transfer request with Cheyenne Mountain to take you over to Star Ranch tomorrow at oh-eight-hundred. I'll issue a corresponding requisition to provide you a Humvee and a driver as assigned by the fella in charge out there. I think his name is Hooper, or Huber."

"Captain Hoover."

"Yes, Hoover. Also, while you're there, I want you to talk to Turnbull about joining us here. Technically, she is no longer an employee of the CDC following her resignation, but I'll be glad to reinstate her with retroactive pay."

Mac had so many things to say in response, but she held her tongue. Her only goal at the moment was to make it twenty-four more hours so she could see Hunter.

"Sounds good, sir. I'll step up my efforts in the lab and begin thinking towards the production of the drug. If you need me, I'll be around. Get it? *A-round*," she repeated while twirling her fingers in a circular motion, making reference to the cylindrical shape of the Den.

Dr. Spielman laughed and shooed her out of his office. Mac soared out into the hallway and began to count the minutes until she left.

CHAPTER 57

Day Ninety-Six
Star Ranch
Colorado Springs

"Here we are, ma'am," announced the driver of the Humvee who brought Mac from the heliport at Peterson. Earlier, when Mac had exited the terminal at Denver Stapleton, she resisted the urge to drop to her knees and kiss the ground like so many freed hostages have done throughout history. In her mind, she was a hostage. Remaining within the protected confines of the Den might have worked for those who weren't prepared mentally to face the ugly world above ground, but it was definitely not for her.

"Thanks for the ride," she said nonchalantly. As if to drive the point home to Mac that she should be careful what she wished for, the driver was forced to take several evasive maneuvers to avoid mobs who attempted to stop the Humvee.

He explained that over the next several days, the National Guard would be taking measures to control the interstate between Colorado Springs and Denver, with several main thoroughfares in each of the surrounding towns next on the list. Mac surmised the additional military presence was in response to her conversation with Morse two days ago. *He was risking their lives based upon my cure and representations.*

Mac exited the vehicle and approached the guarded gate. She presented her credentials to the soldiers, who were distracted by Janie's shouting.

"Mac! Mac! I'm here. Hunter, too!" Janie was jumping up and down on the other side of the fence. The soldiers finally opened the gate and Mac ran into Hunter's arms. The two squeezed each other and she instantly began to cry. A week had seemed like an eternity.

250

Janie, who had eagerly awaited her turn for a hug, eventually lost patience and ran to join them. The three friends were reunited and their emotions poured out.

"Guys," started Mac, "you have no idea what I've seen."

"Mac—" Janie laughed "—our story beats your story, right, Hunter?"

"Trust me, there's lots to discuss," replied Hunter. "This afternoon, we're going to enjoy a dinner that'll blow your mind. The National Guard has taken over a meat processor on the east end of Colorado Springs. They're working with the ranchers to slaughter their beef and pork. Captain Hoover has hooked us up with steaks, ranch-style beans, and cold Budweiser. He says we've all earned it."

"I love Captain Hoover," said Janie with a laugh. "Come on, Mac. Wait'll I tell you about how I was kidnapped."

"What? You're kidding, right?"

"Nope," replied Janie. She began to tell the story to Mac as Hunter excused himself to go speak with Captain Hoover. He promised to be along in a minute.

After Janie was finished, the two women cried as they discussed the pain and humiliation suffered by the other women. Mac considered what Janie had almost endured, and suddenly her captivity in the Den didn't seem so bad.

"Janie, here's the irony, although there's no comparison," started Mac. "I have been underground in a secret facility created by the government decades ago. It's an incredible place with everything you'd ever want during an apocalyptic situation like this one except one thing—the ability to leave."

"Here's what I know," added Janie. "Let's make a pact to never put ourselves in that position again. I'll fight battles with guns and knives before someone will have the type of control over me those Snow people had."

"I agree, which is why we have so much to talk about," said Mac as they reached the home assigned to them by Captain Hoover previously. Mac decided to lighten the conversation until Hunter returned. "I have to ask. Which room did you pick?"

"Ha-ha. You know which one. It's perfect for me and it's right down the hall from Mommy and Daddy."

"The pink one?"

"You know it," Janie said with a laugh as she escorted Mac into the house.

Janie poured a glass of wine and Mac popped the top on a beer when Hunter returned from seeing Captain Hoover. He had a dour look on his face.

"Is everything okay?" asked Mac.

"Things are suddenly moving very quickly," said Hunter. "Two days ago, it seemed like the military was maintaining status quo. You know, protect Star Ranch and limit contact with those outside the perimeter. Cappy shared his new orders with me and laid out the government's strategy for the region. All I can say is their plan is ambitious and even risky."

Mac opened a beer and handed it to him. She gave him a kiss and whispered in his ear, "No worries, my love. We're together and we'll figure it out. But let's promise each other something. Promise we'll never be apart again."

"I promise," said Hunter.

They shared a toast and the group joined in preparing dinner while they discussed the Den. Hunter tried to help Mac understand her sudden paranoia. The isolation and being underground were shocks to her mental stability. The initial conversation she'd had with Sandra Wilkinson had planted the seeds to create a confusing and unsettling experience.

"That said, the place was probably wired with a very sophisticated surveillance system," said Hunter. "In an enclosed environment like that, if somebody loses it and gets access to a weapon, then you've got a mass murder situation on your hands."

"They prohibited guns, except for the guards," interjected Mac.

"It doesn't matter," said Hunter. "Guards can be overpowered or tricked. Heck, they can lose it themselves. It would be a one-sided gunfight."

"It makes me think of the doomsday preppers who plan to hunker down in an abandoned missile silo for months or even years," said Janie. "They don't consider the psychological aspect of doing that. Consider the fact that they all have guns, and you have the potential for a real mess."

"Right, those things look good on paper, but you're throwing a bunch of strangers together with varying attitudes and agendas," said Hunter. "No, thanks. You can have your million-dollar missile-silo condos, or whatever they're called."

CHAPTER 58

Day Ninety-Six
Star Ranch
Colorado Springs

They finished their dinner and then gathered outside on a brick-paver patio surrounded by landscaping. The house was oriented with a view of Cheyenne Mountain from the backyard, which was the perfect backdrop for the remainder of their conversation.

"Let me tell you what I've overheard so I can get your thoughts," started Mac. "Dr. Spielman lied directly to my face, and several times he committed lies of omission by not answering my questions. The first big one was when I asked him about contact with the WHO. He said no, but then I saw a cablegram on their letterhead dated the day before I arrived."

"Maybe he forgot?" asked Janie.

"No, I don't think so," replied Mac. "Once, when I was in his office, I scanned through the paperwork on his desk to learn anything about what was going on. The letter from the WHO specifically said they were frustrated because neither organization had made any progress toward a vaccination or a cure."

Hunter got out of his chair and walked inside the house. He returned with another round of drinks and blankets for the girls. "What else did you learn?"

"It was part of a conversation with Andrew Morse. The two of them tried to speak in code, you know, like I was stupid and couldn't figure out what they were saying. I got the impression that the CDC's directive from the President was to move the clinical trials along very slowly. For some reason, that suddenly changed in the last few days. Now they are on a fast track."

"Cappy just told me something that could explain that,"

254

interrupted Hunter. "There was another ISIS attack on a military installation, this time in Pennsylvania. It was well planned and coordinated. Five or six dozen were killed and RPGs were taken."

"We're at war on our own soil, with ISIS?" asked Janie.

"He and I think this is the logical second phase of the bioterror attack using the plague," replied Hunter. "In traditional warfare, after an air strike, infantry would be sent in to mop up. The ISIS fighters have found their way to America or were here all along. They are attacking us with the intentions of finishing the job while we're at our lowest point."

"Now it all makes sense," said Mac. "The issue of manufacturing and distribution came up while I was at the Den. Our work tomorrow is designed to quickly produce the vials of vancomycin for distribution to our military facilities only, despite the fact clinical trials are less than a week old."

"The President plans to send our guys out to fight terrorists with the drug as a panacea in the event they become infected with the disease. Pretty risky," said Hunter. "This also fits with something Cappy disclosed to me. Mac, the National Guard plans on occupying Breckenridge soon. Their goal is to locate as many as twenty thousand uninfected refugees from Pueblo to Fort Collins. Also, the National Guard will be securing medical facilities and begin treating ill patients."

"Mac, are they going to deploy the vancomycin prematurely, like they did with BALO," asked Janie.

"It appears so," Mac replied. "They need it to convince their soldiers to leave the military bases to secure the cities and to fight the terrorists. If there is an upside to this, at least I know for certain the drug works."

"What happens tomorrow?" asked Hunter.

"First, I need to know if you guys will go with me. Janie, they want you to work at the CDC, specifically at the Den."

"No!" replied Janie emphatically, with a slight chuckle. "That will never happen. Mac, I will stay by your side, but I'll never go underground again."

"Not even Underground Atlanta for drinks at Footprints?" asked Mac.

"Nope."

Mac reached for Hunter's hand and squeezed it. "I got permission from Spielman to hire you as an escort to and from downtown Denver, where the lab is located. I was told by my driver earlier the interstate between the two cities would be cleared and open for travel. Will you do it?"

"Of course," replied Hunter. "I'm not leaving your side."

Mac turned to Janie. "I could use your help, too. There is a much bigger issue I need to tell you guys about."

"What is it?" asked Janie.

"I don't think the President plans on sharing my discovery with the rest of the world, at least not initially. Morse was being coy about this during the phone call, but I got the impression they intend to take the cure, use it for their military and communities like Star Ranch first, and then on Americans only."

Hunter sat up in his chair. "That fits with what I spoke with Cappy about. They are reopening medical facilities to treat the ill with your new drug."

"The President's playing god with the cure," said Janie.

"I think it's much bigger than that," said Hunter as he became suddenly quiet.

Mac and Janie waited for Hunter to continue; then she finally asked him, "What are you thinking?"

"It's starting to add up," replied Hunter. "Spielman lies about contact with other health organizations. He and Morse stumble and let out their initial intention to delay development, but then decide to use the drug on Americans only. There's something going on behind the scenes."

"Let me add one more tidbit from right after Mac left the CDC," said Janie. "Baggett became very controlling over our work. The government brought in IT people one night and installed keylogger programs on our computers, and some suspected they bugged our phones. Our cell phones had to be checked at security when we entered, to be retrieved on exit."

"Why?" asked Mac.

"Baggett gave strict orders to everyone during the staff meetings regarding our progress on finding a vaccine or cure. We could not discuss our findings with anyone, including our families. In fact, do you remember how there would be cooperation with the WHO and the Public Health Agency of Canada?"

"Of course," replied Mac. "It was part of our daily protocol."

"Baggett ordered it stopped. And, I might add, so did Spielman. They wanted to keep all of our clinical research in-house."

"Unbelievable," said Mac. "I'll bet this came from Morse."

The three of them sat on the patio in stunned silence. The clean, crisp air coupled with the bright stars seen over the top of Cheyenne Mountain might have been romantic on any other night prior to the pandemic, but not on this night.

Finally Janie broke the silence and asked, "Guys, this has been like a horror movie. How does it end?"

Mac responded with a nervous laugh. "I'd like to say that all of us are standing on top of Quandary Peak, arm in arm, staring off into the distance with smiles on our faces. We've found the cure and everyone still alive lives happily ever after."

Hunter added, "Yeah, that's how the story usually ends, but somehow this script is written a little different. There are too many moving parts and all three of us agree something is going on within Cheyenne Mountain. Just remember, the bigger the conspiracy, the bigger the people involved. Powerful people like presidents shape world events in a way beyond our knowledge or comprehension. I'm afraid we're right in the middle of it."

CHAPTER 59

Day Ninety-Seven
Upsher-Smith Laboratories
Denver

The trip into Denver was remarkably easy. There was a large military presence along Interstate 25 from Colorado Springs until they exited near Lakewood in central Denver. Captain Hoover assigned Hunter one of the U.S.-based Humvees for ferrying Mac and Janie to the drug-manufacturing facility. This vehicle had low miles and hadn't been abused on the inside like the others deployed in the National Guard fleet, which had been brought back from the Middle East.

Captain Hoover issued travel documents to Hunter, which allowed him to travel anywhere within the Eastern Colorado district established by FEMA and the National Guard. The region split the state in two with the Continental Divide being the difference between east and west. These travel documents allowed Hunter to travel from Cheyenne, Wyoming, to the New Mexico border, or eastward to the state lines of Kansas and Nebraska.

Hunter, while clearly appreciative of the upgraded interior, did piss and moan over the lack of a Ma Deuce on the roof. To make up for the slight, as Captain Hoover sarcastically called it, he issued an AR-10, together with a thousand rounds of ammo, to Hunter to replace the one given to the Vagos motorcycle gang.

He also issued M4s, sidearms and ammunition to Mac and Janie. Despite the fact the interstate was cordoned off by the military, they needed to be prepared to defend themselves in the event of a breakdown in security.

When the trio exited the Humvee at the front door of the Upsher-Smith building, they were greeted by Colonel Clements, who was assigned the task of securing the facility.

"Good to see you again, Colonel," Hunter began as they approached the entrance.

"Likewise, Sergeant. I didn't expect to see you."

"Right. I've been assigned to the protective detail of these scientists. You remember Janie, of course. This is Dr. Mackenzie Hagan with the CDC." Hunter said the words with pride. He was glad Mac had been reinstated.

"The head honcho," quipped Colonel Clements. "I've been expecting you, and the sentries let me know of your arrival. Let me make one thing clear. This building is secured by multiple layers of military protection. Nobody will get past my people. While you're working here, you'll never have to use those." He pointed to their weapons.

"Thank you, Colonel," said Mac. "We're ready to get to work, if you wouldn't mind leading the way."

Upsher-Smith Laboratories was founded by a chemist in England who developed an innovative way to turn foxglove plants into a life-saving medication for cardiac patients. Adopting a *patients first* commitment, the company expanded around the world and was now heavily involved in the Denver community.

The Denver facility was ideally suited for Mac's purposes. As Colonel Clements escorted the entourage through the facility, she was pleased to see how clean and modern their operations were. From molecule to medicine, the process of bringing a new medication to market was a long, complicated journey.

Discovery of the drug together with the R & D was often done in different facilities across the globe. When a researcher created a breakthrough molecule, a facility like Upsher-Smith took that molecular compound and turned it into a medication used exclusively for clinical trials.

The laboratory and manufacturing facility at Upsher-Smith made both oral medications, like tablets and capsules, as well as intravenous drugs. Ultimately, it would be quicker and more cost effective to develop the vancomycin d-ala d-lac for oral use, but the timeframe dictated to her by Morse didn't allow for that.

To a layman, the process of converting her new molecular compound into a medication might seem relatively straightforward. Simply extract the active ingredients, mix it with some inert powder, mold it into a pill, and voilà, a new drug is born.

It wasn't that simple and Mac knew it. The process was phenomenally complicated and posed a real challenge for her and Janie. She'd done it on a small scale in her lab at Quandary Peak. Today, she'd focus on translating her findings into a viable medication to eventually be used on millions.

After another half hour touring the remainder of the facility, Mac was genuinely pleased to meet some of the personnel who worked for Upsher-Smith. Karl and Ingrid Berger, Austrian chemists who were supervisors with the company, had worked their way up through the ranks at Upsher-Smith over the years. The two were familiar with all of the aspects of the process of mass production, including the most critical step, which he was explaining to the entourage.

"Dr. Hagan," started Karl Berger, who still maintained his delightful Austrian accent. He walked her along a vast room protected by thick glass. "These reactors will mix the raw materials together to create the drug. We will work together, wearing our protective body suits, to program the reactors to manipulate certain factors such as heat and saturation. Probes will monitor the process in real time to follow the molecular changes."

"Does the process differ between an oral medication and an intravenous one?" asked Janie.

"Yes, absolutely," said Ingrid Berger. "The time saved with an intravenous option is the biggest benefit under the present circumstances. Also, our facility has a stockpile of vials."

"What about a children's dosage?" asked Mac.

"A very good question," replied Ingrid. "It's not just a matter of halving the dosage. Children's metabolism rates differ to adults, and with young ones, they obviously would prefer a chewable candy flavor. The children don't like shots."

"Neither do most adults." Her husband laughed.

"They'll like this one," said Mac dryly. She wanted to dismiss Colonel Clements, who seemed to be watching her every move. Mac wanted Janie to take detailed notes of the process and she also wanted to fabricate an excuse for creating several doses immediately. Further, the only way to determine if she could trust the Bergers was to get rid of Colonel Clements.

She turned to Hunter and used a voice that was unlike her, hoping he'd pick up on his task. "Hunter, I'm sure you and Colonel Clements are bored by all of this, and I don't know about our new friends, but most scientists don't like to be hovered over. Why don't you boys go talk Army stuff while we get to work?"

"Yeah, sure," replied Hunter, with a puzzled look on his face. Then he seemed to get it. "As a matter of fact, I do want to bring the colonel up to speed on developments in Breckenridge. Colonel, how about some fresh air? Without the HVAC powered up, it's a little musty in here."

"Okay," replied the colonel. "Our generators can only power the lab equipment and lighting. They don't have the capability to fire up the big electrical draws."

"I'll be right outside," said Hunter to Mac.

She smiled and nodded. After they left, Mac turned to Janie and the Bergers.

"Karl, Ingrid, I need to rely heavily upon the two of you during this process. I can guide you through my clinical notes, but you know the actual process of turning the vancomycin compound into a distributable product. Janie, I want you to take copious notes to record our steps for future reference."

"I have a journal," said Janie, holding up Mac's journal from the safe at Quandary Peak. "I'll follow you guys throughout the day. Just don't get annoyed with me if I ask you to verbalize what you're doing."

"Why is this necessary?" asked Karl.

"Please excuse my bluntness, but we've all seen the conditions around Denver. An accident could occur, or worse, once we leave the facility each evening, a dangerous situation may arise, causing us harm. I want us all to be able to do each other's jobs in case we have to move forward without one another, or in another facility."

Janie made eye contact with Mac and then pretended to cast her attention back to the journal. Mac had discussed this necessity with Janie in advance. In the event they were told to work with someone else, whatever they learned each day would walk out the door in their notes as they left. As for sharing information, they'd only disclose enough to keep their co-workers from becoming suspicious.

Like a hairstylist hustling around to secure her client base before she moved on to another salon, Mac was gonna be ready to bring her new drug to *market* elsewhere if the President had other plans.

CHAPTER 60

Day Ninety-Seven
Upsher-Smith Laboratories
Denver

The next morning, after their arrival at the lab, Hunter waited with Colonel Clements's driver while the colonel instructed his men on the day's security detail. The driver advised Hunter that the colonel was assigned to monitor security at Upsher-Smith until he received further orders. The corporal had overheard the colonel in a conversation with General Lauren, the chief of the National Guard Bureau. He was being replaced by a colonel from Peterson Air Force Base. Colonel Clements's new orders would focus solely on securing the interstate, maintaining the hospitals of Denver, and watching over Upsher-Smith.

"Sergeant, are you up for a ride?" asked the colonel when he was finished assigning his men.

"Sure," Hunter replied. After the corporal's loose lips provided him the new change at the top, Hunter hoped to learn more from Colonel Clements, who was tapped into Cheyenne Mountain. Hunter climbed into the backseat of the Humvee and asked, "Where are we headed?"

"You know, Sergeant, nowhere in particular," said the colonel with a defeated tone. "I need to drive around and check on what I've accomplished."

The corporal wheeled them out of the parking lot at Upsher-Smith Laboratories, and another Humvee quickly moved in behind their truck. They rode in silence except for the occasional instructions of the colonel to his driver.

The first stop was Denver Health, where Mac and Dr. Matta had run into trouble after they'd pumped the medical staff for information about the hospital's initial plague cases. The colonel began to open up.

"You know what it's like to follow orders, right, Sergeant?"

"Of course. Yes, sir," Hunter replied.

Colonel Clements continued. "Generally, you do so without question and without expectations of a pat on the back."

Hunter didn't respond as the colonel appeared to be troubled, or perhaps reflective on the nature of his duty. Hunter was glad the corporal spoke of the change in the colonel's assignment. It helped account for his melancholy mood.

"But this is the most difficult challenge I've ever faced in my career and I'm proud to say I accomplished every goal the President set for me. In a matter of days, we secured the drug manufacturer and cleared the hospitals of the dead and the diseased. My men risked their lives to find medical personnel who were hiding in neighborhoods and the inner city so that they could begin treating patients again."

"It's a dangerous place, sir," added Hunter. He had no idea where this conversation was going.

"Sergeant, I don't know Dr. Hagan, but she is a genuinely nice person and obviously very talented. What she is doing for America deserves a medal, but I have to forewarn you, this President will not reward her, nor will he acknowledge her accomplishments. Like me, she'll be cast aside without so much as a pat on the head."

"Colonel, there appear to be quite a few changes locally," started Hunter. "I don't know, but it seems a bit premature."

"Well, that depends on Dr. Hagan's efforts, I suppose," said the colonel as he directed his driver toward the interstate. "I now know fully what she is working on and its importance. It helped me stomach recent changes in my tour of duty, although I don't appreciate how it was handled. Nonetheless, I hope she's successful. America needs a break."

"The country does, but so does the rest of the world," said Hunter, who began his fishing expedition. "This disease didn't discriminate as it spanned the earth. You know, Colonel, up in

Breckenridge, we didn't get any news of outside events. Tell me how other countries are faring."

"About like us," he replied. "During my briefings, this comes up from time to time. Of course, the official word is that communications between world leaders and their nation's health organizations has broken down. I know that isn't true because we wouldn't have nuked ISIS in the mountains on the Iraq-Iran border without some dialogue with China, Russia, and their surrogates."

"Are others working on a cure, too? I mean, the World Health Organization should be leading the charge."

"Here's all I know," replied the colonel as he turned in his seat to address Hunter face-to-face. "They haven't volunteered any of their research and we haven't ponied up any of ours. You know what, that's fine by me. This plague didn't start within our shores. It was brought into America by others. I say we take care of our own first, and then we'll help the other countries. We should have adopted this attitude a long time ago, in my opinion."

Hunter swallowed, choosing his next words carefully. He went for it. "I suppose the President feels that way too, huh?"

Colonel Clements sat up high in his seat. "I know President Garcia does. When he does his first presidential address to the nation in a couple of days, on day one hundred since this whole mess started, I expect he'll reveal his plans to the world."

"Well, I'm glad there is a plan. Whadya think he'll say?" asked Hunter.

"Sergeant, I believe it'll be consistent with the new motto of our government in Cheyenne Mountain, which is America First. I say it's about time, right, Corporal?" The colonel laughed and smacked his driver on the shoulder.

"Dang straight, Colonel! Give 'em the middle finger!" he replied merrily as he pushed the gas pedal and roared down I-25 with no particular destination in mind.

CHAPTER 61

Day Ninety-Eight
Interstate 25
South Denver

"You two had a long day," said Hunter as he cruised down the interstate at seventy miles an hour. He'd give Colonel Clements credit for making a nice, deserted highway to drive for Mac's commute. It had more troops stationed at the exits than earlier in the day and now there was a steady stream of escorted military transports headed toward the city from Colorado Springs. Hunter had total confidence in Mac's new drug, and apparently the President did as well. Clearly, he was prepared to send his military assets out of their protected bases.

"We did," said Mac as she thumbed through the journal kept by Janie. The suede leather-bound book was full of well-worn pages now. Mac closed it up and wrapped the suede string to secure a few loose pages inside. "We have something else, too. Show him, Janie."

Janie retrieved a black duffel bag from the back of the Humvee. "Thank goodness you left the truck unlocked, Hunter. While the Bergers were taking their lunch break, we—"

"Lunch break?" inquired Hunter, looking into the rearview mirror to see Janie's response.

"Oh yes, these two are real clock-punchers," replied Janie. "They take their ten-minute breaks right on schedule, and each day they pack a lunch, which they eat precisely from noon to 12:30."

"I guess that's how they race against time around here," said Hunter. "By the way, what did you guys do for lunch?"

"We broke into the vending machines and stole their Doritos and Reese's Peanut Butter Cups," answered Mac with a laugh and a high-

266

five exchange with Janie.

Janie reached into the duffel and retrieved a Hostess Ding Dong. "You want a treat?"

Hunter laughed and declined. "No, thanks. So you emptied the vending machines and hid the loot in the back of the Humvee?"

"Yup, but there's more," replied Mac. "Show him, Janie."

Janie produced a long, rectangular aluminum case. It was secured with two latches and Janie held a key. Janie turned the key and released the latches. She positioned the case so Hunter could see inside.

"Whoa! Is that what I think it is?" he asked.

"Yes, sir, forty-eight vials of the newest batch of vancomycin d-ala d-lac extravaganza!"

"We snuck out while they ate peanut butter and honey sandwiches," said Mac proudly.

Hunter slowed as an M35 series cargo truck and an Army M1117 Armored Security Vehicle blocked the middle of the interstate. Several fifty-caliber-armed Humvees surrounded the trucks.

Two men dressed in khakis and black shirts stood in the highway behind the trucks, their rifles pointed downward in a low-ready position.

"Mac, in the glove box is an envelope with the travel authorization from Cappy. May I have it, please?"

One of the men approached Hunter and began to speak. "Papers," he said brusquely.

Hunter handed them out the window but eased his hand onto his sidearm. These guys weren't in uniform and looked more like CIA or Delta operatives.

The man studied the documents, looked into the truck at Janie and Mac, and then handed the envelope back to Hunter.

"Where ya headed?" he asked.

"Star Ranch."

"Who's the CO there?" he asked. *A test question.*

"Captain Kevin Hoover."

After glancing through the interior one more time, he instructed

Hunter to pull down the exit ramp and wait. There would be an escort for him shortly.

Hunter obliged and slowly exited the highway. His first question was to Janie.

"Did he see the case?"

"Nope. I stuck it in the bag before he came to the window. Hey, look over there," Janie said. "There are bodies all over the road."

Hunter tried to slow the pace without being obvious. Something had happened here that was beyond the National Guard's normal operations.

The people were not dead, but they were lying facedown on the concrete pavement. Several uniformed soldiers were holding guns on them. A horn honked, drawing Hunter's attention to a military Jeep at the bottom of the exit ramp. The show was over and it was time to get back to Star Ranch.

"Getting back to your case," Hunter began. "I gather you've made up your first batch of the cure."

"We have," replied Mac. "In fact, we now have everything we need to reproduce it if necessary. The samples are ready for use and Janie's notes are better than I could've done."

"Great news! What's in store for tomorrow?" asked Hunter.

"Here, nothing except watching the Bergers mix up more of the vancomycin," replied Mac. "The Bergers aren't expecting us. I told them I haven't had a day off in two months. They said that was unfair and I should take a day to recharge my batteries."

"Really?" asked Hunter. "Do they have any idea of what's been going on around them?"

"I guess not," answered Mac.

"We could take a day off," added Janie. "You know, see the sights. Maybe go to the zoo and see the monkeys?"

"No, thanks," said Mac with a laugh. "Been there, done that."

"I have a better idea," replied Hunter. "I believe it would be a good idea to see your parents and fill them in. I trust your mother's judgment on a lot of these things. I'd like to lay it all out for her and get her opinion."

"Sure, did something else happen today with the colonel?" asked Mac.

Hunter slowed as the Jeep approached Star Ranch. Twin American flags flew from the poles flanking the gated entry. He shrugged and turned to Mac.

"Let's just say our President has sworn himself to an America First approach."

PART FOUR

WEEK FIFTEEN

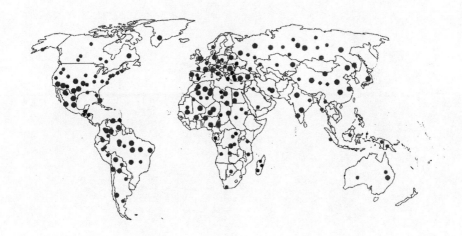

CHAPTER 62

Day Ninety-Nine
Star Ranch
Colorado Springs

Hunter was awakened by a lot of commotion outside reminiscent of the day the ISIS fighters mounted their attack on Star Ranch. He shot out of bed and quickly dressed. Just as he grabbed his rifle, Mac mumbled his name.

"Hunter, what's wrong?"

He ran into the bathroom and looked through the small window overlooking the front gate. "Cappy looks like he's mobilizing his men. I'll check it out. Just in case, you and Janie should get dressed."

He ran back to the side of the bed and kissed Mac.

"Can't we get one day of peace?" she asked.

"Nah," he replied as he darted out the door. Then he yelled over his shoulder, "We'd get bored!"

Hunter tore down the stairs and out the front door onto the lawn. His sudden movement must've caught Captain Hoover's eye because he slowly turned in Hunter's direction as he sipped his coffee. His lack of urgency immediately calmed Hunter down, who approached Captain Hoover at a steady, but brisk pace.

"Hey, Cappy," greeted Hunter. "Everything okay?"

"Yeah, I was about to knock on your door and see if you wanted some coffee."

"Where's everybody goin'?" asked Hunter.

"Not quite everybody, but half of us," replied Captain Hoover. "I got the order an hour or so ago. They want me to redeploy half my men to Breckenridge. I'll go with them today to get everyone positioned and meet with the locals, and then leave the platoon to my lieutenant."

"Is it safe to leave Star Ranch right now?"

"Oh yeah, by the end of the day, we'll have some fresh faces out of Peterson. It'll be a mixed bag of uniforms running around here, but they'll all fall under my command."

Hunter watched the activity for a moment. "What time are you pulling out?"

"Couple of hours," replied Captain Hoover. "Sure you don't want some coffee?"

"Um, no, thanks. Listen, Mac and Janie have the day off. Would you mind if we ride along in the convoy? Mac would love to see her parents."

Captain Hoover handed his empty coffee mug to one of his aides while he signed off on some travel documents and requisition forms.

"Please, join us, but we'll be coming back the day after tomorrow," said Captain Hoover. "Hey, did you hear what happened in the city yesterday?"

"No, what?" asked Hunter.

"Our boys busted a load of terrorists in a stolen M35. They were cruising down the highway like it was nobody's business. However, it does show these guys to be resourceful and fearless."

Hunter nodded. "We caught a glimpse of it on the way back from Denver. Score one for the good guys. Do you know what they were planning?"

"I don't know, but I'm fairly certain waterboarding will be approved again. Also, the President is going to address the nation tomorrow afternoon."

Hunter decided to pick his brain. "Whadya think he'll say?"

"Who knows? That stuff is above my pay grade, but here's what I'm told. This move into Breckenridge is part of an overall plan to separate the well from the ill. That's step one. Second, he is going to make a public statement about rescinding the Level 6 order, which is no longer a secret, thanks to CNN."

"I didn't like it to begin with," interrupted Hunter.

"Neither did I. Seriously, more than you know," said Captain Hoover as he kicked aimlessly at the gravel on the driveway.

"Anyway, the President is kicking off the recovery effort by separating people and reopening medical facilities. Patients will be treated for all types of illnesses. The dying will be treated humanely, so I'm told, with pain medications and antibiotics to ease the dying process."

"I like it," said Hunter. "You seem to be tapped into the grapevine, is there any word on a cure?"

"No, unfortunately. I do believe the President's plan can work. By shifting the healthy population away from the cities and into the small towns, at least we'll have some people alive when this thing goes away."

Hunter now knew information regarding the cure was on a strict need-to-know basis, which explained why Colonel Clements was informed and Captain Hoover was not.

Hunter slapped his friend on the back and started for the house. "Cappy, let me get the ladies up and at 'em. We'll be ready to pull out when you are."

"See ya at oh-nine-hundred," Hoover shouted to Hunter as he jogged down the road.

When he arrived back at the house, Mac and Janie were standing at the door with their noses pressed against the small windows on either side of the entry.

"What's happening?" asked Mac.

"It appears that half of Cappy's people are being redeployed to Breckenridge. They're leaving in a little over an hour."

"Okay, are we going with them?"

"Yes, if you guys agree. Listen, those were ISIS operatives lying in the road yesterday. They'd commandeered that military cargo truck at some point. Guys, there's a war coming, so we have to take our safety into consideration every time we leave Star Ranch."

Mac led them into the kitchen, where the smell of coffee permeated the air. "Hunter, how will we get back on our own?"

"Cappy and some of his men will return the day after tomorrow. That'll give us a couple of nights at Quandary Peak to talk with your parents."

"And I can see Derek," Janie chimed in.

Mac poured everyone a mug of strong, black coffee. "I vote we pack up and head out with the rest of them. We need to get home and think with clear heads, agreed?"

"Agreed."

CHAPTER 63

Day Ninety-Nine
Quandary Peak

Mac's mind wandered as Hunter drove the Humvee through the checkpoint at Blue Lakes Road. To her right stood Red Mountain, where Janie had been held hostage and innocent women were forced to become baby incubators. She closed her eyes and shuddered, revolted by the thought of abusing women that way. The ills of society, from sexual degeneracy to murder and all of man's perversions, had risen to the surface during the apocalypse.

Driving up the road to their home, she admired the beautiful dusting of snow on Quandary Peak rising two thousand feet into the sky to her right. Its beauty gave her hope that the world would right itself and set humanity on a better course than the one it was on.

Finally, driving down the slope to the front of their home, seeing her mom and dad on the front porch reminded her of something her dad had said when they moved from the West Coast to the East Coast when she was seven. They'd had a rough ride and Mac had a terrible cold. They'd had a flat tire in a driving rainstorm and witnessed a deadly accident as well.

When they'd reached their new home, Mac recalled her daddy's words. *The greatest parts of a road trip aren't arriving at your home. It's all the wild and crazy stuff that happens along the way.*

Mac chuckled to herself as she thought of the nearly one hundred days since their discovery of the plague outbreak. She could remember what happened on each and every one of them. What bothered her most was that she couldn't remember what she was doing the day before that fateful trip to Guatemala.

What would I have done differently if I knew the day before was the day before?

"Welcome home, you guys," said Hunter, startling Mac slightly as she was brought back to the present. "It appears we have a welcoming committee."

Tommy and Barb stood on the front porch with their arms wrapped around each other while Flatus ran back and forth in front of the house, unsure of which direction was the best way to go, so he chose them all.

Mac bolted out of the truck and sailed up the stairs until she was in their arms too. The tears flowed from all the Hagans as they were reunited after the most stressful period in their lives.

When they finally stopped hugging, Mac walked around Tommy and assessed his health as if she were tire-kicking a used car. She laughed at herself because it was his insides that needed to be evaluated, not his outward appearance. Nonetheless, she took it all into consideration and then she spontaneously hugged him again.

"Daddy, you're gonna be okay," she whispered in his ear.

"Some doctor you are," he joked. "I could've told you that."

Mac gave him a playful slug followed by a kiss on the cheek. She returned to her mother for another hug. The two made eye contact and smiled. *Everybody is gonna be okay.*

"When they called us from the checkpoint and said you'd arrived, I scrambled around to create a special treat for everyone today, which comes with a bit of good news for you, Janie," announced Barb.

"For me?" asked Janie.

"Yep. Derek and his buddies came by yesterday with some deer meat. He is doing much better although his face is still partially bandaged. He said he misses you."

"I miss him, too," said Janie as the waterworks opened up. Mac quickly hugged her friend.

"I started venison stew in the Crock-Pot for dinner," said Barb. "I suspect we have a lot to discuss, not the least of which are your plans. For now, I think some wine is in order and perhaps Hunter can start us a roaring fire. Temps dip into the thirties every night now."

"Sounds like we just arrived home for Thanksgiving," said Hunter. "Tommy, you wanna join me while we see how our firewood supply is doin'?"

"Yeah, I need the fresh air."

The guys headed off the porch and toward the woods where Hunter had stacked firewood between the pine trees many weeks ago. Mac followed her mom and Janie inside, where the smell of the stew already floated throughout the house. She closed her eyes for a moment and took in the scents. It was like Hunter said, *home for Thanksgiving.*

Barb filled Janie in on Derek's condition and she passed along to Mac the attitude of the town toward the military's presence. As expected, the locals welcomed the soldiers from a security standpoint, but they had no interest in opening up the floodgates to refugees. Barb and Tommy were ambivalent because they were isolated on Quandary Peak and benefited from the proposed upgraded checkpoint expected for the Blue Lakes Road intersection. They looked at it as having their own secured neighborhood.

Tommy and Hunter returned and soon there was a roaring fire. Barb unwrapped some waxed cheese and passed around the Triscuits she'd been saving for a special occasion. Everyone had a comfortable seat in the oversized furniture around a cocktail table.

The carved wood bowl filled with scented pinecones had been removed from the table, and in its place, the aluminum case had been opened with the vials of vancomycin standing upright like soldiers at attention, reporting for duty.

For a minute, the group stared in silence at the case, each contemplating the ramifications of what it stood for. Mac knew this was going to be a long conversation during which the fate of her family, including Hunter and Janie, would be decided. She polished off her glass of wine and quickly refilled it.

"Mom, Daddy, we have a lot to discuss. Can we get it out of the way so we can enjoy our evening together?"

Barb immediately had a concerned look on her face and she leaned forward on the sofa. "Honey, what's wrong?"

"Okay. No, I mean, we're okay." Mac stumbled out of the block. She was having difficulty knowing how to start, so she began to ramble. "Just bear with me. I am so glad we're all together. This feels so right, so homey. For years, we've been separated by a long distance and busy schedules."

"Of course, dear, we're glad you're home too," said Barb. "Are you worried that you have to go back to Colorado Springs? When do you have to return?"

"I don't know. I mean, day after tomorrow, depending—" Mac's voice trailed off and she looked to Hunter. Her mind was racing as she began to realize where the conversation might lead them.

"Barb, we've learned some things that may alter our plans." Hunter rescued Mac. "Let me summarize the good news."

"Yes, please," said Tommy. "As long as all of you are healthy, then the bad news is probably not as bad as you think."

"I agree," Hunter continued. "Yes, we're all safe and healthy. Mac and Janie have successfully reproduced the drug in large quantities, as you can tell from this case."

Mac had recovered from her mental paralysis and was ready to rejoin the conversation. "The president ordered us to accelerate the production of the vancomycin without further laboratory testing or even primate trials."

"But, Mac, that is a mistake—" interrupted Barb.

"I know, Mom, and I voiced my concerns to both Dr. Spielman and Andrew Morse."

"I'm glad Tom's alive and you spoke to him. You also spoke to that weasel Morse?"

"Yes, Mom. That's a longer story, which I'll save for later. Here's the thing. The President accelerated the timetable suddenly, and for the last couple of days, Janie and I worked at a drug-manufacturing facility to produce these doses and thousands more like them."

Barb clapped her hands and said, "Well done, girls. Listen, I know the trials and studies were skipped, but we know the compound works. Your father is living proof."

"I sure am, and so is Flatus, right, boy."

Flatus force some air through his throat and appeared to heartily agree.

Barb continued. "We're finally going to help the people who need it the most."

"No, Mom, that's just it. The President wanted to accelerate the timetable so he could send the doses to the military bases around the country. I believe the infected Americans are about fourth in line to receive the cure."

"Hunter," began Tommy, "why would the President provide the drug exclusively to the military?"

"I believe the President is about to deploy troops around the country to search out ISIS fighters who've been initiating attacks against the military installations. We thwarted one against Star Ranch."

"While you and Mac were there?" asked Barb.

"Yes, Mom. Hunter sniffed it out and suggested an Apache air strike. We blasted them before they could fire their rockets."

Barb shook her head and gulped her wine. "ISIS has rockets?"

"RPGs, but let's not get into the details," replied Hunter, who was trying to get the conversation back on track. "Tommy, I believe the President is beginning his rebuilding effort now and the acceleration in production of the drug is part of that. He has to deploy the troops and be able to guarantee their safety in case they come in contact with the plague-stricken citizens."

"I have to say, it sounds like a viable plan," added Tommy. "The President has to maintain order first before he can begin a viable recovery process. I suppose their presence in Breckenridge is part of that."

"Exactly," said Hunter. "The second aspect of his plan is to separate healthy Americans from those exposed to the plague. They will seek out the well and find them a new place to live in safe zones on a much larger scale than Star Ranch."

"Again, makes sense," said Tommy. "I'm glad to hear he's doing something right for a change."

"Let me add this," said Hunter. "They've dispatched the National Guard to control and reopen health care facilities. The Guard has secured major freeways and cordoned off the medical facilities so they can begin seeing patients again. Hopefully, the vancomycin will be distributed to these locations immediately."

"It seems like there are a lot of unknowns behind the President's plan," Barb added.

"You're right, Mom. We were told the President plans on making an address to the nation tomorrow, his first since the government moved into Cheyenne Mountain."

Tommy, who was sitting next to Mac, leaned forward and patted her knee. "Honey, this doesn't sound like doom and gloom to me. The rebuilding process will be tedious anyway, but the addition of ISIS attacking our military complicates matters. I can see where the President has to take extra precautions to ensure the safety of our troops and probably law enforcement too. Order must be restored."

"I know, Daddy. I can deal with all of that, but there's more."

He squeezed her hand and gave her an encouraging smile. Her dad always knew when she was troubled and had been a great listener when she was a teenage girl growing up. He hadn't changed.

Mac continued. "We also believe the President plans on hoarding the vancomycin for use in the United States only. Both Dr. Spielman and Morse lied to me about their intentions. They don't plan on sharing my research with the WHO or any foreign government. Hunter learned more as to why."

"Some of this is speculation, but most comes from the colonel in charge of the National Guard in the Denver region and Captain Hoover, whom you guys have met," said Hunter. "Basically, the President has adopted an America First policy. It appears his intentions are to protect our military, cure our diseased, and then share the formula with the rest of the world."

"Mom, based upon what I gathered, he may prevent my findings from being disseminated to the WHO for as much as a year. I don't know what the current death toll is, but hundreds of millions could die in that time period."

"Are you sure of this?" asked Barb.

"Everything we learned points to this conclusion," replied Hunter.

Barb slammed her empty glass on the table, causing the fluid in the vials to shake. "That's not his decision to make. Curing the diseased of the world should transcend politics. He's playing god with people's lives just because they're not Americans."

Everyone in the room was silent. Hearing her mother's words angered Mac even more. "Why would he do this? We can take care of our own, but it doesn't need to be at the expense of the rest of the world's population."

"I have a theory," replied Tommy. "Now, I'm not a political person, and as Barb knows, I've lambasted the media, social media, and Hollywood for politicizing everything. It just sickens me. Be that as it may, consider the logical end result of the President's actions."

Hunter chimed in. "Americans are cured and the nation has a tremendous head start on the recovery process."

"To the detriment of other nations," added Tommy. "While we get on our feet and again start to flourish, other countries will sink further into the abyss."

"Daddy, are you saying that we're going to attack them or something while they're down?"

"Not necessarily, Mac. However, we will soon be the only functioning economy on Earth. Our military will be operating on all cylinders. Our markets will be stabilized first, including our currency."

Barb interjected, "In essence, everyone will be coming to us for help, including the world's best kept secret—your clinical notes and the formula for vancomycin d-ala d-lac."

"Mom, this isn't right," started Mac. Then she pointed at herself, Janie and over to her mother. "We swore an oath to help all people inflicted with infectious diseases, not just those who happen to be on American soil."

"Agreed," said Barb.

"Absolutely," said Janie.

Mac stood and walked to the kitchen and rummaged through her backpack until she found her journal. She set it on the cocktail table in front of her mother.

"Here are my clinical notes, from start to finish, including Janie's detailed description of the manufacturing process. It's here, in my head, and nowhere else."

"What are you suggesting, Mac?" asked Barb.

"I risked my life and left my still-recovering father to provide a mechanism to save people from this horrible death. I refuse to be a political pawn on the President's chessboard. I want to discuss our options."

CHAPTER 64

Day Ninety-Nine
Quandary Peak

"We do nothing," said Tommy, who was the first one to provide a reaction. "This is way out of our hands, honey."

Mac looked to Hunter, who had been thinking through their options since they'd started to put the pieces together. He wanted to hear everyone out first before he weighed in.

"Daddy, I'm sorry, but doing nothing is not an option. There has to be someone I can approach."

Tommy responded, "Mac, the entire government is hunkered down in Cheyenne Mountain and therefore inaccessible. You mentioned Dr. Spielman. Could you take this to him?"

"He's in on it too, right, Mac?" asked Janie.

"Yes, sadly. Mom, what do you think?"

Barb fidgeted and glanced at Tommy before she responded. Hunter suspected she was going to make a controversial suggestion. Hunter had learned so much about the family dynamic between Mac and her parents. Outwardly, she was mostly like her father. Inside her head, she and her mother could've been clones.

"Canada," offered Barb, a single-word suggestion that set off a family firestorm.

"The PHAC?" asked Mac.

Janie leaned over to Hunter and whispered, "That's the Public Health Agency of Canada, their version of the CDC."

Hunter smiled and nodded.

Barb continued. "Vanessa Philpott, their chief public health officer, and I have known each other for years. She's someone you can trust to do the right thing."

"How in the world would I find her?" asked Mac.

"Of course, her offices were in Ottawa, but they have regional offices in every province. You could go—" Barb never finished the sentence before Tommy spoke up.

"Hold up! Are you suggesting Mac gallivant halfway across North America to search for an office that may be empty to find this Philpott person, who might be dead?"

"Dear," replied Barb somewhat condescendingly, "that's a little dramatic. Also, I'm not saying she should do it. She asked for options and that was the best I could think of besides cosigning your proposal to do nothing."

"Daddy, Mom is just trying to help. You know I wouldn't undertake anything without considering all of the risks."

Tommy looked at Hunter and asked, "Is that true?"

Hunter wanted no part of this, yet. He held his hands up and leaned back in the chair. He wished the thickly padded leather would swallow him.

Mac turned to him, waiting for his answer. His fight-or-flight reflex was screaming *RUN!*

"Hunter, does Canada have a continuity-of-government plan like we do?" she asked.

He elected to answer this question, conveniently dodging an answer to Tommy's, which would have been *Mac is prone to pushing the envelope, but then again so am I, which is why we're perfect for each other. I wonder how that would've gone over?*

"They do," said Hunter. "Years ago, they built a series of bunkers across the country in anticipation of a potential nuclear war between the U.S. and, well, everybody else. They're called *Diefenbunkers.*"

"Sounds German," said Janie.

"I'm not sure," said Hunter. "I think they're named after an old prime minister from the sixties. Anyway, there are several outside the major cities of Canada. Assuming the Public Health Agency is in the nation's capital, Ottawa, Barb's friend would most likely be in one of them."

"You'd be looking for a needle in a haystack," mumbled Tommy, who sat with his arms crossed. At the moment, Hunter put a checkmark in the *no way Jose* column for Tommy.

"Mac, you do realize I was just trying to provide an answer to your question. I am by no means suggesting you go to Canada. You understand that, right?"

"I do, Mom. And, Daddy, I would never do anything to risk my life. I thought I lost you once, I will not risk losing you because of an irrational decision."

This softened Tommy's heart and he unfolded his arms. He reached out to Mac and mouthed the words *I love you*. Then he immediately looked at Hunter.

Tommy didn't have to say a word, as his eyes conveyed his feelings. *Please take care of my baby.*

"Here's the thing," started Hunter. "We've pieced together a lot of bits of information and created a working theory. We know what the facts are and we have a reasonable belief as to what's happening behind the scenes. May I suggest we wait and hear what the President has to say tomorrow during his radio address? His words will give us a sign as to what we should do."

"I agree with Hunter," added Barb. She raised her glass. "I think we need to eat, enjoy our wine, and each other. While we're together, let's savor every moment."

Tommy raised his glass and said, "Hear! Hear!"

Hunter raised his glass and looked over at Mac. She was swishing her wine around her glass as if she were waiting for a compass needle to point her in the right direction. For the first time since the death of his parents, he felt like he was a part of a family.

He always thought families were like a compass that guides people, but as individuals, we should attack life based upon the moral compass which lies within us. Mac was wrestling with the choice between her family and her principles. Whichever way the compass needle pointed her, Hunter vowed to be by her side.

Chapter 65

Day One Hundred
Quandary Peak

Hunter and Mac loaded their backpacks with energy bars, water, an Eton hand-crank radio, and a military compass. It was an unseasonably warm day for late September in the Rockies. Because the weather could change suddenly, the two dressed in layers for their first hike to the top of Quandary Peak, the fourteen-thousand-foot mountain that had witnessed so many crises in their lives for weeks.

They were unable to pick up the AM or emergency bands on the small radio at the house, so they decided to go on an adventure. They'd hike to the peak, find the station, and listen to the presidential address. Mac also made sure her cell phone was charged so she could take pictures and video for her parents and Janie, who asked Tommy's permission to borrow the Jeep. She was going to Doc Cooley's to visit with Derek for the day.

The Quandary Peak Trail was a six-mile trek on an out-and-back trail. Mac and Hunter were in excellent shape although they were not experienced hikers. Hunter estimated it would take them around three hours up to the peak, but probably half that to return.

He studied the peak through his high-powered binoculars. It appeared the last stretch of the trail was fairly vertical, which would make it a challenge. Even if they didn't make it to the top, at least they'd be able to get radio reception.

With their gear ready, Mac and Hunter were off. Surprisingly, the two didn't discuss the decision that weighed heavily on their minds. After they'd said their goodnights the night before, they went to bed and collapsed into a deep sleep from exhaustion. Mac surprised Hunter by waking up before he did, a trait that she'd carried over from her week underground at the Den.

The first two hours of the hike were pleasantly effortless. It started out as a dirt trail weaving in and out of the forest. They followed the well-built trail as they ascended the eastern ridge, taking in the incredible views as they climbed higher. Once they emerged through the timber line, it got noticeably colder, prompting them to add a sweatshirt to their layers.

There were plenty of photo opportunities, including wildlife sightings. As the two hikers reached the final three-quarters of a mile to the summit, Hunter's predictions regarding the slope smacked them in the face.

The final thousand feet to the peak was on a thirty percent incline. Although the weather was favorable, which made conditions perfect to tackle the last part of the hike, Hunter considered calling this a good spot to listen to the President.

Mac dissuaded him of the notion before he suggested it. After spinning around to take in the view from Breckenridge to Red Mountain and down to Blue Lakes, she asked, "Do you want me to lead the rest of the way?"

"Nope, just follow in my footsteps," replied Hunter, who chuckled to himself. *There is no force equal to that of a determined woman.*

Twenty minutes later after they made their way through the boulder field, which was the home to a dozen Alpine mountain goats with their interesting black tongues, black horns and white hair, they reached the summit.

At the top, Hunter and Mac dropped their packs next to the Quandary Summit gold plat marker, a disc embedded into the rock by the U.S. Coast and Geodetic Survey, a federal agency that mapped and charted the entire United States.

At first they were awestruck at the awesome beauty of the world around them. They looked quietly in all directions, and then suddenly, and simultaneously, they burst into hysterical laughter. The reaction they shared was odd, one that Hunter later attributed to the thin atmosphere.

Mac loved it. She was giddy as she hugged Hunter and took in the spectacle. Once the excitement died down, she took to memorializing their accomplishment with her iPhone's camera. They both provided the camera a few words describing their feelings at the moment.

Hunter decided to film the two of them together. "Mac, come here next to me."

She squeezed herself in the frame and Hunter positioned the camera so that it pointed to the north toward Breckenridge, Wyoming, and beyond to Canada. He pressed the button to begin filming.

"Mac, I love you now more than ever. We've been brought together for a reason greater than just two people falling in love. We've overcome adversity, and now it's time to pursue our dreams. It's time for us to find our happily ever after. Mackenzie Hagan, will you marry me?"

Hunter reached into his pocket and presented Mac with an incredible princess-cut diamond in the center of a diamond-laden double-halo setting. The platinum and diamond engagement ring sparkled in all of its brilliance at fourteen thousand feet in the sky.

Mac sobbed from excitement, but managed to find the words, "Yes, I do love you, and yes, I will marry you."

They shared an extended kiss until Hunter realized they might miss the President's speech. "Mac, I don't want us to forget this moment, and I'm sorry to cut it short, but it's time."

"I know, let's get it over with and hope for the best. Then we'll celebrate!"

Hunter retrieved the radio while Mac took plenty of pictures of the engagement ring on her finger. After cranking it several times, Hunter found the station within the one-minute countdown for the presidential address.

They found a couple of flat rocks to sit on as President Garcia began his address.

"My fellow Americans, one hundred days ago, our families, friends, and neighbors came under attack at the hands of a sinister and evil plot to kill mankind. The deadly plague unleashed on our planet was not just intended to kill people who disagreed with a certain religion, but it was designed to destroy our way of life and the freedoms we hold dear.

"Over the last one hundred days, the world's population has dwindled from over seven billion to what has been estimated to be less than seventy million. Ninety-nine-point-nine percent of the world's population was murdered by a plot instituted by rotten, vile jihadists in the name of their religious beliefs. That's seven and a half billion lives suddenly ended by this despicable act.

"I come to you on this one-hundredth day with a message of hope. This attack may have shaken the foundations of our society, but they cannot be allowed to touch the heart of our great nation. As Americans, we should stand together to show our resolve and reassert ourselves as the brightest beacon of freedom and opportunity in the world.

"Following the attack, I implemented our government's emergency response protocols. Our military personnel from around the world were recalled to the safety of our vast armed forces installations.

"Our first priority was the safety of this great nation from further attack, and our second priority was to annihilate those who've perpetrated the attacks against us. I authorized the attack of an ISIS stronghold in the mountains of Iraq. I'm pleased to tell you the mission was successful, and the command and control structure of the enemy was destroyed.

"That does not mean, however, that the war is over. There are still cells of radical Islamic terrorists prepared to inflict their will upon us. We will not stand for it. The search is now under way for those who are behind these evil acts. I've directed the full resources of our military and law enforcement agencies to find those responsible and deliver a swift blow of justice. Let me be very clear on something. We will make no distinction between those who attack our country and those who harbor them."

Hunter looked at Mac and nodded. "So far our intel is on the money."

Mac nodded in agreement.

The President continued. "With our nation secure and the military hard at work to punish those who would do us harm, it's time for us to turn our attention to rebuilding this great nation. We have a two-pronged approach that will require everyone's cooperation. I have every confidence in you, the American people, to pull together as a family and help one another in these trying times.

"In the coming days, the National Guard will be disseminating leaflets throughout the country, identifying certain safe zones for the uninfected. I want the American people to know we are not abandoning the ill, as I have all of you at the forefront of my mind. By separating the healthy, we can prevent our population from dying off into extinction. We must work together towards that goal."

Mac leaned over to Hunter. "I can't believe he used the word *extinction*."

"He's trying to encourage voluntary compliance," Hunter whispered back.

"For those of you who are infected, or think you have been exposed to the plague either through human or animal contact, or by touching a surface where the disease may have been, we ask that you go to the specially designated health care facilities identified in the leaflets to be distributed by the National Guard.

"I wish I could announce to the world that we've discovered a cure for this deadly strain of the plague, but we have not. We have, however, identified a drug regimen of antibiotics and pain relievers, which will provide you comfort and relief from the symptoms.

"I urge those who are infected to heed my words. We have medications to relieve your symptoms. Take advantage of this opportunity our medical professionals are giving you."

"Hunter, what is he doing?" asked Mac.

"He's walking a fine line. He wants to encourage people to get help, but he doesn't want to make a formal announcement that he has the cure. He's hiding it from the world leaders who are listening to the broadcast."

"But they'll question him about the drug regimen he referenced."

Hunter shrugged. "I guess he'll dance around it and blow sunshine. He's a politician."

President Garcia added these closing words. "Today, I ask for your prayers for all those who grieve their lost loved ones and for all Americans whose sense of safety and security have been threatened.

"This is a day when all Americans from every walk of life should unite to help one another and this great nation as we rise out of the ashes to once again be the greatest nation on earth. As Americans, we've stared down enemies and withstood their attacks. We will do it again this time. I don't want you to ever forget the freedoms we enjoy and our resolve to fight for all that is good and just in our world.

"Thank you and God bless America."

A monotone voice came on the broadcast and announced the presidential address would be continuously broadcasted every half hour. Hunter turned off the radio and rested his elbows on his knees as he joined Mac staring across the mountaintops.

"Do you remember the other night when Janie asked how this horror movie would end?" asked Mac.

"Yeah. You thought we should be on top of Quandary Peak, staring off into the distance with smiles on our faces because we'd found the cure and everybody would live on."

"That's right. So, Hunter, are you smiling?"

"Nope, you?"

"Not after I heard that garbage," she replied. "It's just as we suspected. He lied to the American people and he has an agenda for the cure. This is like a movie. It's surreal."

"It sure is," said Hunter. They both sat in silence for a moment as they processed the President's words and the options they'd considered the night before.

Hunter chuckled, which caught Mac's attention.

"What?"

"Well, Dr. Hagan, the President has placed us in quite a quandary."

"Very funny." She laughed. "I wondered when that line was gonna be written into the script." She gave Hunter a playful shove, causing him to lose his balance and tip over slightly.

"Hey, careful! You don't want me to roll off of here, do you?"

"No," said Mac as she grabbed him by the arm and pulled him upright next to her. "Not before we're married, anyway."

They laughed and then sat there without speaking for another thirty seconds until Hunter asked, "So, Mac, what's the plan?"

Mac stood up, brushed off her khakis and extended her hand to help Hunter off the rocky surface of Quandary Peak. She gave her answer.

"Let's go save the world."

Thanks for joining me on this epic saga!

THANK YOU FOR READING PANDEMIC: QUIETUS!

If you enjoyed it, I'd be grateful if you'd take a moment to write a short review (just a few words are needed) and post it on Amazon. Amazon uses complicated algorithms to determine what books are recommended to readers. Sales are, of course, a factor, but so are the quantities of reviews my books get. By taking a few seconds to leave a review, you help me out, and also help new readers learn about my work.

And before you go...

SIGN UP to Bobby Akart's mailing list to receive special offers, bonus content, and you'll be the first to receive news about new releases in The Pandemic series, The Blackout series, The Boston Brahmin series and The Prepping for Tomorrow series—which includes sixteen Amazon #1 Bestsellers in thirty-nine different genres. Visit Bobby Akart's website for informative blog entries on preparedness, writing, and his latest contribution to the American Preppers Network.

www.BobbyAkart.com

The Blackout Series

36 Hours

Zero Hour

Turning Point

Shiloh Ranch

Hornet's Nest

Devil's Homecoming

The Boston Brahmin Series

The Loyal Nine

Cyber Attack

Martial Law

False Flag

The Mechanics

Choose Freedom

Seeds of Liberty (Companion Guide)

The Prepping for Tomorrow Series

Cyber Warfare

EMP: Electromagnetic Pulse

Economic Collapse

ACRONYMS Used in The Pandemic Series

DHS – Department of Homeland Security

DOD – Department of Defense

CDC – Centers for Disease Control and Prevention

USAMRIID – United States Army Medical Research Institute of Infectious Diseases

EOC – Emergency Operations Center

CEFO – Career Epidemiology Field Officer

WHO – World Health Organization

USCG – United States Coast Guard

NOAA – National Oceanic and Atmospheric Administration

CSPAN – Cable-Satellite Public Affairs Network

FISA – Foreign Intelligence Surveillance Court

DTRA – Defense Threat Reduction Agency

DPRK – Democratic People's Republic of Korea

ISIS – Islamic State of Iraq and Syria

CSL – Cooperative Security Location

OPSEC – Operational Security

SITREP – Situation Report

MARTA – Metro Atlanta Rapid Transit Authority

SARS – Severe Acute Respiratory Syndrome

H1N1 – Influenza A virus subtype H1N1, commonly known as *swine flu*

NDM-1 – New Delhi Metallo-beta-lactamase-1

BALO – Bdellovibrio bacteria

CPSIA information can be obtained
at www.ICGtesting.com
Printed in the USA
LVOW12*0802140917
548718LV00011B/130/P